THUS WITH A KISS I DIE

Books by Christina Dodd

A DAUGHTER OF FAIR VERONA

THUS WITH A KISS I DIE

Published by Kensington Publishing Corp.

THUS WITH A KISS I DIE

CHRISTINA DODD

KENSINGTON PUBLISHING CORP.
kensingtonbooks.com

This book is a work of fiction. Names, characters, businesses, organizations, places, events, and incidents either are the product of the author's imagination or are used fictitiously. Any resemblance to actual persons, living or dead, events, or locales is entirely coincidental.

To the extent that the image or images on the cover of this book depict a person or persons, such person or persons are merely models, and are not intended to portray any character or characters featured in the book.

JOHN SCOGNAMIGLIO BOOKS are published by

Kensington Publishing Corp.
900 Third Ave.
New York, NY 10022

Copyright © 2025 by Christina Dodd

All rights reserved. No part of this book may be reproduced in any form or by any means without the prior written consent of the Publisher, excepting brief quotes used in reviews.

All Kensington titles, imprints and distributed lines are available at special quantity discounts for bulk purchases for sales promotion, premiums, fund-raising, educational or institutional use.

Special book excerpts or customized printings can also be created to fit specific needs. For details, write or phone the office of the Kensington Special Sales Manager: Kensington Publishing Corp., 900 Third Ave., New York, NY, 10022. Attn. Special Sales Department. Phone: 1-800-221-2647.

The JS and John Scognamiglio Books logo is a trademark of Kensington Publishing Corp.

Library of Congress Control Number: 2025932691

ISBN: 978-1-4967-5019-8
First Kensington Hardcover Edition: July 2025

ISBN: 978-1-4967-5021-1 (e-book)

10 9 8 7 6 5 4 3 2 1

Printed in the United States of America

The authorized representative in the EU for product safety and compliance
is eucomply OU, Parnu mnt 139b-14, Apt 123
Tallinn, Berlin 11317, hello@eucompliancepartner.com

For Scott
Who patiently watched with me countless Shakespearean plays,
Shakespearean documentaries,
actors and scholars dissecting Shakespeare,
and so many versions of *Romeo and Juliet*, old and new.
You're the reason I know this enhanced, cheerful and hopeful
narrative of Romeo and Juliet's story is not only possible, but
True Love Personified.

Chapter 1

In fair Verona, where we lay our scene

Are you romantic? Have you found your One True Love? Do you imagine living happily ever after entwined in his passionate embrace?

Good luck with that.

Even a woman as savvy as me can get her tit caught in the wringer of true love. Let me tell you, when you've spent a lifetime congratulating yourself on your cleverness and good sense, and you discover in a moment of nighttime and lit torches that you've won the throne of the land of Humiliatia by being the biggest fool in the history of Suckerdom—that's a moment that *should* cause a moment of thoughtful reflection.

But no. Not me. That night, my temper flamed so hot I could have rendered fat off Old Serpent himself, and even now I lived my sorrow's rage!

The morning after my disgrace, I fled into the garden of Casa Montague to escape the avid and interested gazes that followed me everywhere. My parents, my siblings, the servants, the dogs, the cats, the mice . . .

All right. Maybe not the mice, but only because the cats had recently grown fat and we all know what that means.

Our garden is located behind the house, which was wrapped around an atrium that is so typically Verona. The spacious grounds include a maze, a fountain that included the requisite statue of a little boy gleefully peeing, gravel walks, massive hedges growing along the very high and defensive back wall—defensive because Verona is still, and always, a city-state at war with other city-states, and all noble Verona families jockeyed for position—and little alcoves perfect for assignations, if you're into that kind of thing. Which may I point out that until last night I have never been, and look how *that* turned out. You would think that the woman who, only months ago, single-handedly tracked down and disarmed Verona's first serial killer would be more intelligent than to get herself into such a mess.

Before we go further and I get more cranky, I should introduce myself.

I'm the daughter of Romeo and Juliet.

Yes, that Romeo and Juliet. To quote a future wise man, the rumors of their deaths were greatly exaggerated. The rest is essentially true: the potion, the poison, the self-stabbing, all those theatrics, and those events have been thrillingly repeated around countless Montague and Capulet festivities.

Consequently, our family reeks of melodrama like a badger reeks of musk. But unlike a badger, our family's monologues and diatribes and histrionics have enthralled all of Verona for more than twenty years.

I know this for sure. Except for the first nine months, I've been there for all of it. I'm the oldest child, and for twenty years I've avoided the fights and moaning and madness of passion and marriage. My name is Rosie (formal name Rosaline). I was named for my father's former girlfriend because he admired her chastity and wished that for his newborn baby daughter and, as Mamma repeatedly points out, that name had doomed me to maidenhood. Or I should say *formerly* doomed me to maidenhood, and technically I wasn't doomed. I clung to my maidenhood through machinations that would have impressed every scheming politician who ever lived.

I still can't believe that I . . . and the prince of Verona . . . almost . . .

Deep breath. Back to the facts.

I have five younger sisters and one brother, and Mamma is expecting again. With such wildly romantic, and may I point out, fertile parents, someone has to be practical.

I wish I could still lay claim to that title, but . . . see the opening paragraphs.

Betrothed to the wrong man. Catchy. I could compose a dramatic play with that title. Or a comedy. I'm sure someone would laugh.

Me, Rosie Montague, who has arranged marriages for all the men to whom my parents betrothed me, two of them to my younger sisters . . .

Now, as I recline on a bench and stare at the heartlessly cheerful blue sky, I hear the crunch of gravel on the walk. Someone approaches my private alcove.

Can't everyone leave me alone to brood in peace?

Apparently not, because the footsteps stop. Out of the corner of my eye, I see a male figure. Not Prince Escalus, thank God. This guy is blond. "Whatever you're selling, I'm not interested." With so many younger siblings, I know how to utilize a crushing tone when I wish, but this guy doesn't take the hint.

Slowly I turn my head and—

"Lysander!" I sat up.

Yes. It was he, my One True Love.

I had really hoped this moment would not occur for, well, never.

Lysander is, as always, as glorious as the sun. His straight, dark blond hair is streaked with strawberry, his complexion fair and unmarked by pox. But today, unlike previous moments, his full, soft lips did not smile as if the sight of me filled his soul, and his large green eyes examined me as if seeing the stain of sin.

That air of judgment reeking from a man who had previously regarded me with awe, affection, even love, may have contributed to my inappropriately jocular comment. "You're late!"

He didn't laugh.

My smile died. "Last night, you were supposed to be here in my arms. Nurse would alert my father, Lord Romeo, to our assignation. We would be discovered and forced to wed. It all worked perfectly except—*Where were you?*" It was my cry of anguish.

Lysander recognized it as such. His expression softened. He seated himself beside me and wrapped his arm comfortingly around my shoulders. Which, by the way, was more physical intimacy than we'd ever previously enjoyed. "I was detained."

"How?"

"On my way here, a fight broke out on the street before me. Three men, then four, then five, shouting and throwing punches. Then more. I tried to work my way through the expanding brawl. I was desperate to get to you, to enact our clever scheme and thus ensure our betrothal and future happiness."

Tears filled my eyes and spilled over.

"The prince's men arrived, breaking it up, hauling everyone off to the dungeons."

I nodded. As I'd surmised. "You were caught in Prince Escalus's trap."

"I didn't know it at the time. I shouted my name, over and over, begging the prince's men to pay heed, and at last they did. I was released and sped to Casa Montague, late but ever hopeful, and what greeted my unbelieving ears was—" He stopped. He was unable to speak the fateful words.

"By the news that I was betrothed to Prince Escalus."

"That was this morning's news." Lysander withdrew his arm.

"Last night, I was greeted by much masculine mirth and laughter—"

"Mirth?" What toerags my father's guests had turned out to be! My life had been upended and they were *laughing*?

"—and the news that the longtime virgin Lady Rosaline had been despoiled by Prince Escalus."

"I was not despoiled! It was dark. I didn't know it was Prince Escalus. He kissed me, and you know what that means." It means that society judges women unfairly.

Lysander didn't seem to see it that way. "It means you were despoiled."

"It was merely a few kisses." Experienced kisses, expert kisses, if the turmoil they raised was any indication, but I saw no reason to bring that to Lysander's attention. He seemed to be irritated enough.

"My father was among the men who witnessed the scene. He held one of the torches. He said you were on your back on a bench"—Lysander abruptly stood as if he could no longer bear to sit near—"and in *your* monologue, *you* made it clear Prince Escalus had had his hand on your bare leg *and* you were familiar with his touch."

"I thought he was you!"

"You thought I'd previously had my hand on your bare leg?" Lysander stepped sideways away from me.

"No. No." I had to take control of this conversation. "I thought you were the man who kissed me, for we had planned it thus. Remember our plan?"

"I was delayed, so instead you kissed the prince?"

I repeated, "I told you, I thought he was you!"

Lysander stared at me as if he wanted to strangle me.

"You and I, we've never exchanged a zealous kiss to seal the indenture of our love. How was I supposed to know the difference between your blushing lips and his?"

Chapter 2

To me, that was logical.

Apparently, Lysander didn't view the matter as I did. Leaping up, he said, "You kiss by the book!" and stormed away, leaving me in much the same condition as I was when he arrived, only more wretched and confused.

I put my head in my hands and moaned, then jumped when I heard a thud behind me.

My younger sister Imogene hated to stitch, speak softly, and sit with her knees together. She loved to climb trees, shout, and dig in the dirt. She had just jumped out of the tree that grew beside my alcove and stood looking at me quizzically. "Rosie, you bungled that one."

"I know, but I don't know why."

She seated herself beside me. "You know how men say, 'All cats are gray in the dark'? And they snigger?"

"Yes." I didn't get it.

"I didn't know what that meant, so I asked Mamma. Everyone says you're the smart one, Rosie. Can't you figure it out?"

I thought. "You mean Lysander thought that, despite my inexperience, I should be able to discern the difference between my One True Love and the very prince of deceit." I thought some more. "Lysander was insulted."

"Yeah."

"I am fortune's fool! I pass the crown. You're the smart one."

She stuck a finger through the hole in her gown. In tones of great gloom, she said, "Nurse is going to yell at me. She'll tell me I'm twelve years old, that Mamma married Papà when she was thirteen, and I need to stop having fun."

I'd heard that lecture myself. Had heard it for years and years. "I'll fix it for you. I owe you for the explanation. Nurse doesn't have to know."

"Thank you, Rosaline." Imogene swung her feet. "Are you still mad at everybody?"

"Honey, I'm not mad at *everybody*. I'm mad at me for being so careless and"—I remembered what Lysander said about the men laughing at me—"I'm . . . humiliated."

"Why?"

"I have to marry Verona's podestà, Prince Escalus the younger of the house of Leonardi. Because he decided he wanted a wife and I would do nicely because of my organizational abilities, my virginity, and my nice *tette*."

"He said that?" Even Imogene was horrified.

"That was the gist of it. After he . . . he . . ."

"Despoiled you?"

"No, he did *not* despoil me. It was merely a few kisses."

"Oh. Because I was in the oak over by the wall and I heard Lady Luce and Lady Perdita talking on the street and they said he despoiled you."

"They have ever been monstrous neighbors." I didn't want to know, but I had to ask. "Were they mirthful?"

"Um. Sort of. Snorting and smirking." Imogene got a worrisome smile on her face. "You know those nasty worms that spin those webs and eat all the leaves on the trees?"

I glanced up at the white webs on the ends of the branches. "Yes. Gardener has been trying to get rid of them, but he says it's an infestation and we'll have to wait for winter to put an end to them."

"I threw a branch full of worms and webs on the ladies."

After I got done laughing, I asked, "Did they see you?"

Grinning, she shook her head. "They screamed and did the icky worm dance."

I hugged her. "I love you—and not merely for that!"

"But you don't love the prince?"

"No. No! Aside from the fact Lysander is my One True Love, and I'll never love another, organizational ability, virginity, and *tette*? Makes you swoon at the romance, doesn't it?"

"No." Imogene might be a hoyden, but she understood romance. As a daughter of Romeo and Juliet, it was required.

"Me neither." Yet that was the essence of last night's coup d'état speech masquerading as a proposal. Or maybe it was a proposal masquerading as a coup d'état speech. Hard to tell.

She slipped her hand into mine. "What are you going to do, Rosie?"

"I'll marry, for this time even this unready maid must bear the yoke."

"No!" She squeezed my fingers. "You don't have to. You could stay here with us. We could be a family forever and ever!"

This time, I wrapped both arms around her. "Honey, we *are* a family forever and ever. But although I'm still a virgin"—Blessed Mary, how I'd come to hate that word!—"my virtue has been besmirched. I must either get me to a nunnery or get married to the man who did the besmirching."

"Why?" she wailed. "Why can't you stay here?"

"Prince Escalus is not a bad man. I don't believe he'll beat me or lock me up or tell me to change to be a wife more suitable for the podestà. Indeed, he was married once before to Princess Chiarretta, and he treated her with great deference and mourned when she died in childbirth with his son. Prince Escalus seems very aware of what I am like—"

"Nice *tette*," Imogene muttered.

"Yes. For that, and other reasons, is why he graced me . . .

with the honor . . . of being his wife." I was descending into bitterness and sarcasm, and that wasn't the purpose of this conversation. My duty now was to explain clearly to Imogene the results of her earnestly given suggestion, so I pulled up my big-girl *camicia* and said, "If I fail to marry or retire with my shame to a convent, the family will be ostracized. *You'll* be ostracized. No other family will allow their son to marry you."

"I don't care."

She meant it, I knew . . . now. "There's more." I lifted one finger. "No other family will allow their sons to marry Katherina or Emilia. Cesario will never be able to find a bride to carry on the noble line of Montague. Our married sisters won't be allowed to visit us. We'll wither and die in Casa Montague. Last but not least, my darling Imogene, the legend and romance that is Romeo and Juliet will be forever tarnished."

She swallowed and gave a curt nod of understanding. "Then it is thus. Can I help you prepare for your wedding?"

"I'll *need* you to help me prepare for the wedding. We'll make it a proper Montague celebration."

Imogene brightened. "That would serve the ol' prince right!"

Chapter 3

*On Tuesday next at 8 p.m.,
Princess Isabella of the House of Leonardi
Requests the Honor of the Presence of Rosaline of
the House of Montague,
Her Honored Parents, and Beloved Siblings
for a Tour of the Palace and its Gardens
and a Simple Family Dinner to Celebrate the
Upcoming Nuptials of
Lady Rosaline to Prince Escalus of the House of
Leonardi*

**Please send your acceptance via return messenger
within the hour.**

"Oh, man, do we have to?"
"It could be fun."
"A tour of the palace? Nuh-uh."
"Probably there'll be art and, you know, culture."
Gloomy silence.
"It won't be so bad. We *like* Princess Isabella."
"I *love* Princess Isabella." Cesario was six years old and in-

fatuated with Prince Escalus's sister, who was twelve. He saw no impediment in the age gap—like my father, he had incredible confidence in himself and his own powers of persuasion.

"And we like food." Katherina, thirteen, was trying hard to look on the bright side.

"The palace is *infamous* for its kitchen." Emilia had just turned eight; she was the family wit and food critic.

"We'll have to use our best manners." For Imogene, this was clearly the worst of the upcoming ordeal.

"Tuesday is *tomorrow night*."

More gloomy silence.

"'Within the hour'? Who says that?" Papà was incredulous.

"One assumes the prince," Mamma said sensibly.

"We're stuck." Imogene expressed solid despair better than any of us.

Gloom deepened over my family: my parents, Romeo and Juliet, and my younger, still-living-at-home siblings Katherina, Imogene, Emilia, and Cesario. Mamma had called us to the family table in the atrium of our spacious home in Verona for the reading of the invitation. It was chilly out here; autumn had arrived early, but she was at the overheated portion of her pregnancy.

I spoke up. "I'll write back and accept?" I asked brightly.

"Better let me do it." Mamma lifted herself carefully out of her chair, hand on her back. Papà's hand hovered behind her, but he didn't dare help. She was also at the snappish part of her pregnancy. "I'm tactful, unlike everyone else in the family."

Our faithful family nurse hurried over to offer her arm. Mamma took it and we watched them enter the library.

"It's true," Papà said. "Juliet can tell you to go to hell and make you look forward to the journey."

"You would know." Katherina grinned at him.

He didn't grin back. "Yes . . . there's something about having a baby that makes her look unfavorably on men in general—

and me specifically. It might have something to do with waking up all night long to piss."

"You could get up with her," Imogene suggested.

"I tried that. It makes her angrier. Like a serpent maddened by night's candleflames, she *hisses* at me." The greatest swordsman in Verona actually looked frightened.

My mother is one of the kindest, most gentlewomen on the face of this flat earth and, it goes without saying, the most beautiful. She was also one of the most formidable as the rude, curious, and unwary frequently discovered to their dismay. I half hoped Prince Escalus would step over the line and find out the hard way, but I also half hoped Prince Escalus tripped and fell face-first in a pile of donkey dung, so you could say that, no matter my advanced age, my maturity was not to be admired.

"I'm sorry, dear *famiglia,* for being such an idiot." If I'd apologized once, I'd apologized a hundred times.

Emilia asked what all my siblings were wondering. "Rosie, did you really f—"

Papà and I answered at the same time. "No!"

"Why not?" She may have been only eight, but in our family, what with the noises that came from our parents' bedroom, we all had a good grasp of human nature, or at least human nature as related to Romeo and Juliet. Romance and flirting led to passion, which led to singing bed ropes, which led to Mamma tossing her biscotti every morning and another baby in the family.

To Papà, the answer was easy. "We caught them in time."

The real reason was a little different. "I realized I had the wrong gentleman in my arms and kicked him in the hairy hangers," I replied.

Cesario and Papà winced and flinched.

"You kicked the prince? Good for you!" Imogene imitated a solid kick.

"Did you bring him to his knees?" More than the rest of us sisters, Emilia felt the indignation of being subservient to men, and fully supported bloodlust to right the unbalance.

"Not quite, but his breath's release made a gratifying whooshing noise." I'd lived on the satisfaction of that sound ever since.

Emilia got right to the heart of the matter. "Who was the *right* gentleman?"

I looked at her. Just looked at her.

Emilia had the makings of the second most sensible of the Montagues after me; now she exploded with exasperation. "You were going out to meet Lysander? In the garden? In the dark? You could have been debauched! You could have been kidnapped! You could have been found with a knife in your chest! Remember Duke Stephano, your most recent betrothed, who was stabbed in that very garden!" She pointed, as if I didn't remember the location of Duke Stephano's stabbing. "Rosaline, what were you thinking?"

I exploded back at her. "I was thinking that Lysander's family had said no to a match with me, and he loves me and asked me to figure out a way we could be together, and, you know, the swiftest path to marriage is the one through the bedroom!"

"That's also the swiftest path to the nunnery!"

"The plan should have worked!"

"It didn't!"

At the same time, Emilia and I realized our mother had returned from the library and stood viewing us both with disfavor. She handed the sealed paper to our footman and in a soft voice said, "Please make sure that is delivered to Princess Isabella." She turned to her family and said in an even softer voice, "The volume of Montague voices is most displeasing in young ladies and"—her own volume rose—"for at least the next two months or until I deliver this blessed babe, could I please have evidence that my daughters show some semblance of a proper upbringing rather than shaming me by braying like two donkeys?"

At once, Emilia and I were on our feet and curtsying. "Yes, Madam Mother. As you command, Madam Mother."

Mamma continued, "Tomorrow night, we leave at seven. Before we leave, make sure you're clean, dressed in the proper garments, and lined up for inspection. There will be *smiles*. There will be *manners*. There will be *no excuses accepted*." She waited until everyone was on their feet and bowing and curtsying and announcing, "Yes, Madam Mother. As you command, Madam Mother." Then she pinned me with a level look that promised bloody retribution should I defy her. "We go to support our beloved Rosie as she faces the future *she* created for *herself,* and to that end, Rosie will sweep aside her disgraceful indulgence in self-pity."

"That's not fair!" I protested. "Prince Escalus admits he eavesdropped on the plan to unite Lysander and me as a couple, diverted Lysander, and substituted himself—"

"Rosie's disgraceful indulgence in self-pity, and her whining complaints of what is fair and not fair, will now end. Because what have I always told you children?" Mamma pointed a finger at us.

We cowered and recited, "'Justice and life seldom walk hand in hand.'"

Her attention returned to me. "What does that mean?"

"'Life ain't fair.'" I now believed it fervently.

She used her gaze to hold mine. "Neither by word nor deed will Rosie sabotage her betrothal to the prince. With her deliberate attempt to take destiny in her own hands, she has angered the Fates and now she must face the consequences, which most in her position would consider an honor."

While the prince's union with me formed a short footbridge

over a small social chasm and was in itself perfectly unremarkable, nevertheless the Montagues and the Capulets, wildly successful merchants all, didn't regularly intermarry with the dukes and princes of Verona.

"Do you understand me, Rosaline Hortensa Magdelina Eleanor?" Mamma demanded.

It was always bad news when she called me by my full name. I curtsied and said, "Yes, Madam Mother."

"What do I mean?"

I muttered, "That I can't secretly meet Lysander ever again and I can't say anything to Prince Escalus that will give him a disgust of me."

"More than that, you'll display the sweet side of your nature, which we as your family well know, to the prince, your betrothed."

I nodded sullenly.

"What?" she snapped.

"Yes, Madam Mother. I will do as you instruct, Madam Mother." I dared not put the slightest hint of defiance in my tone, and my deep curtsy reflected my absolute obedience to her as my commanding officer.

If her waiting stillness was anything to go by, she still wasn't satisfied.

As I knew I must, I added, "I do so swear."

Mamma's gaze swept across me and my siblings like a scythe, leaving us awed, afraid and silent. In that tone that both condemned and commanded, she said, "Love teaches even asses to dance."

The quiet continued until she entered her bedroom and Nurse delicately shut the door behind them.

"Not sure, Rosie," Imogene said, "but I think Mamma is irritated with you."

Heads nodded in unison.

"At least it's not me," Papà said cheerfully, and strode off whistling.

I'm so glad someone had something to be happy about.

Gentle reader, in case you don't know . . . that was also sarcasm.

Please don't tell my mother.

Chapter 4

The Montague family was preparing to go to the palace for that intimate dinner. The image should have conjured up glamour, excitement, music, food, and wine.

Alas, it was not so.

Earlier, Nurse had helped Mamma into her voluminous gown with a high waist to accommodate the baby bump. As always, Mamma personified glamour and beauty, Verona's ideal noblewoman ripe with child.

Now in my bedroom, she reclined on my bed with pillows behind her shoulders and supervised as Nurse and her staff helped Katherina, Imogene, Emilia, and me into our layers of chemises, stockings, underskirts, bodices, and skirts.

In the adjoining bedroom, Papà had volunteered himself and his manservant to wrestle Cesario into his formal clothing.

For my sake, my sisters attempted to maintain their good humor, joking that because of the reported dismal state of dining at the palace, I should strap on the scabbard Nurse had given me, but leave out the dagger and instead stuff it full of bread, cheese, and dates.

Yet, as Emilia said morosely, that wasn't funny when it sounded like such a good idea.

We did, of course, each have our eating knives attached to

our belts with a scabbard, but we couldn't leave those home any more than we could walk the streets without shoes. A guest who arrived at a meal without a blade would likely go home hungry and defenseless.

I had a new silk gown—bodice and skirt, never worn—made for Mamma before she fell pregnant. The color, an intense teal, should have been too bold for an ingenue, but as Mamma said, I was too old to play that role, the prince was too sensible to expect it, and because she'd passed her dramatic coloring on to me, the color presented me like a dewy pearl in a velvet setting. Overnight, Nurse had driven our seamstresses to lengthen the hem (I was taller than Mamma), let out the bodice (my shoulders and rib cage were broader than Mamma's), and create a matching pearled cap to cover my dark hair and matching beaded sleeves to be laced onto the bodice.

I felt like the prize pig at an auction.

"*Should* she carry a dagger?" Nurse was serious. "For the first time, she's going to the palace as the prince's betrothed, an important role in these treacherous times, and enemies may lurk in the dark corners and hidden places."

No one scoffed. My recent ordeal with Verona's first serial killer had left more scars than the one on my chest. We had discovered by grisly experience that a woman, no matter how protected, could discover danger where she least expected it.

"Yes!" Imogene was all about fighting.

"Not Lysander's dagger," Mamma warned. "Nor yours, good Nurse. The prince's dagger is correct."

When danger had first reared its head, both Nurse and Lysander had given me daggers, to strap one each onto my arms.

Prince Escalus had given me a dagger also, this one a stiletto to strap onto my ankle.

I had put them all to good use, and his dagger I had slipped into a scabbard lined with ribs and extinguished a beating heart. His dagger, wielded by me, had saved my own most wretched flesh, and for that, at least, I was grateful.

Nurse fetched the blade from the cupboard, knelt and buckled the worn leather onto my leg, then straightened my linen underskirt and velvet overskirt so no sign of it showed.

Now dressed, we girls lined up in front of the bed for Mamma's preliminary inspection.

She clasped her hands over her heart. "My beautiful daughters!"

We were, of course. That's not narcissism; when you're raised knowing your parents are the most beautiful, romantic, admired couple in the known world, it follows that you, too, are a beauty. We all have varying degrees of raven hair, golden skin, and well-lashed, large brown eyes. Katherina and I had developed curvaceous figures; we assumed the younger girls would, too. With another vision of pulchritude always following close behind me, I didn't waste time on conceit.

Yet standing here, a jewelry box of silks and satins, gold embroidered sleeves and soft shawls woven in Nepal, we knew we were striking, even intimidating.

Nurse helped Mamma sit up.

"Now!" Mamma said. "Emilia, stop picking your nose. Katherina, lift your chin! No one will notice the pimple on your forehead."

"How can they not?" Katherina snapped. "It's a unicorn horn!"

Nurse studied it, then produced a yellow-colored salve that reduced the redness.

"Imogene, show me your hands." Mamma looked at Imogene's nails and shook her head. "Nurse, take her and use soap and a brush."

As Nurse dragged her away, Imogene wailed a protest.

Mamma continued, "Emilia, forget you have a nose. Rosie,

come here." She held out her hand. I came and took it. "You're handling this calmly. Are you feeling well?"

"Mamma, I would rage and cry if I thought it would do any good, but I recognize the truth of your words yesterday. I do take responsibility for my actions." The certainty was, my world had fallen apart and I had moved from hot wrath to numb horror. "I'm resigned to my fate."

Katherina snorted.

I looked at her. "In sooth, I am. I'll be the wife of the podestà. I'll be wealthy, wear beautiful clothing, host parties, be the envy of all Verona—"

"You don't care about any of that stuff!" Emilia protested.

"No, but that's what my life now will be. Before Lysander, I'd schemed to stay here in the heart of Family Montague and be the maiden aunt to all the babies you would have. I'd have been happy. To my surprise, I met Lysander and dared to dream I had at last discovered a love worthy of a progeny of Romeo and Juliet's. Then . . ." I lifted a despairing hand and let it fall.

Katherina was the daughter who always asked the right questions. "Did Prince Escalus explain *why* he was there instead of Lysander?"

"He said quite a few things. He wants a wife and he had specifications. Apparently, despite my temper and my unappreciated ability to shout loudly enough to make myself heard, he values me a master diplomat." In reference to my ability to tactfully maneuver myself out of unwanted betrothals . . . except the last one in which my betrothed was stabbed to death by the aforesaid serial killer. That happened without any maneuvering on my part.

I promise you, it did.

"Diplomacy is good for the wife of the podestà." Katherina nodded.

I shot her a glare, then remembered my resolve to remain stoic in the face of this adversity. "He said he liked my charming family."

"Emilia, stop picking your nose!" Mamma commanded.

"It itches!" Emilia protested.

"Come here, child." Mamma held a linen towel to Emilia's face. "Now blow."

Emilia honked.

"He's in for a rude shock," Katherina told me. "What else?"

"He wants an older sister to care for Princess Isabella."

"You have the creds for that." Katherina tried always to look on the bright side, but now in a biting tone, she added, "It would be pleasant if you could have been left in place to act the older sister to *us*."

I hugged her. "I'll always be there when you have need of me."

"Don't wrinkle!" Nurse shrieked from the basin, where she scrubbed at Imogene's hands.

We deftly separated.

"He said I'd proved myself to be a good household manager." (This was true; Mamma was a grand woman, but a disaster at managing the Casa Montague and I'd early taken the reins.) "And because I come from fertile stock, I'll provide him with a crew of strong sons to row his barge and a flock of lovely daughters to listen, enraptured, as he spins the same tale over and over of his past triumphs."

The last was a jest of a kind; at the dinner table, Papà did enjoy repeating tales of his youth until we all cried, "Desist!" Not that he ever listened.

"He's the prince. Of course, he wants heirs." Mamma sounded prosaic.

"He did mention that," I said, "and he seemed enthralled with filling the empty, echoing corridors of the palace with progeny."

"Ahhh." Mamma and Katherina sighed sentimentally. "How sweet."

I covered my face with my hands. I know my place in society, but the hop from lifelong virgin to breeder of nations seemed sudden, jarring, and—considering the bedroom duties necessary to bring this about and the partner who had elected himself as my mate—a lot of work for a few minutes of what I assumed would be pleasure.

Someone tugged at my arm. I looked down into Emilia's wide eyes. "Yuck," she said.

"Thank you, Emilia. I couldn't agree more." I stared at the others. "Then he cited that I'd trusted him to rescue me from murder charges."

"He did do that," Katherina agreed.

"A lot of people helped with that," I snapped. "He said I teased him. He seemed much struck by that."

Mamma's soft heart was wrung. "No laughter, no teasing. Since the deaths of his parents, Escalus the elder by assassination and dear Eleanor after she gave birth to Princess Isabella, Prince Escalus has lacked a normal family life."

"He's not like us," Emilia said, and it wasn't a compliment.

"He said something about admiring my courage." Then I lied. "And that's all."

Imogene arrived holding out her distinctly cleaner hands as if they belonged to someone else, someone she didn't know or like.

Nurse followed close on her heels, and she mocked me. "That's all? Really? What about what he gave you?"

This woman had been my mother's nurse and my nurse and supervised the care of all the children. She slept in my room, she bossed us all, and now she butted into the conversation when I least wanted her.

I glared, conveying my displeasure without words. "He didn't give me *anything*." That I wanted to admit.

As was her wont, she blithely ignored my palpable hint. "After you met with him, you clutched something in your hand and held it to your heart."

Mamma and my sisters all began to smile.

"Let me assist your faulty memory," Nurse said. "When I asked you about it, you said he gave you something to think about."

In exasperation, I said, "*La merda,* woman, do you never cease your babbling?"

"Don't be vulgar, Rosaline," Mamma said automatically.

Nurse put on an innocent expression. "To be silent when I know the truth would be a sin of omission."

My three sisters began circling like the brats they are. "What did he give you, Rosie? Did he give you a ring? Did he give you a kiss? Did he give his heart?"

"Definitely not his heart." If he'd said he loved me, I might not return his affection, but I wouldn't be quite so aggravated.

"We haven't seen a ring," Imogene said, "so—"

Katherina and Emilia chanted, "Oooo, a kiss. Rosie got a kiss. Rosie got a kiss. Rosie got a—"

"That's enough, girls." Mamma was firm, but smiling. "We must leave Rosie her secrets."

"Humph." Like that was going to happen in this household.

Papà staggered in, sweaty and exhausted, pushing Cesario ahead of him. Tommaso, our young footman recently promoted to the position as Papà's manservant, stood behind him, looking equally worn. "Behold my son, perfectly dressed. Now I have to go change again. Don't let him get dirty or tear anything. I'll be right back!" He sprinted out of my room and down the corridor to our parents' suite, with Tommaso on his heels.

Cesario smiled, a cheerful imp, and struck a pose. "Princess Isabella will think I'm handsome and love me more than ever."

"You're a blister on the bottom of humanity"—if there was

a choice between diplomacy and insult, Emilia always chose the insult—"and Princess Isabella knows it."

"I am not!" Cesario shoved her with his hand.

"Are too." Emilia shoved back.

"She does not!" He shoved.

"Does too!" She body shoved.

Nurse caught them both by the backs of the necks and held them apart. "You will both remain clean and unwrinkled until you arrive at the palace or I'll personally wash and iron you while you're in your clothing."

Both kids relaxed so abruptly, they fell to the floor, where they remained until Papà arrived clad in an entirely different outfit. "To think I used to take an hour to dress," he marveled. "Children have an unexpected way of changing your priorities."

Mamma put her hand on her belly and half closed her eyes. "This child is much more placid than Cesario. Probably a girl."

"No, Mamma, it's a boy." Imogene threw that off as if everyone should know. "He looks like Grandpapa Montague and he'll make famous wines."

We stared at her. Imogene had a most disconcerting way of predicting the future, which wouldn't be a concern if she was wrong, but she was always right.

Time to turn the subject before someone mentioned witchcraft. "One thing about this visit," I announced with robust, if unlikely, good humor, "there's no way it can be as bad as we fear."

Chapter 5

"The central atrium of the palace contains exotic trees and plants from far-distant lands, like Persia and Aksum. You can tell this tree, commonly called a palmyra by the long, hanging leaves and the rough, scaly bark." Prince Escalus used his long fingers to display the leaves to the whole Montague family, who nodded in unison, holding their eyes open as wide as they could to keep from nodding off. "It is said to grow to great heights far to the east, in the warmer parts of Jambudv pa."

In the big scheme of things, this oratory was nothing more than a fleeting moment of discomfort, but . . . my fault. My fault that my beloved family was bored almost to tears and we all now knew that we faced many more moments of excruciating ennui. Moments that would stretch into hours, and hours into years . . .

Because I was betrothed to Prince Escalus, soon to be married to him. I'd doomed my family and myself to an eternity of listening to him expound about his peculiar enthusiasms as if they were interesting.

I groaned gloomily.

Prince Escalus stopped talking and looked at me in inquiry.

Mamma and Katherina viewed me in warning.

Cesario piped up, "Rosie, you sound like Mamma. Does your tummy hurt like hers?"

I put my hand on my belly. "Sweet Jesus, no!"

Papà glared at my hand.

I dropped it to my side and faked a smile. "Prince Escalus, while as an apprentice apothecary, I admire your enthusiasm for your garden—you have so many gardeners!"

I'd glimpsed a dozen men and women lurking in the bushes, kneeling in the dirt holding a trowel, carrying plants in pots.

Prince Escalus flicked a glance around. "My garden is dear to me."

"Obviously."

"As an apprentice apothecary, would you like to tour the herb garden?" He gestured toward the walls that separated the common herbs from his more exotic plants.

"No, I thank you." Heaven forbid! "I fear my family doesn't share my enthusiasm for herbal preparations. While we have our whole lives to enjoy this marvelous space, I'd hoped to hear more about the palace art and culture." A lousy excuse, and one that had my siblings rolling their eyes, but better than any suspicion that I might be with child.

Prince Escalus strode over, loomed over me (I was to discover he used looming to great effect), and looked into my eyes. "I was going to tell you about this spring-blooming plant, commonly known as *rhododendron*. But whatever my future bride desires is my command."

Behind us, Imogene faked sticking her finger down her throat.

Mamma slapped her lightly on the back of the head.

I grinned.

One side of Prince Escalus's mouth lifted. I think it was supposed to be a smile, but with this melancholy guy, who knew? Anyway, why was he smiling? He hadn't seen the byplay.

The word "melancholy" fit Prince Escalus like a well-tailored coat. He'd never been a handsome boy, and, in fact, before the battles, I remember him comporting himself like the self-important youth he knew himself to be. Son of the podestà, heir to the rule of Verona—how learned, how glorious, and how commanding in his every word and deed! Even young as I was, I disdained him. Not that it mattered; I was a girl and unworthy of his notice.

Then, eleven years ago, his life had been split in two. The house of Acquasasso tried by stealth, violence, and deception to take the office of podestà for their own. Prince Escalus the elder put down their rebellion, for he was a warrior of renown, and in the aftermath was assassinated. To this day, the assassin remained at large and undetected.

Barely thirteen, Prince Escalus the younger survived imprisonment and torture. He rose from the dungeons to take command of the city, and now his importance was indeed as great as he'd previously imagined. Still, suffering had marked the unremarkable countenance, and not in a good way. Although he was now but twenty-four, he wore black, and black, and more black, lightened by occasional trims of midnight blue, mold green, and gloomy maroon. Streaks of white marked his shoulder-length black hair, his brown skin bore a gray tinge of dungeon, and his scarred complexion would eternally show signs of the knife and the heated rod. He limped slightly from the iron bar they had used on the bones of his right leg, and although I'd never seen him in action, he'd earned a fearsome reputation as a swordsman.

In other words, Prince Escalus was the complete opposite of my One True Love, Lysander of the house of Marcketti.

Cesario's patience had been tested long enough, and he blurted, "Prince Escalus, where's Princess Isabella? I *love* Princess Isabella. I want to see *her*."

Prince Escalus glanced around as if puzzled. "I don't know. I believed she would join us for this part of the tour. She always seems so interested in my garden."

In other words, she was staying the hell away.

"I'm sure directing a formal dinner could be a challenge for a twelve-year-old." Mamma had already established herself as the orphaned Princess Isabella's surrogate mother. "Perhaps I should find her and offer my assistance."

"And me!" Katherina said.

"And me!" Imogene said.

"And me!" Emilia said.

"And me!" Cesario said.

Papà put his hand on Cesario's shoulder. "Son, men don't interfere in the business of women."

"That's not fair!" Cesario protested. "I'm the one who asked about her!"

"Princess Isabella is surprisingly accomplished at such formalities," Prince Escalus assured us, "and needs no assistance."

"If you have no taste," Katherina said to me out of the corner of her mouth.

I widened my eyes to keep from cackling.

The prince continued, "If you come this way, this door leads into the long walk."

As with most rich homes in Verona, the palace stood as a private enclave surrounded by tall stone walls built to keep intruders out and the residents safe, for Veronese families fought for power, and at any moment, another city-state could march to bring us under their control. Yet while the palace walls were the tallest and most heavily fortified, and the towers were created to support the prince's archers and watchmen, the interior reflected all the wealth and comfort of a master family. The atrium at the center of the house was the largest I'd ever seen, and the balconies and stairways and great carved wood doors led into the home itself. Despite my recent humiliations at the prince's hands, the interior of the palace interested me.

Prince Escalus led the way. "Within the great walk, we display the works we collect for public display."

"You allow the public to view?" Papà knew very well he did not. Since the revolt, the prince had instigated a security shut-down and no one entered the palace except to speak privately to the prince, and that in one designated and well-guarded office chamber.

"No." Prince Escalus was brief, blunt, and unapologetic. "The best works of art we keep above with the bedrooms for our private enjoyment." He turned to me and without appearing to move closer, again he loomed. "I look forward to giving you, Rosie, a private showing."

Gentle reader, what was I supposed to say to that?

I'm looking forward to it, too?

Because while I'm not a subtle person, I knew his private showing had little to do with works of art.

Papà made a low, rumbling growl.

That was never a good sign.

Mamma, bless her, stepped in with a firm hand on Papà's arm and a pleasant reprimand. "As you know, Prince Escalus, Romeo is one of the most renowned swordsmen in Verona—"

Cesario interrupted, "*The* most renowned." He knew the legend as well as anybody, and although he didn't quite understand Prince Escalus's subtext, he did know he didn't like the tone of the conversation.

Mamma placed her other hand on the top of Cesario's head. "—and should anyone unsheathe their works of art prematurely, I don't know if I could stop my beloved husband, Romeo, from removing said works of art from their hooks on the wall."

Chapter 6

A prolonged pause.

Prince Escalus looked around at the Montagues. Mamma was now gripping Papà's straining elbow with both hands. Katherina kept a straight face. Imogene openly giggled. Emilia was whispering to Cesario what Mamma's code meant. (Remember, Cesario was only six, and a boy; subtlety was beyond him.)

At last, Prince Escalus's gaze landed on me.

I explained, "In a large family, a member must always be aware that what one says may be overheard and subject to interpretation by other members. Discretion is advised."

Prince Escalus looked around again at the Montagues, and I think it was the first time he truly realized that in marrying me, he married the whole family.

I felt obliged to add, "Please recall, I have two sisters not present who are equally opinionated and outspoken."

Katherina had to spoil my warning with an opinion of her own. "No one's as opinionated and outspoken as you, Rosie."

Prince Escalus's mouth did that sideways twitch, which might indicate horror in this case, but I'd come to suspect might be humor. He bowed first to Mamma and Papà. "I beg your pardon. I hold the greatest respect for your daughter's virginity."

Only I recognized that as a thrust (if you'll pardon the term) at my irritation with that virtue that has given me fame among the vulgar of Verona.

Papà gave another growl, not quite as menacing, but, still, a warning. "Step carefully, my prince. Montague loyalty flows to the house of Leonardi. But above and beyond all other duty, I am the papà. I stand *with* my noble family in joy and peace, and *before* my family as a bulwark against harm."

Imogene's giggles abruptly halted. The other children straightened and nodded solemnly.

"I understand, Lord Montague." Prince Escalus bowed more deeply to Papà and Mamma. "And madam."

"We know our roles in our world," I said softly.

He viewed my siblings with what I thought must be a new comprehension, inclined his head to them, and offered me his arm. "Would you walk beside me, Rosaline, as we lead our family to the grand walk?"

I placed one fingertip on his velvet-clad arm. "As you command, my prince."

He looked at that fingertip, then into my eyes, and I knew he saw too much.

He said nothing, and merely led me toward the palace's massive doors of walnut and worked bronze. At our approach, two footmen in livery flung wide the entrance, and once inside, Prince Escalus waved an encompassing hand.

No one spoke a word, our reticence not because of ennui, as in the garden, but because this place, this home, this monument to beauty conquered us with parts equally glowing and impressive. The high ceilings, the wooden floors, the long carpets, the statues, the framed paintings, the murals, the gilding, the candles, the fresh flowers . . . the rich, warm colors of the tapestries threaded with gold and the velvet curtains.

Each breath felt alive with color, as if I was standing inside a sunset, and for the first time in days, my humbled soul eased.

Mamma broke the silence. "My prince, who decorated this?"

"My mother, Princess Eleanor," Prince Escalus answered.

"I knew it!" Mamma's eyes sparkled with joy. "When Eleanor walked into a room, she lit the very air with warmth."

"You knew my mother?" Prince Escalus asked without expression.

"I did. She was my dear friend. Her death robbed the world of light." Suddenly Mamma looked tired, and she gripped Papà's arm.

At once, Papà said, "Prince Escalus, the wife of my heart needs rest before our meal. Where may I take her?"

"This way." Prince Escalus gestured the Montague offspring to the right along the great walk. "If you like, you may preview the works and I'll be along later to help you understand them."

While Prince Escalus escorted my parents into a quiet room close by, I noted a great many maids dusting, and a footman or two hovered to give advice. Such a display seemed excessive to me, but it wasn't yet any of my business how the prince ran his household. What was my business was my doleful siblings, who stood eyeing each other and me.

"This is nice," Emilia said, "but—"

"Art . . ." Imogene moaned softly.

Cesario wasn't a whiny boy, but he whined now. "Do we have to? Look at the pictures and the statues?"

"Don't worry, the prince will be 'along later,' " Imogene imitated Escalus's superior tone, " 'to help you understand them.' "

The art tour stretched before us in excruciating boredom, and without Mamma's diplomacy, we had no chance of escaping.

"Psst!" I heard. "Psst! Emilia!"

In unison, we looked around. Princess Isabella stood behind a heavy velvet curtain, beckoning to my youngest sister.

It took only a moment for us to realize Princess Isabella offered escape, and Emilia leaped toward her and vanished into the folds.

Cesario started to rush toward concealment, but Princess Isabella held up a hand. "Wait. You're the boy. My brother will immediately realize you're missing. You must stay until almost the end."

Cesario sagged. "Noooo!"

Emilia stuck her head out. "You get to be the youngest. You get to be the boy. You get to do all the fun stuff. Balls up, kid!" She disappeared again.

Princess Isabella blew him a kiss, and she followed Emilia.

Cesario looked around at Katherina, Imogene, and me, and we nodded. "She's right," I told him.

He sagged and with dragging feet wandered toward me.

Prince Escalus stepped into the great walk and made a shooing gesture with his fingers. The servants vanished and my sisters scattered as if admiring the works of art; in fact, they had placed themselves in such a manner to make it difficult for him to realize we had lost a sibling. I pointed toward the ornate mosaic that covered part of one wall and projected my voice to fill the space. "You're right, Cesario, you *can* see the Moorish influence in the brightly colored tiles and elaborate design."

The prince joined us. "Did you recognize the Moorish influence, Cesario?"

Cesario fixed his gaze firmly on the prince's chin and lied like a trouper. "Uh-huh."

"Do you know the two reasons we have a Moorish influence in Verona?" Prince Escalus asked in an instructional tone.

"Nuh-huh."

"Because the Moors captured the island of Sicily and there spread their culture, art, and architecture. What do you think the other reason is?"

Cesario looked like a mouse trapped in the mouth of a scrawny cat. In what was clearly a wild guess based on his tutor's current teaching, he said, "The Holy Father's Crusades?"

"That's right!" Clearly delighted, Prince Escalus hugged Cesario's skinny little shoulder, while Cesario looked at me in alarm.

Prince Escalus looked around at the girls. "Come with me and I'll show you . . . Weren't there more children—"

Katherina joined us and widened her brown eyes, exotic in their upward tilt—Mamma's eyes—at him. "I can't wait to see what else you have to show us."

He fell for it. Of course.

Imogene lagged behind as Prince Escalus led us onward through the gallery, and whenever he glanced back, she would appear to be studying a sculpture or a textile.

He seemed gratified by her fascination, and by the questions with which Katherina and I plied him, and before too long, Imogene had vanished.

When the prince failed to notice, I nodded at Katherina and interrupted him midsentence. "Cesario, do you need to use the facilities?"

Cesario was squirming from boredom, an action easily misinterpreted by Prince Escalus.

"I'll have a footman take him," the prince said.

Two footmen popped out from beside the drapes and hurried toward us.

"It's a large palace and he's a small boy. With Mamma resting and Papà tending to her, I'm in charge." I spoke crisply, for I *was* the oldest sister and I *was* in charge. "I'd feel more at ease if Katherina escorted him. Perhaps the footman can show them where to go?"

"As you wish, but that leaves us quite—"

Katherina snatched Cesario's hand and fled, chased by the footman.

"—alone," the prince finished. He looked around. "Where did the other children disappear?"

"I'm sure they'll appear momentarily." I saw a nearby drape move.

A pale, sad-faced female peeked out at me, but as soon as my gaze met hers, she pulled back.

"Who was that?" I asked in a low voice.

"Orsa of the kitchen. She wants to view you, I trow."

"Yes. I do seem to be a moving display." I had suspicions that the parade of servants worked to observe their future mistress—she who would hold their futures in her hands. Testing my theory, I said, "The palace seems well tended, if perhaps a little dusty."

At once, two maids popped out of hiding holding cloths and wiped at vases and tables.

Craning my neck, I looked up. "Especially the cove molding and drapes. There are cobwebs!" I managed to sound scandalized.

Three footmen appeared, one carrying a ladder; in moments, the neglected upper parts of the great walk were being tended.

Prince Escalus seemed not to notice my manipulations. "Your siblings . . . as you said, it's a large palace, and I hope they're not lost."

"I'm sure they're fine." As I prepared to launch myself into scintillating conversation to keep him occupied, a large portrait had caught my eye, a man of impressive physique and weathered beauty. His shoulder-length blond hair had been artfully highlighted, his dark eyebrows served as a frame for his alert green eyes, his unsmiling mouth, sculptured cheekbones, and determined chin bespoke a man of authority and responsibility. I wandered toward it, trying to comprehend how it was possible for mere wood plank and paint to portray a face so alert his gaze seemed to be watching me. "Who is this?"

"My father, Prince Escalus the elder. Alberti painted him as Papà received the first rumbles of rebellion, and captured a mighty likeness of his sense of responsibility for the unrest and his ongoing schemes to turn the tide. After the uprising, much strife had changed his countenance. When he rescued me from the Acquasasso dungeons, he spoke more wisely and looked more haggard, a man who'd given all for his city and feared for the future of his family."

"When was he . . . ?"

"That very night, he was drugged and stabbed in his bed, and I, to my eternal shame, have not been able to find his killer."

Chapter 7

I knew the story, comprehended the prince's tragedy, loss, and sense of responsibility. As I looked up at the picture, my betrothed joined me, standing behind and to the right, and I looked between Prince Escalus, a man of shadow and scars, and the portrait. "You don't look like your father at all. He's very handsome."

Prince Escalus gave a bark.

I'd heard that sound once before. I was fairly sure it was his form of laughter, and immediately I realized what I'd said. "I didn't mean it that way. I meant—"

"I know what you meant. I resemble my paternal grandmother, a formidable woman who spreads terror before her like a farmer spreads manure."

I sputtered a laugh. "I have indeed heard such."

"Soon enough, you can form your own opinion."

Without thinking, I snipped, "One more thing to look forward to." At once, I realized I had broken my vow to my mother and myself, and swept around to face him. "Not that I—"

He was leaning down, leaning close, eyes closed, nostrils quivering.

"What are you doing?" I demanded.

His eyes popped open, and we stood face-to-face.

"Were you *smelling* me?" How bizarre was that?

He didn't straighten up or back away. "In the past, I've noted your hair smells like a flower."

"A flower."

"A rose. A dark red rose. One with velvety petals."

"Dark red? You know what a color smells like?" Then, "In the past, you've smelled my hair?" I didn't know how to respond. Outrage? Confusion? Laughter? I experienced them all.

"I don't know why dark red. Your hair's so black, it has blue highlights. I saw the whole glorious length of it, do you recall? In the moonlight?"

"Yes. I recall." Thank God, my mother had made me promise to be all that was polite because the memory was so uncomfortable I'd have punched him in the *pizzle* right there. "When you made the list of my virtues and my undesirable characteristics, which side did 'her hair smells like a dark red rose' go on?"

As you recall, gentle reader, by his own account, he'd done exactly that: made a list of what qualities I had that would make me a good wife and what qualities I embodied that weighed against me. Not that I held that cold, logical approach against him . . .

You're right. In my family, we looked not for riches or pulchritude—*everlasting love* ruled our lives.

He said, "I like the scent of a dark red rose. It inspires me with . . . dark red passion."

An almost inscrutable answer, except that now, as daylight fled and the autumn evening began its reign, I noted many things. Although he was scarred by the tortures he'd endured at the hands of the house of Acquasasso and not (as I've said) a handsome man, his eyes were large and heavy-lidded, changeable as the sea, seductive in their intense focus . . . on me. I, who had felt nothing but a burning humiliation at the clever and public way he'd entrapped me, now recalled how he'd laid me across his lap, wrapped himself around me, kissed me until wit had flown, and what took its place burned under my skin like cold, still silver heated to liquid lust.

The lust had not, as I thought, dissipated in the cold light of day, but only awaited the dusk and the man to heat again, and course through my veins, my nerves, my mind.

He grasped my left hand and looked into my palm. "Do you still have the betrothal kiss I placed therein?"

I nodded, because that was, in fact, what he'd given me on the night of my dishonor and our betrothal. He'd spoken of his admiration for my courage and my loyalty to saving my family. He'd pressed a kiss on my skin and wrapped my fingers around it and bade me keep it close to my heart, and, as Nurse had loudly and publicly noted, to my dismay, I did find myself occasionally and unexpectedly holding my fist to my chest.

Now the prince leaned in. His breath feathered across my skin. "A more solid token will soon take its place on your hand. A ring of precious diamonds that will with its magic stones protect you from harm and be a warning to all that the prince has claimed you . . . forever." His gaze compelled my eyes to close and—

Carried on the breeze, a voice called my name. "Rosaline . . ."

Chapter 8

I wrenched my head around. I looked down the gallery, expecting to see the figure of a man.

Nobody was there. No breeze ruffled the air.

"What?" Prince Escalus's dagger sang as he drew it, and he searched, too. "What's wrong?"

"Didn't you hear that?" I trod the carpet toward the far, dim end of the long walk. "Someone called me."

Prince Escalus looked around again, and gradually resheathed his dagger. "I heard nothing. Who called you?"

"I don't know."

"Are you making sport of me, Lady Rosaline?" In a moment, the prince's voice had changed from summer warm to winter chill.

"I am not, sir!"

"Is the man you heard Lysander, forever with you in your head and heart?"

"No, I . . . No! I wouldn't so dishonor your home by such pretense."

"For I tell you now, I'll not have the ghost of that youth haunting my marriage bed."

With those words, my promise to my mother burned to cinders. "In your marriage bed, sir, you'll get, sir, what you've earned by your cold analysis and unworthy deception. Now, on my own, sir, I'll explore the palace further and trust that no man from within or without will summon me in any unprovoked manner." By the time I was done with my magnificently indignant speech, I may have been shouting, for as I stormed away, Prince Escalus winced.

Served him right, the arrogant, petulant, anticipated-by-him master of me.

I walked—nay, I stalked—down the great walk to the far corner, aware the whole time he watched with a judgmental gaze. I wondered if he'd be foolish enough to try to stop me. I entertained myself with imagining his apology and my haughty rejection thereof. I turned the corner and gave rein to my increasing outrage with dire mutterings and a good, solid kick at one of the finely carved, heavy wooden tables.

To my horror, the tall vase thereon rattled and tipped, and I caught it barely in time. As I cradled it in my arms, I remembered my father's admonitions, my mother's lectures, and the scar that had been my constant companion since the last time I'd lost my temper.

Besides, my toe hurt from the impact.

Meticulously I returned the vase to the table. Shouting imprecations at the prince and storming away was greatly satisfying, but I'd learned from other iterations the return usually involved some form of uncomfortable apology. And I was pretty sure it would have to come from me, because apparently the Lord God's Eleventh Commandment was: *Men do not apologize, no matter how wrong they are.*

I really hated that one.

"Lady Rosaline . . ." I heard the faint call again. But from where?

I whirled to face . . . nothing. No one stood behind me. For as far as I could see, the great walk was empty. "Who's there?"

No reply.

"You kids better stop teasing me." For that was the only thing that made sense; Princess Isabella had led my siblings into a hidden passage—great Veronese houses were riddled with hidden passages—or they'd slipped from curtain to curtain in a nefarious intention to frighten me. Surely, the palace servants, for all their skulking, wouldn't play such a trick. No. That made no sense. It had to be the kids. At any moment, I'd hear a childish giggle and . . .

"Lady Rosaline . . ."

A door stood open that had previously been shut and the mysterious voice seemed to originate there.

Why, you ask, would a sensible woman follow an eerie voice up a narrow, steep, dark staircase? Surely, that was as ill-advised as going into the cellar in a thunderstorm to investigate a noise when a murderer is on the loose.

The answer was simple—because the alternative was apologizing to the prince for my impetuous speech, while at the same time practicing restraint so I don't kindly point out what an ass he'd been and that he deserved every word.

I climbed that stairway, climbed another stairway, climbed another, paused to gasp (my recovery was not yet complete and my layers of clothing heavy) and considered whether I was being a deluded fool.

Probably.

I almost turned back, but again I heard the voice call my name. Leaning down, I pulled the stiletto from the sheath on my ankle. I exited the last open door onto the stone balcony that surrounded the top of the tallest palace tower, there to find myself alone.

I did not doubt that I'd conjured the man's voice out of my own longing to be out of this marriage trap in which I found myself—but you'd think that the prince was right. If I was going to hallucinate, it would be Lysander's voice I'd hear.

Sheathing the stiletto at my ankle, I straightened to study the view.

All of Verona lay beneath me bathed in twilight: the hills, the Roman arena, and the expansive piazzas. I leaned my elbows on the rail and watched the shadows of the sun-kissed clouds slip across Verona's red stone streets, sprawling markets, golden buildings with their rosy roofs, and wander along the showy crescents of the Adige River. I stared, enraptured, as the occasional torch moved through the streets and the glow of firelight and candles spilled from the public houses. It was beautiful, my city, and I loved it with all my heart; yet right now, if I could follow those clouds and those shadows, and travel the countryside and escape even for a few moments these city walls, how swiftly I'd leave this all behind!

"Lady Rosaline."

The voice, much amplified, spoke near me, and I jumped so hard I bit my tongue. I whirled to face—a man emerging from the stone wall. I mean, like, *materializing through cold, hard rock.*

I'd seen this man recently.

Prince Escalus the elder. The man in the portrait. The man with the golden hair and the striking green eyes. The father of Prince Escalus the younger and Princess Isabella, who, for lo these many years, had been moldering in the grave.

"Wait." I pointed an accusing finger at him. "You're dead."

Chapter 9

"Your father always bragged you were an unusually clever girl." Elder ladled on the sarcasm with a liberal hand.

"So I am." I considered him. He did indeed look like the portrait . . . almost. He seemed more worn, so I supposed this apparition resembled his appearance at the moment of his death. While the center of his being looked solid, as my gaze moved to the edges, I realized his outline wavered as if blown by the breezes of eternity. I remarked conversationally, "I wonder what vapors are in the air to bring about a phantom's appearance in my mind."

"I might be an illusion caused by food or drink," Elder offered.

"I've had nothing to eat or drink since my arrival at the palace. Maybe your appearance is caused by hunger?"

Elder sagged and sighed. "It's a good thing you're going to marry my boy. Not to offer refreshments before dragging his betrothed and her family along on a tour of his tedious—"

"Ha! Now I know you're not real. You're telling me what's in *my* mind."

"You don't believe I'm real?" He seemed offended. "You don't believe in ghosts?"

"I'm all of twenty years, and while I've heard much about them, I've never before witnessed one."

"Until now."

"I'm not seeing you. You might not know this, but I'm quite an accomplished herbalist and an apprentice apothecary—"

"Now who's lying? Your father would never allow such a thing."

"I work with Friar Laurence. Do you remember him? He who performed the secret marriage of my parents, and when Mamma's father wished her to marry Lord Paris, he provided her with a potion that lent the appearance of death for two and forty hours."

"Of course, I remember Friar Laurence. *He's* an accomplished apothecary."

"He is."

"Ladies are unfit for such work."

I smiled with chilly disdain. "I'm unfit for many things, Elder, especially becoming the wife of Verona's podestà. Yet here I am, being rushed to the altar by your son." I took a clarifying breath. Why was I arguing with a phantasm? More to myself than him, I said, "In the prince's garden of exotic plants, one has pollen that causes hallucinations." I thought of Friar Laurence's teachings. "Or perhaps I brushed against a leaf or flower that contains intoxicants."

Yet for all my good sense, Elder didn't disappear. "Quiz me. Ask me questions you don't know, but I do."

"How will I know if you answer true?"

That seemed to stump him.

"Ha!" Again I gloated at him.

He took it ill. "Like all women, you imagine victory in petty pleasures and tiny triumphs."

Since I *was* enjoying my tiny triumph, I continued the conversation. "I hadn't heard that the palace is haunted. Do you often lure guests up here?"

"No one else can see or hear me."

Startled, I spoke unwisely. "The hell you say. Your son?"

"No. Do you think I wouldn't have rather communicated with a sensible man than a foolish woman?"

I tapped my foot. "I see now where your son got his high-handed manner and unjustified sense of superiority."

Elder broke into a smile that lit up his elderly, handsome face. "*Now* you sound like my wife."

I looked around. "Is she here, too, gliding through the air and speaking to the unwary?"

"Is she not still in the convent where I sent her in safety to have the child?" He viewed me intently.

That gave me pause. "Your wife, the princess Eleanor, gave birth to your daughter, Princess Isabella, and, on hearing of your own demise, fell into a decline and died of sorrow."

He seemed unmoved . . . for a moment. He drifted toward the railing and looked out at the city, as I had, and I saw him struggle to contain a fresh grief. "I'd feared that was so. When I arrived back in the palace and saw that the child was here and she was not . . . Eleanor was the wife of my heart. She would never have left the little girl alone unless she had no choice."

I joined him at the railing. "I'm sorry for your loss, but please enlighten me. How could you not know? Is she not nearby?"

"She died in a state of grace. She has gone on. I fear I'm condemned to wander until justice is done."

He looked at me, and I saw the diamond glint of ghostly tears. "She was fragile, you know. After Escalus, she lost the babies, one after another. I should never have touched her again, but we loved each other."

"I comprehend."

Swiftly he turned on me, no longer a man discussing his lost love, but a judge. "How do you know such a thing? Are you not a virgin?"

I tossed my arms in the air. "Everybody in Verona! Even the ghosts! Why this huge concern with my virginity?"

He looked me over—not like a man looks at a woman, but as a farmer looks at a farm animal purchased for breeding. "I admit I was surprised at my son's choice. You're very old."

"A withered crone."

"A trifle overripe, perhaps."

It sounded as if he was trying to comfort me, which made me grind my teeth.

He continued, "I suppose he thinks your maturity will stand you in good stead as you deal with the social and political divisiveness of Verona."

"So he informed me."

"Also, your mother Juliet is exceptionally fertile. How many children are there now?"

"Seven, and one on the way."

"I'm sure that played into my son's decision."

"He told me that, too. A girl could swoon over the romance."

"Surely, a woman of your advanced years—"

"I'm perfectly healthy, thank you."

"—has enjoyed her previous moments of silly swooning."

"Until very recently, no."

"You fell in love with my son." That pleased him.

"No."

That *dis*pleased him. His facial expressions were remarkably lifelike for a figment. "Who then is your lover?"

"I . . . don't . . . have . . . a . . . lover," I said between my teeth. "Lysander of the Venitian house of Marcketti is my One True Love. We've never done more than touch hands, and because of your son's hateful maneuvering, my darling is forever lost to me."

Elder was interested. He questioned me. I told him of the

events in the garden, how Prince Escalus deliberately tricked me into kissing him rather than Lysander, how we were caught and now must be wed. *And* how when I explained to Lysander that I was misled, he had taken it amiss that I'd failed to discern the switch. "I'd never kissed either of them before, so how would I know the difference?"

After Elder got done laughing—FYI, laughing from a ghost sounds like an off-key madrigal—the judgmental old fart said, "Sounds like my son did the right thing by agreeing to marry you."

"You mean, like a *favor*? Prince Escalus is doing me a *favor*? Did you hear the part about *deliberately*? He *deliberately* tricked me, because when he made a list of my wifely attributes and my decayed faults, I came out on the plus side."

"He was ever a logical boy." Elder approved.

I charged on. "He decided he wanted to marry me and rather than deal with messy emotions and actually being pleasant to me, or even proposing the match to my father like a civilized male, he publicly humiliated me. All Verona has heard the tittle-tattle and is laughing at me, and I haven't dared to set foot out of Casa Montague since the scandal, at least not in daylight except to come here, and that in a covered sedan chair guarded by the prince's bodyguards, and by the way, as I was carried through the streets, I could hear sniggering." By the time I finished, I was bellowing. I knew I was bellowing, but I assured myself that it didn't count as breaking my promise to my mother because Elder didn't really exist.

Interestingly, Elder's expression now grew serious. "I believed my son had a good brain for strategy, but Cal made a stupid mistake there."

"Who's Cal?"

"Escalus. His mother used to call him Callie, so I shortened it to Cal."

Callie. Heh. I filed that away in my mind for future use. "I'm curious. What stupid mistake is that? Until this moment, you were his champion."

"The greatest love shrivels at the sound of laughter. If he wishes for an amiable marriage, he should never have exposed you to scandal and mockery."

"There's nothing to shrivel. There's no love between us."

"Nor can there be until he makes amends. I'll speak to him."

"You said he couldn't hear you."

"I can still speak." Elder's voice held such a tone of royal command, I didn't understand why he couldn't make himself known to whomever he wished.

Probably because he was merely a phantom of my mind, the result of a plant exhalation. Maybe I was, in truth, unconscious somewhere—my recent fever had forced me to live through amazing and terrifying nightmares and memories, and I knew that was possible.

I asked, "What difference does it make? I vowed never to wed unless I loved and he loved, and the union between us would be as amorous and devoted as has been shown to me in my own home."

"We can't all be Romeo and Juliet." Elder sounded prosaic.

"To be truly together, body and soul—it can be done." I believed that, although few others seemed to. "All else is distant politeness, infidelity, indifference, and, all too often, loathing."

"I thought youth was a time of idealism and romance."

"I have a mind, sir, and my logic is the match of any man's. All that a woman of good sense has to do is look around at the misery created by two ill-joined people to want to avoid that state."

"With an attitude like that, I don't think you should marry my son!"

"We are agreed on one thing, then. The only one who

should have compromised me is Lysander!" I kicked the stone post and winced at the twinge to my already bruised toe. "Now I have to get married to . . . to . . . to the prince of Verona!" For the first time, the enormity of what now faced me—social leadership, political maneuvering, being a wife and chattel to a man I didn't love—struck me and I burst into tears.

Chapter 10

"Oh, blast," I heard Elder mutter. "I don't like crying women."

"Then go away!" I sank down on the floor, pulled my knees up to my chin, and rocked and wept. Loudly. Freely. Whenever I opened my eyes, I could see his feet uncomfortably shifting back and forth. I closed my eyes and wept some more. I don't cry often, so when I do, I make a good job of it.

At last, Elder sat beside me and said, "I'd hug you, but you wouldn't enjoy the sensation."

I shook my head. "Don't hug me. Don't comfort me. Go away. I don't want anybody to see me like this."

"I don't have a body, so I'm not strictly any *body*. Anyway, I can't go away. I need you."

That made my breath catch and my tears slow. "Of course. The former podestà isn't merely a ghost who appears randomly to me. You want something." At this moment, I loathed all men, living and dead.

"I *need* something," Elder corrected.

"What?"

"When you stop crying and wipe your nose, I'll tell you."

"Turn your head," I instructed.

"Why?"

"I'm going to tear off some of my underskirt and I don't want you looking at my legs."

"Woman, I'm a ghost!"

"Turn your head or I'll sit here with a snotty nose." Experience had taught me that a man who hates a crying woman hates a snotty nose worse.

He sighed loudly and turned his head.

I lifted my skirt, yanked free a piece of linen—no small feat, for linen is tough—and lowered my skirt.

He pointed toward my foot. "That's *my* stiletto you have strapped to your leg. Where did you get *my* stiletto?"

"You looked!" I used the linen to wipe my eyes and blow my nose.

"Of course, I looked. I'm dead, not"—he struggled to find a word—"cold!"

"You lied!"

"I prevaricated."

"Why? Why look at my leg? The priests tell us when you die, you leave all earthly desire behind."

"How would they know? They're not dead, are they? Anyway, I don't desire you; I simply enjoyed the view. A woman's well-turned ankle warms me without purgatory's pain." He smiled reminiscently. "Now, tell me, how did you get my stiletto?"

I reached down and pulled it free of its scabbard. "Are you sure this is it?"

"Indeed, for I know my weapons well."

"Your son gave it to me."

Elder got a most peculiar expression on his faintly obscure face. "I gave it to him. He gave it to you."

"He believed I was in danger. He's exceptionally responsible, your son. He carries the weight of his office as he walks the streets of Verona, speaks to the people, listens to what they say, makes sure that they're content, and at the same time, he listens for any rumblings of another to overthrow the house of Leonardi." I thought Elder, who seemed to have blanks in his knowledge of Verona's happenings, would be glad to know that his son ruled so wisely.

Instead he gazed at me as if he knew something I didn't. "So out of all the weapons in the palace he could have given you, he gifted you the stiletto I gifted to him on the day before my untimely death."

"Really? Are you perturbed with him? Because I can give it back."

"No. Keep it. You may have need of it."

"Indeed, I have already put it to good use."

"Your father is wrong," Elder said obscurely. "You're not clever at all . . . I have no idea how long we have before my son misses you and mounts a search, so let me tell you what you must do."

I was not amused by his high-handedness. "What I must *do*?"

"Yes. What I need." He tilted his head as if listening, and spoke more swiftly. "Find out who murdered me."

Chapter 11

I was frankly startled. "Find out who murdered you? Don't *you* know?"

"No. That night in my bedroom, my bodyguard and friend, Barnadine of the house of Bianchi, and I shared a toast to celebrate our victory over the Acquasasso. Afterward, I fell onto my bed. Barnadine fell onto the pallet against the wall. I slept, unsuspecting that the wine in the flagon had been drugged by persons unknown. As dawn's light first caressed the sky, I woke as the door creaked open. I looked. A man with a horrible face entered."

"What kind of horrible face?"

"A demon's visage: flat black silk on which was painted bloodred lips, red eyeballs, and pointed red brows. The nose appeared unformed, bones displayed like a decomposing corpse."

"A mask, I hope."

"Yes. After the first moment of terror, I recognized that thing as a man who clothed himself in cowardice. Then terror struck deeper, for I knew what that signified."

"Assassin," I said.

Elder nodded. "I reached for my sword close at hand. I couldn't command my hand. I couldn't grasp the hilt in my fingers. I dropped it. The blade hit the floor with a clang and woke Barnadine. He stood, fell to one knee, then flat on his face. The bedposts, the curtains, in my sight grew long and wavy. With my faulty vision, I saw the masked assassin unsheathe a knife from his belt and advance in catlike steps toward the bed. I resisted the drug's bonds. As he climbed on the bed, I pulled a dagger from under my pillow." His voice grew strong with the memory of his struggle and he stabbed with the imaginary blade. "I wounded him. I know I did. I swear—blood drenched the tip of the knife and my fingers, and he screamed." Elder looked at me as if to convince me.

He seemed to need my very human assurance. "I believe you."

"I kicked the demon off the bed. He hit the floor and screamed again. I heard a scuffle. Barnadine had recovered himself enough to fight, and I tried mightily to sit up, to defend myself and support my bodyguard!"

I discovered I had my hand over my rapidly beating heart, wishing as if in an unfolding onstage drama that Elder would win the battle, survive and live to guide Verona to peace. Even though I knew how this must end, still I hoped.

Elder dropped his head and in a flat tone continued, "Yet it was not to be so. Barnadine remained out of sight, unconscious, perhaps dead, and once more the demon's mask rose above me, untouched, unbloodied, menacing in his silence."

"This man, what did he look like?"

Impatient with me, Elder said, "He wore a mask."

"No! His skin color, his weight, his height, his hair—"

"His hair was tied back in a black cloth, his mask was as I said. He wore black gloves, a wide cape of heavy black cloth. His height, I cannot say, for I couldn't stand to measure myself against him, and the drug made me doubt my own senses. His weight... he was a sturdy man, strongly built, good with a blade, a dishonorable warrior who killed for whim, for money, for family?" Elder's figure wavered as if heated by wrath's flame. "Almost certainly for family, an Acquasasso who imagined that by my death they could return to our most beloved Verona and rule."

I couldn't contain my frustration. "Did you not see after your death who lifted his fist in triumph?"

"I was nothing. I was not there. I was cold. I was dead."

"What a waste of opportunity! Could you not somehow find him, track to his lair to view his countenance?"

"From that moment to this, I have been nowhere. O that this too solid flesh would melt . . ." Elder gestured at his ghostly self. "Well, it did. Only when you entered the palace gate was I animated, complete in memory of what had occurred and thirsting for justice. *At last!*"

"Oh." Probably not a coincidence.

"With a single thought, I sped to Cal's side and spoke to my son." Elder gestured, alive with excitement.

Well . . . not *alive,* but you know what I mean.

"Cal seemed to be unaware, heedless of me. Me—his father! He hurried to greet you and your family and it was only when I tried to block his path that he reacted."

In that, I was quite interested. "What happened?"

"He walked through me, stopped, shivered, looked about as if sensing me, but not understanding."

"Interesting."

"Despite my shouts, he walked on."

"He can be quite single-minded." I experienced a burst of the kind of smug exaltation I previously had only experienced when successfully deflecting a marital suit aimed at me. "Let's make a deal. I'll find out who murdered you, and you promise in return that I'll marry my One True Love."

"I can't do that. I'm a prince, not a matchmaker!"

"You're a ghost."

"As you wish. I'm a ghost, not a wishing well!"

"That's the deal. Take it or leave it. If I'm going to put my life in peril searching for a killer who—for what? eleven years?—has eluded capture, I want something in return."

"There might be no danger. He might be dead." Elder groped to give me reassurance, then thought it through and shook his head. "Although if there's no chance for justice—"

"You wouldn't have returned." I had to agree.

"Yes. He's out there . . . somewhere."

"Stop being such a misogynist. The killer might be a woman."

Elder honked like an angry gander. "Women are, by nature, gentle, sweet, and unfit for dangerous pursuits."

"Yet you want me to find the person who stuck a knife in your chest and stopped your heart."

"Yes!"

I folded my hands in my lap. "I can't. I'm, 'by nature, gentle, sweet, and unfit for dangerous pursuits.'"

Elder had talked himself into a corner. He knew it. I knew it. We stared at each other, him in scowling frustration and me in smug triumph.

Then from the stairwell, I heard a now-familiar voice. "To whom are you speaking?"

I stood and faced my betrothed, Prince Escalus.

Chapter 12

I looked between Prince Escalus the younger and Prince Escalus the elder. "To your father."

Younger looked around, past the elder, then focused again on me. "My father is dead."

"He can't see me," Elder said in my ear.

"Obviously!" I was talking to Elder.

But Prince Escalus answered me. "Therefore, he's not here."

"Or hear me," Elder said.

"Obviously! Now would you go away?"

"I came to find you for dinner." Younger spoke slowly and carefully. "Don't you want to eat with our families?"

"Yes, I'm starving." Sparring with Elder had given me an appetite. "But I'm about to set my seal on this pact."

"'This pact'?" Younger said.

"With your father! He wants me to find his murderer."

Prince Escalus walked over to me, took my face in his hands, and pressed his lips to my forehead. "No fever. Do you feel quite all right?"

I pulled myself back. "Yes. I'm fine! Why wouldn't I be?"

"You were recently very ill."

"Why were you very ill?" Elder asked.

Younger grew stern. "Is this pretense because of your success in discovering the dreadful killer of Duke Stephano and all the others?"

"Serial killer," I muttered. "No. It's because your father asked me to—"

Elder advanced to a cackle, and I swung on him. "Oh, shut up!"

"Did you really do that? Discover a killer?" Elder was definitely interested in that information.

"He wants to know if I really discovered a killer," I told Younger. "I did more than discover the killer, didn't I?"

"You eliminated the killer at great cost to yourself. When I proposed, I did speak of my admiration for your steadfast courage and loyalty to your family, did I not? Are you fishing to hear it again?"

I considered him with a shock that shouldn't have occurred. "You don't think much of me, do you?"

"I do. What more proof of my esteem could you command than the princely betrothal with which I've graced you?"

"Be still, my heart."

I had noted on previous occasions, occasions that occurred before Prince Escalus fixed his attention on me, that he was a man given to words spoken only with forethought. He paused now and seemed to retrace our discourse, and seemed to decide a change might improve its tenor. "Lady Rosaline, my father would never ask a gentlewoman to search for his killer. He believes women to be—"

"'Gentle, sweet, and unfit for dangerous pursuits'?"

"His exact words! How did you know?" The stupid man still wasn't getting it.

Elder chortled.

I crossed my arms and stared at Prince Escalus.

"Someone told you. He is not here." But his gaze searched around me.

I'd put doubt in his mind. "This is mean," I said to Elder. "Somehow show yourself to him!"

"Don't you think if I could have spoken to him about finding my murderer, I would have?" Elder demanded.

"Don't you think I've searched for his murderer to wipe him off the face of the earth?" Prince Escalus asked.

They were talking over each other, about each other, and both were tormented.

I placed my forefinger on my prince's arm. "I know you have searched, sir, for the safety of Verona and your family, as well as vengeance for that bloody treachery, and I grieve with you for the loss of your father." To Elder, I said, "*Why* can you show yourself only to me?"

"The rules of beyond? I can only show myself to my reluctant future daughter-in-law?" He waved vaporous arms in exasperation. "I don't know!"

"Lady Rosaline, do you talk to yourself often?" Prince Escalus asked. "Or is this a ploy to convince me you're deranged so I'll back out of the marriage?"

I didn't lose my temper, exactly, but I was severely exasperated. Really, gentle reader, can you blame me? I pinned him with my most severe, elderly spinster stare and snapped, "How deranged do I have to be for you to back out?"

In wondering tones, Elder said, "You truly don't want to marry him."

The damnable man/ghost finally had the gist of the matter. I glared down at him. "Did you miss the obvious clue? Like the bargain I'm demanding in return for my cooperation?"

Elder jumped to his feet—actually, he rose a little above the floor—and shouted, "You'll be the princess!"

"I don't care!" I shouted back.

"I must go and think." Elder slid backward into the stone and vanished.

I stared at the spot and sighed. "He's gone. How I wish he'd never come."

"Confess." Prince Escalus tried hard to sound jocular. "This is all a game you made up to discourage me."

"Let's go to dinner." I swept ahead of him through the passage, down the stairs, and into the great walk. There I waited for him to catch up. "For your information, I don't play games . . . Cal."

Chapter 13

Younger grabbed my arm and turned me to face him. "*What did you call me?*"

"Cal."

"My parents used to call me Cal."

"Only your father," I corrected him smugly. "Your mother called you—"

"Don't say it!"

"Callie."

He stared at me with a gratifyingly intent air. "Who told you that?"

I sighed and walked away from him, back toward (I hoped) the dining room. Because I wasn't kidding, all this arguing had helped me develop an appetite.

He caught up with me at once. "You must see you're asking me to believe something so unlikely that—"

"I am not asking you to believe anything." I stopped walking and spoke aloud my wonder. "I don't even believe it myself. But then, everything that's happening in the last few days has been . . . I don't know what happened to my life! I used to be in control. I ran the household. I dealt with the crises. I was the captain of my own ship! Now I'm lost in a storm-tossed dark-wine sea and land is nowhere in sight." I shook my head, and shook it again. "*And* there's a ghost."

For the first time, I saw a real smile on Prince Escalus's face. It was quizzical and rather one-sided, as if he wasn't sure how his lips were supposed to create the condition of amusement, but it was a smile.

"I've never done this before," I added. "Seen a ghost. I wonder why it had to be your father. He's obnoxious, you know."

Prince Escalus clasped his hands behind his back and paced slowly ahead of me.

I followed. I sensed his turmoil; indeed, any female with half the normal instincts could sense it, but unlike any other female, I was more than usually invested in the results.

"You're determined on this course? Of investigating my father's murder?"

"Sir. If you hadn't unexpectedly come upon me speaking to Elder, I would have never told you of the incident. I know what madness this seems." I paced slightly behind him. "I assure you, I'm not determined to investigate his murder. If the elder podestà's murderer is in Verona still, and living"—I gave a nod to Elder's beliefs—"he, or she, has a willingness to kill, and a wiliness to remain hidden for all these years. That is a dangerous endeavor."

"Exactly!" Prince Escalus faced me, obviously pleased at my good sense. "So you won't do it."

"Until Elder agrees to my terms, no."

"What are those terms?"

"*My* terms. Since apparently I'm the only one who can see and hear him, I've got him by the short hairs." I delivered that idiom triumphantly, for Cal had spoken it during his "proposal" of marriage, and I had not at first understood.

"My father was an old-fashioned man. He would never appreciate a woman who . . . is as independent, stubborn, and firmly spoken as you are. My mother was a sweet gentlewoman, and she loved and adored him. As he loved and adored her."

I nodded. "Indeed, so he said, and his churlish countenance softened when he spoke her name. I do remember her well.

She and my mother used to laugh . . . What?" For Cal's countenance had developed a diplomatic smoothness, a still sheen.

"People often presume that if they claim a connection to the house of Leonardi, it will increase their consequence. I assure you, your mother need not resort to such subterfuges. I've already connected myself to the house of Montague." He started to walk away from me.

I grabbed him with both hands by the back of his jacket.

The sudden yank brought him stumbling backward.

I shoved him around, clutched a fistful of black linen of his shirtfront, and jerked him toward me. "If you value your life, do not ever speak of my mother to me in such a manner ever again. No!" I pointed my finger in his face. "Do not ever speak of my mother in such a manner at any time, to anyone. Do not even think it!" My finger shook with rage. "You have the effrontery to imagine the Montagues need the connection to the Leonardi family to increase our consequence? Do you know *who* we *are*? What our worth is in estates and lands, in wine and grapes, in gold coins and good family—and loyalty to you?" I flung both hands up as if flinging him and his Leonardi consequence to the winds. "Lady Juliet and your mother were best friends throughout my childhood. And your childhood, too, Prince Escalus! If you hadn't been such a self-righteous, inflated, conceited pee-bladder of a boy-prince, you would have known that!"

My tirade had wiped the smoothness off that fiercely ugly face.

Okay, he wasn't *fiercely* ugly, but he was no Lysander of the house of You'reSoBeautiful; and right now, to me, Prince Escalus looked like a troll.

He drew a breath to speak.

I wasn't done with him. "I'll still marry you. I'll make the sacrifice because you so carefully ruined me, and for the sake of my family's reputation, and I hope you're happy with the icy temperature of your marriage bed." I turned to storm away.

Elder popped out of the air in front of me.

I shrieked, and without knowing how, I found myself standing next to my betrothed. Pretty sure I jumped. "Don't do that!" I told Elder.

He pointed at me. "You have your deal."

"What?"

"You win. Your tirade was so loud it pulled me from the depths of cold stone to agree to your deal."

"My *tirade*?" I gestured up and down at Prince Escalus. "Did you hear what he *said*?"

"Yes." Elder wore that same smooth expression his son had worn; I guess I knew where Younger had learned it. "It was unworthy of him."

This conversation did nothing to improve my rage. "But he's your *son* and a *man,* so you're giving him a pass?"

"I'd speak to him if he could hear me, about the courtesy owed to Lady Juliet and your family." Then, as if I must need clarification, he enunciated clearly, "He can't hear me." More briskly he added, "Anyway, you did a fine job of stripping him of pretension. You'd be a good wife to him. But you wouldn't be a merry wife, so again I say—you have your deal. When you discover my killer, I'll deliver you to your One True Love."

Wisely, I was not without suspicion. "Why do you care whether I'm a merry wife?"

Elder quoted the old adage. " 'Merry wife, have no strife.' My son deserves a pliant wife who adores him."

"As do all men, no doubt. What do women deserve in a husband?"

Puzzled, he frowned. "I don't comprehend the question."

"Of course, you don't." I nodded to him. "So it shall be done."

Elder popped away as suddenly as he'd come.

In a neutral tone, my betrothed asked, "My father returned? For what reason?"

"He believes you deserve a 'pliant wife' who 'adores' you."

"I want *you*."

That was funny, in its way, and telling, but I was on a rampage. "You've got a damned funny way of showing it!" I drew breath. "I have four given names, did you know that?"

"No." He was cautious, for not even his most royal and exalted self bore no more than one name and the name of his house.

"My name is Rosaline Hortensa Magdelina . . . Eleanor. My father chose Rosaline in the hopes his baby daughter would be chaste and worthy. Hortensa and Magdelina are my grandmothers, and necessary to keep the tenuous peace between the families. Eleanor was the name my mother chose. Perhaps even you can discern her intention to honor her friend." I flounced away from Prince Escalus.

He hurried after me and touched my arm.

I swung on him. "What?"

"If we wish to go to dinner, it's back that way." He pointed in the opposite direction.

"Of course. I'm off course." Spinning again, I stalked toward the candlelight that spilled from a broad opening.

He murmured something I knew I didn't want to hear and followed me.

As I passed, I glimpsed movement off to the side. Once more from behind the drapes, I saw the thin, pale, sad face. Orsa of the kitchen. Not a girl as I'd first thought, but a woman, peering pitifully at me, and when I looked right at her, she dropped the brocade to cover herself.

As I advanced toward the dining room, I could hear the ever-increasing murmur of conversation, and I knew a vast relief that I was about to join the families and a vast perturbation that despite all vows, I'd lost my temper.

Not *frequently*, but more than once. Yes, definitely it could be described as more than once, but not frequently. More frequently than I had for years, and more vigorously, but—

Prince Escalus gently gripped my shoulder.

I stopped, but did not face him.

"I must beg your pardon, Lady Rosaline, and that of your beloved mother. You're right."

You're right? That got my attention. I didn't know if I'd ever before heard a male use those two words together.

"I was a pompous youth with no interest in my mother's life or any female not available to me as a . . . dance partner. With shame, I do remember my youthful behavior, and regret my neglect of my own dear mother, a regret sharpened by the realization I can never again speak with her, feel her loving embrace, see her sweet face. I confess to jealousy of even her memory, and it sat ill with me to know that Lady Juliet knew her as I never will. I most humbly beg your forgiveness for my arrogance, and humbly beg that you not inform Lady Juliet of my . . ." He hesitated, unable to choose an adequate description.

I'm always eager to offer a suggestion. "Assholeyness?"

His solemnity did not break. "Precisely. I fear my outburst would grieve her. I also fear the sharp point of Lord Romeo's sword." At this last, the shadow on his face lightened. He did now perhaps feel protected by bounds of family.

I didn't spare him. "You're wise to worry about my father. He's a good man who easily takes offense and remedies his perturbation with violence. He doesn't kill as many men as he used to, not for lack of irascibility but because of the tempering influence of my mother. However, he did once use the point of his sword to remove a lord's clothes, leaving him naked on one of Verona's streets. The fool had to go into exile, and I hear even as far away as Geneva, mockery follows him."

"Will you pardon and protect me from such a fate?"

I examined my fiancé, my podestà, and my prince. He did look as humble as that man could look, which was not at all, but he managed to seem anxious and as if my response mattered to him, and what else could a woman expect?

"I'll pardon you on your understanding that should you ever

again speak ill of my beloved parents or of my siblings, aggravating as they can be, I'll serve your oysters as pâté on toast."

His half an eyebrow, deformed by the torture he'd suffered, rose. "Have I noted that your colorful way of speaking fills me with delight?"

"It is not colorful when it is truthful."

Prince Escalus crooked his neck as if easing a tension therein. "Noted. If you would do me the honor of going in to dinner with me?" He presented his arm.

I stared at it, knew that while Elder might be sincere in his decision to help me marry my One True Love, I didn't trust the ghost, or a politician, and most especially not the ghost of a politician, much less the father who must want only the best for his son. As Prince Escalus and I agreed, searching for Elder's killer would be a perilous endeavor and by no means would I come out unharmed, or even alive.

"We arrive together for the comfort it will give my family." I hovered my fingertips above his forearm.

Again he noted the separation between us, but he did nothing to force my compliance.

We entered the brightly lit dining room together.

Chapter 14

Papà stood speaking to the prince's boon companions and bodyguards, Dion, Marcellus, and Holofernes. From Papà's animated and pointed gestures, I assumed he was discussing past sword battles and his almost unbroken line of successes. The companions listened intently, not three younger warriors humoring an old knight, but men learning from the greatest swordsman to ever grace Verona's streets. Even at the advanced age of thirty-seven, Papà handled a sword with skill, speed, and strategy.

My siblings were gathered around Princess Isabella, giggling as she stealthily passed grilled skewers of figs, bread cubes, and cheese to appease their hunger.

Our beloved Friar Laurence stood with the children, laughing with them and snatching the occasional fig. His humble brown robes and shaved head denoted that he had taken vows of poverty as a Franciscan monk, and the three knots on his corded rope cincture stood for poverty, chastity, and obedience. This good brother had in secret joined my parents in matrimony and, as a skilled apothecary, prepared for my mother the potion that put her into the sleep of death for two and forty hours. A respectful pupil, I weekly went to his shop and learned the apothecary arts, thus he'd earned a seat at this most momentous meal.

As soon as everyone saw Cal and myself, and saw that we were together, a palpable air of relief swept the assembly.

Mamma sat beside an old woman, older even than Nurse, a woman of seventy years or more, with iron-gray hair pulled back under a black veil and tucked into a beaded and bejeweled headdress. Loss and worry had worn deep, dry wrinkles around her mouth and eyes. Her shoulders were stooped, her frame skinny, and she leaned close to listen to Mamma.

"My grandmother," Cal murmured in my ear.

"She who 'spreads terror before her like a farmer spreads manure'?"

"The very one. Are you afraid?"

"Introduce me and I'll know."

"Dowager, here is my daughter Rosaline." Mamma beckoned me.

As a young gentlewoman should, I glided majestically toward them.

"Hurry up, girl!" the old lady shouted. "I'm slipping toward the grave quickly enough without having to wait on your airs!"

I picked up my pace.

"Kneel down." She pointed to the floor before her. "Let me look at you."

Surprised, I looked at Mamma, who nodded, and I knelt before the old woman.

Now I understood. She was almost blind, her brown eyes clouded white with the obscurity of age, and when I realized she waited on me, I took hold of her twisted claws and put them on my face.

She slid them down from my forehead, over my chin, and back up again. "Let me see your teeth," she ordered.

I bared them in a semi-snarl.

She used her finger to poke at them; her skin tasted like garlic. She pronounced judgment. "Strong teeth. Good complexion. Good bones—although, of course, that's required from the daughter of Romeo and Juliet. Name is Rosaline?"

"Yes, Dowager. Rosie, should you wish it." Keeping in mind the way she'd leaned to hear my mother, I spoke loudly.

She tapped her chest with one of those bent fingers. "I'm Ursula. It means 'bear.'"

"I'll keep that in mind, Dowager."

"You may call me Nonna Ursula."

"As you command, Nonna Ursula."

"You give the proper answers. Are you an obedient woman?"

Cal gave the bark that passed for a laugh.

She tilted her head toward him. "My grandson doesn't think so."

"Of course, your grandson is always right." I could slide the implied knife between the ribs as well as any society matron.

She cackled, and it sounded ungodly, like the laugh of her eldest son, Prince Escalus the elder. "You're impudent."

"Yes, Nonna Ursula."

"Good. Sit next to me at dinner. You can entertain me."

Cal and Papà leaped to help her to her feet.

She whacked at them with her cane. "Get off. Get! Off! I can still stand on my own."

She could, although she wavered and scowled. "Give me your arm, girl."

I offered it. She tucked her hand in my elbow and I led her to the long table covered by a brilliant-colored Persian carpet, to the chair Prince Escalus pulled out for her.

Her arrival was the signal for dinner to begin. Seating had been assigned, not according to station, but with a wise view of letting the two families gain in acquaintance. Set at each place was a round pewter dish, a goblet of swirled color glass made on the isle of Murano, a silver spoon, and a trencher of bread. Very elegant, although in the case of Emilia and Cesario, perhaps the glass was ill-advised.

Servers in the prince's livery arrived for the hands-cleansing ritual. One held an ornate pitcher, one a matching bowl, one linen towels. Starting with the prince, the man with the pitcher poured water over his hands; another man caught the water; the last handed him a towel to dry his hands. As the men worked their way down the table, I observed the clever seating arrangement.

Prince Escalus sat at the head of the table. I sat at his right hand, and Nonna Ursula sat beside me. As the dowager princess, she deserved to grace the foot of the table, but seating her toward the center allowed her to follow the conversations. Papà sat next to her, then Katherina, then Holofernes. Imogene sat next to him, and Friar Laurence next to her. Across the table, Cesario sat on a tall seat between Mamma and Marcellus—Marcellus being the most stern and unsmiling of the prince's companions.

I grinned. Cesario would take care of that.

Each place had a small olive-wood bowl filled with white flakes of salt. I viewed my bowl, then looked at Princess Isabella and lifted my brows. She nodded proudly. At this table, no one sat below the salt, a signal that all were equal—her idea.

We had two empty chairs across the table, I knew not why, and I was curious to see who came to fill it.

Eight-year-old Emilia sat at the foot of the table between Princess Isabella and Dion; she had been boosted up on her seat, too, and she looked around as if amazed to find herself in such a position of honor.

She settled back and, with her own particular insouciance, took command of the discussion, with special care to speak clearly and toward Nonna Ursula. "Papà brought one of our special wines to celebrate this evening, a full-bodied blend of

Sangiovese and Barbera grapes set down in the year of Rosie's birth." From the cradle, the Montague family trained in wines. We grew grapes at our vineyards north of the city, and there processed them into wines revered throughout Italy and beyond.

Papà signaled to Tommaso, who stood guard by the door, and the youth disappeared and returned lugging a small wooden cask. Papà rose and together the two men pulled the cork plug, and Papà, with a small hammer, gently tapped in the spigot. Tommaso presented him with a glass, he sampled the wine, and pronounced, "Strong, flavorful, aged with dark fruit to perfection . . . like our daughter Rosaline."

Everyone applauded and smiled at me, and I found myself blushing. I found it uncomfortable being the center of attention, and told myself I'd better get used to it, for as wife to the podestà, I'd be the princess upon whom all eyes would be fixed.

I then assured myself I wouldn't mind, since under normal circumstances, I'd be busy, not sitting like a scrap-cloth doll on display.

Papà himself served the wines, and on this occasion, I received the first glass. Then Nonna Ursula, then Mamma, then Cal and his bodyguards, then Friar Laurence. The children received their wines well-watered. Everyone waited until Papà had filled his glass and lifted it. "The house of Montague welcomes the joining of Prince Escalus of the house of Leonardi to our beloved daughter Rosaline Hortensa Magdelina Eleanor in matrimony, and may you both be blessed with long years of love and happiness!"

Glasses raised, clinked, and congratulations were exchanged with various amounts of enthusiasm.

Cal rose to answer Papà in like tones—and a man stumbled into the dining room.

"Barnadine," Nonna Ursula said crisply, "how good of you to join us at last."

Barnadine. I recognized that name: faithful bodyguard to Elder, the servant who failed to protect his master.

That would explain his distressing appearance.

That, or guilt. Had this man been the one to assassinate Elder?

Chapter 15

A man of great height and formerly great muscle, Barnadine now carried scarce enough flesh to stew in a pot. He wore once-expensive clothing, worn thin with use and crumpled as if he'd slept in them. Nervously he finger combed his thinning brown hair, and he bowed to Nonna Ursula, then the prince, then my father, then my mother, then me . . .

He couldn't seem to stop bowing until Nonna Ursula snapped, "Sit down, Barnadine, you're making us all weary."

Cal frowned. "Did you not bring your protégé, Barnadine?"

"I did, indeed. He's shy. He lingers in the great walk."

"Bid him come in so I may welcome him."

Barnadine hustled back to the entrance and gestured, then followed the young man into the room. "This is Friar Camillo, friend and blessing to our family."

A solemn Franciscan monk of less than twenty years entered, and on seeing Friar Laurence, he broke into a smile. Friar Laurence hefted himself to his feet and ambled around to greet the young man. They embraced, and Friar Laurence turned Friar Camillo to face the group. "This youth is most pious and excellent in his service to the sick and poor, and as well he speaks kind words and witty, when he chooses."

All murmured greetings and beamed at Friar Camillo, for he

was one of those blessed people who when they smiled, the whole world experienced his joy.

I know one should never gaze upon a man of the cloth with the eyes of a sinner, but Friar Camillo had a noble visage, unmarked by disease, with strong features and wide eyes, and a manly structure that had benefited from much prayer, walking, and labor.

Cal bade him sit, and Papà commanded, "Tommaso, give the good brother and Barnadine each a glass so they might join in our celebration."

Friar Camillo accepted his glass with thanks and sipped, and praised its contents.

Barnadine took his glass, drank it down, and passed it back for more.

Cal didn't wait, but answered Papà's toast. "The house of Leonardi welcomes this alliance with the house of Montague, and—"

Barnadine lurched to his feet. "I have a toast, too."

Everyone paused in that awful, cringing moment that waited to see if this drunken speech would cause embarrassment to all, or merely to the speaker himself. Thankfully, Barnadine rose to the occasion. "Let us toast Verona, that beating heart of our adoration whose walls enclose the greatest, most prosperous, and most beautiful city of all the lands on God's green earth!"

He had redeemed himself, and in gratitude and enthusiasm, we proclaimed, *"Cin, cin!"* and *"Salute!"*

Friar Camillo came to his feet. "May I offer a blessing on this union, beseeching Jesus that it will bring continued peace and prosperity to the families and churches and businesses of Verona?"

Cal and Papà gave their consent; Friar Camillo said a short, heartfelt prayer; again we drank. Friar Laurence followed suit with another blessing, this time including a prayer for a fertile marriage. We followed with more wine, and I wanted to groan at the expectations piled so high on my head . . . and my loins.

"With so many holy blessings, this union cannot fail," Barnadine proclaimed, and sloshed wine out of his goblet onto his waistcoat.

"Say not so!" Papà commanded.

The Montagues murmured reprovingly, for in my family, we do not so challenge the Fates.

Nonna Ursula must have subscribed to the old superstitions, for she spit lightly on my head.

I thanked her and wiped off the damp with my napkin.

She turned her head so she appeared to look up and down the table. "How soon will this blessed event take place?"

"Immediately," Cal said.

The outcry appeared to startle his royal I-don't-have-to-worry-about-the-details–ness. "Immediately!" he repeated, as if that would vanquish our protests.

Every Montague at the table looked to me.

"We need time to send the invitations, receive the responses, allow our friends and families to pack, to travel from their homes," I explained. "They'll want to attend the wedding."

"How many relatives can there be?" He sounded incredulous.

Foolish man. Of course, with both his father and mother deceased, and only young Princess Isabella, elderly Nonna Ursula, and perhaps a few aunts, uncles, and cousins as family, he couldn't comprehend the vast undertaking he proposed.

Mamma started counting on her fingers, and I already knew she would need to use Papà's hands, too, and mine, and all the digits at the table. "My mother, Lady Capulet, is currently visiting my aunt Samaritana, her sister, in Padua. Romeo's parents, Lord and Lady Montague, currently reside at the Montague estate and vineyard, and his siblings and their children, of which there are many, live in Verona or are scattered across the lands. Our two married daughters, Susanna and Vittoria, live respectively in Venice and Florence with their husbands." She looked at me. "*Their husbands,* who were formerly suitors to Rosaline's hand, although those marriages were thwarted by Rosaline's own machinations."

A sore subject for her, but Cal gestured it aside. "For my sake, I am glad for her machinations, but why must we wait on so many to attend? Are not the people of Verona enough to celebrate properly?"

Another outcry, louder than the first, and many words about "My sisters!" and "My parents!" and "Family!"

Papà put an end to it with loud harumph. "Podestà, you haven't thought this through. The feud between the Capulets and Montagues is in the past, but among the many hotheads in our families—"

Which was funny . . . because he was the easiest to ignite.

"—the feud is ever ready to take flame once more, and if a slight is perceived, if one minor relative is not given their due in hospitality, the rebellion that left you and Princess Isabella without the loving care of your parents will seem a minor conflagration."

Cal looked at me for confirmation.

I nodded.

He stood, came around to me, and offered his hand. "Let us promenade."

I rose and, without touching him, continued ahead of him to the great walk.

"Shouldn't they have a chaperone?" I heard my mother ask worriedly.

"It's a little late for that," Papà said.

Chapter 16

I flung out an arm toward the dining room. "There's the other reason the wedding must proceed at a majestic pace."

"What reason will you give me now?" Cal might have been testy, might have been irritated.

Which I did not appreciate. "What do you mean by that?"

"Is this not all a tactic to stall the wedding as long as possible?"

A question designed to send me into a frenzy and so I framed a question to return the favor. "Who ever said men were the logical sex? I've never seen that to be true!"

He snapped at the bait. "What do *you* mean by *that*?"

"My parents have every reason to wish that this union take place immediately, as you command. They were stunned at my good sense in capturing a prince, not quite comprehending that, in all truth, you captured me. And for all that the torches that lit us that night showed us both clothed, I spoke unwisely and it's believed that we engaged in previous trysts."

"As we did."

At that injustice, I took fire. "I don't think that you sneaking up on me while I stood alone outside on our veranda qualifies as a tryst. I believe to be a tryst, both must be involved in the arrangements."

"Perhaps." It was, at best, a grudging agreement to that, and at the same time, a deliberate reminder of an evening that seemed to me almost a dream, yet a vision of a heady future.

It would not do to dwell on past moments, and so I calmed myself. "I simply point out that word has gone out to all Verona that I was despoiled by the prince. If we wed as soon as you wish, that will be seen as a confirmation."

"For fear a child is on the way?"

Did I really need to talk him through every arguing point? "If there's no apparent hurry, doubt will be cast and my reputation restored."

"No one will dare to disparage your reputation." He drew himself up to his full height and exuded chilly dignity. "I'm the prince of Verona. I will forbid it!"

He was more unseeing than his blind and elderly grandmother. "When you look upon the sky, do you see muddy earth? When you gaze upon beautiful Verona, do you see the grandeur of ancient Rome?"

He didn't so much deflate as stand down. "I don't understand."

"You suffer from the worst sort of powerful illusion if you believe that your forbidding will do more than confirm their suspicions. Please, Cal, I beg you, don't do such a thing. The sniggering at my expense is already loud enough."

He seated himself in a velvet-upholstered chair, put his fingertips together, and pretended to think. Or maybe he did think, but they were man thoughts and thus indecipherable to me. Finally he looked up. "I never meant for laughter to be the burden of this match."

"I acquit you of that. Mockery is not something that could afflict you as prince." Again I thought to clarify that which seemed beyond his experience. "Although for the most part, men don't suffer the ordeal of sniggering amusement due to, for instance, their skill at swordplay."

"You're accomplished at swordplay yourself."

That was true. My father, Romeo the quick with a blade, believed all his children—his daughters, as well as his son—should know how to defend themselves. "Unless provoked unto death, I lack the mettle to eviscerate an opponent."

"I suspect I'm grateful for that."

I remembered that night, the unruly passion lit by torches, the nasty flavor of mortification, of knowing I'd been so befooled, and the resultant betrothal. With all the sincerity in my being, I assured him, "You are."

Wisely, Cal didn't even so much as hint at a smile, but offered his hand, palm up.

Gentle reader, let's stop and discuss my moral quandary. Do you understand that a man's hand that does not grasp or insist is an invitation, and palm up means even more? It was an offering of peace and a hope it will be accepted. Thus the question is . . . should I accept the gesture and return it with a handclasp?

Since that night of the humiliating scene in the garden and its postmortem of a marriage offer, I'd steered away from any deliberate contact of my skin to his. I didn't want to remember those moments of passion, with all the stars of the dark night that fell from the sky and wrapped us in their flame. I still felt the burn; I waited impatiently for it to fade. Would this simple touch ignite it again?

Yet to ignore his gesture would indicate a decline of his goodwill, and in the marriage of my Capulet grandparents, I'd seen what damage could be done to a family when warfare lives between the couple.

I was the Montagues' sensible daughter. Should I be sensible now?

The prince was not a man to long wait for rejection; his hand had gradually begun to retreat and close.

With unromantic haste, I snatched it in mine.

There. It was done. I had maintained my good sense. A handclasp was a simple thing, a common thing. I held my mother's hand, my father's hand, my sisters' hands, Cesario's hand. This gesture was no more than that. I was myself, Rosaline of the Montagues, prudent, rational, not given to flights of unreasonable and unforeseen craving for a man I barely knew. I was comfortable, nothing more.

Cal gazed at our hands and rearranged the grasp so his fingers deliberately intersected mine, reaching between, pressing our palms together. As if to give reign to sensation, he closed his eyes. With his thumb, he stroked my palm, creating the agitation that I'd told myself lacked importance; and in his still face, I saw the truth. I could scoff at myself, at my own passionate imaginings. It was Cal's passionate imaginings of which I should beware.

He opened his eyes and caught the sunrise of comprehension that lit my face. He gazed; then in an austere voice, he asked, "Are you thinking of Lysander?"

"I am not, and I'll be uncomfortable if you are."

He gave that bark of a laugh, then lifted my hand to his lips and kissed it. "We progress."

"About time," Elder's voice chimed.

Way to spoil the moment. Exasperated, I asked, "Would you go away?"

"Until justice is done, I fear we're stuck with each other," Elder said.

Cal glanced around. "My father again, I presume? How long has he been here?"

Elder clarified, "I merely observed briefly."

"Because I must say," Cal told me, "knowing my father can linger through any intimate moment lends our encounters an element of horror I haven't felt since my adolescence."

Elder barked a laugh that was more full-bodied than Cal's, more openly amused, but still so similar as to send a chill up my spine. "I'll be in the dining room." He made that ridiculous little pop-out sound and disappeared.

"He's gone." I tightened my grip on Cal's hand, a practical grasp that vanquished all sense of dalliance, and pulled him to his feet. Releasing him, I said, "Let us return to reassure my family you now comprehend the reasons we must linger at the church door for yet a while."

"Yes, let us do so." He straightened his doublet, then stalked ahead down the corridor. "But I don't like it."

Chapter 17

I caught up with Cal. "You have no relatives whom we must invite to the wedding?"

He slowed. "Uncle Yago and his wife, Lugrezia."

"Right." I glanced around the great walk as if expecting them to materialize. "Don't they live in Verona? Shouldn't they be here? Now? At your table awaiting their dinner?"

"They were invited. So yes. They were quite surly about my marriage to my Chiarretta. It seems history repeats itself."

"'Surly'? That makes no sense. If you remove from this world without heirs, your uncle will inherit the role of podestà, will he not?"

"He flatters himself so. He certainly intended it when my father was murdered, and my aunt vociferously urged him on, but he faltered at the last moment."

"'Faltered'? Why?" I viewed the still, smooth countenance that, now that I knew how, gave clarity to the subject. "Not out of loyalty and kindness to you, I assume?"

"Uncle Yago's greatest concern is his health, which he laments daily."

At once, I recalled Elder's belief that he'd stabbed the assassin with the tip of his knife, and I asked, "What issue has he?"

"At the same time my father was dispatched by so cowardly

a villain, my uncle had been celebrating with friends the Leonardi triumph over the Acquasassos. On his way home, sabotage delayed his sedan chair. He barely fended off an attack by armed knaves. The wound to his abdomen has never healed—or so he claims. My uncle has always been a man of many vapors and ill humors, much disgruntlement and discontent."

"Hm." Had Uncle Yago drugged Elder and worn the assassin's devil's mask?

"When he dies, I swear his tombstone will say, 'See, I told you I was sick.'"

Startled from my grim concentrations, I burst into laughter hearty enough to bring tears to my eyes.

Cal stopped to view me as if the burst of unreserved merriment unnerved him.

Had I offended? I promptly brought myself under control and glanced around. "Is it inappropriate for me to laugh here?"

"No. Not at all! Don't stop. Your laughter is delightful."

"Why do you stare at me in such astonishment?"

He spoke with painful slowness. "I can't remember the last time someone laughed out loud in this palace. I can't remember if anyone has ever laughed so restrainedly at some small witticism I said."

Without a thought to my "don't touch" policy, I tucked my hand into his arm. "That was no small witticism. I don't know your uncle, but that was funny." Now that I knew I could, I grinned.

"Not funny. It's true."

"Wit is truth wrapped in delicate glass beads threaded with gold." While thinking that whenever Elder's brother made an appearance at our festivities, I'd make a study of him, I started once more toward the dining room.

Cal didn't, and as I turned to face him, I realized that once more, he'd wrapped himself in a dark cloak of passion, and only the lights were the dark flames that glowed in his eyes. I thought, *Merda! He's going to kiss me again. What good is a ghost if he can't hover and nag as a chaperon should, and why am I leaning into Cal?*

My own mind answered me, *Because he may not be your One True Love, but he can kiss until the blood sings like rich red wine in your veins.*

Then . . . in a lightning-swift change, I lost his attention. He looked over my head toward the dining room, and I looked, too.

Papà stood there as Imogene and Emilia trooped past him, directing them to the open door of the palace's atrium.

"What are the children doing? Where are they going?" Cal asked me.

"If I were to guess, I'd say Mamma arranged for them to have a separate feast. Probably there's a children's table set up where they can laugh as loud as they want, sing, jump up, and run around—" Cal looked so dumbfounded, I stopped. "It's all right, Cal, in Veronese society, it's actually normal for children to eat independently of the adults. It's only in the Montague household where we insist on keeping the family together for meals."

"Princess Isabella will remain, and be lonely!"

"I don't think so." I nodded as Katherina, Princess Isabella, and Cesario walked out, hand in hand.

"The kitchen will be overwhelmed with two meals!"

"I hope not, since that's a clear sign of an ill-functioning cook"—which didn't surprise me, considering the palace's reputation—"but in any case, Mamma will have also arranged a simple repast for the children."

"Without supervision, they'll be wild!"

"Who says they're without supervision?" I indicated Nurse's muscular figure stalking after the children. "She'll keep them under control. Cal, why so concerned that the kidlets are at a separate table?"

"I wanted our families to visit, to get to know each other. I want us to be . . . close."

"One of the reasons you chose me was for my family." I was repeating one of the things the romantic fool (sarcasm) had mentioned that night after he'd arranged to have us caught in a compromising position. "You said it's important to like your in-laws."

"Yes."

"In the next months, Cal, I promise, we'll have more togetherness with the Montagues and Capulets than you could possibly desire, and as the children get to know you and lose their awe, you'll think twice about this match you've brought upon us."

He did that "looming" trick of his. "I will not."

I did that "not cringing" trick of mine. "Let them go now and both the adults and the children will retain their polish a little longer."

Chapter 18

As we reentered the dining room, the long table held empty chairs where the children had sat, and the adults wore varying expressions of reprieve or boredom or satisfaction.

Marcellus, I noted, looked like a killer granted a reprieve from hanging—Cesario, with his incessant questions, had a way of making grown men fear him.

Friar Camillo viewed Barnadine with some alarm, for Barnadine sat, face buried in his goblet, covered with splashes of the red wine he'd spilled.

Cal escorted me back to my chair by Nonna Ursula, then moved to stand at the head of the table. "The wedding will take place on the first day of winter. No later. Whatever relative and friend wishes to attend and cannot make arrangements in that amount of time need never wait upon us again."

Zoinds, Cal. Way to put it plainly.

He nodded his head to me, a confirmation that he'd done as I asked, and done as he wished.

"It shall be done." Mamma sounded so calm, there might never have been a discussion.

I seated myself. He seated himself. The first course arrived, and everyone breathed a sigh of relief. Simple platters of cheeses, salamis, and fruits were passed from hand to hand, and ample baskets of breads and bowls of first-press olive oil followed. We used forks to spear whatever foods we desired.

All except Nonna Ursula, who scowled and proclaimed, "That silly new gadget will never last when fingers do the job so well." She proceeded to use her hands to load her plate. When she passed me the platter, she advised, "Eat up! The rest of the meal will be wretched. If your reputation be true, and the famed Montague meals be as delicious as I've heard, I look forward to the moment when you take over the palace kitchens. I'm too old, Cal's too busy, and my granddaughter too inexperienced."

Sadly, she was correct. After the first course, one cold and mediocre dish followed another. I watched as the food was returned, barely touched, to the kitchen, and wondered who profited from the sale of the foods. As future wife of the podestà, I knew I'd find out soon enough.

Yet for all that, we were a merry table of good company. Cal got his wish; the families and attendants grew to know each other in conversation and temperament.

Nonna Ursula pulled her shawl up on her shoulders. "I feel a chill."

As did I, and when I turned to look at her, I knew why. Elder hovered in the air between us, seemingly seated on an invisible chair. I gasped and pulled away.

"What? Did someone walk on your grave?" Papà joked; the ancients believed that when a shiver ran up your spine, someone had placed a footstep on your eventual resting place.

"Not *my* grave," I said crisply.

"My mother is a font of information," Elder informed me. "She may be the meanest old lady in the world, but she's never wrong and she never forgets a detail."

I glanced toward him and nodded, hoping that without me saying anything, he'd understand that I knew what he wanted me to do.

"Are you nodding at me, girl?" Nonna Ursula shouted. "I didn't say anything."

I examined her and that wrinkled, alert face. I leaned close and murmured, "You're not blind."

"I'm blind . . . almost completely." She closed one eye as if to see me better. "And you are too observant."

I guessed, "Your hearing is—"

"Not good. But I see more and hear more than anyone realizes." She relaxed, choosing to trust me. "Don't tell, hm?"

My mouth twitched in a smile. "Not a soul."

"The old faker," Elder marveled.

"She's not a faker," I chided. "She's using her disabilities to her advantage."

"Are you talking to yourself?" Nonna Ursula asked.

I took a chance. "No, I'm talking to the ghost of your son."

Nonna Ursula leaned back and laughed heartily. "Now that is an idea to shake out the villains." Her expression changed, became contemplation.

Elder watched Barnadine help himself to another full glass of wine. "Barnadine's parents came to Verona from Sicily, fleeing the vendettas that had taken three of their sons. The family crafted in leather, wonderful pieces of art and clothing. I recognized their talent and the possibilities, and welcomed them to the city. I suggested to Old Barnadine that he could serve me by providing protection against attack, and within days, he arrived with a shirt of leather, light, supple, to be worn in secret beneath my formal clothing." In satisfaction, he said, "More than once, it foiled an assassin's blade, and I gained a reputation for invincibility."

I glanced at him. He smiled a smug smile.

"I raised the family to prominence, gave them well-deserved honors, took Barnadine to train in my forces, and when he proved himself, took him as my bodyguard. His family ranks among my most loyal subjects, bound to the house of Leonardi and to Verona in joy and gratitude."

I understood entirely. For us, the Montagues, who owned vineyards in the countryside, Verona and its walls had provided safety in times of war and rampage, and because our wines were the best in the world, when our vineyards were threatened, the podestà marched out in defense and kept them safe. Verona's red-stoned streets, the golden buildings, the bustling markets, formed the bones of our very beings.

I leaned toward Nonna Ursula and spoke in her ear. "I'm surprised Barnadine joined us for dinner." Cal could invite whomever he wished, of course, but one expected more decorum of the guests than Barnadine presented.

She did hear me, for she sighed. "I always insist he have a place at the table. He was my son's most faithful bodyguard, a good man who failed in his duty, and to this day blames himself."

Elder observed, "Every time I see Barnadine, he looks more worn, more ragged, more guilty."

I asked Nonna Ursula, "Why does Barnadine look so worn, so ragged, so guilty?"

She well understood the need for discretion, for she answered harshly, but in low tones. "He drinks too much."

I challenged her. "A simple explanation with much of substance behind it, I trow."

"Barnadine is the tragedy birthed of calamity." Nonna Ursula spoke with pity. "He's not the man he was. Even before the revolt, he foiled one assassination attempt on my son after another. In the battles with the Acquasasso for control of Verona, Barnadine fought next to Escalus in battle after battle, each more perilous than before. He guarded Escalus fiercely, throwing himself into the fray ahead of him. Then . . . then when the combats were won and victory was ours, when all danger was past, a vile craven drugged them both and murdered him who held our safety in his hands. Barnadine blames himself." She nodded toward Cal. "Others blame him, too. My grandson is young and judgmental, without the tempering that time gives a man—or a woman. For at some point, have we all not failed in our duties?"

To my surprise, she had tears in her eyes. "In what way have you failed, Nonna Ursula? I've heard naught but good about your faithful support of your son, your grandson, and your loving care for your granddaughter."

"I—"

Urgently Elder spoke in my ear. "He's coming."

"Someone's coming," I said to Nonna Ursula. "Someone of importance."

She looked toward the door, straining to see. "Who?"

Chapter 19

Elder answered her question. "Yago, my brother. He of the schemes and laments and displeasures and personal injuries unwitnessed by others."

"It's your son, Duke Yago," I told Nonna Ursula.

"He comes late and will leave soon," she said.

Elder continued, "He brings with him his wife, Lugrezia, who in her dappled girlhood cast her net toward me, and when I loved Eleanor, turned her craft toward Yago and caught the fool. Her sour face was always enough to curdle fresh milk, and the years have set that fateful resentment in sneers that can never be erased."

"He brings with him Duchess Lugrezia, his wife," I said to Nonna Ursula.

She grimaced. "The woman's a mumble-news. She speaks softly and so works to leave me isolated among the company."

Thus we were not surprised when Yago and Lugrezia appeared in the doorway and posed, like two bolts of dark lightning sent to obliterate the candles and plunge us into dark.

Conversation hushed, and Elder said, "Ever they have affected a jolly revelry like two turds tossed in the punch bowl."

I didn't laugh—but it was a close thing. Clearly, Cal got his turn of phrase from his father.

When Cal noticed them, he rose slowly to his feet and smiled a grin so faulty, I thanked the Madonna that he'd not felt obliged to create that terrible contortion for me. "Welcome, my noble uncle and gracious aunt. Come sit at the table with this merry company and celebrate my blessed betrothal to Lady Rosaline of the house of Montague." He gestured toward me, his broad hand a graceful, gracious sweep.

I stood and curtsied. I didn't remember previously meeting the couple; yet from the expressions on their sour lemon faces, one would have thought Cal had introduced them to a voluptuary.

Duke Yago resembled Elder in his features and form, but even as a ghost, Elder appeared more robust, for Yago's sallow complexion, crumpled chest, and skinny shoulders gave him the appearance of a soon-likely visit to the boneyard's stone slab.

Duchess Lugrezia stood taller than her husband, an impressive woman, clearly once so beautiful she had put the stars to shame; and now to clutch at youth, she wore white hair painted yellow, wild eyebrows penciled brown, and narrow lips overstained with red.

The couple dressed alike in magnificent well-padded scarlet velvets and fur-trimmed sleeves—people of consequence not in themselves, but because their clothes declared them to be. In unison, they strode forward, clearly intending that Yago take his seat at the foot of the table, but Cal gestured them forward. "We sit close so Nonna Ursula can hear our conversations."

They surveyed the table, looking for the most prominent seats among people they clearly considered beneath them.

Papà rose. "Please take my seat. You'll wish to greet your mother with affection and respect."

Yago seemed only now to notice Nonna Ursula. He shuffled over, kissed her cheek, murmured, "Madam Mother, I rejoice to see you."

For all that his voice was pitched low, she heard him, for she loudly answered, "You rejoice too seldom, Yago. I have only one son left on this earth and he arrives with a tardy gait."

Duke Yago grimaced in contemptuous and unhidden disdain.

I wanted to warn him of Nonna Ursula's not-so-impaired vision, but would never deliberately remove the elderly woman's camouflage, although I saw that his contempt pained her.

The tension at the table thickened, for my kind family had welcomed Nonna Ursula to their hearts, and Cal, for all his dire warnings, obviously loved his grandmother.

Yago remained oblivious, or perhaps he cared nothing for family, friends, and a merry company. He groaned like a swaybacked horse as he lowered himself into my father's seat next to Nonna Ursula. Cal directed Lugrezia to Cesario's empty chair across the table, next to Mamma, and ordered they both be given plates and foods to sate their hunger.

Duchess Lugrezia pulled the entire stuffed and refeathered peacock toward her, and with her eating knife, she began the process of removing a joint.

Good luck to her. None of the rest of us had been able to dismember the tough old bird.

Papà walked around to stand behind Mamma, to hold her shoulders and give support, and, I thought, to stand above Duke Yago in height and placement at the table. It was a gesture quite unlike Papà, and made me realize he had no fondness for the man and his inflated consequence.

Without waiting on wine or greetings or to discover the tenor and direction of the conversation, Duke Yago said, "Nephew, did you know the flagellants have returned to Verona?"

Periodically the flagellants, men and women filthy, unhoused, and with their faces covered and their backs bared, arrived in a pack to wander the streets, mortifying their flesh with whips in penance for their sins. And our sins, too, if one was to believe their accounts. They called themselves *disciplinati,* and in return they required bread and wine, blankets and shoes.

"I'd heard that report, Uncle." Cal settled into his chair at the head of the table. "Indeed, as podestà, I had to allow them to cross through the city gate, direct them to the arena where they can sleep, and tell them which routes to follow through the city."

Duke Yago appeared not to note the reminder of Cal's position. "What do you intend to do? Wherever go the flagellants, so goes trouble."

That was true. Some citizens welcomed them and the holy frenzy they brought with them. Others feared them, and justly, for they had no stake in Verona's peace or property, and yes, trouble followed them like the stench of dried black blood.

"I would ban them, but such a move puts them on the roads around the city, blocking merchants and visitors. I prefer to keep them here, under my eye, regulated and hemmed in by Verona's laws."

"They cover their faces to hide their lawlessness."

"I won't allow such behavior."

"They won't listen to you!" Duke Yago used his own whip of scorn.

"Then they'll visit our dungeons and scatter like autumn leaves under the wind of my displeasure." Indeed, the icy breath of Cal's assurance made me shiver; he would not allow the *disciplinati* to defy him, or his uncle to chide him.

Duchess Lugrezia smiled so charmingly, I wanted to raise a shield to protect us all, and in a voice as welcoming and cordial as a courtesan's, she said, "Come, Yago, these many years since your wounding, Callie has done well without your avuncular advice, or at least well enough"—she put down her knife—"if one discounts the food at the palace." Her gaze swooped in on me. "I hope, my dear Rosaline, your advent will improve matters."

Perhaps this will amaze you, gentle reader, but if my temper abruptly gains the upper hand over my tact . . . tact will lose. "I promise, Duchess Lugrezia—"

I must have had that tone in my voice, for Mamma shook her head at me.

"—that when I'm mistress of the palace, my improvements will start with a value-enhanced guest list." I smiled with at least as much charm as she had.

Mamma dropped her head into her hand.

Lugrezia nodded with approval. "That is exactly what I hoped you would say, dear Rosaline. Because our nephew brings to table plebeians who would be better served a meal on the paving stones of the street, and when reproached, he talks about his duty to Verona's citizens." She flapped a hand at Cal, and that warm voice echoed of amused affection. "He will be, I anticipate, guided by you in household matters at least." She picked up her knife and began poking at the peacock again.

I couldn't believe it. She hadn't comprehended my insult. She remained untouched by my scorn. I looked around the table, and saw equally stunned expressions to match the one I wore, and some warm commiserations from those who had encountered Duchess Lugrezia before. In fact, Papà grinned at me, Mamma still frowned a reprimand, and Cal wore such a smooth expression I knew he was hiding something, probably a loud bark of laughter. At me.

Damn it, I was tired of getting it wrong every damned time.

"Did I neglect to mention that Lugrezia has the shell-covered hide of a sea cow?" Elder asked.

"You did so neglect," I answered shortly.

"Both of them do, and neither has been blessed with humor. Look not for jesting in any future dealings."

"Does she talk to herself?" Duke Yago was staring at me. "Sign of madness, you know."

I found myself releasing my breath. The whole evening had

been one simple-wittedness after another, and this was no worse than the rest.

Mayhap Nonna Ursula and I thought alike, or mayhap she heard my thoughts the way she heard Elder's words, for she sat with chin firm, eyes bright, hands caressing the rough knob at the top of her cane. She leaned close and said, "Rosie, you have given me a marvelous idea. We've had enough of the meal and the company, and I can offer an excuse of fatigue and you can offer to help me to my fainting couch. Come, let's find a private place where we can talk with no one overhearing."

Chapter 20

Nonna Ursula didn't wait for my reply; obviously, I'd do as she wished.

Everyone should do as she wished.

"I'm weary," she announced. Silence fell, the men leaped up and all eyes fixed on her. The company waited, breath bated, for a pronouncement—*spreads terror like manure,* I remembered—but she merely smiled with those strong teeth. "Rosie will help me. Good night."

The company slumped as if released from a great stress.

I didn't make the mistake of helping her out of her chair—which irritated her no end. "Give me a hand, girl, give me a hand! How many times do you think I can stand on my own?"

"Madam, I do not assume anything about a lady of your age and strength." I added more philosophically, "And I scheme to never get on the rude side of your cane."

"Help me up, then. I promise not to thump you." Between the two of us, we got her out of the chair. As she walked past her son, she whacked the back of his head with her open palm. "Come back on the morrow," she commanded. "Bring your wife."

Duke Yago would not, I thought, dare disobey a direct command from his formidable mother.

We walked slowly down the corridor. "Here." She pointed into a small, cozy chamber.

When we'd entered, I realized this opened into a greater room, with a bed spread with woven blankets and fur skins, and a variety of pillows piled at the ornate headboard. A large casement window filled with small panes of heavy, clouded glass would in the daytime allow light into the chamber, and more than portraits or statues or exotic plants marked the wealth of the palace. "Your sitting room and bedchamber?" I inquired.

"Indeed. I can't climb the stairs, and this places me in the center of things, where I can keep track of the household." She added, "Shut the door. No spy holes gaze in here, no secret passages lead in or out. We can talk." She tried to sit in a comfortable chaise, and wavered.

I leaped forward and steadied her, then helped her sit, then recline, and tucked pillows behind her head.

"You know how to care for the elderly," she observed, and closed her eyes wearily.

"I helped Nurse with my Capulet grandfather as he faded."

"It irritates that company fatigues me, that I can't hear the words, much less the nuances, that I must strain to see." She opened her eyes. "But I can see and hear my son and his contempt. What a cabbage-cask he is, smelling of vinegar, shrunken with salt, puckering the mouth, and offending the nose."

I gave her a summation of Papà's philosophy. "Everyone does the best they can. Sadly, some are shit-crawling worm-suckers, and their best reeks of funk and failure."

"Perhaps." She smiled bitterly. "Yet I'm his mother and he's *my* funk and failure."

"She always did blame herself for his failings." Of course, Elder had tagged along. "Yet I remember—he was born bound in pity for himself and lacking care and compassion for others. It's in himself that the blemishes lie."

"He's not dead yet," I said to both of them. "He may improve."

"God grant," they both answered.

Neither believed it.

"Nonna Ursula." I took the coverlet folded at the foot of the chaise and tucked it around her slight figure. "I've heard naught but good about your faithful support of your son, your grandson, and your loving care for your granddaughter, yet you fret. Do you wish to unburden yourself?"

In the first nervous gesture I'd seen from her, she plucked at the heavy material. "I should never have gone with Eleanor to the convent. I should never have left Escalus alone. Eleanor was the woman who made all Verona see that the brusque, hearty, insensitive man had a tender side. She feared for him. She begged to stay with him. With the unrest, she had no choice; she had to leave Verona to have her child, so turned her pleas to me, asking that I stay with him."

"Did he not command that you go with her?"

"All his fears were for her, yes. Yet should I have decided to stay, my will would have been done."

I examined her. "Eleanor needed you, did she not?"

"Indeed. For all that Princess Isabella is a comfort, Eleanor should never . . . they should never have taken the chance of begetting another child. The difficult birth left her exhausted, yet when she took the baby in her arms, she was revived. It was the news of Escalus's death that put her in the grave. If I'd been here watching his back, that wouldn't have happened. I'm good at sniffing out treachery, for most men believe women are stupid and old women are senile, and I, in particular, as we discussed, am blind and deaf."

"Then you have some suspicions about who might have arranged for the assassination."

"I do. I did. Escalus was at the height of his powers at the time of his untimely death, thirty-three years old, a strong man and virile. When he had fought and won Verona back from the Acquasassos, no one in his right mind would have attacked him face on, so it had to be drugs and a knife in the dark."

"Not poison?" I asked.

"I told you not poison," Elder said in irritation.

I gestured him to silence.

"No. That makes me say it's not a woman. Women who kill use poison. Men want blood on the blade. But"—Nonna Ursula lifted her hands in that unknowing gesture—"we all know women can be deadly in every way, and my son was not . . ."

I went on alert. "Not?"

"Men are weak." She made her pronouncement without a hint of doubt.

Elder glared at his mother.

"Escalus loved Eleanor, but when she couldn't bear a child and each pregnancy weakened her," Nonna Ursula said, "he resolved to no longer touch her."

I dug into the marrow of the matter. "He was a fleshmonger?"

"I was not!" he protested.

"No," Nonna Ursula said. "There were not many women. He was fastidious and circumspect, careful never to bruise Eleanor's kind heart."

Sarcasm rolled off me like fog off the Adige River. "How magnificently controlled of him."

Elder lifted his hands toward heaven. Which was funny in a peculiar way.

"Men." Nonna Ursula lifted one shoulder. "They think they're strong, in control. If one of them ever gave birth, all of Adam and Eve's children would disappear off the face of the earth."

"She's right about that," Elder told me.

I answered them both. "I know."

"I've recently felt he's near, but that's perhaps my own procession toward the spirit world."

"She seems pretty lively to me," Elder observed.

"Rosie, when you claimed you'd seen the ghost of my son"—clearly, she didn't believe a word of it—"you gave me an idea."

"What is that, Nonna Ursula?"

She leaned forward. "When I was younger, I was adept at contacting the spirits."

Torn between astonishment and alarm, I said, *"Really?"*

"She's an old fraud. She never saw a single spirit," Elder declared.

"No, I'm an old fraud. I never saw a single spirit," Nonna Ursula echoed.

"Ha! I knew it." Elder rubbed his hands in glee.

Nonna Ursula continued, "Yet if my son's killer is still living among us, and hears of our visits with the dead—and he will, for there's nothing the people love more than royal gossip of a celestial nature—he will perhaps reveal himself with suspicious behavior."

I considered the idea from all angles. I thought it would work, but . . . "Might that suspicious behavior be violence?"

"You'd think she would have thought of that, wouldn't you?" Elder viewed his mother with ghostly irritation.

Nonna Ursula said, "I hear you're quite good at defending yourself."

Someone must have told her about the incident a few months before.

"And you'll be on your guard, will you not?"

"Yes." I took her hand. "But I'm not the only one who might be harmed."

Nonna Ursula drew herself up. "No one has the guts and nerve to touch me."

"I admire her confidence." Rising ghostly irritation.

"My dowager, I admire your confidence." I was more gentle in my tone than he. "But you're elderly, nearly blind, nearly deaf, and a woman."

"The meanest old woman in Verona," Elder reminded me.

"I'm also the meanest old woman in Verona, Padua, and Mantua." Again Nonna Ursula, more or less, echoed Elder. Could she in some hidden part of her mind hear him?

"I'd wear the meanest old woman tiara for Venice, too, but last I heard that Acquasasso bitch is still alive. Lady Pulissena, cursed be her name. But, girl, do you have a better idea to find out if our assassin is still living? And for flushing out the villain?"

I couldn't, and I looked to Elder.

He shook his head. "She told me I had a talent for intrigue, and that I inherited it from her."

Nonna Ursula took my continued silence as acquiescence. "Tomorrow evening, as the sun goes down, we'll gather a convocation of sympathetic women to lure the castle ghosts with chants and charms, and discover what they witnessed on that blood-soaked night of murder, treachery, and sorrow."

Chapter 21

After the dinner at the palace, as my family rode through the streets of Verona in the sedan chairs, we heard shouts; and peeking through the curtains, we saw torch light in the distance.

"What is it?" Cesario's clear voice echoed down the empty street.

Papà hushed him, and said, "The flagellants. Let us not attract their attention."

The bearers picked up speed, the prince's bodyguards ran beside us, swords drawn, and we arrived at Casa Montague safely, if much jolted by the pace, and worried as all must be at the disruption of Verona's fair streets.

Mamma, especially, had been sickened by the movements. Nurse and I put her to bed, while Papà carried the drooping Cesario to his chamber and commanded my sisters to theirs.

Nurse placed a cool, damp cloth on Mamma's forehead. Tonight the strain of her pregnancy showed, for her long, dark lashes rested on her pale cheeks and she patted her belly as if urging calm on a restless child.

I took Mamma's limp hand and felt her wrist. "Better now? Can you sleep?" Her heart beat true and strong.

"The nausea recedes. The activity does not."

I saw a thump of a fist or foot up by her ribs and winced.

Her brown eyes popped open. "But my daughter Rosie, I would know why tonight you shed the chaperonage of your siblings to wander alone with Prince Escalus, then wander the palace alone by yourself, then disappear with Princess Ursula."

I knew what she wanted; she wanted to know whether and how well I'd obeyed her commands in regard to the prince and our betrothal. Yet in her current delicate state, I debated what and how much to tell her. "You know why I allowed the children to disappear." My gaze followed Nurse as she puttered around the room, her head turned to provide her ears clarity. I raised my voice to help her. "They had listened to enough of Prince Escalus's odd enthusiasms. He is my burden to bear, and when Princess Isabella offered them escape, I sent them forth."

Mamma nodded, pleased with my answer. "As I come to know Princess Isabella, her resemblance to dear Eleanor grows stronger. I feel as if my friend has requested me to act as mother and guide." She grimaced and massaged her belly. "While you were alone with Prince Escalus, did he give your father cause to slaughter him?"

"Before he could do that, he was interrupted."

"Who would dare?"

"Who, indeed?" I hovered on the edge of confession, unsure if I should mention Elder. If I told Mamma I'd seen him, she would certainly believe me. She knew lying was not my modus operandi. Manipulating and finagling, yes. Lying, no. But would she wonder at my sanity?

While I contemplated, Mamma struggled up onto her elbows, then flopped back on the pillows. "Would you calm down?" She spoke fiercely, and not to me and not to any ghost. She spoke to the coming Montague, and she was as exasperated as any woman carrying a child could be.

Nurse hurried over. "What do you want, my lady?"

"I want to stand up. Or rather, the little tyrant wants to stand up."

"You should sleep." Nurse glared at me as if I were keeping Mamma awake.

"He wants me to stand and"—Nurse helped Mamma to her feet—"he wants to be walked."

I sighed and put away my desire to tell about Elder. Mamma was burdened enough with a woman's holy duty nurturing a new life, and while she might deal with equanimity at the news of a haunting, she would most definitely forbid me to seek the villain who'd murdered Elder. I didn't blame her, it did seem foolish to the extreme, but I had to keep in mind my reward. When I succeeded, Elder would owe me, and he'd agreed to guide me into the arms of my One True Love.

More pragmatically, although I'd be leaving Cal without a wife, I'd also be ensuring his safety and the safety of his sister, for they were in danger as long as the assassin remained free. And if he'd allow me, I'd arrange a more suitable match for Cal. That obsession that drew us together was powerful, I acknowledge, and he'd proved to me he hid within his undemonstrative facade the means to persuade me to . . . view his art collection, and with pleasure.

But what would we talk about subsequently? I knit my brow. "Mamma, what do you and Papà talk about in bed? After?" I spoke without forethought, and when Mamma and Nurse turned their amused gazes on me, I wished I'd kept my mouth shut.

Of course, I also constantly wished I was more adept at keeping my mouth shut. It seemed as if maturity should have cured me of that unhappy attribute. But nope. Twenty years old and still as mouthy as ever.

"After. Hm. Generally, while I loll in a lovely golden glow, your father proudly announces he taught Emilia how to spit through her two missing front teeth. I chide him. He asks if I think it's time we purchase a new sedan chair, and when I cast a sardonic look upon him, for I know what he's up to, he cites as his reasoning the new addition." Mamma put her hands under her belly and adjusted as if she could move the babe into a more comfortable position. "Then he wonders if we could manage to keep a pony in the garden, which he knows I won't allow, but he thinks by suggesting something I vehemently oppose, I'll be more likely to yield to his wish of a new sedan chair. Then—"

By now, I was laughing, and hurrying to her side, I helped Nurse lower her into a cushioned chair.

As I leaned over her, she cupped my cheek. "It's simply life, Rosie. It goes on with its great griefs and its marvelous joys and all the day-to-day bits and pieces and irritations, and love is the oil that gives it traction."

"I wasn't talking about love, Mamma."

"I know." Mamma caught at her belly. "A foot," she told me, "and another foot." She followed up by saying, "Passion is the lemon zest that gives the pudding of life flavor."

I laughed again. "If I must only have lemon zest . . . well, that won't be so bad."

Mamma nodded and smiled, but mostly she kneaded her belly.

Katherina stuck her head in the door. "Can I come in?"

Nurse clucked like a disapproving hen.

Mamma looked up with a smile. "Of course, child. Why are you awake?"

"I went to ask Rosie what happened between her and the prince tonight," Katherina explained.

Nurse put her hands to her hips. "Are all the girls awake?"

"I waited until the others fell asleep. Then when I went to Rosie's room, she wasn't abed, and I determined that I would find her before she wandered into the garden seeking another tryst." Katherina glared.

I yelped in indignation. "When did my younger sister become my arbiter of propriety?"

Katherina pointed her finger at me. "Your outrageous actions have made Emilia replace you as the sensible one. Or me! I'm not happy about it, and neither is she."

I argued, "I hardly think one little—"

"It was more than one, and it was huge!"

"Some of the events of recent days aren't my lone responsibility." I threaded my fingers at my chin. "Isn't that right, Mamma?"

Mamma made a motion meant to pacify. "My children . . ."

Katherina's eyes sparked. "Mamma, it's Rosie's eyebrows, isn't it? Satan's eyebrows?"

I sparked right back. "If that's what it is, it took long enough for Satan to gain ascendency over me, and Papà is still without the evil one's influence!"

"Papà has his moments!" Katherina snapped.

"Katherina!" Mamma said in that shocked and disappointed tone that always brought us to heel.

Katherina's gaze fell to the floor, and she mumbled, "I'm sorry, Mamma."

"You should be. Your papà is a good man, if a little too quick with his wit and unable to see that he might offend. Your sister is a good woman, wayward sometimes—"

"One crummy tryst!" I said.

"You couldn't even rendezvous with the right tomcat!" Katherina shot back.

"Maybe if I had more practice, I'd get better at it!" The bell clanged in my head. *Wrong. Wrong! See above about my mouthiness.* "I didn't mean that," I added into the following outcry. "But really, am I never going to hear the end of this?"

"No!" Nurse and Katherina yelled.

Mamma murmured calming words to her belly, then called Katherina and me over. "You girls rub him for a while, and no more shouting." As she knew it would, having Katherina and me kneel together and care for her child calmed us all. Nurse joined in by rubbing Mamma's shoulders, and as we patted and caressed, the child visibly slowed its thrashing. Mamma told Katherina, "This evening, I was helping Rosie understand the joys and duties of a wife, and she was telling me—"

"About Nonna Ursula and the séance." One glance proved I'd successfully diverted Mamma and Katherina from any further discussion of Cal's passions, and for the moment, at least, no whisper of Elder would cross my lips. "Nonna Ursula bade me tell you—while she should be enjoying the closing moments of her life, she is instead disturbed in her mind about the fugitive assassin who slayed her son."

"Poor woman." Sympathetic tears welled in Mamma's eyes.

"She fears what we all fear, that he walks among us and he'll strike again. To bring the villain out of hiding, she suggests we conduct a séance to reach to the other side and ask for the truth from those who have gone before."

Imogene bounced into the room from the doorway. "How cool! Can I come?"

Mamma seemed not at all surprised. Did she always pay attention to who listened at the door? "Honey, you're awfully young. I think if we limit the attendance to Rosie and me—"

"You're not to attend," I said to Mamma.

At the same time, Katherina said, "I'm coming, too!"

"No. No!" This was not at all what I intended. "I wasn't issuing an invitation, simply explaining what—"

"You can't imagine I'd let you go into a séance alone?" Mamma sounded shocked and insulted. "Indeed, I'd forbid such a nefarious undertaking, but Nonna Ursula had a reputation in the past for communing with the spirits for good. Her intervention gave dear Lady Alba the assurance that her little child had joined the angels, and Lady Alba was at last able to leave mourning behind and live again."

Katherina clasped her hands in supplication.

Mamma sighed and nodded at her. "So it shall be."

"It's not fair," Imogene whined. "I wanna go. I wanna talk to Zuann!"

"What do I tell you?" Mamma used her reproving voice.

Imogene's lip trembled. "'Justice and life seldom walk hand in hand.'"

"What does that mean?" Mamma asked.

"'Life ain't fair.'" Imogene's eyes filled with tears.

I couldn't stand it. She was such a dear sister, hounded by the oncoming and inevitable baggage-train wreck of adolescence, and she'd be miserable at home. I beckoned her over and put her hand on Mamma's belly. As she rubbed, I saw her tears subside, and I smiled. "Mamma, if we're going en masse ... the more the merrier."

"Not Emilia!" Nurse said sharply.

"No, and not Cesario." Mamma gave Imogene consent without words, and my dear wayward sister lit up like an overfilled oil lantern.

"In the morning, I'll write a note to Nonna Ursula," I decided. "So she won't be surprised."

"We won't tell Papà, will we?" Mamma requested. "We'll keep this our secret?"

"Tell me what?" Papà asked from the door.

"Girl stuff," Mamma said airily.

"I beg you, don't tell me." Papà came over and lifted us, one by one, to our feet. "It's been a big night and you should all be abed. Nurse, will you take them?" He knelt beside his Juliet, gently pressed both his hands on her belly, and called, "Imogene, is it still a boy?"

Imogene laughed out loud. "So much boy!" She raced down the galley toward the girls' room.

Katherina sighed in exasperation, then raced after her.

Nurse stepped out, glared at me as if it was my fault, and followed me into the corridor.

I glanced back as I exited to see Mamma murmuring to

Papà, showing him where to touch, then using both her own hands to press on the babe, and they both had such expressions on their faces that I had never seen. I stopped in place. "Mamma, are you well? Is the babe? Do you need me?"

She looked up. "Are you still here, child?" For a woman so attuned to her children, her surprise seemed, well, surprising.

Papà stood and walked toward me. "Leave me to take care of your mamma. In this matter, little apprentice, my experience is more extensive than yours."

Gently he urged me out the door and shut it behind me. I felt as if I'd missed some secret communication between them—which wasn't that usual. But . . . huh. They really had both looked quite peculiar.

Chapter 22

The next evening, Nonna Ursula, holding a small cloth bag, hobbled on my arm into the castle's library. The setting sun shone through the glass windows. As convocations go, this one was not large. Mamma, Princess Isabella, Katherina, and Imogene sat on wooden chairs around a small parquet table, a lit candelabra in the middle. Princess Isabella and Katherina looked wide-eyed and scared. Imogene was all energy and excitement, ready to leap out of her skin at a moment's notice.

Nurse leaned against the wall, arms folded, her mouth puckered in disapproval.

Elder slipped in through the unlit fireplace. "I've never witnessed one of these," he told me. "It's always been ladies-only entertainment."

I ignored him for all I was worth, and tried not to consider that if he was within my vision, other spirits could join.

Nonna Ursula asked, "Rosie, who's attending this gathering?"

I didn't know if Nonna Ursula was playing her "I can't see" card, or if the angle of the sun and the arrangement of the candles obscured her sight. "In this chamber are Lady Juliet, two of my sisters, Katherina and Imogene, and Princess Isabella." I didn't mention Elder. That seemed premature.

Nonna Ursula peered toward the flickering candlelight. "You

have a third sister, the little charmer at the end of last night's table. Where's she?"

"Emilia is eight and I didn't want her to view our proceedings," Mamma explained.

"Because afterward she'll wet the bed with fear?" Nonna Ursula asked.

Nurse snorted.

"No, because she's brave to foolishness, and she'll burn down our house attempting to lure the spirits by herself." Mamma knew her daughters very well.

Nonna Ursula cackled. "I like your children, Lady Juliet."

"Thank you, Nonna Ursula." Mamma accepted the compliment with complacent ease. "I like them, too."

Today she seemed less uncomfortable, less on edge, and may I say it? Placid. Papà was right. He did indeed know how to care for Mamma.

I guided Nonna Ursula to the chair with arms and helped her seat herself. Katherina and Princess Isabella scooted her close to the table.

"Rosie, take what's in the bag and place it in the center of the table." Nonna Ursula may have been amused.

I opened the bag, reached down, and grabbed what felt like a bony, oblong ball, pulled it out and . . .

Listen, I'm not much of a screamer, but I screamed.

So did Katherina and Princess Isabella.

I dropped the skull on the floor.

It rolled to rest at Nonna Ursula's side. She picked it up, looked into its empty eye sockets, and said, "Alas, poor Yorick, such rough treatment, when soon you'll be called upon for assistance!"

"Is that truly the legendary Yorick?" Mamma asked in a conversational tone.

"Who's Yorick and why is he legendary?" Imogene seemed much less perturbed at the sight of a skull than the other girls.

Or than me, for that matter. I wiped my hand on my skirt and glared at Elder, who tried *not* very hard to smother a grin.

"Yorick was our jester, a man of infinite jest, of most excellent fancy." Nonna Ursula placed Yorick next to the candles. "He was the only man I ever allowed to attend me at my séances, and after his untimely death, I've kept him close to call in the spirits."

Imogene could contain herself no longer. "Are we really going to contact the spirits of the dead?"

"If they wish to be contacted." Nonna Ursula smiled a mysterious smile, and as she did, the last rosy ray of the sun struck her face, flushing her with the pink of artificial youth and making her cloudy eyes glow with a fiery red.

The children gasped—I admit to a tremor myself—and Elder said, "*That's* a neat trick."

Princess Isabella asked, "Nonna, are you . . . yourself?"

"Yes, yes, who else would I be?" As she spoke, the light faded, and she was once more a wrinkled woman with white-blind eyes and an impatient expression. "First, let us pray that Jesus, Mary, and all the saints guide and protect us in our undertaking this day, for should the spirits venture forth, we seek only enlightenment, and not a haunting."

At her closing words, I looked meaningfully at Elder. Who, of course, ignored me. I then closed my eyes, bent my head, and listened to Nonna Ursula's surprisingly fervent prayer. But not so surprising, really, for everyone believed in ghoulies and ghosties, although few claimed to have met them, and fewer still really had. I was in an exclusive club—the only person I knew who had actually visited with a ghost. I admit to some hope that after the "Amen," Elder would be gone from me.

He must have read my mind, for he said, "No such luck for you."

Nonna Ursula firmly tapped on the skull with her knuckles, then indicated Mamma should repeat.

Mamma knocked. Imogene knocked. Then—reluctantly—Katherina, Princess Isabella, and I.

Each strike on the hollow bone sounded startling in its suddenness, contributing to the eerie ambience.

"Yorick has now summoned the ghosts. You"—Nonna Ursula pointed a crooked finger at Imogene—"blow out all but one candle."

Imogene blew, and left the candle in the middle burning. As the sunset turned to purple dusk, the circle of light around us drew in like a warning, and the empty spaces where Yorick's eyes and nose had once been seemed to come alive.

I could hear humming in my ears; it was the sound of my listening.

"My mother is good at this," Elder observed. "Even I'm spooked."

I shot him a glare. I was not amused.

"Let us hold hands so none of us wander alone." Nonna Ursula offered one hand to Imogene. "Are you frightened?"

"A little. Mostly, I want to see my Zuann!" Imogene offered her hand to Princess Isabella, and they entwined fingers.

"Your Zuann?" In bewilderment, Nonna Ursula turned to Mamma.

As Mamma took Princess Isabella's fingers and then Katherina's, a smile played around her mouth. "Zuann is her dog. He died last year after a good long life."

"Then your Zuann is at peace and we mustn't disturb his slumber," Nonna Ursula advised Imogene.

Imogene sighed. "Mamma said you'd say that."

Nonna Ursula continued, "We seek to speak to the spirits who wish to give guidance about their untimely deaths."

"The palace should be full of those." Princess Isabella glanced over her shoulder.

"We won't call them all," Nonna Ursula answered. "Only the ones who witnessed the death of my son, your father."

"Why doesn't Rosie ask him who killed him?" Imogene suggested.

Elder cackled a laugh.

Everyone jumped as if they'd heard him, and jumped again when Katherina grabbed my hand as if it was driftwood bobbing in the Adige River. The completed circle of touch seemed to send a spark through us that forged us into one.

"Imogene, why would Rosie be able to inquire of our murdered prince on any matter?" Mamma asked.

"You gave Rosie the name of your friend and his love, Princess Eleanor, so Rosie's connected to them both." Imogene explained it as if everyone should know.

"Hm." Elder hovered behind his mother, and mused, "As good an explanation as any. Does your sister have the Sight?"

"Yes, but we don't speak of it." Then I cursed myself, for looking at him, answering him out loud. He was so . . . there.

Imogene added, "Also, Mamma, if she's not, then she's gone mad, for she sees things that aren't there and replies to questions we don't hear."

Heads turned between Imogene and me.

Mamma used both of her joined hands to stroke her belly in her calming manner, and perhaps she brought the child into the circle, for he subsided.

Yes, I'd said I'd communicated with Elder; that was what had given Nonna Ursula the idea of a séance. However, for the first time, she considered that what she viewed as a jest could be the truth, and turned to me. "Do you truly see him? Is he here?"

I should lie and save myself from possible incarceration or accusations of witchcraft. I knew it. But the meanest old woman in Verona trembled and looked on the verge of tears, carried there by hope and a half-realized belief that her son was almost within reach. "Yes."

Nonna Ursula brushed at her damp lashes, recovered in typical iron-lady fashion, and fixed her ruined vision on me. "Why does *he* not tell you who killed him?"

"He doesn't know. He was drugged. The villain wore a mask." I'd quickly reached the point where speaking to and for Elder seemed—dare I say it—normal?

Nonna Ursula leaned back in astonishment. "You really have confidence my son's ghost is haunting you."

"I'm not haunting her," Elder snapped at his mother. "I gave her a task, and she's doing a damnable poor job of accomplishing it."

"You know why we're sitting around this little table holding hands." I was speaking to him. "This is for you!"

But Nonna Ursula answered: "Don't use that tone with me!"

"Not you. *Him.*" I tried to point toward the hovering spirit.

Katherina hung on to my hand as though I was drowning, and only she could save me.

"My son?" Nonna Ursula was clearly disbelieving. "You're talking to *my son* in that tone?"

"What's he going to do, Nonna? *Haunt* me some more?"

"I said I'm not haunting, I'm—" Elder caught sight of my smirk. "You're mocking me."

"You and your son are such upright autocrats, it's hard not to tweak you both a little," I told her.

Elder stared at me as if I was quacking a message. "Tweak me a little? I'm the prince of Verona!"

"You're the *murdered* prince of Verona. The long-dead, moldering-in-the-grave prince of Verona." I was not trying to put him in his place, but to give him a sense of historical perspective. "Which, by the way, helps not at all. If you seek to know who killed you, why are you hanging around the palace? Surely, it would be easier if you wandered about Verona or Padua or Venice or wherever the suspects inhabit and see what they're up to!"

"I can't leave the palace. The bounds of this property hold me."

"You didn't tell me that!"

"When I first returned, after I tested Cal and realized he couldn't help me, I determined that in Verona, there must be some wise man who could help me. I hurried toward the gate that guards the palazzo—and it was like lightning striking. With a flash of light and pain, I was flung back into the garden, weakened and amazed. I tried again."

"Of course, you did," I muttered.

"I'm confined, unable to leave these boundaries. I can't move beyond these walls."

"Why?"

"No one explained the rules," he said testily. "I was alive, then I woke up dead. There wasn't a 'Dear Prince Escalus the elder, Welcome to the Other Realm Dinner Party and Ball.'"

"Probably because you'd argue about who should sit at the head of the table, you or the Lord God Himself." I clapped my hand over my mouth. Blasphemy most dreadful, and I waited to be wiped from the face of the earth.

Hands separated.

Everyone at the table crossed themselves.

Mamma crossed herself. "Rosaline Hortensa Magdelina Eleanor!"

Elder himself looked around as if alarmed.

With a crash as loud as thunder, the heavy wood door slammed open. "What is going on here?"

We all jumped, but it wasn't the voice of God.

It was Prince Escalus the younger. Papà stood with him, the bodyguards and Barnadine stood behind, and they all wore faces that promised that impressive masculine shouting would commence.

Chapter 23

Nonna Ursula settled in her chair like a satisfied hen on its nest and announced in ringing tones, "We're contacting the spirits of the next world."

Barnadine, red-faced and perspiring, looked around as if terrified and, pulling a bottle from his jacket, took a swig.

Marcellus crossed his arms and muttered something . . . uncomplimentary.

Cal marched into the room and focused on me. "This is your doing!"

He had every reason to be upset, and I intended to pacify him. "Actually—"

Cal interrupted, "You claim to see my father's ghost!"

Papà gaped at me. "You claim to see a ghost?"

I didn't appreciate his choice of words. "Papà, I'm not *claiming* anything."

Holofernes and Dion exchanged wide-eyed glances, nodded at each other, and sidled out of the room.

"You're pretending to be mad to avoid yet another match?" Papà acted as if I spent my life scheming. While there could be some justification for his belief, it wasn't true—except in the matter of marriage.

"No!" I answered.

Apparently, Mamma thought his phrasing could be improved, also, for she said, "Romeo, our Rosie is not a liar. You know this."

"In a most unfeminine way, she does seek to change the course of her fate!" Papà pronounced. "You yourself assured me of this, Juliet!"

"Yes," Mamma said, "but—"

Cal had a fire in his eyes. "She asked how crazed she had to be for me to cancel our betrothal."

Together, in tones of despair, Papà and Mamma said, "Oh, Rosie."

I pointed at Cal. "He made me angry."

"That's no excuse!" Mamma said.

"I'm not excusing myself. It's the truth!"

Cal's voice was low and intense. "I'll tell you." He grew more hushed and more intense with each word. "I'm going to marry you, regardless of your pretense of madness. And bed you until you forget this nonsense. A babe or two will bring you to your senses!"

"Good God, man." Papà placed his palm flat on his own chest as if suffering palpitations. "You take your life in your hands."

I ignored him—my own dear papà—igniting instead in rage at Cal. I pushed back my chair and advanced on my sarcastic, disbelieving betrothed. "Marriage and babes are a man's fix for every woman's complaint, from constipation to how many maids to hire to clean the bed drapes!"

Papà lifted his despairing hands at Mamma. "Sweet Virgin Mary, she doesn't need a ploy when she's got that viperous tongue! We'll never get her married off!"

"You will." Cal extended his arm and pointed his finger toward the chapel. "She's marrying me if I have to carry her over my shoulder to the altar!"

"That's enough!" Nonna Ursula's voice had the power to

shatter marble. "You'll have eternity to battle when you're married. For now—no, Grandson, this meeting with the spirits is my idea."

"*You're* covering for *her.*" Cal snapped at his grandmother. He actually snapped!

Papà and Elder groaned.

Imogene, Katherina, and Princess Isabella whimpered.

Barnadine squeezed himself into a dim corner as if that hid him from sight.

Marcellus decided Holofernes and Dion had the right of it, and without taking his gaze off the scene, he backed slowly and silently out the door.

Torn between horror and humor, I said, "Cal, this is not your best moment."

Mamma released a brief laugh and settled back to enjoy the pyrotechnics.

Nonna Ursula did not disappoint. She rose to her feet without help, without a wince or a struggle, buoyed by vivid, visible choler. "Am I so feeble and bitten by age you can't comprehend I could have a thought on how to find my son's killer? Do you think me so toothless and without claws that I can't seize the past by the throat and wring its neck until it spews forth justice?"

Cal seemed to realize that he'd angered the whirlwind and he would be lifted into the cloud and slammed to earth, bleeding and broken. In a placating tone, he said, "Nonna, I never meant—"

She chopped her hand down.

He stopped midsentence.

Her voice gained the strength of an orator exhorting a crowd. "What can you possibly mean that won't insult me? It's a good thing I have you, Prince Escalus the younger, to build me a marble shithouse and help me piss in a fur-lined pee-pot!"

Whew. Nonna Ursula had a way with an insult.

Cal clasped his hand into a fist, placed it on his chest, and bowed to her. "Forgive me, Nonna. I doubt not your power and wisdom."

"You may meditate on your foolishness while I retire and ponder what the spirits have told me this evening." In a voice laden with mystery, she said, "If I read the portents correctly, your noble father's butcher is closer than we realize."

At that moment, the door from the atrium swung open and Yago, Elder's brother, stepped onstage. "As you commanded, Mamma, I am here!"

Chapter 24

Nonna Ursula cackled, then laughed until she collapsed back into her chair.

Horribly, after a few moments of shock, so did we all, leaving Yago standing in the doorway, the framed picture of puffed velvet indignation. In chilly tones, he asked, "What is the jest?"

When Nonna Ursula gained control of her amusement, she told her son about the séance and that he'd walked into a Situation.

Cal apologized to his uncle for his misplaced mirth, and offered him a seat.

Expressions of acute dislike passed across Yago's face as he realized he'd been summarily dismissed as his brother's killer. He was insulted as only a weak man could be, and Elder agreed with me. "Yago wants to think he *could* kill me if he desired, but he doesn't have the gut or the wit. Yet I wonder about the wife. She has cunning, ambition, frustration. Where is she this night?"

"Yago, where is Lugrezia?" Nonna Ursula spoke as if Elder's question had prompted her. "I commanded she come, too."

"Alas, she begs your forgiveness, Mamma." Yago sat in the

seat offered him and fussily arranged his puffed sleeves. "Last night she took ill of a bellyache."

"That peacock was undercooked," Mamma murmured.

Yago continued, "It's too bad. She would have loved to attend one of your séances." He shot his mother an evil glance. "What ghosts did you meet? What wisdom was given you? None, I surmise, for young Escalus's sword remains sheathed and I hear nothing of the ballyhoo after the assassin or the search for his whereabouts."

"In sooth, we learned far more than I expected." Nonna Ursula smiled enigmatically. "Assist me, Grandson, and you, Rosaline. I am to bed."

"But I just got here!" Yago complained.

"Too late. Too late! And without the required wife." She dismissed him with a gesture. "I'll summon you another time, with a specific schedule, and you'll attend as you're told. You are, after all, the lesser son."

"If she's deliberately prodding him—" Elder began.

"She is," I replied.

"—She's doing a good job of it. But why? Does she suspect him of my murder? Or does she have an ulterior motive?"

I didn't know, and Yago stared at me so oddly, I knew he'd heard my comment to Elder and wondered at me.

"Rosie, bring the skull."

Thankfully, with an insouciance I admired, and had no desire to match, Imogene loaded the skull into its bag. I grasped the ties in one hand. With the other, I took Nonna Ursula's arm.

Cal grasped her other arm, and together we assisted her toward the great walk, past the bodyguards hovering close enough to hear every word from within, and toward her bedchamber.

"What are you doing, Nonna?" Cal asked close to her ear. "You anger Yago for no reason."

"Ha!" Elder kept pace with us and grinned at me. "That's my boy, asking the right questions. He's a bright one."

"Indeed," I said. It could be taken as a reply to both Cal and Elder. But also . . . why was Elder gloating about his son doing the smart thing? The podestà who had guided Verona for how many years now and increased his influence and power? I supposed it must be simply a father/son thing, like when Papà went to Cesario and wrestled with him, teaching him holds and praising his manly prowess. Elder's sentiments were, I suppose, an indication of how much Elder had missed of his son's growing-up years, and the guidance he would have given him. Elder would probably be horrified to know I considered him rather sweet.

"I have reason." Nonna Ursula's feet kept catching on the smooth floor, as if weariness meant she couldn't lift them high enough to clear the surface. "I would replace Yago's heart of a mouse with that of a lion, and if not him, let the surgery be done to his wife."

"If one of them hides the heart of a sly rat, slinking through the piles of garbage with blood on its claws—what, then?" Cal asked.

"We wait for it to slink into our trap." Nonna sighed; the idea of her only living child as traitor disheartened her.

As we walked, I heard a low buzz of conversation; the hive of servants passed gossip too juicy to contain. About the séance? Of course. About Cal's unexpected and uncontrolled anger? Yes, for one skill that Cal had learned in the dungeon, and in all the years after, was to withhold his emotions. If he had them, he hid them. They were his, and not for display, for fear someone would use them as weakness.

I understood and even agreed. In my family, every emotion was laid bare and shouted to the rooftops, and with exuberant parents and so many siblings, I sometimes felt buffeted by laughter, love, sorrow, anger. Yet . . . interaction with a man who, at least in the daylight hours, seemed without expression, and without feelings, could lead to . . . No, not *could* lead. *Did* lead to misinterpretations.

I'll say this for Cal; he might not be handsome, and he might not be my One True Love, but he had piqued my interest enough that I dissected his motivations.

Ghost or not, Elder excelled in displaying emotions, mostly exasperation, and perhaps if he had lived, he would have humanized his son a little.

I cast an eye on Cal. If I did wed him, or almost certainly, *when* I did wed him, that would be my chosen task.

I grinned. He wanted to use me for my various household skills and breeding abilities. I wanted to fix his faults. Could this be a good basis for a marriage?

Possibly not, but it might be exhilarating.

We escorted Nonna Ursula into her bedroom, where her serving maids, Old Maria and Pasqueta, waited with mulled wine and fresh nightclothes. Nonna Ursula sank into her chair and gestured Cal close. Putting her hands on either side of his face, she said, "You started this, my darling boy, when you brought Rosie into our family. A new light permeates the palace, a new rhythm moves us to dance. Nevertheless we must first lay the dead to rest. Escalus wanders. He disturbs my rest and yours."

Cal turned his head and looked at me darkly. "If Rosie is to be believed, he speaks to her."

Nonna Ursula didn't hesitate. "If you believe she lies, why marry her?"

"I didn't say I thought she lies."

"You didn't say you believed her."

"I do believe her."

Well. Good for you, Cal. I like your clear declaration, even if it is accompanied by a darkling glare. I did not smirk.

Elder was not so kind. He smirked for me. "See? He loves

you, or he'd have you committed to a holy hospital in care of nuns."

I corrected him. "Cal admires me and my attributes of character and figure." And I carefully deposited Yorick's skull still wrapped in its bag onto the table before the fire. Let Old Maria or Pasqueta put it in its proper place.

Him in his proper place? Was a skull a *him* or an *it*? I shuddered. I didn't know, and I turned my attention back to the conversation.

Cal said, "I dare not proclaim my faith in Rosie. Nonna, you know very well what that would lead to. I pray your workings of this night will remain within the palace walls." He sensibly recognized the Pandora's box we had opened.

"That would defeat the purpose, would it not? Dear boy, safety is no longer our sole goal."

"Nonna, you could be hurt." When he looked at his grandmother, I could see the love he held for her—and the apprehension.

"How?" she asked. "This palace is guarded. My window is barred on the outside. Your men are loyal, are they not?"

"I bind them to me with responsibility, praise, payment, and my loyalty to them."

"He is a smart boy," Elder said to me.

I nodded.

"He got that from me," Elder added.

I cast him an amused glance.

He grinned back, so cocky I realized with a shock I liked the man.

"And from Princess Eleanor?" I asked.

In a softened voice, the ghost said, "She gave him her grace, her endurance, her upright strength, and her endless capacity for love."

That startled me. To me, love is frequently, loudly proclaimed, and generous with its application. Cal's affection for sister and grandmother was obvious, fervent and protective, yet he dispensed his emotions like a miser dispensed his gold.

Being a man, maybe he didn't know what they were.

I noticed Cal and Nonna Ursula scrutinizing me and the space around me.

Elder was right. If I didn't get this mystery solved soon, I could find my pragmatic repute overlaid by whispers of madness. May God grant that Nonna Ursula's séance prove fruitful in my quest to find Elder's killer.

Chapter 25

Grimly, Papà and Cal loaded the frail females into two sedan chairs—Mamma, Imogene, and Nurse crowded into one chair; Katherina and I were in the other. Not that we were actually frail, but one could never convince the manly men of that.

Although in this case, I conceded they might have a point. An unusual silence had settled over Verona, and what Nonna Ursula and I had considered a clever stratagem to force the hand of Elder's assassin had turned into an after-dark excursion through the shadowy streets. Our citizens huddled on street corners or peeked through windows. It felt as if the world waited on indrawn breath for a battle to start.

With the armed accompaniment of the bodyguards, Marcellus, Holofernes, and Dion, and the prince's most experienced bearers carrying us, and four outrunners carrying lit torches, we set out, brocade curtains drawn, to Casa Montague.

"Rosie, why . . . ?" Katherina huddled forward on her seat and whispered.

"It's the *disciplinati*." I didn't whisper, but I was very quiet. "They march along in masks and whip themselves for their sins and ours, so they say, and perhaps some are true penitents, but because they cover their faces, it's possible for trouble to lurk among them. Many times, riots and unrest accompany them.

Prince Escalus has given them a specific route to travel through the streets. We will avoid those streets, but—"

Katherina jerked her head around. "Listen!"

I heard it, too. The shuffle of many feet, the slaps of whips, and the moans and prayers rising like a ghostly mist among the buildings.

Cal gave a command. The bearers picked up the pace.

I clutched Katherina's hand and shushed her comfortingly. Only the torches gave us light within the sedan chair, and that flickered with the swaying of the curtains.

Katherina had her head down, her hands clasped in prayer.

I risked a glance between the gap.

The sounds of the *disciplinati* grew, a muttering magnified by the tall stone buildings and the narrow pavement, but I could see nothing of them.

Then!

We passed through an intersection and there they were, men dressed in grubby robes of blue and white, hoods up, shuffling toward us, their eyes lowered, their backs bared, their whips slapping their flesh. They reeked of blood and sweat, and when I would have drawn back, one of them looked up and caught my gaze upon him. Through the slit in the cloth over his face, I saw his eyes: black pools of anger, contempt, fanaticism.

With a gasp, I drew back.

Katherina whispered, "Rosie, are you witless?" She took the edges of the curtains and tied them together.

I sank back against the seat. "I am. That was unwise."

I listened to see if that creature put up a cry against us.

Yet the bearers ran steadily on, the sounds of the *disciplinati* faded behind us, and Papà and Cal began to speak in normal tones.

The crisis was over, at least for this night, at least for us.

Surely, it was over for all, yet I . . . felt dirtied, and I feared.

Chapter 26

The party covered the last way more slowly and stopped in front of our home, where the servants at once flung the door wide and greeted us with light and warmth and hushed, worried voices. When the bearers set the steps, my knees trembled unsteadily as I descended. As if sensing my need of support, Cal caught my gloved hand, then turned to do the same for Katherina. Papà helped Imogene and Nurse; then he and Nurse turned and helped Mamma down onto the street and held her while she swayed.

I hurried to her side. "Mamma, are you ill?"

She smiled faintly, eyes closed. "The motion of the sedan chair did not sit well with our young winemaker."

"Madam, good Lord Romeo and I will help you inside and lay you down." Nurse pointed a somehow peevish finger at me. "Get these children in the house and get you all to bed, and let me hear no more about plots to unmask a killer or ghosts who speak to you or any other matter, except your upcoming nuptials to"—she pointed a much politer finger at Cal—"this prince, who you must go out of your way to please and appease that he might not change his mind before joining his life with an incendiary!"

Imogene watched them go into the house, then glanced at

Cal. "Rosie, I don't think she helped your cause at all." She followed.

Katherina said, "My prince, Nurse didn't mean that. Rosie never sets anything on fire that doesn't deserve to be on fire." She winced, realizing she also hadn't helped my cause, and skittered into the house.

Indecisive, I stood on the street. Should I curtsy and enter the door held by Tommaso? Or should I speak to Cal, who stood immobile, his feet firmly planted on the stones of Verona's street, gazing at me as if he . . .

I don't know how he was gazing at me. So far, we'd firmly established I didn't understand him at all.

I only knew that what I did now mattered. If I was alone with Cal, I'd talk to him frankly about Elder's desire to rest at last; Nonna Ursula, who sensed her son walked; and Cal's own need to find Elder's killer. I'd assure him that our betrothal, while reluctant on my part, hadn't changed my loyalty to Verona's podestà. I'd do nothing to harm his reign. I thought he knew that, believed in me, yet sometimes such reassurance needed to be given and to be accepted.

Only . . . people were watching: his bodyguards, the outrunners, the sedan bearers, the neighbors, hungry for gossip, who peered out of their windows. If I could, I'd ask him to return, to arrive through the postern gate in their back wall and, as he'd done before, visit me on the back terrace—although that posed a danger of a different sort.

I knew he would not; the silence in the city had mutated into a low, menacing mutter. The *disciplinati* were on the move, and as the podestà, Cal would take matters in hand.

I made my decision, bowed my head, began to sink into a curtsy . . . and he caught my fingers. He eased the glove from my hand, thrust the leather into my other hand to grasp. He leaned close, and in his dark, velvety, quiet, seductive tone, which invariably pulled my focus to him, only him, and painted his shadowy face with passion, he said, "If you only set on fire that which deserves to be on fire, then I am deserving, for I . . . burn." Pressing a kiss in my palm, as he seemed wont to do, he flicked my cloak back to bare my gown and pressed my hand, and his kiss, on the skin above my heart.

His gestures grew ever more heady and I grew ever more uneasily aware of how, now and previously, he eased me toward . . . intimacy.

"Good night, sweet Rosaline. Sleep in safety and dream of . . . dark red roses." He released me and turned away.

Great farewell. Almost poetry. I hated to stomp on it, but I really needed to tell him. "I'll dream of your safety in this night."

He turned back. "Why would I not be safe?"

"My podestà, I saw a man, one of the flagellants, whose eyes flamed with a demon's fire. He would burn Verona to the ground, bring anarchy to the world, and as he climbed the piles of bodies, he'd call it God's work."

He focused on me, and in the light of the torches, his eyes flamed a bit, too. "When did you see this man, Rosie?"

"Tonight. I looked through the gap in the sedan's curtains."

Holofernes covered his eyes. Dion groaned.

All that lovely romance evaporated from Cal's expression, and his voice exploded in exasperation. "Rosaline! Why?"

"So I could see him and warn you."

He reached out as if to clasp my shoulders and shake me, but his hands stopped merely inches away and he trembled as if fighting his urges. "Because you're curious as a cat and as likely to die from it!"

"I pray that the Virgin Mother watches over you as you undertake your duties this night." I curtsied and backed inside, my gaze held captive by his, and when Tommaso would have shut the door behind me—call me Nosy Rosie if you want—I caught it and held it open a crack.

Cal spoke to the bearers. "Take the chairs back to the palace. Holofernes, Dion, and I will take the outrunners and escort the *disciplinati* to their rightful route through the city."

I was right. Softly I shut the door.

Katherina, Imogene, and Papà waited, holding candles. "Is he still yours?" Papà asked.

I looked at my open palm, flexed my fingers, and nodded.

Katherina and Imogene, breathing identical sighs of relief, went up to bed.

"But, Papà," I said, "he goes to confront the *disciplinati*."

"I'll suggest to your mamma that she rest, plan your wedding, and joyously carry our baby. After that, I'll join our new son-by-betrothal, for he may have use for an extra blade." Papà ran up the stairs in a spritely step.

I stood, thinking, working my way around recent events. Although I'd become betrothed, seen a ghost, and participated in a séance, none of that impressed me so much as the hellfire in the flagellant's eyes . . . and tonight the prince would seek him. Them. Prince Escalus and his men would run toward danger, armed merely with swords, and I feared for them.

Was the flagellant a demon?

No, worse. He was a man. One glance could sum up a man if that man sent a message of all-encompassing hatred. Of what, though? Wealth? Power? Or, more likely, of a woman, any woman regardless of her place in life, for a woman was a cause of man's expulsion from Eden and forever she tempted men to sin.

As a sensible woman with a family who depended on me and a betrothed who led the city, I knew I needed to protect myself in a responsible way, or I would find myself confined or surrounded by bodyguards better used to shield others . . . or taken by men such as I'd seen this night and, at best, held for ransom. Or worse. The latter didn't bear thinking of.

I called, "Tommaso."

Our young footman appeared at once. He hadn't been far away.

"Yes, Lady Rosaline?"

"Do you know how to fight?"

"Yes, Lady Rosaline. Not like a lord or like you, my lady, with a sword. I grew up fighting with the street pigs for a scrap of food. Your mother found me and brought me here, but I remember well how to battle with fists and desperation and a blade honed from bare bone."

"I hoped that would be your answer." I pinned my gaze on him. "In the future, when I travel the streets of Verona, you'll come with me."

"Yes, my lady. Thank you, my lady." He bowed as if I'd given him an honor.

Papà bounded down the stairs, sword buckled, thrusting a stiletto up his sleeve and smiling gleefully. "Nurse is caring for my beloved Juliet, so I'll be off to join the prince and bring peace to the streets of Verona." He pressed a kiss on my forehead, Tommaso opened the door for him, and he ran into the street. Really, the man was happiest fighting and . . .

But with Mamma so far gone with child, he was confined to fighting.

To Tommaso, I said, "In becoming the betrothed of the podestà, I have, perhaps, become a target for"—I hesitated—"rogues, villains, and desperate men."

"Your lady mother saved me from such men, and I've waited long to repay the debt to her. I am your faithful servant and soldier, and I swear I'd die before I allow harm to befall a daughter of the house of Montague." Such a dramatic declaration spoken in a prosaic tone.

Then, "Who'll be footman? Who will assist Lord Romeo? Who'll help him when required to care for Cesario?" He asked me because Mamma, as a household manager, would have made a good grape-stomper. -

Thus I ran Casa Montague, and I pondered his question with the care it deserved. "In the morning, send me Teodor." Because Tommaso had proved to be a *giocatore* of astute judgment, I asked, "Do you agree with my choice?"

Tommaso gave the question the consideration it deserved. "He's young, raw, and uncertain, but he learns quickly, and when I'm not out with you or my lord Romeo, I'll train him. Also he's handsome, which allows forgiveness when there is none for the less fortunate." Although he no doubt spoke from experience, for smallpox had brutally pitted his skin, he didn't sound bitter. He had that which compensated for all distortions: a nimble mind and a strong muscularity.

"Send him to me, but wait until the morning is advanced, for I wish to sleep." And worry, for Cal and Papà were out bringing order to Verona, and although I wished it otherwise, the memory of the flagellant's hate-flamed eyes made me think of demons abroad in the street. I climbed wearily to my room.

My desire for a long sleep was not to be fulfilled, for dawn had not yet cast its gray net when a candle flame thrust into my face made me flinch away and the shadowy figure of Nurse shook me awake. "A sedan chair arrived from the palace. You must go at once. The dowager princess was attacked and lies bloody, unconscious, and barely breathing. Friar Laurence is at her side, and he begs that you go to his shop, compound the healing poultice he taught you, and bring it to him, for you alone can create his formula."

Chapter 27

Nurse dressed me in my plainest garb, strapped on my three knives, and followed me as I slipped into my parents' bedchamber to wake Mamma. No need. She sat in a chair, surrounded by glowing candles, brow puckered as she hemmed a baby blanket. She put it down at once and stretched out her arms to me. "Nurse told me." Her gaze flicked into the shadows where Nurse hovered, silent and discreet for once.

I rushed into Mamma's arms, needing her embrace and knowing she needed mine. To think of Nonna Ursula hurt by cruel hands, her spark of vitality dimmed, brought tears to our eyes. As the scent of smoke drifted on the breeze, and flames glowed on the horizon toward the river, she feared for Papà, and now, as I ventured out, for me.

Yet when I lifted my head from her shoulder, neither of us wasted time in lament.

"Mamma," I said, "I have come to think that with recent events, I'll be wise to have protection. Last night, I spoke to Tommaso, and he boasts a good fighting record, a good mind, and a fervent dedication to our family. He'll train Teodor to take his place as footman and as manservant. May I have him as my personal bodyguard?"

Mamma placed a soft hand on my cheek. "Rosie, you're the

best daughter any woman can have. You look to the future so frankly and take measures to handle any future problems and relieve my mind of worry. Of course, you may take Tommaso!"

I warmed to her praise.

She continued without a hitch. "Two of the house guards will escort the sedan chair on your journey to Friar Laurence's and the palace."

"Mamma, no!" My protest was shocked and sincere. "To leave Casa Montague unguarded on such a night—"

"We are not unguarded. We are sending two of our own to protect our precious diamond jewel of a daughter. That is our decision." When Mamma started talking like a queen, using plural pronouns, she left no room for argument or negotiation.

"As soon as I arrive at the palace," I declared, "I'll send them home."

"Of course." She smoothed my hair. "You'll take Nurse."

Nurse moved restlessly in the shadows. She was torn.

"No. She must remain with you, Mamma." I put my hands on her belly, where the babe kicked and rolled. "This little one is now lively, and you have two months before you can let him out!"

"He'll come when God announces his arrival. In the meantime, Rosie, my daughter, you'll be careful." She hadn't argued that I must take Nurse.

I noted that, and that worried me. But fate had caught us in its fangs and we had no escape, so I assured her, "Mamma, I must be, for Nonna Ursula's life may depend on it."

Leaning forward, she kissed my cheek, and flinched as the babe shoved its foot under her ribs. "You children," she muttered darkly.

I gave her belly a last rub, rose, and made my way to the prince's sedan chair waiting at the door. The luxurious conveyance couldn't keep out the smoke or subdue the sound of men's shouts and the clash of steel. Cal and Papà would be in the thick of battle, and knowing their expertise, I fervently believed they would be unharmed, lest it be by unscrupulous means.

When I again remembered the flagellant's hellfire eyes, I knew that creature could embrace and justify treachery.

The chair carried me through the slowly brightening streets at a speed I hadn't imagined possible.

Tommaso and Papà's guards ran with their knives drawn.

I touched the blades Nurse had given me, tucked into the scabbards strapped to my arms, and I had also Cal's blade strapped to my ankle. Knowing they were at the ready strengthened my courage. Preparedness had a way of doing that.

We halted at Friar Laurence's shop, and while the men paced outside, I compounded the poultice for Nonna Ursula. I heard their low voices muttering in ominous worry, but I dared not hurry. The complex preparation required concentration and exact measures, so I moved deliberately through the formula. I owed that to Nonna Ursula.

When the poultice rested safely in a jar, we proceeded to the palace in silence and at the same brisk pace; I was glad to reach our destination. As soon as I dismounted from the sedan chair, I ordered the Casa Montague guards home, and they went willingly and at haste.

I entered the palace and hurried to Nonna Ursula's suite, and there found Friar Laurence on a bench beside the bed where Nonna Ursula reclined, streaks of dried blood staining her slack, pale face. "A resourceful villain broke in to plunder the riches of the palace," Friar Laurence said in a low voice. "Princess Ursula's mind dwelled on her son and the heartless murder that took him too soon. While she rested on the bed, she sent Pasqueta to the kitchen to make her a posset. The villain came through the window, and when she perhaps spoke or sat up, he struck her on the side of the head, not once but twice, probably with the pry he used to rip the iron bars off the wall and enter. She fell, and he escaped the same way."

I leaned over the old grande dame, already so dear to me—I liked women who spread terror like a farmer spreads manure—and stroked her brow with a cool cloth. By the time I had arrived at the palace, and carried the poultice inside, Friar Laurence had staunched Nonna Ursula's profuse bleeding, had calmed her two maids, and had set them to work cleaning the evidence, with the stern admonition that when their mistress returned to consciousness, she would not want to wake on bloody linens.

Now, using the poultice, he bandaged the wounds.

"Did no one see or hear anything?" I looked around when I said that, seeking Elder as a source of information.

"When Pasqueta arrived with the tisane, she found the princess unconscious on the bed and . . . this." Friar Laurence gestured at the destruction of the room and its contents. "She screamed, but even that didn't wake Old Maria, for she was asleep in her bed and she's as deaf as Princess Ursula."

I examined the clutter of belongings that had been flung hither and yon, then walked to the open window and looked out. Two of the bars had been wrenched from the stone wall. "A mighty effort for one man."

Friar Laurence came to look, too. "Perhaps more than one man?"

"Perhaps. It's known there are treasures to be found here. Let me at once send for the metalworker to repair the damage." I spoke to one of the prince's messenger boys and sent him off, then returned to the good brother. "Nonna Ursula is not so deaf as she presents, and I suspect she heard the disturbance. Perhaps confronted the creeping reptile of hell."

"Thus she would know him by sight. No wonder the attack was so brutal."

"He left in a panic, for the prince would rightly order him racked, drawn, and quartered, to make an example of him—"

Friar Laurence grasped my upraised, clenched fist. "'Vengeance is mine,' saith the Lord.'"

"I can exalt in the Lord's vengeance."

"When it occurs," he conceded.

I looked around again. Where was Elder? Why was he never where he could do some good? If his only task in the afterlife was to haunt me and make sarcastic comments, he might as well be dead.

Yes, gentle reader, I was aware of the irony of that thought. "What was taken?" For all the mess, I saw nothing awry.

"Nothing. The waiting ladies say nothing is gone that they know, but a jewel is a little thing and hard to note, and the princess owns many jewels. Or maybe the wrongdoer came to steal and had to flee before he found something he deemed of value."

In a second sweep of the room, I stiffened like a hunting dog on point. The bag containing Yorick's skull was gone. I'd left it there for Nonna Ursula's maids to put away; had they? Or had the intruder removed it for some unknown reason? In a chamber filled with treasures, only someone who feared his guilt would be discovered would remove Yorick's skull. Right?

Before I could inquire of Old Maria or Pasqueta, a timid knock sounded on the door.

Princess Isabella stood there, wreathed in worry and twisting her hands. When she chose to don her royal presence, she was the very portrait of composure, but now I remembered how young she was and how few family members peopled her life. I gestured her in, and she hurried to her grandmother's bedside and whimpered at the sight of the sagging wrinkles that no one noticed when Nonna Ursula's sharp tongue spoke and her dark eyes snapped. "Will she recover?" the princess whispered like a child who fears the coming dark.

I knew Friar Laurence couldn't tell her; all his learned knowledge couldn't speak to the vagaries of human frailty.

Yet, like Princess Isabella, I begged for reassurance. "Yes, will she?"

He understood. "A head injury is grievous, for we know not what happens within the skull. If God favors us, the lady will live. But you must both know her age works against us, and the longer she's without wit, the more grievous and desperate the danger."

I nodded, and when Princess Isabella sobbed into her hand, I embraced her.

"She needs sustenance. She needs wine. She must come awake to partake of life or we have no hope." He told me what I already knew.

I tightened my grip on Princess Isabella's shoulders. "What can we do?"

"Sit with her," he commanded. "Hold her hand. Brush her hair. Speak to her."

Princess Isabella caught back her sobs and looked up. "Of what?"

"Of what you do all day. Of your weaving, your readings. Talk about the paintings in this room, your friendships, what you eat. Remind her of life." He looked sideways at me. "You could speak to her about last night's séance and your repentance for the sin that you committed."

Now, how had the good brother learned of that? For I had rather hoped he wouldn't know until told in the confessional.

He gathered up his bag. "I can now do no more here. Other injuries occurred during last night's disturbances, and I go where I'm needed. I'll be back later. Send for me if you see change."

As the sun rose and light filled the chamber, I sat with Nonna Ursula, hoping for a sign of consciousness, while Princess Isabella flitted in and out, chatting as Friar Laurence instructed, telling Nonna Ursula of her palace duties, complaining the cooks didn't listen to her, asking for advice.

One of the palace guards stood at the door. Tommaso guarded the open window. Both Old Maria and Pasqueta tried to close it; I insisted it remain open. Old Maria argued that Princess Ursula could catch a chill in her lungs.

I assured her the fire on the hearth would keep Princess Ursula from such a fate.

How I wished Nurse could have accompanied me to handle the maids, to cheer me through the long morning, to be my right hand as she often was! But someone had to stay at Casa Montague to supervise the children, the staff, and to care for my pregnant mamma, who was, I knew, fretting about Papà.

As the hours progressed, the tumult created by the *disciplinati* faded, and I hoped that would serve to reassure Nonna Ursula's sleeping mind that her grandson had triumphed. When the normal sounds of the city and the smells of the street, good and ill, wafted in on the drafts, I reminded her of the teeming life beyond the palace and how much she loved it.

I also discussed her son, Prince Escalus the elder, suggesting irritably that he could have hung around to witness the attack on her and give his report to me. But even under my provocation, he remained unseen and unheard, and I reflected aloud and with bitterness of how useless a ghost he had turned out to be.

I also listened for the prince's return.

I told Nonna Ursula all that, too, showed her my knives—they quieted Old Maria's muttering about the open window—assured her that on the prince's arrival, he would visit her and suggested if she would wake and tell us who attacked her, that would assist in the hunt for the hell-bound beast who had dared lay hands on the dowager princess of Verona.

At midmorning, Pasqueta brought me bread, cheese, fruit, and watered wine. I thanked her and recognized the opportunity for what it was. "Speak to your princess," I said. "It is Friar Laurence's command that we speak to her."

Pasqueta glanced at me, tears in her eyes, leaned over her mistress, and pushed her white hair off her forehead. "Forgive me for leaving you alone. I never dreamed someone would enter the palace and bludgeon you." Lowering her face into her hands, she wept.

I gave her a wiping cloth and studied the poor woman.

Pasqueta wasn't so young. Her black curly hair was threaded with gray, and around her dark eyes, fine lines had begun to form.

"How long have you been with the princess?" I asked.

She mopped at her face. "More than twenty years. She chose me when I was fourteen to be the legs and strength for Old Maria."

"You're very fond of Princess Ursula."

"She saved me from . . . My father wished to sell me. She bought me for a fair price, and when he tried to . . . take me back, she set the guards on him. He's never returned." Fiercely she added, "I hope he died in the mud of the street."

She was the last person to see Nonna Ursula unharmed, and absent during the attack. Conveniently? Perhaps, but her emotion and ferocious dedication appeared to be genuine enough.

"Last night. You went to the kitchen to make her a posset."

"Princess Ursula waited until Old Maria was asleep. She's impossible to wake, jealous of our mistress"—Pasqueta gave a sideways twitch of the head to indicate the aged serving woman, who watched us suspiciously—"and Princess Ursula likes my posset better. I add honey to bitter herbs to soften the flavor, and I always make sure the water is at a rolling boil. Everything dissolves so much better and it's not so grainy on the tongue."

To make her feel as though she was instructing a person inexperienced in the preparation of medicines, I kept my wide gaze fastened on her face. "Before you left, did you notice anything amiss? Hear anything outside the window?"

"Nothing. I keep thinking, trying to remember a hint of . . . but . . ." She burst forth, "I was only gone as long as it takes to boil water!"

"Does the cook not keep water simmering on the fire?" Our cook did.

"The palace cook is a slovenly brute who feeds the household and the prince's men bad food and bad wine and—" She abruptly stopped talking.

"And sells the good outside the palace?" I offered.

She sighed in relief. "Aye. You understand. He does nothing if it doesn't benefit him."

From that information, I deduced that Pasqueta was gone long enough for someone to break the bars and enter. "When you crossed the threshold, you found—"

"Princess Ursula's belongings had been overturned and she was unconscious, bleeding, so white—" Pasqueta turned pale and put her hand to her mouth as if to contain sickness.

I wet a rag, wrung it out, and put it to her forehead. She murmured a thanks and leaned forward, holding it in place with one hand and clutching her gut with the other.

I watched her steadily, trying to decide if that twinge of guilt I'd spied meant she'd set up the robbery—such suspicious timing!—and yet had been horrified by her accomplice's brutal attack.

When she lifted her head, the color had begun to return to her cheeks. "I'm sorry, Lady Rosaline. I hadn't spoken of it, and in this moment, I was overcome."

I took the rag, wet it again, and once more put it on her forehead. "Better now?"

"Yes," she whispered, and glanced sideways at Old Maria. "But I . . ." She swallowed.

"Tell me."

"I saw something."

Chapter 28

"*S*omething?" Although Pasqueta was older than me, I used my firm, encouraging, elder-sister voice.

"It was dark. Even in the palace, the corridors are full of shadows at night. Here and there, a night candle is lit, but"—she shivered—"the restless ghost of Prince Escalus the elder walks."

"You've seen him?"

"Last night, I did."

Elder, you said I was the only one. Where are you? "This ghost was in Nonna Ursula's bedchamber?"

"I saw a dark cloaked form slip from her sitting room and drift toward the tower." Pasqueta kept shivering, little quivers of remembered terror. "He wore the old prince's cloak. The one from the portrait! I saw it. I knew it!"

"What did you do?"

She blushed, such a rapid change from her previous pale complexion I was afraid she'd keel over from the change. "I ran in the other direction, back the way I came."

"And?"

"I'm so ashamed. I splashed half the posset out of the cup."

My gaze fell to her flexing hands; livid blisters had risen and discolored her skin.

The worse was yet to come. "I left Princess Ursula alone while I worked up my nerve to creep back. I'm such a coward. When my princess said she'd hold a séance, I knew she would rouse the spirits, and she did. She did!"

Although Elder had found a way of defusing my trembling fear of ghosts—his caustic sentiments made him seem less a phantom from beyond and more an in-law to be avoided—yet I could still comprehend her overwhelming fright. "You didn't confess to Friar Laurence because . . . ?"

"Old Maria was right to sound the warning against me. I failed in my duty to my beloved mistress." Her eyes, wretched with guilt, overflowed and she wept in true remorse.

I patted her shoulder, and when she'd gained control, I grasped her wrist. "A ghost is a spirit without a body. Without flesh, it cannot pick up a weapon. It cannot beat an old woman senseless."

"But you don't know what a ghost can do . . ."

I stared, impressing on her my true knowledge.

"You've seen a ghost?" Her voice grew hoarse. "You've seen the spirit of the murdered prince?"

"Have you not heard such claims?"

"The palace gossip claims it's so, but to me, you seem so . . . normal."

Fooled her! "Do you understand what I'm saying? If the figure you saw is a ghost, he couldn't have hurt Nonna Ursula. Plus, Prince Escalus the elder truly loves and admires his mother."

Pasqueta scooted her chair back from mine.

I continued, "If the villain who attacked the dowager princess is a man—"

"But the window!" She pointed. "He escaped out the window!"

"Perhaps not. Perhaps he came in the window and left through the door. If he found the right place to hide, he might still be within the palace."

"'Within the palace'?" She clutched at her chest.

I didn't know whether she feared the ghost or the intruder more. Or me, because she continued to scoot backward. "We're all in danger!" She stood in a rush.

I still gripped her wrist. "We have guards. Tommaso stands by the window, and two of the palace men are outside the outer door. We're safe."

Pasqueta's gaze swung from Tommaso, who watched and listened, toward the sitting room and back again. "I dare not stay!"

My opinion of her started a steep downward slide. "You'd leave Princess Ursula in her time of need?"

"No. No, I don't mean that." Pasqueta wrung her hands. "But a man in the palace. And a ghost. The guards can stop a man, if that's what it was, but they can't stop a ghost!"

She had me there. So I added, "Old Maria will be glad to know she's won the competition as the most loyal of Princess Ursula's serving maids."

Pasqueta looked at Old Maria.

Old Maria stared back at her, and although she couldn't know what we'd been discussing, her malevolent gaze gave her opinion of her rival.

"Where will you go?" I asked.

"I can't leave here. I have nowhere to go and . . . and Princess Ursula saved me. I'm loyal to her." Pasqueta took a long breath. "I'll be brave. I'll protect her, no matter the horrors waiting around every corner."

"You've helped by telling me about the man's figure you saw. It was a man?"

She looked startled at the idea a woman could be so perfidious. "Of course!" When I studied her, she said, "I saw him come out of the door. He was tall." With her hand, she indicated a height above her head.

"What else did you observe?"

Her eyes drooped as she tried to recall. "He'd pulled the hood up on his cloak, so I didn't see his hair. He wore gloves. I heard boots on the floor."

So definitely not a ghost. "How did he move? Did he walk in fury? Was he running away?"

Her eyes popped wide. "He moaned. That's why I thought he was a ghost. He put his hand to his face and moaned like someone facing an eternity of damnation."

"If he fears eternity, he's a man." Remembering the bag containing Yorick's skull, I asked, "Was he carrying anything?"

"Not that I remember or saw."

"Did you or Old Maria remove the"—how to describe it?—"bag from the table and put it away for the princess?"

"I didn't. Old Maria is ruthless in her pursuit of tidiness. I'm sure she did."

I nodded. "Pasqueta, thank you, you've helped so much. Now . . . trust no one. Tell no one. If you do, you could be in danger."

Pasqueta crept away, weeping in fear and sorrow, and I returned to my care of Nonna Ursula, updating her with the newest information.

Justice must be served for Elder . . . and for her.

When Friar Laurence returned, he dismissed me and Tommaso, commanding we find food and drink. I rose from my chair to find the cook had prepared an unappetizing spread for me, and if I hadn't been so weary at heart, I would have gone up and created such a havoc in the palace kitchens they would have trembled before me. Instead I pushed the plate toward Tommaso—that child of the streets didn't disdain food, no matter how unappetizing—and climbed the stairs to the tower where I'd first met Prince Escalus the elder. Where had he been? What had he seen?

Where was his son and my papà?

But when I arrived, I saw not Elder floating slightly above the floor, but rather Lysander of the house of Gorgeous standing on a ladder, next to the column that held the city's night candle, and muttering like a madman.

May I remind you, gentle reader, it was four stories to the ground.

Chapter 29

Lysander placed one firm foot on the rail.

My heart leaped in my bosom. "Lysander," I called softly, for I didn't want to frighten him. "Don't jump!"

His muttering ceased, he looked around in surprise, and in a completely normal tone, he said, "Rosie! What are you doing here?"

I rushed toward him.

He did jump, off the rail and onto the floor of the tower before me. "Never mind. You're betrothed to the prince. I trow you can visit the palace whenever you wish. My lady." His voice held the tang of bitter.

I didn't care. I stood with my hand on my heart. "I thought you were going to—"

He looked over the edge, four stories down, and laughed. "No. Not even for the lack of your love, Rosie."

Frazzled and piqued, I said, "That's not what . . ." *Don't say that!* "What are *you* doing here?"

"I came on commission from Prince Escalus." He gestured, and I realized he wore a workman's rough garb, and leather bags, tools, and paraphernalia littered the floor. "Word went out to all of the Veneto that he wishes to light the city towers at night with a flame that does not extinguish in wind or rain, so

I went home to Venice, to the island of Murano, and spoke with the great glassmaker, Marietta Barovier. I designed a lamp, she created the clear glass *cristallo* to fit within the dimension." He lifted a large lamp of dark metal that contrasted with the milky glass. "When I presented it to Prince Escalus, he declared himself my patron and is financing a great many lamps to be installed on all the palace towers and eventually on the city walls."

"Oh. Oh!" I smiled at him. "How wonderful you are!"

He cocked his head and examined me. "Even after my rude dismissal of you in your time of need, you are so kind?"

He meant his anger in the garden, and I appreciated his near apology. Well done . . . for a man. "I'm not kind. It's truth. To be able to provide light to the city and country on the darkest night, to guide the weary traveler to shelter and a meal, to assure Verona's citizens that the prince is in his home and in command—what a gift you give."

"Well." He pretended modesty. "I must make it work."

"Will it work?" I asked in concern.

"Of course. It's so simple that I'm amazed no one has done it before."

At his self-confidence, I laughed out loud and touched his hand.

As if my approval meant much to him, he glowed like one of his lamps. "What are you doing up here?"

Recalled to the circumstances, I leaned my elbows on the rail, looked out over the city, and drew in a deep breath. "The dowager princess was attacked by a thief and a villain. She survives, but barely, and I've been at her side all day. I needed . . . air."

"No. No!" His distress seemed genuine and was, to me, surprising for a man who was not a native of Verona. "Princess Ursula is famed in Murano for her patronage. I've been told that as a young woman, she ordered a window made for her with glass, and, of course, so many years ago, the glass was lumpy and cloudy, and the window very heavy, but she started a fashion and the glassmakers remember."

"That window is still in place. *La canaglia* wrenched it from its hinges, but the glass is unharmed." I swung on him as if he was responsible. "Nonna Ursula possesses many beautiful things, no doubt envy and evil reign in one man's heart, but to attack an elderly woman with such brutality—" For the first time since I'd been summoned to the palace, rage choked me.

Lysander handed me a wineskin. "Drink."

I did. I took a breath and drank again.

"When you're angry, you flush the color of a ripe pomegranate."

I glared. *Flatterer. Not.*

He rummaged in his brocade bag, brought out part of a loaf of bread, and tore off a chunk. He handed me that and used his knife to slice cheese, and watched while I devoured it all, and again washed it down with wine. I wiped my mouth on my sleeve. Revived, I said, "Friend, my thanks. I hadn't realized how hungry I was."

"You have to eat and drink for Princess Ursula. She needs you."

"I know." I did know, and I turned back to look out over the city. I sipped again, then handed him the wineskin. "I've lived my life being the practical one. Then I met you and fell in love, solved a crime, kissed a prince, was betrothed for the hundredth time—"

"'Hundredth'?" Lysander sounded amused and sympathetic.

"Approximately. Now a ghost demands I find his killer—"

Lysander choked on the wine, sputtered, and did a double take. "What? What did you say?"

I paused and thought. Lysander and I had fallen into our previous easy companionship, I hadn't realized . . . "I haven't told you that, have I?"

"No, you have not! What ghost? What . . . ?" His wide-eyed alarm would have done any actor proud.

"Prince Escalus the elder. Cal's father." Where *was* Elder? I'd expected to find him here.

"What killer?" Lysander did a double–double take. "Wait . . . Cal?"

"My betrothed. Probably best not to repeat that. *Cal*, I mean. It's a family nickname." Not his favorite nickname, either, but not as bad as Callie.

I wasn't sure whether Lysander gaped at me about the ghost or the nickname, but I rather briskly announced, "I am not a liar and dramatist. A ghost, Prince Escalus the elder, haunts the palace seeking justice, and only I can see him."

Lysander drank again, deeply, then handed me the wineskin and climbed back up the ladder. When he got up high enough to see the top of the column, he rested his arms on the stone and examined his perch. He nodded, as if he saw something that pleased him, and asked, "Can you hand me the lamp?"

"No. How tall do you think I am?"

He glanced down at me, smiled as if my irritated, upturned face gave him pleasure, and climbed back down as I lifted the heavy lamp over my head. He gripped the handle in one hand and the base in the other, and even watching him made me breathe deeply to calm my heart. The round steps looked precarious to me, the ground was very far, and the breeze tossed his fair hair in its loving fingers.

"Are you showing off?" I asked.

"Perhaps." His eyes glinted green with humor. "Are you impressed?"

"With what? Your foolhardy disregard for your handsome neck?"

"It is handsome, isn't it?"

I lowered my gaze to the rear of his breeches. "Marvelous." To think, previously I'd been uninterested in the finer points of male anatomy. Perhaps I'd been slow to mature, or perhaps I was making up for lost time. Either way, the view of his *culo* pleasured me more than his neck.

In a conversational tone of voice, he asked, "Is the ghost why you held a séance?"

"How did you hear about the séance?" I asked sharply.

"When I hear your name, I listen, and this morning when I dropped into our kitchen to cajole food and drink for this evening, the cook was gossiping with the baker's lad about last night's ghostly visitation called up by Princess Ursula."

"Your kitchen? In the Marcketti household?"

"Yes."

My horror overflowed. "Everyone in Verona knows?"

"Yes."

"*How* do these things get around?"

"The actions of the prince and his family are always of interest to everyone, and the servants see all. Romeo and Juliet are famous for the reasons we all know, and thus the scandal of your impetuous betrothal created a buzz, like a beehive in swarm." He descended the steps and looked me in the eyes. "Isn't that what you intended when you arranged the séance?"

"It's what Nonna Ursula intended, but I didn't realize . . ." This tiding put a different complexion on the break-in, and I couldn't contain my troubled thoughts. "I didn't realize this swarm would travel so swiftly. News of the séance is on the street, but not of Elder's visits to me?"

"Princess Ursula, being who and what she is, is assumed to have taken command of you and your training as future wife of the podestà. The interest in you is more avid and . . ." He hesitated.

"Salacious?" I suggested.

In a nonverbal confirmation, Lysander confessed, "Last night, I punched my cousin Rugir and busted his lip."

"Rugir? You hit Rugir?" I was wildly impressed, and not at

all surprised. He'd been a pig about me. He detested intelligent women. "He's the best fistfighter in Verona! I had no idea that you—"

"I can't. I'm not. That's the only reason I managed to lay a hand on him. He never thought I had it in me."

"Oh." That explained it. "Did he hit you back?"

"No, he bought me a drink. He was very proud. He thinks that what I do"—Lysander gestured around at the paraphernalia of his work—"is for foreigners and peasants."

"Certainly not for an intellectual superior like *him*!" I was sarcastic enough to make Lysander grin.

"His reputation as a sodden lackwit has never sullied his charm or prowess with the ladies."

"Naturally not." I knelt beside the second lamp. "Tell me how it works."

"You don't really care. You're indulging me." After that feeble protestation, he said, *"Va bene!"* He knelt beside me. "The oil is placed here, in the cistern, and when the wick is lit, it will burn clear and true. The roof will protect it from rain, the glass will protect it from wind, and the vents here"—he moved the sliding metal doors at the top and bottom—"can be adjusted to raise or lower the flame."

"Genius," I breathed.

He huffed and scowled. "The pale glass can be removed and exchanged for gold, used in the time of celebration, or red, used in the time of war or unrest. Verona's citizens need only look up to realize what message their podestà sends."

"Even more genius!" I stood and dusted my knees. "Why your displeasure?"

"I wish I'd thought of the colors, but it wasn't my idea. It was his. Prince Escalus. He's a smart man, your . . ." He looked down, then looked up into my eyes, and in a moment, I realized his casually friendly behavior was but a front for his true love and passion. In a husky voice, deeper than normal, he said, "If I can't have you, he's the one other man who's worthy of you."

I put my hand over his and pressed his fingers. "Thank you. That's very kind."

He cracked a grin. "And, of course, he's a better catch."

I slapped his hand hard. "You were doing so well!"

He cackled like the fiend he was, and I realized he had deliberately stuck a knife in my conceit. I couldn't help it, but I laughed, too, and shoved at his shoulder with mine.

Behind us, Cal cleared his throat.

Chapter 30

I whirled and ran to my betrothed. "Nonna Ursula? Is she . . . awake?" As if by strength of will, I would bring her back.

He looked down at me oddly, as if that wasn't the response he'd expected. "She's unconscious. Unchanged from the morning, Friar Laurence tells me."

I sagged in relief that she still lived, and frustration that there'd been no improvement. "Inside her head, wherever she is, she must want to shout at us to return her to life."

"Friar Laurence told me she moves not, nor does she show signs of sleep. She's still as death, but he says . . . he says that's what she needs now to heal the damage to her mind." His voice, usually so deep, still and enduring, developed a rasp of pain.

"I know. I know. I'm impatient, and the results of this violence cannot be borne."

Lysander, who had been standing silent and still at the railing, appeared beside us. "Prince Escalus, may I express my horror at the attack on Princess Ursula, and the distress of the Marcketti family at her suffering?" He bowed, his hand over his heart.

Cal gazed at Lysander, then at me, then at Lysander, then at me, and I realized what he'd seen when he reached the top of the stairs and stepped onto the floor of the tower. We'd been together, alone, talking easily, like friends . . . or lovers. And I'd held Lysander's hand.

I started to explain.

But why? Anything I said would sound defensive. Anyway, since when had Cal become the Rosie Montague vice squad? Sooner or later, he had to learn to trust me, and it had better be sooner.

Before I could cross my arms and tap my toe, Cal replied to Lysander. "Your horror and the distress of your family help ease my saddened heart, as well as the hearts of my sister, Princess Isabella, and my betrothed, Lady Rosaline."

That response soundly put Lysander in his place—and me in mine. I was now part of the ruling family, and Lysander should not forget it. Nor should I.

Lysander bowed again, and backed away, returning to his work on the lights.

"Cal, that was unnecessary. We have enough crises to handle without adding one filled with imaginary emotions."

"Your emotions for Lysander of the Marcketti are imaginary?" Cal asked in a neutral tone.

Lysander could hear him, and both could hear me; and what I had to say, they had both better heed. "My feelings are my own, and not for display or discussion, and in this time of anguish for Princess Ursula's suffering, I indulge in no flagrant madness of passion for *anyone.*" Now *I* gazed from Cal to Lysander, Lysander to Cal, and any passion expressed in my eyes could only be called icy.

Before they could react with the proper groveling and apologies (I know—obviously, my weariness and anxiety had unhinged me, for they were men and incapable of either), Elder, who'd been surprisingly absent, appeared with a pop and a hiss of irritation. "My mother's been attacked? Who would dare?"

I wanted to snarl at him, demand he explain himself. Where had he been at the time of the attack? Why couldn't he do one little thing right? What did he have to say for himself? Instead I spared him a glare, then said, "What use is a ghost when he's not around to witness the crime?"

"Indeed," Cal said, "when I learned of the attack on my grandmother, I thought of your ghost."

"He's not *my* ghost." I didn't want to own Elder, and I most definitely didn't want to be like him. I enjoyed my earthly state very well—indeed, even with all the murders and misunderstandings—and I would do my best to remain among the living.

Probably that explained Elder's constant state of crabbiness. He'd enjoyed his earthly state, too, and left it too soon.

"What did he witness?" Cal asked.

I gestured to Elder to explain himself.

Elder spoke directly to his son. "When Lady Rosaline is not within the palace, I'm not . . . anywhere. Somehow her presence brings me to a semblance of life."

"You jest!" I said.

Now he spoke to me. "Last night when you left, I faded."

Turning back to Cal, we both realized he hadn't heard a word Elder had spoken. He merely stared at the space Elder occupied because there I spoke. "He can't move beyond these walls, and he's not present unless I'm in the palace. Somehow I animate him."

"What is the purpose of his appearance if he can't help?" It was the cry of a grandson in distress.

"I don't know. He doesn't know. He said he wasn't given a list of rules. He said that there wasn't a 'Welcome to the Other Realm Dinner Party and Ball.'"

Cal's strong white teeth snapped together. "Is that supposed to be funny?"

"You'd have to ask him," I snapped back, and moved to the

next earthly crisis. "Cal, what about Papà? And you? And your men? What happened with the *disciplinati*?"

"Your papà is unharmed, and a good man to have in a fight. He's returned home to rest. The rest of us are fine. Unharmed."

I snapped, "Except?"

Lysander gasped, I assume at my brusque manner, then hurriedly returned to tinkering with his lamp.

Elder said, "Testy, are we?"

Maybe I wasn't diplomatic, but I recognized Cal's tone from Papà's use of it to Mamma, and it meant Verona had overnight become an unweeded garden gone to seed, given over to wicked thorny thistles that pierced the hand and heart and hurt all who dared fight them.

In other words, *la merda* had been flung and the flagellants had flung it.

Cal's expression mixed guilt, exasperation, and a touch of accusation. "Marcellus took a blow to the face; his eye is swollen shut. Holofernes received a knife in the back—not deep, but long—and Barnadine caught a blade under his chin."

"As long as everything's *fine,* if by 'fine,' you mean—not dead."

"How I wish I could hold a blade!" Elder exclaimed.

I started toward the stairway, rolling up my sleeves. "Friar Laurence requires me for the stitching and the bandaging? How many lesser men of your guard were injured?"

My forthright action must have taken Cal by surprise, for it was a moment before he caught up with me. "Eight. Mostly bruises and broken bones. The flagellants were for the most part armed only with their whips, but a few held weapons, some crude, some so well-honed . . ." He shook his head. "I should never have let them in the city."

I turned on the stair and faced him. "Was there a good choice, Cal?"

"No. To exclude them would have fomented unrest in the country. To allow them in took the viper to my bosom."

"To be the prince is to carry a burden too heavy for most to bear, to make decisions when all decisions are terrible. It gives comfort to Verona's citizens to know their podestà protects them. I admire you, my prince." A truthful tribute and one I didn't hesitate to give.

He stood above me, two steps up, and looked down at my face as if weighing my honesty. I must have landed on the side of sincerity, for he offered, "You may call me Cal."

My mouth twitched. I curtsied. "You are very kind."

Elder played dumb. "Weren't you already calling him that?"

"You're not helping," I answered. Then to Cal, "Let's go."

He caught up with me at the bottom of the stairs. He was alone; Elder had vanished again, and I was glad for that. I didn't need his point of view in this scene!

At once, I heard moans and saw the bodies stretched out on rugs and cushions and sitting on chairs. A weary-looking Friar Laurence grunted as he finished smearing ointment on Barnadine's stitched chin. "Rosie, there you are," he said in relief. "That boy won't let me examine him, and he's crying. Can you coax him to tell you what's wrong?"

"Of course." I started toward the young soldier sitting on the floor, knees bent, arms on top, sobbing into his sleeves.

Cal caught my arm and brought me to a halt. "This is my personal guard, the men who surround their leader, and they faced the worst of the fighting and took the worst of the injuries. The others sleep and eat. I don't want you here."

"Do you want Friar Laurence to work alone? For in the case of wounds, time is of the essence."

"There are other apothecaries in the city."

"Busy, no doubt. And of more consequence, they're not present." I placed my hand on his arm. "Cal, I know what I'm doing. Your men are safe with me."

He reacted with irritation. "I know that! But you are my lady and such bloody work should not be your lot."

"The care of your men is surely the duty of your lady." I had no time for such debate. I indicated the young guard. "What's his name?"

"Biasio."

"Did you see what happened to him?"

"I saw no injury to him. He fought well."

I viewed Cal's smooth face and knew *something* hung in his mind. "Why do you think he's crying?"

"He's a young warrior who made his first kill." Sorrow touched him as he watched Biasio. "For most of us, the first time the steel slides into a man and separates him from life . . . it is an unexpected horror and a loss."

"I comprehend." Indeed, I did, for I'd experienced the same thing after my adventure in the spring.

"I know you do." Cal cupped my cheek. "I'll talk to him."

"He'll be ashamed in front of his podestà. Friar Laurence is about to set that man's arm. Assist, and I'll speak to Biasio." I did, and found Cal's intuition was correct. The lad was unharmed, but sick at heart and ashamed of the violence of his reaction. To warm him, I put a rug around his shoulders, called for mulled wine dressed with honey, and assured him Prince Escalus had praised him for his proficiency. I dared not linger too long; others needed my skills. As I had hoped, Cal was now fully involved with helping his men, but when I left him, Biasio leaned his head against the wall and listened with respect to Marcellus, who held cloth-wrapped chips of ice to his eye.

It seemed the palace had access to an icehouse stocked with winter ice cut on Lake Garda. *Classy!*

Friar Laurence examined the injuries, each man in his turn, and I followed, speaking easily, observing each warrior as I asked about the fighting in the streets, what they'd faced, and so slyly uncovered the news of a thrust to Dion's gut. He believed it to be nothing, but when I quietly told Friar Laurence, he examined Dion and, over Dion's protestations, ordered ice compresses and bedrest.

Barnadine's usually overly florid complexion was pale and his eyes bloodshot, so I demanded another look at his chin. Which was fine, but when I had him lift his chin, he wasn't able. When I gently tried to help, he cried out in pain. A second examination by Friar Laurence proved Barnadine had been clubbed at the back of the neck, and he confessed to searing pain down his arm and numbness in his hand. Yet his eyes brimmed as he begged to be allowed to fight again; Elder's bodyguard feared for his young prince's safety.

When told, Cal looked grave. "The ways of the worthy could not be easily abandoned, and I have no doubt that if I left him, he'd find his way into the thick of battle. Better keep him by me. It's safer for us both."

When Friar Laurence gave Barnadine the news, he sighed in relief. "I'll survive," he told the good friar. "I know tricks in battle these whipped peasants can't imagine." His gaze shifted back and forth between us. "If I may presume—Princess Ursula had been good to me regardless of my merits. Has she recovered consciousness?"

Chapter 31

On hearing the question, the other men moved closer to hear, and all wore expressions of somber concern.

Friar Laurence looked to me. I raised my voice for all to hear, and put hope in their hearts. "Not yet. But you know, Barnadine, she has a will of iron and she is not easy to kill."

His gaze shifted to look around at the men, but he spoke to me. "My whole life, she's been there, directing and managing."

The other men nodded.

I understood. I didn't remember a time when the valiant princess hadn't stood as a power and a presence in the house of Leonardi.

"She was kind when I . . . failed in my duty." Barnadine meant when he failed to stop the assassination of Elder, and he wiped his nose on his sleeve. "Before . . . I used to bring her flowers, those little pink blossoms because she loved the scent, and she thanked me most graciously. She said her husband used to cut them all—which infuriated her. He'd put them in a glass and give them to her. Then she couldn't be angry. She said the flowers reminded her of him. I'd forgotten that, and now I wish . . ." He passed a shaking hand over his wet eyes. "The wine calls me, so I forget it all."

"Do we have no idea what villain perpetrated this outrage

on the old princess?" Holofernes had suffered slashing bruises on his legs and back, the result of a whip expertly applied; fury filled his voice and his expression was murderous.

"Someone who took advantage of the disturbance in Verona's streets to enter the palace and plunder. One of the flagellants." Dion's voice seethed and condemned.

Marcellus eyed me with more cold disdain than ever before. "Or one of our own citizens encouraged by the unrest and the rumors of nefarious dealings in the palace."

My mind skittered around, trying to decipher what I'd done this time to incur Marcellus's disfavor. With so much to choose from, it was difficult to decide, but I settled on the séance. I did want to point out that Nonna Ursula had so commanded, but to put the blame on a woman so beloved and in jeopardy was the act of a she-goat. Too bad Marcellus was like salt applied to a happy bed of spring-blooming columbine; around him, spring color and gaiety shriveled and died.

Cal turned to Friar Laurence. "You've worked hard all night and you're weary. Take a few hours rest here before you return to your duties."

Friar Laurence shook his head. "I must return to the shop to compound more medicines. I'll take my rest there."

"Should I come to help?" I had to offer, although I knew the answer.

"No!" The response came from several throats.

Cal said, "The streets aren't safe for a female, and we can't escort you."

Friar Laurence nodded agreement, blessed us all, and made his way toward the great door on the street. He would always do his duty, but age and weariness had begun to make their mark.

With his departure, Cal looked around at his men. "It's necessary we take this time to rest, and so you all should."

Marcellus hauled himself to his feet. "I'll speak to the rest of the guard, give them your commands to eat and sleep. With the proper behavior of all"—with his one open eye, he was looking at me—"we'll recover enough to fight again."

With chilly disdain, I said, "I'm sure *all* will do *everything* to your specifications of proper." I congratulated myself on delivering a proper verbal slap.

Unfortunately, Lysander of the Marcketti chose that moment to descend the tower stairs.

The men turned to look at him.

They gazed at Cal.

They gazed at me.

With all the gazing and head turning, both above on the tower and here in the corridor, unspoken messages were being passed and assumptions being made. Too clearly, they'd seen Cal and me descend the stairs and found naught amiss, but the unexpected appearance of another man—handsome, young, and rumored to be my suitor—caused suspicions to stir.

The way Lysander avoided glancing at me didn't help. Staring fixedly at Cal, he cleared his throat and said, "My prince, if I may, I would request your noble company on the tower. I have a question about the placement of the lights."

Cal appeared to notice nothing amiss with Lysander or his men or me, for he was ever the clever diplomat, and perhaps—oh, perhaps—had listened when I had made my thoughts clear above. "Of course, Marcketti. I come at once." He bowed to me. "Thank you, Lady Rosaline, for your kind care of me and my guard. My lady's generosity will be long remembered. You should now return to Princess Ursula's side."

I curtsied in return, feeling much as if I'd stepped onto a silent, possibly hostile theater stage, and I enunciated my lines the way I knew they should be written. "My first care is for you, my prince, and your valiant guard of Verona are also my guard. Now I do indeed return to my conscientious attention to our wounded princess Ursula."

Cal nodded approval at me, hurried to Lysander's side, and at once engaged him in lively conversation as they climbed the stairs. Clearly, Cal delighted in this innovation he'd envisioned.

I turned on my heel and walked with dignity toward Nonna Ursula's room and saw Tommaso pacing outside her door, watching for me.

I heard a man's booted step and turned to glance behind.

As Marcellus passed, I heard the single, hissed, and scornful word: "Proper . . ."

Tommaso started toward me and *somehow* his shoulder connected, hard, with Marcellus's shoulder. Caught by surprise, Marcellus stumbled and righted himself.

Tommaso made him a mocking bow. "My pardon, Lord. That was clumsy and not courteous, not behavior fitting of the palace's exalted atmosphere."

Marcellus started to retort, glanced at me, got the message, and stalked off.

Looking every inch a lad from the streets, Tommaso grinned, bowed, and fell in behind me. Although I appreciated Tommaso for his brawn and bravery, I had no idea he could provide a message with such pointed subtlety. Bravo to him!

In Nonna Ursula's room, I found Elder hovering over his mother, while Princess Isabella argued loudly with Old Maria about whether the window should be closed. Tommaso stopped and stood stoically in front of its opening.

I paid them no heed, but hurried to Nonna Ursula's side.

She was unchanged, except she'd begun to show the ravages of being too long without water; her eyelids looked almost transparent and her cheeks were gaunt. When I held her wrist, I could feel sluggish movement of blood in her veins. I glanced up at Elder.

He looked grim. "She's very close, and as unwilling as I was. What can I do?"

"Talk to her. I think she hears you, maybe now more than

ever. Talk to her. Convince her to come back before I have *her ghost* demanding I find her killer."

"Maybe she knows."

"Maybe she does."

Cal arrived from his visit with Lysander and the window combatants cast themselves on him and argued their differing views about fresh air and deadly miasmas of the oncoming night.

With a hand on my shoulder, Cal broke into my despair. "I partially shut the window and sent them both away." Going to his grandmother, he leaned over the bed and smoothed her hair back from her forehead. "I don't understand how this could happen. She's not one to allow a thief to harm her."

As I stepped back, I saw the thing I hadn't noticed before. Her cane with its heavy head rested close to her hand. Inspiration's lightning flared around me. "What if it's not a thief?"

"What?" Cal was clearly startled. "What?"

I gripped his arm. "I hadn't thought . . . I was in such anguish . . . But only last night, we held the séance and hoped the word would spread that we were investigating Elder's murder. The word has spread, indeed."

"How do you know that?"

"Lysander. He heard it this morning in the kitchen of the Marcketti. Oh! And Friar Laurence also knew."

"So soon!"

"Could we have frightened the killer so much that he watched until Pasqueta left to make her a poultice, entered Nonna Ursula's chamber, and—"

"You're saying he was within the palace? He didn't break in, he . . . broke out?"

Chapter 32

"Her cane rested on the bed with her, close at hand. She didn't grasp it and land a blow because—"

"She did indeed know her attacker," Cal finished my sentence. His face cleared of all emotion.

I began to understand him. He wouldn't reveal emotions or thoughts until he'd contemplated them, worked through the possibilities in his mind—and maybe not even then. I added an important component to my theory. "Her serving maids say nothing is missing."

He strode to the window and looked out once more to the damage on the bars.

I joined him. "Could a man have got in through such a small hole?"

"Perhaps. But a man couldn't wriggle in."

"Perhaps a boy. Or a woman?"

He nodded, a bare movement of the head, but he had observed the surroundings and he'd decided the intruder had invaded and attacked from within. "She knew them all. My guard. Our household. She believed them loyal, and she believed she was indestructible."

"That makes sense. That's why whoever it was, was able to hurt her . . ." My voice wavered.

Cal, bless him, gathered me close. Not a heated embrace, but one of comfort, and I put my forehead on his chest and my arms around his waist and gave back the solace in equal measure. I had so much family—so many boisterous, emotional, loud siblings and grandparents and uncles and cousins—and Cal had so few people he cherished. Like the men, he had never had a time when Nonna Ursula hadn't been a force in his life, and he loved her, would have given her anything to keep her happy until the natural end of her days. He'd failed in the most basic way, and while I longed to reassure him, I knew nothing I could say would change his unwavering sense of responsibility. His love for her made him all the more bound to her safety and happiness, and I'd do anything to help bring her back to us.

Yet if there was a way, not even Friar Laurence knew it.

Trying to give comfort, I tightened my grip on Cal, and felt him flinch. Pulling back, I observed him more closely. Exhaustion ringed his eyes, and his mouth had a tightness I hadn't observed before. The tightness of pain.

"Now that we're alone"—except for an unconscious woman and her ghost son—"I can ask, what injuries have you amassed in the battle?"

"I'm uninjured."

Yeah, sure. "Uninjured as those men were out there?"

He flexed a shoulder in what might have been a shrug, but wasn't.

I reached up to the seams of his jacket. "Let me see."

"It's nothing."

"I wasn't asking. Let me see." He was on the verge of refusing, and I didn't want to push him into that corner. Hastily I said, "Must I undress you? For I tell you, my prince, I've wrestled many a reluctant three-year-old sibling into clothes, and wrestling an injured, full-grown man out of his garments provides no challenge to me."

My mostly proper prince shook his head. "We are unchaperoned."

"If only."

Cal looked around. "My father . . . ?"

"He speaks with Nonna Ursula, commanding her to come to consciousness."

"She can't hear him," he said testily.

"Perhaps, Cal, she can now hear him better than she can hear us."

"Someone from within," he murmured. "Someone she trusts."

"Such treachery strips away all our security and leaves us brokenhearted and suspicious."

"This explains why no one saw the invader enter or leave through the window. He slithered in and out through the door."

I hated to throw acid on an already burning pain, but I had to ask. "How do we feel about Pasqueta, who conveniently left Nonna Ursula unprotected, and now claims to have seen a remorseful ghost slip from the room? And Old Maria, who slept through the clamor?"

In the face of such grim reality, his mouth lost its generous outline. "When you must leave Nonna alone, call Princess Isabella to stay with her. We don't need to tell her more than that we—"

"That I sense improvement in Nonna when we speak to her," I finished his thought.

"Do you?"

"What I sense is, Princess Isabella is getting discouraged by our lack of progress. She lingers in the corridor rather than come in to face the disheartening prospect of viewing Nonna slip further and further from us."

"Yes, I too." His gaze lingered on his grandmother, slack-jawed and unresponsive, and he returned to her side to pet her hand, lift it to his lips, and speak lovingly in her ear.

Elder watched his son. "Poor boy," he whispered. "So much has been taken from you."

I allowed Cal his moment, but time was of the essence. Grasping his hand, I pulled him toward a chair. "Strip down and let me see that shoulder."

Irritably he said, "I didn't say it was my shoulder."

I wasn't letting him get away with that. "Is there *more* than your shoulder?"

"Merely bruises." It was an unwilling admission. "It was an all-out brawl." He looked at his bloody knuckles, sat down, and eased off his jacket with a groan.

I unlaced his sleeve from his black shirt and that gave me a big enough gap in the linen to push it back and view the joint. *Merely bruising?* Maybe, but this was a dark, angry red. I put one hand on the joint—it was warm—and with the other took his wrist. "I'm going to move your arm for you. Don't assist me, but do tell me where the worst of the pain is."

"I don't need you to make it hurt *more*."

I smiled into his face, all charm and chiding. "Don't be a baby. In the end, I might be able to make it hurt less. You do want to know if something is broken, don't you?"

"It won't make any difference," he said.

Of course not. When violence flared again, Verona's prince had to go out and bring order to our world.

As I began to move the joint, he grunted and winced. "You were laughing with him."

I concentrated on the inner workings of the shoulder, trying to discern anything loose or clicking or slipping. "Who?" I asked.

"Young Marcketti."

I stopped in surprise. What had Cal seen? Heard? I have no idea how long he stood there and listened, but I could remember nothing but Lysander's heartfelt declaration that if he couldn't have me, only the prince was worthy. Surely, that was okay? Then Lysander teased and I laughed and . . .

"Lysander's funny. And he's not that much younger than you."

"He seems younger." Cal gasped as I took the arm back.

I eased it forward and observed his face, which relaxed from its clench of pain. "I don't actually know all about his life, but I believe he hasn't had the burdens thrust upon him that you've had, and certainly not the torments." I brought the arm up and back.

"That hurts!" He was talking about his shoulder.

"Show me where."

He pointed at the front of the joint.

I lowered his arm, but kept my hand cupped to his shoulder and gently examined the site. "What hit you?"

"The point of a pole wielded by a flagellant well-versed in its use."

"Was he aiming for merely one of the warriors, or was he aiming at the prince of Verona?"

"Does it make a difference?"

"I don't know." I wondered at my own query. "I just . . . I told you about the man with the flaming eyes. His memory disturbs me." I meant that more than I could say.

Taking my fingers, he kissed them. "Be not afraid, fair Rosaline, I'll protect you."

"I'm not afraid for my safety. I've taken precautions." I told him about retaining Tommaso as my bodyguard. "You see, I'm not as rattle-skulled as you imagine."

"Not rattle-skulled, but impetuous and far too dauntless."

You're wrong. I'm the sensible one! But he continued to hold my hand as if I were fragile, and gazed at me as if he saw a woman different than I knew. I asked, "Did you kill the brute with the pole?"

"Not I. Barnadine took his feet out from under him, and I lost him in the mêlée. Perhaps he was trampled to death."

I clenched my fist. "We can only hope."

He looked down at it and smiled as if my feeble defense amused him. I wanted to remind him I'm a fighter, but he knew it. He also knew, better than I did, that even armed and prepared as I was, I'd be at a loss in a fight with a man. Any man. That truth was one of the Lord God's most unjust decrees.

Cal's smile dissipated by degrees. "The *disciplinati* have divided into two groups. Most are holy, devoted to their penance and their mission, but as you saw, Rosie, a few are anarchists who want to burn the world to the ground and bring it back in their image. Those men fought us last night, then disappeared into the old underground."

"How do they know about it?"

"It's accessible through the arena where I ordered them to camp. But I fear the group includes local warriors and soldiers without a war. They're too good at battle." He breathed deeply, his chest rising and falling as if he sought the words to explain. "Last night, I judge you saw the leader of the flagellants who rampage through the city, deliberately causing death and destruction. I heard the talk. They believe a messiah walks among them, a man called Baal, a false god who tells them when they take down our beloved Verona, they will own its women and riches, and he will be their lord that favors them."

Cal struck fear into my heart. "How many flagellants serve Baal?"

"In the heat of battle, it's hard to tell. Not all. Most of the *disciplinati* are the holy men of sacred sacrifice they claim to be. But last night in Verona . . . fifty rebels fought for Baal." Cal took my hand, but he didn't see me. He saw the previous night's battle. "Baal is driven by a demonic passion and he urges his men to the edge of destruction. They believe *him* invincible, and that in serving him, *they're* invincible. They fight with a fervor that fears nothing, for he assures them that even if they die in his service, they'll gain paradise."

"What can stop them?"

His attention returned to me, and he seemed to find relief in my countenance. "We'll find out."

"You'll go into battle again tonight." I didn't like him returning to fight, but one picks the combats one can win, and forbidding him would provide nothing but grief for us both. I made my diagnosis. "As far as I can tell, everything inside your shoulder is working as it should, but the swelling must be contained. You'll recline on Nonna Ursula's chaise and get much-needed sleep while I apply ice to your joint."

I didn't wait for an argument, but used his good arm to help him up. He let me, which made me wonder if he was truly weak or taking the opportunity to remind me what we shared in our physical connection. Maybe both, for the way he clasped my shoulders and leaned on me no longer gave me comfort. He made me breathless with more than exertion and that starfalling sensation of passion and turmoil.

I saw Elder accessing us and speaking rapidly to Nonna Ursula, urging consciousness on her, I suppose, for the entertainment of our awkward courtship.

Reluctantly Cal released me to sink down on the chaise and I hurried to the door to find Princess Isabella and Old Maria and Pasqueta prowling the corridor outside. "Ice for Prince Escalus," I commanded. "As swiftly as possible! Two cloths full. At once!"

They jumped and disappeared in the direction of the, um, icehouse?

I really needed to explore the palace.

I returned to Cal, who appeared to be drowsing, but as soon as I nudged my hip against his hip, he clasped me by the wrist. "You laughed with him," he said again.

He had been truly disturbed by seeing me with Lysander, and I was sorry for that. "Cal, I swear to you, I won't dishonor you. Lysander's my first love, my first passion—"

Cal's eyes slitted open to stare at me.

"—But you and I are betrothed. Perhaps the deed was done by a dishonorable trickery on your part—" I caught myself, recalled that harping on the past was a betrayal of my vow to my mother. And bitchy, considering there was no going back. Added to that, Cal was injured. "Nevertheless, Lysander is not just another pretty face. You know that. You gave him the commission for the lights on the tower."

"He's got an inventive mind," Cal allowed.

"He does. He was also quite clear that the lamps were your idea, as was the different colors, so—"

"Don't patronize me!"

I blinked at Cal's vehemence.

"We're different men. Lysander's only responsibility is to prove himself to his family and the world. He will, perhaps, make a never-to-be-forgotten mark with his unique ingenuity. I carry the same burden every ruler has carried since the dawn of time. I'll be remembered only in case of some great disaster during my reign. If all is well, I'll be but a fond remembrance that rapidly fades."

I was fascinated by this glimpse of Cal's inner thoughts. "Do you seek greatness and the long tail of memory?"

"If greatness comes with keeping the peace in Verona, then yes, I seek it. The long tail of memory? No. Death finds every man. Time erodes the slab on which he rests. His name and body become dust."

Wow. Way to raise all our spirits, Cal.

"Let death not find you tonight," I instructed.

"Tonight will bring a finish to this crisis, one way or the other, but the challenges will never stop." The pallor of the dungeon, always faintly etched on Cal's face, increased with his weariness. "I do seek a home with the woman I . . ."

I hung on his hesitation like a piece of meat on a hook.

". . . I respect."

Way to rip that hook right out of me.

Elder spoke in my ear. "Either the boy handles you so cleverly, I am all admiration, or he handles you so badly, I fear for his long life."

I whipped my head around to find Elder hovering beside me. "You, sir, are the winner of the 'Least Desirable Father-in-Law' contest."

"I'm the only contestant." Elder seemed to think he was being logical.

I wanted to be able to slap his smug, ghostly face, but I didn't want to pass through his miasma. "I am not a stupid woman. I observe human nature. Cal may not seem like you now, but you're his father. You're his kin *and* he knew you, so he well remembers what you're like. Sooner or later, he's going to get comfortable enough with me to be just like you."

"With some of his mother mixed in," Elder said.

"Not enough of his mother. Not enough to compensate for you! Knowing you does not make him a value-added husband!"

"Humph. Most women think I'm charming." Elder vanished.

Cal watched me as if nothing of my one-sided dialogue could surprise him anymore. "You don't like my father?"

"He doesn't know how to keep his tongue between his teeth."

His mouth twitched. Just once.

I easily saw what he so badly wanted to say.

Who was I to talk?

"Shut up." I stood and flounced to Nonna Ursula's side.

Who knew I could flounce? Not me.

These men with their fights and their megrims and their inventions and their deep, dark mysteries were turning me into a silly creature—and I didn't like it.

Chapter 33

While Cal slept, I kept his shoulder packed in ice to make him comfortable, and simultaneously considered whether to smother him with a pillow. Unfortunately, that would create more problems than it solved.

See? I still contained a small ration of sense.

Instead I contented myself with the occasional belligerent glare. Since he didn't know it, he couldn't be offended—or worse, amused.

Yet also, I knew that tonight he would put himself at the front of his men in this battle for Verona's soul and safety, and the disciples of Baal had proved to be worthy opponents, inflicting pain and injury despite their pious protestations.

I paced back and forth between my two patients. I feared for them both; Nonna Ursula in the moment, Cal in tonight's mêlée, and in sooth, my hostility was nothing more than a mask and a distraction from worry. As twilight drew nigh and Cal began to stir, knowing he would need sustenance for the long night ahead, I sent to the kitchen and . . .

In my own defense, it had been many long hours of work and worry, *and* I was growing hungry myself, *and* when I'm hungry, I find myself giving into an impatience some might describe as outright temper. *And* when I tasted the palace cook's piss-pot soup, for I have no better way to describe it, and realized this was the offering he would place before the men who had rushed into battle to preserve the cook's worthless hide—the time had come. Indeed, the time was long past.

I instructed Tommaso to stand watch over my patients, and rode the storm of rage through the corridors, past a wide-eyed Princess Isabella, past the men sleeping sprawled in the atrium, and I started up the stairs toward the kitchen.

A hand on my shoulder jerked me to a stop.

Who dared interrupt my righteous intention?

Marcellus, of course. He spoke as if he had the right to demand, "Where are you going?"

"'My lady,'" I said.

"What?" Startled. He was startled at my rebuke.

"'Where are you going, *my lady*?'"

Marcellus had a strong, agile body built by years of fighting, a handsome enough face, if a little glare-y toward me, and an attitude of superiority that needed a good slap-down. Our eyes clashed in enmity; then he made a courtly bow. "Where are you going, *my lady*?"

"'If I could be so presumptuous to ask,'" I suggested, but I didn't have time to teach him more manners. "I'm going to deal with the palace cook and the palace kitchens, and you're exactly the man I need with me. Come on." I swung around hard enough to whack his legs with my skirts and returned to my stair climb. I didn't have to listen for Marcellus; I knew he wouldn't let me go alone. Indeed, I depended on it.

As in all elegant homes in Verona, the kitchens were on the top floor, to keep the heat and odors out of the living quarters, and to contain the possibility of fire. Better a cooking fire start from the top than the bottom.

In a normal home, I would have expected words of warning to fly ahead of me via the other servants. But the palace staff had to eat the same wretched food served by the same wretched cook, as had been presented to me, and so I found the kitchen as it was, awash with filth, smelling of rotting produce and offal, and littered with lolling cook's assistants. The cook himself engaged in negotiating with the innkeeper over the cost of two immense baskets of palace meats, vegetables, fruits, breads, and cheese.

A single scrawny scullery maid labored to clean the long wooden table with sand, and when she looked up and saw us, her eyes widened and she backed into the corner.

I recognized her, the girl from the great walk who hid behind the curtains. I indicated her to Marcellus. "She can stay."

Marcellus said, "Yes, my lady," then fixed his gaze on the cook and flexed his fists.

The innkeeper dropped the goods and bolted.

As he passed, Marcellus grabbed him by the throat and picked him up. While the man choked and turned purple, Marcellus stared into his face. "I know you. You're Rollo from the Village Inn. When the prince is done with you, you'll wish you'd joined the flagellants." He released him. Rollo fell to the floor, crawled to the top of the stairs, then bounded to his feet and took them three at a time.

The cook, a man as large, disgusting, and smelly as his kitchen, started toward me, his large hands raised as if to slap me against the wall. I didn't move, not because I'm foolish, but because I honestly couldn't believe he'd be unbalanced enough to think he could hit a noblewoman, much less the podestà's intended. I wouldn't allow him to later boast he'd made me flinch.

But as he came closer, I believe my eyes widened in alarm, for Marcellus stood immobile and the cook smiled a nasty smile. Just as I feared my faith in the cook's good sense and Marcellus's loyalty was misplaced, the cook lunged and swung—and

Marcellus's swift fist met Cook's face in a teeth-shattering blow.

I ducked, and glad I was, for blood flew like wild strawberries mashed by an overenthusiastic chef. The collective gasp sucked all the air from the room, and I stepped aside to avoid the stampede of former cook's assistants, many of whom wore a marked resemblance to him.

Ah, nepotism. A marvelous tradition by which entire families can be unemployed all at the same time.

The cook staggered backward, hand over his nose, eyes bulging at Marcellus. "You hate her!"

Marcellus grabbed him by the greasy apron and brought him face-to-face. "She is my podestà's, and therefore mine to protect."

When the dust had cleared, the cook rested unconscious at the bottom of the stairs, Marcellus stood by my side, the scullery maid had stopped squeaking, and I surveyed the shabby battlefield I'd won.

"Now what?" Marcellus asked.

"Wash that man's filth off your hands. We're making a meal." Going to the laden baskets that had come so close to escaping the kitchen, I found myself satisfied that this food, at least, was eatable. I gestured the scullery maid closer. "You're Orsa? Yes? Orsa, are there any clean aprons around here?"

Orsa opened a greasy wooden cupboard against the wall and brought out one clean white apron.

"One for him and a clean one for you, too." I tied it around my neck and at my waist. "You scrubbed the table well. Can you scrub that big iron pot in which to make soup?"

She nodded.

"Make your arms strong and swift." I had no wish to poison Cal's troops. I asked Marcellus, "Do you know how to chop?"

"I'm a soldier. I know how to fix a meal."

"Good." I handed him one of the baskets. "I want whatever meats are in there minced." I dug through the second basket and tossed vegetables on the table: leeks, onions, garlic, cabbage, turnips, green beans, and some marvelous dried mushrooms. I looked up at him. "Is there smoked fat pork?"

"Yes. Pigeon, plucked and cleaned. Chicken, plucked and cleaned. A stag haunch?"

I looked over his shoulder. "We're in business. Chop the smoked fat pork as fine as you can. In fact, cut all the meats fine. We don't have much time." Before we had to feed the men, I meant.

I thought Marcellus might balk at doing as I commanded, but he apparently understood the necessity of putting food into soldiers marching to battle, for he minced meats without comment.

I turned back to the scullery maid. "Orsa, as soon as you're done cleaning that pot, hang it on the hook over the fire. Then wash and chop the vegetables."

"I'm not allowed to use a knife," she quavered.

"Do you know how?" I asked.

She nodded.

"I, Rosaline Montague, betrothed of Prince Escalus the younger, give you permission to use a knife." I pulled my blade out of my sleeve. "Here. It's sharp."

Orsa took the knife, tested the edge with her thumb, smiled in a way that transformed her plain, thin face into something remarkable, and went to work on the dried mushrooms, the carrots, and the green beans. Good. She knew to cut the tough vegetables first.

I watched long enough to know she was competent; then I went to the door where one skinny, brave, and very young houseboy hovered, peering in anxiously, probably sent by the more experienced staff to investigate. "Petro, yes?"

"Yes, my lady." He bowed, all awkward legs and arms.

"Petro, send a sedan chair to Casa Montague for Old Cook. Tell her Lady Rosaline requires her presence at the palace, and to pick a staff large enough to get her started in the kitchens. Bring her back here as soon as possible."

"Yes, my lady." He started to run down the stairs.

"Petro!"

He paused.

"Bid the men bring her with the care they would offer a treasure, for Old Cook is the key to all future meals at the palace. When she's comfortable, each morsel you eat will sing a glorious angel chorus in your mouth."

His bright eyes gleamed. "Aye, my lady!"

"You promise much of this Old Cook." Marcellus didn't stop chopping, but his abrasive tone set my teeth on edge.

"She's the reason people in Verona and beyond fight to feast at the Montague table."

"Why isn't she in charge of the Montague kitchens now?"

"The bone-bending disease struck her early, taking her from a tall young woman into a bent, wizened still-young woman blessed with a happy talent for food. She tires easily and some days can't get up from her bed. When she's able, she's in the kitchen providing advice and inspiration, and there she's much beloved." I threw the minced smoked pork into the hot iron pot and listened to the sizzle as the pork rendered. "After the first meal here, when I realized how soon Prince Escalus insisted the wedding would be, and how bad the food was, I appealed to Old Cook for help. She had gladly consented. Her enforced repose leaves her bored and restless, yet she warned me her command in this kitchen could be only temporary." With a long wooden paddle, I stirred the pork and, satisfied, threw in handfuls of meat and bones chopped fine, as I instructed.

I added the slow-cooking vegetables, pitchers of water, and herbs: sage, thyme, parsley, nettles, then turnips, leeks, onions, garlic, and cabbage. When the soup was bubbling, I turned back to Marcellus. "For you to question my authority and decisions in the palace kitchen is akin to me questioning Prince Escalus about his battle plans. You know nothing about my skills. Don't presume, and don't let it happen again."

Chapter 34

I didn't smile, and I held Marcellus's gaze.

He blinked as if startled. During the short time he'd known me, he'd seen me as a fragile female, buffeted by earthshaking events, by turbulent emotions, and in the end neatly trapped by his prince into a betrothal. He hadn't seen me as spinster Rosie Montague, captain of her own destiny, commander of the Montague household, organizer of adult parties and children's events, and beloved sibling and cousin to half the people in Verona and beyond. I had my strengths, I knew them, and it was time he knew them, too, and gave them the respect they deserved.

No. Gave *me* the respect *I* deserved.

Marcellus recovered, inclined his head, and bowed like a courtier. "My apologies, my lady. I'm a churl in the face of your authority."

"I wouldn't go that far," I said. "More of a braying donkey. Much of the staff is hovering at the door. Order them in, organize them into a crew, and let's get this pigpen cleaned and restored before Old Cook arrives to create order and marvelous meals." I figured Marcellus could handle that. Whatever else he was, he was, after all, Cal's trusted commander. He knew how to coordinate an attack, even if it be on filth.

I feared the fancy footmen, the frilly maids, the calloused hostlers, would hesitate, but they piled through the door and went eagerly to work clearing away the years of rotting debris and ingrown dirt; the entire palace had been forced to eat the moldy, repulsive, dried-up foods, and I knew I couldn't have done more to win their loyalty and appreciation.

The soup wasn't fancy, but its meaty, herbaceous scents filtered through the kitchen, down the stairs, and I sensed a lifting of hearts and a return of appetite. As soon as the vegetables were cooked through, I ordered Orsa to stir while I grated day-old bread into the broth to thicken it. With a ladle, I filled a medium pot for the staff working in the kitchen and a small pot for Cal, then ordered two robust manservants to wrap towels around the iron handle, lift it from its hook, and carry it down to the men. With them went a maid carrying bread, cheese, and dried fruit from the baskets. Everyone was smiling.

It's amazing how good food can lift the heart.

Marcellus went to the wine cellar, and I, carrying a bowl of bread, cheese, and fruits, went back to Nonna Ursula's room, with a boy carrying the small pot and grinning all over his face.

Before we entered the room, I put my finger to my lips. Cal was still deeply asleep. Nonna Ursula was unmoving. Old Maria sat in a chair by the window, sniffing as the fresh air choked her, using the last of the sunlight to embroider in the Florentine way.

Tommaso sat on a bench with his back against the wall, looking bored, but as the smell of the soup reached him, he rose to help the boy hang it on the hook over the fire. "Bless you, Lady Rosaline, my belly thinks my throat's been slit."

I collected bowls from Nonna Ursula's cupboard, filled two of them, put them in front of Tommaso and the boy, and softly commanded, "Eat!" As they pulled the spoons off their belts, I picked up a basket and prepared to go out into the garden.

I had fragrant pink flowers to pick.

Tommaso stood. "I shall go with you, my lady."

His sincere intention moved my heart, for he was almost salivating over the soup. I replied, "It's not yet night, and I'm going into the prince's own garden. I'll be safe. You should eat." He looked undecided, so I put my hand on his shoulder and pressed him back down in his seat. "Eat," I said again, and left.

The garden much resembled the evening the Montagues had come for Cal's family dinner: shadowy, fragrant, and softened by twilight. Yet . . .

Elder wanted me to find his killer.

Papà and Mamma wanted me to stay chaste and, with their own experience as an example, and despite my exemplary and prolonged virginity, they worried I couldn't make it to my wedding night.

My siblings wanted me to be good ol' dependable Rosie.

Cal demanded I yield to him my trust, my troth, my thoughts, my much-vaulted virginity, without a promise of anything of himself in return.

Lysander was the only one who didn't want anything from me, except . . . me, and although I knew whom to blame for that night when I'd been caught in Cal's arms, still I felt guilty when Lysander worshipped me with his gaze. I mean, really, how many worshipful men does a woman get in one lifetime?

Maybe one. If you're lucky.

The *disciplinati* simply wanted me to die.

And someone close to the podestà had tried to kill Nonna Ursula because that person believed that during that séance, she had discovered the villain who had killed her son.

I realized how very overcome I had become by the constant barrage of voices, faces, hungers, demands. All my world roiled in confusion, upending my security and stripping away my serenity. My own skin no longer fit on my body. I feared what was to come, and for all our sakes, I needed to do as Elder required and find his killer before he struck again. At Cal, at my family, or at me.

I took a deep breath and sought the peace of the garden to clear my mind.

Nearby, a man's voice said, "God's blessings to you, Lady Rosaline!"

Perhaps I was a little jumpy, for I reached for the dagger in my sleeve—and came up empty.

I'd given my knife to Orsa to use in the kitchen, and had not yet retrieved it.

Chapter 35

"My apologies, Lady Rosaline. To startle you was never my intent." Friar Camillo rose from his knees, his heavy wooden bead rosary in one hand. He'd been praying at the small shrine dedicated to the Virgin Mary; he was almost invisible clad in his brown robes and concealed by twilight.

I felt foolish with my hand at my wrist, searching for a knife that wasn't there, but . . . why was he praying at this shrine? Now? I had too many suspicions floating in my mind to ignore that he was here where he should not be; and for all that he was a monk, he was also a tall, strapping man. I retreated a step. "Friar Camillo, I didn't mean to disturb you."

"Indeed, you did not. I had finished my devotions." He lowered his hood, and again his youth, strength, and good looks struck me. "On this beautiful autumn evening, may I walk with you?"

Not really. "I didn't expect to see anyone in the garden."

He took that as assent, probably because no one refused a monk, and joined me on the path.

"They're expecting me back as soon as possible." With suspicion weighing on me, I sensed it was wise to tell him someone inside knew where I'd gone and when I'd be back. As we walked, I asked, "Why are you here?"

"Friar Laurence sent me to do what I could for the prince of Verona's soldiers."

"Right." That explained why he was in the palace; the guards would always grant a holy brother entrance. "How are the men?"

"Much cheered by your good soup. I blessed the healthy going into battle this night and cared for the wounded." He smiled down at me. "You have made many friends with your clean sweep of the kitchen and your skill with a pot and spoon."

I may have smirked with self-satisfaction. "I'm glad to hear that."

"On my way out, I discovered the shrine to the Virgin and took a moment to say a prayer for my own mother. She's suffering and will soon join our dear Lord in heaven." He sounded composed, considering the topic.

I crossed myself. "May a choir of angels carry her forth."

He also crossed himself. "Amen."

Now I felt thoroughly foolish for suspecting the monk of any ill-doing. He was too young to have taken Elder's life, Friar Laurence trusted him, and Barnadine had sponsored him at the prince's table. What more credentials did he need?

"Is your mother in your family home?"

"Indeed, no. She is a holy sister in the convent attached to mine."

I blinked. It was not unusual for a widow to join a convent rather than remarry, yet his tone indicated there was more to the story.

Indeed, I was right; for without self-consciousness, he confessed. "Unwed, she joined the convent on her sixteenth birthday and there gave birth to me. My future was thus predestined by her past."

"Your father?"

"Unknown. Nor did I know her for all my boyhood. It was

not until I took my vows and began serious work among the poor and ailing that I met her, Sister Agnese." No wonder he'd been composed; he had known her for a short time, and without the relationship of mother and son.

"Sister Agnese also cares for the poor and ailing?"

"The convent sponsors lodging for those whose lives are ending and have no resources or kin to care for them. A most holy sister, she worked tirelessly to ease their passages into the next life, and so the disease that eats the flesh took her as well. Now Sister Agnese fills a bed in the lodging and there lifts everyone's spirit with her cheerful acceptance of her impending passage."

I don't know that I'd have the strength and the resignation to cheerfully accept what sounded like a painful passing. "When she met you, did she know you?"

"She did, although she said nothing, but eventually I comprehended why we were allowed time together." He walked with his hands folded and a smile on his handsome face.

The spicy perfume of dianthus recalled me to my duty, and I stopped before the bed of flowers so pink they glowed in the setting sun. "Do you have your eating knife?" It was a question asked while fully recognizing that if my foolish suspicions were not, in fact, foolish, I could be putting my life at risk.

Without hesitation, he pulled the small sharp implement from the scabbard on his belt and handed it to me, hilt first. I thanked him, and with well-hidden relief, I knelt beside the flowers and cut them with one sweep. I placed them in my basket and handed his knife back to him. "Thank you. I'm collecting fragrances to place under Princess Ursula's nose. In that way, I hope to rouse her."

"I'd heard she was attacked." He looked grave.

"By a cruel and brutal villain." As I spoke, I watched closely and thought I saw a shadow of trouble cross his face.

"Is there no improvement?" At my sad denial, he said, "I

pray that God's will be done; her return to health or her quiet passing to the heavenly gates."

I lifted the flowers. "I prefer to draw her back to life."

"An excellent strategy! Scent can be invigorating." Energy infused him. He strode into the herb garden, blade in his grip. As he moved from plant to plant, he said, "Mint to rouse the mind, oregano to remind her of God's gift of food, lemon balm to brew, garlic chives . . . ah, the savory glory! And lavender to bring serenity, should she embrace her passage into paradise."

He used his knife swiftly, skillfully—clearly, a healer at home in an herbal garden. In only a few moments, I had a basketful of fragrances for Nonna Ursula, and felt more at ease with Friar Camillo. He was a nice young man, caring and generous, and again I assured myself he had no ulterior motive for his appearance in the palace garden, except, perhaps, to ingratiate himself to the podestà and his intended bride. That was not such a terrible ambition for a young monk, was it?

Nevertheless, I escorted him to the door onto the street and raised my hand to him, urging him to go in peace . . . but to please go. (I didn't say that last part.) When the door had shut behind him, I moved in all speed to Nonna Ursula's chambers.

I found the kitchen boy gone, Old Maria sitting beside the fire looking more like a withered crone every time I saw her, Tommaso standing at attention, and Princess Isabella and Cal scraping the last of the soup from the pot.

Cal looked better for his sleep, rested and less pained. He dressed himself once again in the dark and brooding prince of Verona uniform; the warrior had returned. Really, it was too bad; I enjoyed having him at a disadvantage.

"Rosie, you tossed our cook from the house!" Princess Isabella said in awe and gratitude.

"To be precise, Marcellus tossed him." I grinned in remembrance of that well-placed fist.

Cal looked up with interest. "Did he?"

"I merely had to duck away from the flying body fluids," I assured him. I placed the basket on the table and reached for him; I thought to examine his shoulder.

With a single cool glance, he refused my support.

I halted, feeling an ego-deflating sense of rejection.

His gaze slid to his sister, to Old Maria, to Tommaso, all watching with interest.

I understood. He'd allowed me to care for him when he needed it, but now we returned to the proper-in-public, hands-off betrothal, and maybe some sneak-around, hair-sniffing behavior in private. I wished that he'd make up his mind! I asked, "How is the shoulder?"

He placed his hand on the joint and carefully exercised it. "It will do."

Gentle reader, can you say, "Damned with faint praise"?

He added, "You're a good apprentice apothecary." Considering what scoffing had ensued when he had discovered me working in Friar Laurence's shop, this was a vast improvement.

"Yes, I am." I saw no reason for false modesty.

Cal placed his spoon in his now-empty bowl and pushed it away. He folded his hands on the table and stared at me. "How was your walk in the garden with Friar Camillo?"

Princess Isabella sat straight up, and her eyes sparkled. "Friar Camillo was here? I wished I'd seen him. He's so handsome!"

Cal and I both looked at her.

"And charming!" she added artlessly.

We turned back to each other.

"I went out to find you and saw you rushing after him into the herb garden," Cal said.

"You . . . watched me? Us?"

"I didn't watch you. I simply didn't know he was visiting you."

"He wasn't visiting me. Friar Laurence sent him to see what

more he could do for your soldiers and he stopped at the shrine to pray." I could have told Cal about my mission in the garden, but I didn't appreciate the sensation of being interrogated. "Friar Camillo was helpful to me."

"He's very at ease for a young man." Cal seemed to find that offensive.

"From what he told me of his early life, I think he has reason to behave in a manner that increases his social value."

"You discussed his early life?"

"He was praying for his mother, who is ill." Cal couldn't be jealous of a monk, could he? "Is there a *problem* with Friar Camillo?"

"Not that I know of."

"Because Barnadine introduced him into the house and Friar Laurence likes him."

"True." Cal was agreeing with me, but he was clearly not backing down from . . . whatever stupid stance he had taken.

"If you think I should be warned about him, please say so." I was still miffed . . . or miffed again.

Princess Isabella watched us lob conversation, challenging back and forth, as if we were in a ball court. "Cal, are you jealous because I said Friar Camillo is handsome and charming? You're not handsome, but you can be charming." In a doubtful tone, she added, "Sometimes."

I confess, I smiled in mockery. "When you put yourself out."

Chapter 36

Cal drew himself up into his most haughty, princely posture. "If I seek insults, I don't need to converse with you two. I could sit with my men."

Princess Isabella giggled.

Slightly mollified, I laughed out loud. "Your men's complaints will have diminished significantly due to their full bellies."

"That brings us to my second issue. You replaced my cook with the Montagues' discarded cook? Who is lame and skinny?" For a man who enjoyed a good meal, thanks to me, Cal behaved like an ungrateful churl.

Mollified vanished in a flash of rage and indignation. "She is not lame! She has been early stricken by a challenge that faces the elderly."

"She's skinny," he said. "I want a cook who'll sample the food, not leave for me to discover it's been poisoned."

I wound up for a snap-his-head-off rebuff, such as I'd given Marcellus. "Mark my words, with her expertise, she'll make your kitchens the envy of Verona. Ladies will try to bribe her to work for them, but she works only for the Montagues. Only for us!" I pointed my thumb at my chest. "For that you can be thankful. And—"

"*Va bene,*" he said.

I almost staggered when he knocked the prop of indignation out from under me. "What?"

"If you're going to make such a sweeping change in the household, I want to know you're passionate about it. The soup is good, too. Thank you."

Rather than pick up the iron pot and swing it at his head, I took my basket, swirled around, and hurried to Nonna Ursula's side.

As I did, I heard Princess Isabella chide, "Cal, the prince of Verona should never be so ungracious. Rosie has saved us from starvation, and our new cook has already transformed our kitchen into a place of glorious appetite."

I didn't bother to hide my grin. The child had found her woman's voice.

I could see that the onset of night made Nonna sink more heavily toward the moment when life must end, and hurriedly I plucked up the mint and crushed it under her nose. Speaking loudly and slowly, I said, "Smell that, Nonna Ursula. Of what does that remind you? For me, it's hot summers in the garden, the sun on my hair, picking mint to be crushed with wild strawberries. And this."

She didn't stir. Nothing on her face changed.

I replaced the mint with crushed oregano. "Imagine this stuffed beneath the skin of a roast goose, flavoring the drippings."

"Rosie . . ." Cal put a gentle hand on my shoulder. "She can't hear you. Even when she was alive, she couldn't hear well, and now—"

I shook him off. "Lemon balm, so bright and lively brewed in a tea with chamomile!" For a moment, I thought I saw a flicker of life cross her face. But before I was sure, it had disappeared and she was as she'd been before. Probably my own desperate desire made me see things that weren't there.

I waved a dried frond of lavender under her nose.

Princess Isabella had joined us. "She hates lavender. Violently. She says it smells like mildew and it makes her sneeze."

"Really?" Hm. In my mind, I could see Nonna Ursula rousing to bat it out of my hand.

She didn't, and I heard Cal and Princess Isabella sigh in disappointment. They, too, had begun to cherish a gleam of hope that this would bring her back to us.

When I crushed the garlic chives, we all blinked at the pungent odor, but nothing moved on Nonna Ursula's face. Finally I indicated the pink flowers to Cal. "These hold sentiment for her. Hold them under her nose and talk to her in your man-voice. Remind her of her past when youth and love were sweet, and her lord husband brought her flowers like this to warm her heart."

Cal looked at the flowers, then looked at me. In his gaze, I saw something deep and dark, brooding and sure. Gathering the blossoms, he cupped them in his palms and leaned close to Nonna Ursula's ear; with the scent wafting over us all, he spoke of his grandfather, how much he'd adored his wife and family, his strength in his role as podestà, and how before his death, he taught his son and grandson about ruling justly.

Princess Isabella sniffled and rubbed her nose on her sleeve.

The first I knew of Elder's presence was a manly sob and his deep voice saying, "God bless the boy, I'm glad he remembers my father so fondly."

Cal finished by saying, "Nonna, I'm going to put these flowers in a bowl by your bedside where all night you can smell them, and when the morning comes and the sun rises, you'll rise, too. You'll look on the world made new, and we'll be glad of your return."

I teared up, too, and hugged Princess Isabella, and Cal hugged us both together, and if Elder had had breath, he would have honked his nose like one of Hannibal's elephants.

From the corridor, we heard a clatter of blades and the thump of many booted feet.

In a brotherly gesture, Cal kissed first Princess Isabella, then me, on the forehead. "I'm off! Say a prayer for our victorious delivery of Verona from this turbulence. Watch over Nonna Ursula." He fixed his stern gaze on me. "For this night at least, stay safe within the palace."

"Of course." Although I wished mightily to go home to see my family and sleep in my own bed.

Reaching into his black shirt, from the place over his heart, he brought forth a slightly crushed, dark red rose. He pressed his lips to the opening bud, and taking my hand, he placed it in my fingers and lifted it to my lips. "Drink in the scent. It is you. Watch the blossom unfold. It is my heart triumphant." He spoke in a quiet voice meant to reach only him and me.

He was loud, though, for even Tommaso sighed at the romance.

"*Rosa centifolia,* the rose of many petals, came from the Far East, from Cathay, and grows in dirt laced with well-rotted manure. The intoxicating fragrance and glorious color attracts bees and butterflies, while the thorns keep browsing animals away." He clutched the stem into my hands in reassurance. "I removed all thorns from this rose for you."

"Thanks." *Well-rotted manure?*

In his deep, soft, passionate tone, Cal continued. "God in His power created the thorns to protect the rose's beauty, and perhaps in the far-distant reaches of the desert and dunes, to catch sand that blows in the wind and thus bring shelter to its roots. Birds feast on the fruit of the rose, and when at long last I've made you my wife, I'll brew you a posset of flavorful rose hips, a drink so healthful and rich your hair will gleam, your fingernails will grow strong, and you'll stalk like a wild beast across the world of men."

"Our cats are like that when we feed them venison liver." I winced at my own ineptitude.

He smiled, apparently undeterred. "All will fear you, and you'll easily give birth to our healthy sons and daughters."

Just like our cats produce too many kittens. But no. What could a woman say to such a declaration of, um, horticulture? "As they fear you tonight, Prince Escalus, my betrothed, as you plunge into battle to save our fair Verona." That sounded so silly I felt as if I had fumbled the ball.

Cal crushed me to him in a swift embrace, pressed his cheek against my forehead, then departed, leaving me holding a battered rose and feeling quizzically unbalanced.

Princess Isabella lamented. "For a moment there, he was doing so well."

Chapter 37

Actually, on the rare occasion, Cal had been quite accomplished with poetry. Not that I'm a poet, but all my life I'd been surrounded by iambic pentameter and romantic declarations and glorious moments that required lovers to go somewhere . . . to the spangled heavens, to faraway imagined white-sand beaches, to the cliffs of romance towering over the clawing tidal waves of tragedy . . .

I really hate poetry. All that unnecessary traveling.

I suppose, when push came to shove, I preferred the earthy monologues of horticulture and Cal—passionate Cal who loved his exotic plants and found all the details about them enticing, never noticed my lack of true rose culture enthusiasm. He was, perhaps, unable to conceive of a person who wouldn't look upon the petals of a rose and think of its origins, its preferred growing medium, and what use to make of its parts.

I smiled at the dark red rose.

"Hey! You! Lady Rosaline!" Old Maria beckoned me over, and for the first time it seemed she viewed me with respect. "I didn't believe it before, but you're smarter than hair."

"Thank you." *I guess.*

She gestured toward the basket of flowers and herbs. "The words weren't working, and neither was all that rubbing her, but the odors—when I smell something I knew long ago, for a moment, I'm back in that place. Maybe she will be, too; be back here with us." She stared at her mistress. "Although not yet."

"No, not yet. Maria, after the séance, did you remove the skull bag from the table by the fire?"

She barely glanced in that direction. "I keep this room tidy. I don't let clutter overcome the order, which at all times Princess Ursula demands."

"Um." I nodded, looked around, and realized what truly was missing, what had been missing for the last few hours. "Where's Pasqueta?"

"Gone," Old Maria said in relish.

"Gone? As in—"

"Disappeared. I told the princess that girl was useless. I told her I could handle the caring for her without help. But nooo." Old Maria snatched up her sewing, put in a couple of stitches, put it down. "She had to bring in a strong young skirt who wanted dancing and laughter and men. I told her so. I told the princess, and now I'm proved right."

Doubtfully I said, "Pasqueta didn't seem that young."

Old Maria's glare could have withered ripe apples on the tree. "Her tenure here is nothing compared to the time I've spent with Princess Ursula."

I backtracked. I needed Old Maria cooperative, not angry with me. "Right away, I recognized your loyalty. I said to myself, 'That is a loyal woman.' Yet I wonder, why would Pasqueta leave a position serving the dowager princess of Verona, with its privileges and the respect accorded her, and the knowledge that every woman in Verona would gladly take her place? She didn't seem stupid to me. Did she seem so to you?"

"Not stupid at all." In a tone scornful and disbelieving, she asked, "Why do you suppose she left to *make a posset*?"

"Because Princess Ursula asked her?"

"She left the princess alone to be attacked."

"She wasn't alone. You were with her."

"Princess Ursula and I are of an age and with like losses." She flipped her hand at her ear. "I didn't wake, because I didn't hear. Come, girl! You know what I'm saying. You must have thought it yourself. Pasqueta's timing was too convenient. It takes a man to tear the bars off the wall outside, but it takes a woman with the morals of Eden's snake to open the window from the inside to ease his way."

Yes, I had thought it. Despite Pasqueta's assurances, I knew it was a possibility. But she'd seemed too truly frightened of the ghost, and then of a man inside the palace. "Yet . . . her disappearance is disturbing, too. Violence has been done to beloved Princess Ursula. Is someone methodically removing the protections set around her?"

Old Maria squinted at me, reluctant to abandon her pet theory, but recognizing if I was right, she was in the line of sight. As she thought, her eyes moved craftily from side to side. Abruptly she pulled her silver sewing needle from the cushion and pointed it around like a blade, thrusting it at Tommaso, at Cal's guard, at me. "I'll defend the dowager princess to my death!"

I leaned back. "Thank you. I'm proud to know I can depend on you."

"Rosie!" Nurse stood in the entrance, dagger out, clad in a dark cloak.

I jumped to my feet, glad to see her; and at the same time, I knew at once I was needed. "Is it Mamma?"

"The babe is coming early." Nurse leaned against the doorframe to catch her breath. "The midwife is nowhere to be found. Friar Laurence is busy with the wounded."

I ran to get her a goblet of watered wine, and as she drank, I said, "And . . . ?" Because why couldn't Nurse handle this birth? She had experience, more than I did.

"Lady Juliet fears I know not what, but she sent for you. She begs for you. You must come at once!"

Chapter 38

Princess Isabella begged me to remain, and then commanded in her most royal tone that I not go, but to no avail. I kissed her forehead, looked into her pleading blue eyes, and said, "My mother needs me."

I sent Tommaso to find Dion and bring him to me.

Princess Isabella demanded I take a sedan chair, but Cal had left a skeleton crew of men to guard the palace. "I will not leave you unguarded," I told her.

"What about Nonna Ursula?" She gestured at the poor, thin, broken woman on the bed. "Will you leave her unguarded?"

Dion strode in, looking pale, but strong and impatient, a man forced from the field of battle and unhappy about it. "You summoned me, my lady?"

"I must go to Casa Montague," I told him.

"No." Like his friends, like his master, he seemed to think he'd had the final word.

"My mother, Lady Juliet, is in child labor with no one to help her."

He opened his mouth to refuse again, but he'd met my mother, and like every other man in the world, he worshipped her. Something shifted in his countenance. "I'll accompany you."

"Tommaso will accompany me. You must stay to guard Nonna Ursula."

Dion looked between me and Tommaso, me and Nonna Ursula, me and Nurse.

"Dion, did you not think you were injured for a reason? That, by God's foresight, you have been remanded in the palace, while your fellows go into battle, so you can remain to watch over your young princess and your old?"

Princess Isabella wrung her hands. "Cal will kill me if I let you go unprotected. You *must* take the sedan chair."

"To travel in the prince's chair would make her a broader target to the flagellants," Dion said.

I nodded agreement and showed Princess Isabella the knife up my sleeve and the stiletto at my ankle, and indicated Tommaso, who stood, arms crossed over his chest, looking grim, solid, and dependable—ready to protect me. "Last night, we could hear the shouts, see the flames, smell the smoke. Tonight we hear nothing, see nothing, smell nothing. The *disciplinati* have been cowed by the efforts of Prince Escalus and his men."

Nurse assured her, "I slipped through the streets prepared for trouble"—she touched the glittering tip of her knife—"but all was quiet." Her voice dropped on the last word, as if she feared challenging that *quiet*.

"We must hurry." I allowed Nurse to toss my dark cloak around my shoulders. She tied it close to my throat and pulled the hood around my head. "The longer we tarry, the later it grows, and my dear mamma needs me. If Cal should return, tell him. He'll understand." For he had lost his own dear mother, Princess Eleanor, not long after the birth of Princess Isabella.

I smiled at the young woman, so beautiful and untouched, and kissed her cheeks. I promised her and Dion that I'd keep my knife in hand; and in return, Dion promised he would die before the two princesses were harmed.

Old Maria was on her feet, needle in hand.

As I led the way toward the door, Elder appeared beside me. "You can't stop me," I said.

"I'm not trying to," Nurse said in irritation.

"It's the ghost of Prince Escalus the elder," I told her.

Both Nurse and Tommaso dropped back.

"Of course, I can't stop you." Elder looked less corporeal than the first time I'd seen him, thinner, more transparent. "You're a stubborn, foolish woman who imagines you can face any challenge in the pursuit of right."

I didn't stop walking. "My mother needs me."

"I know. I need you, too, but Lady Juliet holds first claim to your heart." He sighed as if he had breath. "As she should. I can hear what's happening out there. Be careful, Rosie. Be strong. Be smart."

"You sound like my father."

"Who else would I sound like? I'm your father-in-law!"

"Not yet."

"Exactly." He seemed to think he'd made his point. "You do no good to your mother or me or Cal if you die on the way."

"Exactly," I said back to him. "I'll be careful, strong, and smart, and come back to find your killer." The guards opened the door for me. "We're getting close, you know. Nonna Ursula was almost killed. Pasqueta has disappeared. Someone is desperate to hide the truth, and we will find him."

"Soon. It must be soon." His voice sounded wispy and sad.

"There's no choice, Elder." I halted. "While I'm gone, sit with Nonna Ursula. Continue to talk to her."

"How can I do that? It's ridiculous. I'm not *here* unless *you* are."

"She's your mother. Try!" I threw him a kiss, then willingly left the safety of the palace. I heard the great door thunk firmly behind me and the rattle of locks. Following Tommaso, and with Nurse taking up the rear, I now sallied forth onto Verona's streets, seemingly undaunted.

Yet in my heart, I remembered and feared the man with the hellfire eyes.

Chapter 39

Verona was not Verona tonight. Shutters covered the windows of each house. I clutched my cape closer, kept my head down, tried to move swiftly and softly, to silence the rustle of my skirts and the sound of my breathing.

All was hushed, as if a snowstorm blanketed the city. The wind held its breath, and a sliver of moon had risen above the horizon.

Our citizens remained behind locked doors. Not even in the distance could I hear the clash of battle. No fires lit the skies, and if the *disciplinati* were out, they'd changed their strategy.

What was it Cal had said? *I fear the group includes local warriors and soldiers without a war. They're too good at battle.*

And: *They believe a messiah walks among them, a man called Baal, a false god who tells them when they take down our beloved Verona, they will own its women and riches, and he will be their lord that favors them.*

I imagined Cal and his men, hunting while the flagellants waited in ambush, their whips, knives, and poles in hand.

In the empty market square, boards had been nailed across the shop doors, and we skittered along the perimeter, ducking from shadow to shadow. When we entered the narrow streets on the other side, I sighed in relief. Not too much farther to go and I would be with Mamma and help her deliver the babe who arrived before his time. Please, our dear Lord in heaven, and with the help of His Blessed Mother, Mary, my own mamma would be delivered safely of the child . . .

Perhaps I should never have allowed my focus to waver, to worry about Mamma rather than our surroundings, for as we turned onto a dark, narrow street, not far from Casa Montague, a man's voice broke the silence. "There she is! The prince's whore!"

The crowd surged out of doorways and darkness, stampeding toward us like wild wolves, sharp teeth bared. To remain unseen, the flagellants had discarded their costumes, but not their poles and whips, and before we had done more than turn to run, they overwhelmed us in a swirling wind of howls and fury.

Tommaso laid about him with his knives and fists, and more than one flagellant screamed in pain, but they took him down to the ground, fighting and kicking.

Nurse and I stood, back-to-back, using our blades to widen a circle around us. We circled and moved toward the end of the street, but the sullen crowd grew larger.

Silence fell, a silence of anticipation. They enjoyed our fear, tasting it with flickering tongues and black-toothed grins, and they waited for . . . something.

Or someone.

When he stepped forward, I knew him. Baal. The man with the flame-red eyes. He reached for me—

Nurse slashed his outstretched arm with her knife. "Get away from her, demon!"

In the stunned silence, he held up his wound and stared as if he couldn't believe the gash in his skin and the gush of blood. With the howl of a lead wolf, he let loose the pack.

Nurse disappeared as Tommaso had done, fighting, bringing them down with her knife, her fists, her kicks, and yet inevitably overwhelmed by the sheer numbers.

When the pack would have closed on me, the demon waved them away.

In the feeble moonlight, I could see his outline. He looked like a man: hair, teeth, eyes (two), nose and mouth (one of each). He stood a little taller than me, broad at the shoulder, ignoring the blood that dripped from his arm. A mercenary and, perhaps, a minor nobleman from the south, for when he spoke, his crisp diction sounded clean to my ears.

His words did not. "I've never raped a prince's whore before."

I didn't wait. I whirled and used my knife to carve a path through the remnants of the crowd, fighting to get to the crossroads. What would I find there? No safety, yet it seemed in my panic to be a station of safety, a place where I could escape.

The flagellants could have overwhelmed me, but the demon shouted orders and they fell back on his command.

No matter. I stood no chance.

He put his hand on my shoulder.

I whirled and slashed.

He knocked the blade out of my hand. "The prince's whore!" He laughed in triumph, and he grabbed my arm.

"I'm not a whore!" I shouted. "I am Prince Escalus's betrothed!"

"Even better. The prince's virgin. Your fall will signal the fall of Verona, and you will burn. On the flames we set here, we'll build a new world for *us*!"

A cheer went up—and a light flashed on.

Every head turned to look into the sky. On the top of the tower, a flame burned white and pure.

Lysander's lamp.

Chapter 40

The flagellants gasped.

On the far side of the tower, another light ignited, bright against the dark, dark sky.

A murmur ran through the crowd. "The light of God!"

The demon dragged me forward, his chin uplifted, his gaze transfixed. "No, it's not. It's a trick!"

I saw an opening and I shouted, "God's eye is seeing your rebellious sins!"

Without even looking, the demon slapped me hard enough to make me fall to the ground. But I couldn't fall, for he still held my arm, held me up; and when my knees buckled, he kicked me in the belly.

I couldn't scream because I couldn't breathe. My face bled, my gut heaved, and when I vomited, he tossed me aside.

Cretin! I reached under my skirt, pulled the stiletto from the scabbard at my ankle, and stabbed him in the thigh.

He could scream. As he collapsed, he did.

I jerked the stiletto free and rolled away. I had to *hide*. Hide in among the forest of men's legs, still and taut.

"You . . . woman!" Baal's voice writhed with amazement, contempt . . . and pain.

"The messiah has collapsed!" one man shouted.

Another yelled, "God is judging us!"

"He's a false messiah!" the first voice shouted.

I landed close to one man's pole planted in the street while he stared upward, and yanked it from his lax grasp. Glancing behind me, I saw the demon crawling toward me, holding his thigh as if to contain the bleeding. His eyes were fixed on me; they flamed in manic fury. I had hurt him. He had been invincible, a messiah worshipped by men, and a mere woman had bloodied him at last.

As the third light ignited, murmurs swept the mob with wonder and increasing panic.

I feared Baal. I feared his mission, his vengeance. I feared the crowd would stampede and grind me into the stones of the street. I urged myself to get up and run. Run! Only then did I stand a chance.

I couldn't stand. The kick to my gut had broken me. Every movement sent bile into my throat, and I choked on each breath.

I glanced back again.

Baal was gaining on me, his grim face intent on winning. Not rape, not anymore.

Murder. He would kill me, if it was the last thing he did.

I had no choice. I swung the pole, scattering the men around me with blows to their shins, and having cleared the battlefield, I turned to face Baal, stiletto in one hand, pole in the other.

He sneered. He had retrieved the knife he'd knocked out of my hand and he held it pointed at my heart. Pitching his voice to reach my ears, and the ears of his men, he said, "Justice. You'll die on your own blade."

I probably would, for that blade was long and so was his reach. But Papà had taught me to fight, and I would make Baal suffer, too.

He rose off the ground, a demon invincible once more.

Behind him, a man politely cleared his throat. "Excuse me? God's wrath will ignite one more light. Then you will die."

Baal swung around to face... Lysander, dressed in his rough work clothes.

Lysander shouted, "You will all die!" In a theatric flourish, he pointed his finger to the tower.

The fourth lamp blazed.

With his sword, Lysander stabbed Baal through the heart.

Chapter 41

Lysander leaped over Baal's body to pick me up.

Barely in time, for the stampede I had feared ensued.

With one arm around me, and one arm and sword cutting a path through the fleeing *disciplinati,* he helped me into the safety of a doorway. He propped me up against the cool wall and stood guard in front of me, his bloodied blade at the ready.

Men ran in every direction, fought to get away, got knocked over and trampled. The shrieks of the downed men pierced the night, and a man's voice shouted, "The prince is coming! Prince Escalus is here!"

"If the prince is here, he has no chance to restore order among this chaos." Lysander spoke in a low voice, pitched to reach my ears.

"Agreed. The riot must run its course." I wrapped my arm around my aching belly. "Do you see Nurse and Tommaso?"

"Not a sign. With luck, they are sheltering in a doorway, too."

I so hoped and prayed. "How did you find me?"

"After I instructed one of the guards on how to light the lamps, I came down to ask if you wished to watch. You were gone. Princess Isabella was in tears, that mean-eyed Old Maria lamented your inevitable demise, Dion stood guard over Princess Ursula—"

"Who hasn't roused?"

"No, she has not. *Il mio cuore è spezzato.*" He put his hand over his broken heart, for he'd already declared his admiration for Princess Ursula. "I questioned Princess Isabella, discovered your companions and destination, and with my sword and knife, I hurried forth to—"

"Rescue me." I began to breathe more easily; the pain in my gut slowly transformed into a deep, raw ache.

"I had hoped not to find you in need of rescue." He returned to scanning the mob. "I had hoped simply to guard you."

More and more of the rioters rushed past: bleeding, limping, crying.

"You arrived at exactly the right moment. Thank you. The way the lamps lit! I've never seen anything like it, and neither had the mob. When that man shouted, 'The light of God!' that was all it took. Scared them all into submission."

"I shouted that."

I gripped his arm. "Lysander, that was inspired!"

"You shouted, too. I heard you."

"Nothing more than a riff off your brilliance." My pain was easing, and I managed a smile. "How did you time the last lamp lighting?"

"I knew how long it took to drag the ladder around, climb it, put the flame to the wick, so I had an idea I could make it work for me. But mostly, it was luck."

I'm a good Catholic girl, and I said, "It was God's mercy."

He crossed himself. "You're on an errand to help Lady Juliet and you must not fall." Suddenly he darted into the last of the men staggering past, and in only a moment, he returned with Nurse.

She, too, was bloodied and limping, but when she saw me, she burst into tears and reached out to embrace me.

Lysander stopped her. "Don't. She was slapped and kicked. She's in pain."

"Ohhh." Nurse's cupped hands hovered close to my face. "My poor baby!"

"And you, Nurse?" I asked. "What has been done to you?"

"I've been thoroughly trampled, but I never lost my knife, and not one of those *canaglia* will forget me, I vow!" Her voice blared in fury.

"Shhh," Lysander hushed her. "There aren't many left, but let's not attract their attention."

Too late. We had attracted attention, for Tommaso bellowed, "Nurse? Have you found them?"

"Here!" she bellowed back.

He cut a swath through the dwindling mob, targeting each flagellant and taking him down with a well-wielded staff and sword. Not the sword he'd started out with, either. As he drew near, it was clear that of all of us, he'd suffered the most damage—and probably had inflicted the most.

He looked us over. "If you need help, say so and I'll carry you, but let us flee now before the flagellants regroup." He lowered his voice. "And before the vultures swoop in." The people who would come to dispatch any of the living and pick over the bodies, he meant.

We pulled up our hoods and huddled in our capes. Tommaso led the way, weapons in hand. Nurse supported me. Lysander followed behind, sword out.

When we passed the body of Baal, Nurse tried to get me to turn my head, but I insisted. I stopped and looked at him.

Not a demon. Not a messiah. Those open, empty eyes stared at the stars, and I saw that he was nothing but a man.

"The Fallen will feast on his liver," Lysander said.

"I hope it doesn't choke them." Tommaso obviously hoped the opposite.

"He's burning in hell." Nurse pronounced his eternal sentence.

"Yes." I turned away. "Hurry. Mamma needs me."

Chapter 42

Even before the footman opened the door, I heard Mamma scream. I pushed Nurse away and, holding my gut, I sprinted up the stairs. Nurse followed and we found Mamma on her back, struggling to produce the babe.

I had attended the last three births, fetched towels and water, murmured support and encouragement. I wasn't Friar Laurence or a midwife, experienced in childbirth, but I'd listened and learned, and I understood if the child would not come, we had to use every advantage our world could give us.

Nurse wet a cloth I thought she'd bathe Mamma's face, but she wiped mine gently, yet the pain reminded me I had been slapped hard enough to cause damage, and I didn't want to frighten my mother. I wiped my hands, too, then grasped my mamma's face in both my hands and turned her to see me. "Mamma. Mamma, we must get you on your knees."

So wrapped was she in the labors of birth, she didn't seem to see me, but keened with the pain that gripped her. "I can't. I can't." Sweat stained her brow and dribbled off her chin.

"You can." I glared at Nurse, who stood bleeding, sobbing, and wringing her apron in her hands. "We'll help you. Come, Mamma, on your knees. Grip the bedpost. Hold on and scream when you need to. Together we'll bring my brother forth!"

I spared a thought to my siblings. I knew they had gathered in the chapel, praying to God for their mother and, as an aside, the baby she would bear. But mostly for Juliet, who held our family together—so kind, so stern, so our mother in every sense.

Nurse and I helped Mamma to her knees and put her hands on the bedpost, and she screamed again as the downward pressure carried the child toward the world of today.

Nurse massaged her belly.

Fluid gushed between her legs.

I saw a head start to emerge and cupped my hands to catch him.

He slid out by the spasms of her belly and the downward motion of the force that led us to earth.

He was perfect. Beautiful. A boy in all his parts. Screaming his indignation at this exposure into the world of man.

I heard my siblings cheering. I wept to hold his tiny form, alive, breathing, happy it had been so easy.

I handed my brother, the son of my house, to Nurse, who held ties and scissors and made swift work of the umbilical cord, then wrapped him and returned him to me.

"Mamma! Mamma! He's here and you're—"

She was still screaming. Mamma was still screaming.

Why? Why? I didn't know enough. I held the babe up to her face. "He's here!"

Papà burst into the room, a projectile of male vigor that melted before her pain and compulsion. "One more," he said to her, and his tone pleaded and cajoled.

What was he talking about?

Then I knew.

No. Not another baby. She was so weak. She couldn't do it.

But Papà knew. Somehow my parents had realized she carried two children. No wonder she delivered early. Now Papà lent her his strength, supported her, held her hands against the bedpost, spoke encouraging words in her ear.

Who was I to declare Lady Juliet Montague could not bring forth another baby from her loins?

Returning my brother to Nurse, I said, "He's tiny. Keep him near the hearth. Keep him warm. There's more to be done."

Nurse held him close to her bosom and hurried to do my command.

Returning to the bed, I bent to our purpose. "Mamma, you bring forth our newest sweetheart. Our bonus baby. You'll push him out and the whole family will rejoice in him, kiss his sweet cheeks, and hold him . . . just hold him. Think how excited Cesario will be to know he has two brothers. Two! He'll be such a good big brother." I was sort of sobbing. Not that I meant to. What good did it do to be so emotional?

Mamma still screamed, the sound thinning as she tired, and I knew I had to go somewhere I hadn't been since the day of my birth. I gathered air into my lungs and, with all compassion and gentleness, slid my hands into the birth canal.

The shriek Mamma gave made me understand that nothing could be gentle enough.

The baby was there, still in his sac, but wrongly placed, butt first. He had to be turned.

I knew how the method worked. I did. But I'd never performed such a service.

None of that mattered. Mamma needed me. The baby needed me. I had to make this birth happen, or mother and child could perish.

Papà stared at me, pleading, his mouth moving without sound. "Please, please, please."

I could feel the weight of my siblings, kneeling in the chapel, begging God to deliver their mother from pain.

I wasn't God. I couldn't deliver her, but I could, perhaps, turn this baby and bring him into the world. As gently as I could, I rotated the baby, urging him, nudging him into the proper position.

How could I ignore Mamma's screams?

Yet . . . how could I not do what must be done?

Papà nodded at me, encouraging me, begging me to help his Juliet.

Everything in her contracted and clamped down on my hands. "Try not to push, Mamma," I begged. "Not yet."

"Breathe," Papà urged her. "Breathe."

I breathed, too, waiting for the contraction to end, then began again. The sac was slippery and sagged as if ready to break, but I begged God to wait until my brother was head down, for that slippery fluid would ease the way. Then—oh, then! Mamma would be delivered of her labor and she could rest. With gentle touches, I urged the babe to bring himself around and out. Maybe I annoyed him. Maybe he'd needed guidance. But suddenly he punched at me and flipped.

I cupped his tiny skull in my palm, then released him and slid my hand down and out. "Push, Mamma! Push!"

The sac broke. The fluid eased his way, and my brother was born.

Twins. Twin boys. I had delivered them both. I heard Mamma laugh. I heard Papà praise her and me. I heard Nurse announce she would cut the cord, and when she shoved me to the side . . . I collapsed.

Chapter 43

Landing on the floor brought me to consciousness, and reminded me of the injuries I'd forgotten in the excitement and the demands of tending to Mamma and the babes. Dimly I heard the tumult of crying infants, men's voices, Mamma's frantic worry, but in my mind, I knew all was well. I surrendered to my body's demands for rest.

I woke in my own room, dawn's first touch of sunlight on the wall, and through half-closed lids took inventory of my body.

My face throbbed. Towels had been stuffed under my nightgown, so I was bleeding and not at the right time of the month. I felt bruises on bruises. But all in all, considering what the previous day had been, I was *fine*.

I'd wakened before dawn to the news that Nonna Ursula had been attacked.

I'd gone to Friar Laurence's shop to prepare a healing poultice and had taken it to the palace.

I'd sat with her all the hours, touching her and talking to her.

I'd comforted and counseled Princess Isabella.

I'd gone up to the tower to find Elder and instead found my One True Love and Fabulous Inventor, Lysander placing lamps on the four upright thrusting corner posts—no penile subtlety there!

He'd given me food, thank God, and showed me his luminary intent.

We'd been discovered by my betrothed, Prince Escalus, during an intimate moment. He hadn't been pleased at our friendly banter, but in my worry about Nonna Ursula, I really hadn't immediately registered the depth of his disquiet.

I'd descended to care for the prince's wounded men, and when that was done, to care for Prince Escalus himself.

In a frenzy of horror at the palace kitchen, I'd gone up and, using Master Disapproving Marcellus for muscle, I'd re-created the food-prep, and with my own hands made a delicious soup to feed the men.

I'd gone to the garden and gathered scents, herbs, and flowers, hoping to guide Nonna Ursula back to life, and suffered a few worrisome moments with Friar Camillo, who had been all that was holy, proper, and helpful.

Returning to Nonna Ursula, I'd discovered Cal and Princess Isabella gobbling the rest of my soup, while Cal criticized me . . . I mean, really, what was wrong with the man? With my scents, I attempted to revive Nonna Ursula.

Unsuccessful and frustrated, I'd more or less promised Cal I wouldn't leave the palace, for he and his men now marched on the *disciplinati,* who were rioting throughout Verona. What kind of idiot would go out on such a night?

This kind of idiot.

I'd spoken with Old Maria and realized Pasqueta had disappeared, but before I could investigate, Nurse had arrived with the news my mother, Lady Juliet, desperately needed me. I arranged protection for Nonna Ursula and Princess Isabella and went into the streets with Tommaso and Nurse and . . . well, you remember what happened then. Certainly, I did, in far too great a detail.

And I had delivered my brothers.

I pressed my hand to my gut and tried to lift myself off the pillows.

A hand slid under my back and helped me, and startled, I turned to face the stern face of Prince Escalus.

I must have been a little woozy still, for I smiled, let him support me, and said, "Greetings." Feeble, but I was alive; he was alive; I was happy.

His stern mouth didn't smile—of course not. He seldom understood how to tilt his lips up at the corners—but his eyes softened. "Let me help you."

Other hands plumped my pillows and he put me on them so gently I was almost not in pain. Almost. I touched his dark-stubbled chin. "You were successful."

"Indeed. Your courage and Lysander's lights dissipated the riot and the only duty for me and my men was to mop up the last of Baal's madmen. The real *disciplinati,* the flagellants, exited the city gates still alight with holy fervor." Holding a cup to my lips, he fed me broth thickened with porridge. "Their leader spoke of the dark angel Baal who joined them on the road, and subverted men to his will. He accepted no blame for bringing Baal into Verona, but assured me that through your intervention, God had taken his justice on the demon."

"In the future, I'd prefer not to intervene in such matters."

"That would be best."

"Nonna Ursula?" He wouldn't be here, would he, if she had passed?

"She stirs." No smile, but he radiated pleasure. "Wakes, drinks, eats, sleeps."

I touched the place over my heart. "Such good news. Does she remember?"

"She doesn't speak."

That was disappointing. "She needs time. It will come." It must! "How's your shoulder?"

He rotated it. "Good. The fighting improved it."

"Of course, it did." I closed my eyes for only a moment, but when I opened them, it was afternoon and Lysander sat where Cal had been, holding a tiny, sleeping infant.

Gentle reader, if you're of the female persuasion, you can probably imagine my thoughts at the sight.

Itty-bitty baby resting asleep on that warm manly chest, utterly trusting and secure. One miniature foot, with its soft, curling toes falling from the blankets, and Lysander fussing, tucking it back in while he pats and rubs and jiggles. Seeing him holding that sweetums, that precious newborn... if I weren't already in love with Lysander, I would be now.

Although... two men in my bedroom, one after another... What had the family given me that I was hallucinating?

Lysander observed me looking at him and the babe. "He's so tiny!" he said in awe.

Maybe not a hallucination. Maybe an apparition, like Elder?

Don't even think it, Rosie. "Another two months in the womb would have been beneficial." I sounded like Friar Laurence, and that wasn't whom I wanted Lysander to think of when he saw me. "What's his name?"

"Adino!" Cesario shouted.

The babe didn't even flinch. Already he was used to the loud and lusty Montague voices.

I looked toward the sound of Cesario's voice.

Ah. That explained the male presence by my bedside. All of my siblings and my papà were crowded into the room, watching me. Lysander and I had sufficient chaperonage.

"Adino means 'adornment,'" Cesario added. He held baby #2 against his shoulder with an older brother's insouciance. "This one's Efron. It means 'doubly blessed.'"

I laughed gently, careful not to hurt myself. "Perfect. May I...?"

Lysander stood and placed Adino beside me in bed. I wrapped

my arms around him. "Look at you," I crooned. Tears seeped from my eyes.

"Rosie, don't you like our babies?" Cesario sounded shocked and concerned.

Imogene bumped him. "She's crying because she's happy."

"That's stupid," Cesario said.

"It's a girl thing," Lysander told him.

"Ah. *Va bene.*" From Imogene, Cesario thought it was stupid. From Lysander, Cesario accepted and gazed at him in wide-eyed hero worship.

I looked to Papà. "Mamma?"

"She's well. Nurse is with her. She grows restless to see you, but the midwife demands she remain in bed."

"I'll go to her tomorrow."

Papà removed Efron from Cesario's grasp and brought him to lie beside his brother. "They sleep better together."

My siblings crowded close.

I touched the babes' wrinkled foreheads, their tiny chins. Every other part of them was swaddled in layers of blankets. "They are perfect?" I asked. "They suckle?"

Papà nodded. "Friar Laurence came at once to christen them, and he said they're miracles. Too small, but they breathe easily and vigorously take the teat."

"Miracles," I agreed. "I don't know how we'll tell one from the other."

"They both look like Grandpapa Montague, and they'll change as they grow." Imogene stroked Efron's head. "This is our winemaker. Adino"—she stroked his head, too—"will be an inventor like Lysander."

"I want to be an inventor like Lysander!" Cesario proclaimed.

"I thought you wanted to be a great swordsman like Papà," Emilia said.

"I'll be a great swordsman inventor! You're jealous because you can't do either, because you're a girl."

Cesario sometimes forgot that Emilia could beat him up, but now she reminded him.

Papà sighed and separated them. "Come on. Kiss Rosie, and then we'll feed the animals."

"What animals, Papà?" Cesario asked.

"You animals," Papà said.

My siblings lined up, youngest to oldest, and kissed me on the forehead. Emilia whispered, "Your black eye is awesome."

Katherina laid her cheek against mine for a long moment. "You scared us so much!"

Lysander was next to the last in line, ahead of Papà; and with Papà watching, he didn't kiss me, but he did cup my cheek. "Your black eye *is* awesome," he said, and lifted Efron from the bed and, hugging him, took him from my room.

Papà kissed me on the forehead and nodded in approval. "Your black eye is the badge of a warrior, as if we needed proof that our eldest daughter has a brave, loving, and true heart." He took Adino and that tiny face screwed up as if to complain about his loss of warmth. "Thank you for coming to your mamma's aid, Rosie, and helping us produce two more blessings. May God reward you for your valor."

I smiled to see him with his son. "Papà, this animal would like to eat, too."

"Your meal is here." Papà moved toward the door and revealed Cal behind him.

Chapter 44

Cal put the tray beside the bed. "Thanks to you, my own sister now calls me Cal."

I tried not to grin, but he sounded so resigned, and I didn't believe that for a minute. Always the man was in the right place at the right time, and always he steered himself there. "Earlier, you were here alone."

"Even then, Emilia remained in the chamber with us and I trembled under her critical gaze." He plumped the pillows and helped me sit up. He handed me a cold, damp, folded cloth. "Here. Put that on your eye."

Ah, the palace ice. I had indeed achieved warrior status. I placed it on my bruised face, and both winced and sighed at the prospect of relief. "Nonna Ursula—has she spoken?"

"Not yet. But as you do, she drinks and eats and life comes back into her countenance."

"That is the best news of all!"

"She's guarded at all times, as is my sister and your sisters here in Casa Montague. Thank you for putting Dion on duty when you left." He didn't reproach me for leaving. He knew and understood duty and love, but he had expressly commanded I not go out, and the trip to Casa Montague had been a disaster almost unto death. Baal of the flame eyes crawling toward me would live on in my nightmares.

Yet I would have gone even if I'd foreseen the events, and he knew it. "Shouldn't you be out patrolling the streets?"

"Verona is Verona once more. Loud, busy, angry about the *disciplinati* rioters and the damage they caused, blaming me and my men for failing them. Except the people who for a price repair damage—they're busy and pleasant."

I enjoyed his wry humor, knowing he gladly shouldered his burden as both podestà and scapegoat of Verona. "Why do you do it?"

"For my people. For my place." He placed a hand over his heart and gestured out my window: "For this city on the silver river.

"These red stones glowing in the sun.

"This arena, ancient monument among the ancients.

"This fortress built by Roman gods against the barbarians of the north.

"These men and women who live happily within these ancient walls.

"This blessed plot, this earth, this realm, this home . . . this Verona."

All right, I confess, it was poetry, yet I tingled at that magnificent summing up of the beauty that was my city-state.

Prosaically, he handed me a mug. "Here."

I drank, then peered into it in disgust. It was the same broth and porridge he'd given me earlier. "That's it?"

"Bread? Cheese?" he suggested.

"Fruit! Honey!" I demanded, and handed back the mug.

Under my eager gaze, he cut an apple into quarters, dipped it in golden honey, and, with his cupped hand under it, put it to my lips. As I bit eagerly into it, he utilized his handsome eyes and his deep, poetry-reciting voice. " 'Stay me with flagons, comfort me with apples: for I *am* sick of love.' "

Cheating! He'd gone biblical on me, quoting a verse from the Song of Solomon 2. I chewed and swallowed, plucked the apple from his hand, and said, "Yes, I'd like bread and cheese, too, please. And wine, since you offer it."

He poured a deep red wine, from a flagon, of course, and put it to my lips.

I didn't like being suckered twice, so I placed the cloth-wrapped ice on the bed—yes, I knew I was going to have a damp spot on the blankets—then took the goblet and sipped.

He wasn't smiling. He never smiled. But he radiated a manly glee at feeding me and offering wine and making me as aware of him as I would be of a generous lover. In so many words, I wanted to tell him I got the message and to knock it off, but sometimes (frequently) that didn't work out for me. In his hands, my plainspokenness tended to rebound in unforeseen ways. In other words, I was not a chess player, and he was, able to predict my movements far ahead of me and counter them in the way he considered most advantageous for him.

"Why did my father let you remain in my bedchamber?" I suppose I should have asked that first thing.

"I vowed to be on my best behavior." Plucking the cup from my fingers, he turned it to drink from the exact place my lips had rested.

It didn't take Eros to figure out *that* symbolism. "This is your best behavior?"

"Not at all. One day soon, I'll pleasure you with my best behavior. But for today, I keep the implication of my promise to your father." Cal carved a trencher out of the crusty bread, cut a slice of blue-veined cheese, finished slicing the apple, and placed them all in the bread bowl with a pool of honey. "I merely provide you with food and drink. Call it reciprocity for preparing soup to hearten the bodies and souls of me, my sister, and my men."

"Don't forget about restoring the palace kitchens to respectability," I advised him.

He settled into the chair and cut himself a slice of cheese

and broke off a stem of grapes, and ate them as if the last few days in battle had been generous in violence, but sparse with food. "If you're right and the attack on Nonna Ursula came from within the palace, and was generated by my father's killer—"

Maybe I was bruised and exhausted, but the way he changed subjects made my head whip around in a complete circle.

"—who do you suspect?" he finished.

Marcellus. But why? Because he didn't like me and I didn't like him? I knew better than to propose that solution. Shaking my head, I ate an apple quarter dipped in honey and followed it with a bite of cheese.

At my non-answer, Cal asked, "Who does my father suspect killed him?"

"He saw a man in a mask. He fought and then your father was dead. He doesn't know."

"Mayhap the spirit is lying. Mayhap the spirit is not my father, but one come to deceive us." Cal made a good point.

But—"He looks like the portrait."

"Can a ghost change its appearance?"

"I don't know the rules, Cal. No one does, not even your father, or so he says, but I assure you, no ghost who wanted to gull me would be so rude and arrogant. If he drew breath, I would smother him."

"Sounds like my father," Cal grudgingly agreed.

Randomly I ripped off a chunk of bread and waved it as I took a stab at a suspect's name. "Barnadine."

"He saved my father's life time and again on the battlefield. Nonna Ursula has treasured him all the years since. Why murder Papà and years later attack my grandmother?" He drank the wine again, then handed me the cup.

"Whoever attacked Nonna Ursula believes that in her séance and with the assistance of Yorick's skull, she discovered the assassin's treachery." I drank, making sure I did not drink from the same place that his lips had touched.

He observed, and if anything, my skittishness pleased him. Men. Who understands them?

"If she discovered the truth, the killer would already be hanging from a gibbet on the bridge over the Adige River." He slipped a grape between my lips.

What was I supposed to do? Spit it out? I chewed and swallowed, and responded sensibly. "Your grandmother, being who she is, very well might not tell you what she knows. She might intend to handle it herself, and everyone in the palace and beyond realizes that."

I could see Cal struggle with that truth. "Damn," he said. "Yes, Barnadine would grasp that better than anyone, but he has no reason—"

"Unless he killed your father."

"He fought valiantly with my father and valiantly at my side these last days, while in great pain. Does he really seem to you to be an assassin?"

"If so, I can't discern why."

Cal inclined his head in agreement. "Who else?"

Simultaneously we heard a crunching sound and turned to see Cesario standing behind Cal, looking curiously at us both and eating a crust of bread. Seeing that we'd noticed him, he came around to stand between us, forehead puckered, and examine us.

"Cesario, what are you doing?" Cal asked.

"Papà said I should come in here and see if you were canoodling with Rosie."

Chapter 45

Cal had wanted me for my family.

I hoped we were everything he'd ever imagined.

"I can't tell," Cesario said. "Are you? Canoodling?"

Cal sighed mightily. "I vowed I would not, and I am not."

"Papà says he's made vows like that, but then Mamma smiles at him and he forgets all but the pleasure of her company." Cesario grinned. "Then we have babies!"

"In the future, if we could have them one at a time, that would be less strenuous," I suggested.

"Papà said twins are efficient."

Cal put his head down to hide his . . . yes, his grin.

In exasperation, I replied, "Having an entire litter at one time would be even more efficient, but Papà is not the one who has to give birth!"

Katherina stuck her head in the door. "Cesario, Mamma says you are to come out of Rosie's bedchamber."

Cesario said, "Papà said I was to stay and watch for canoodling."

Katherina shot Cal and me a glance that showed a fair amount of curiosity. "Who are you going to listen to, Papà or Mamma?"

Cesario dragged his feet toward the door. Katherina put her arm around his shoulder and they disappeared toward Mamma's bedchamber.

Cal and I ate more, slowing as we filled, and gathered our thoughts, then returned to our investigation.

"Could my father's assassination and the attack on Nonna Ursula be separate?" he proposed. "Not linked?"

I contemplated a slice of apple and that idea. "With the timing, it seems unlikely. But perhaps . . . if that is the case, what about Nonna Ursula's serving maids? Could one of them have been bribed to leave the room and allow an intruder to steal what he wished, and Nonna caught the intruder in the act?"

"Which maid? Old Maria, who has been with Nonna forever, or Pasqueta, who owes her everything?"

"Pasqueta has disappeared. Or at least, when I left last night, Old Maria assumed she'd gone off for some frivolous reason."

"Well. Old Maria." His tone indicated dismissal. "She's been jealous of Pasqueta since the day Nonna Ursula brought her to the palace."

"I spoke with Pasqueta when we were sitting by Nonna Ursula's bedside because I thought her timing—leaving Nonna Ursula alone in time for the attack—did seem suspicious. She confessed to seeing Elder's ghost leaving the chamber."

Cal leaned forward. "What did she do?"

"She fled in fear."

"I thought if you weren't in the palace, my father's ghost couldn't materialize."

"True. Pasqueta was already spooked because of the séance and my sightings, so she saw a *man* in a cape and assumed it was the ghost."

Imogene popped in. "Prince Escalus, Mamma wants to know if you're staying for the meal."

"I wouldn't be so unkind as to task your mother with preparing food."

"Usually, Rosie handles that, but I suppose she's going to duck out now." Imogene grinned at me. "In case you haven't heard, nice black eye, Rosie."

I made an ancient, discreet, rude gesture involving one finger.

Katherina joined Imogene. "I've taken over the kitchen. Honestly, Rosie has everyone so well trained, all I have to do is agree to the menus. She's going to make you a good wife."

I put the ice on my face again, closed my eyes, and tapped the rude gesture at my giggling sisters.

"She will, in all respects." Cal held up the bread and cheese. "Nevertheless, this is sufficient for my meal. When I'm done with my discussion here, I'll walk back to the palace and converse with my men, and I have faith that our new cook will graciously provide me with whatever sustenance I need tonight." To Katherina, Imogene, and me, he said, "I'll send word back about Nonna Ursula. I hope to find her awake and speaking."

The girls sobered and I opened my eyes. "Thank you," we said.

"Are you going now?" Imogene asked.

"Not quite yet. Your sister and I are discussing a puzzle."

"Do you need help?" Imogene liked puzzles.

"An emotional puzzle," I said.

"No!" Imogene skittered out as if chased by a swarm of hornets.

"We'll leave you two alone." Katherina drifted out after Imogene.

"For how long?" Cal mused. He had the game figured out now.

"We'd best hurry before Emilia arrives." I put the ice on the bed again, then trailed my finger through the honey and licked it, tasting the sweet, golden, thick gift of summer, and giving it its due in pleasure. I contemplated our next suspect. "Duke Yago? Do you consider your uncle on the list of suspects?"

Cal took an unusually long time to reply.

When I glanced up, his gaze was intent on my finger and my mouth, his lids were half shut over his eyes, his lips were slightly open, and he breathed as though he had run too far and too fast.

Chapter 46

Gentle reader, you and everyone in Verona is well informed about the pristine state of my virginity, and while I made the gesture in all innocence, and because there is something so tactile about honey on the tongue . . . I was perfectly able to comprehend what intimacy Cal had envisioned.

Placing my hands on my trencher, I kept them absolutely still and said again, "Your uncle, Duke Yago?"

Cal leaped up and walked toward the door onto my balcony and threw it open to the fresh air. "Uncle Yago! Yes. I do suspect him. But he seems so . . . limp."

I had no answer to that unfortunate choice of words.

Silence reigned.

Many minutes later, Cal turned to face me, but couldn't seem to quite *look* at me. "Yet Yago's my father's brother! How is it possible that he should be so . . . ineffective? Is he really ill, or is it all an act to disguise his treachery?"

"Has anyone examined this supposed wound of his?"

"Not that I know." He cautiously glanced toward me.

Still, I didn't move. "I wonder if he could be coaxed to show it to Friar Laurence."

Cal seemed to be returning to a less excitable state. "Not if it doesn't exist!"

Point taken. "Lugrezia?"

He dismissed her. "She's a woman."

"And you're a fool."

He looked fully into my face.

Yes, I was a fool, too, for what I'd done, and for my continued provocation, regardless how inadvertent, but I plowed ahead with my argument. "She's ambitious, wife to a man whom you previously described as, er, limp. The events that have unfolded—Elder's assassination, the attack on Nonna Ursula, the flash fire of violence and unrest in the city—all could have been hired and encouraged by one person. One woman. She is a power, is she not?" I asked.

"A power, yes. Unlikeable, but a power."

"And never a suspect, because she's a woman."

He nodded, conceding the point.

"Friar Camillo," I suggested.

Cal sputtered, which was kind of fun. "A monk? What reason have you for such an accusation?"

I had to think how to phrase my answer. "He is young, handsome, clean, helpful."

"Suspicious!" Ah. Under the right provocation, Cal *could* indulge in sarcasm.

"He plucked the herbs and flowers for Nonna Ursula. He assisted Friar Laurence with your wounded. He prayed at the shrine of the Blessed Virgin in your garden. My point is, Friar Laurence is always hurrying to and fro, busy at all times. Friar Camillo seems to linger in the palace."

Cal moved to allow the light full into my chamber. "It's not unknown for a monk to be lazy."

"Or for a monk to have ambitions to be valuable to the prince's household."

"Or for a monk to fall in love with a beautiful woman," Cal observed darkly.

"Me?" I touched my bruised face. "If that's the case, he's in for a rude surprise."

Cal paced toward me. "A temporary bruise and, so I tell all my warriors, a badge of courage."

I liked knowing Cal considered me warrior enough to claim a badge of courage. I smiled at him. "Actually, men have fallen in love with me before. I recognize the symptoms."

"Do you?" He had that neutral tone in his voice again.

"Yes, and I don't believe that's the case with Friar Camillo." Articulating my uneasiness made this sound foolish to me. "I'm not really sure why he bothers me, Friar Laurence has borne witness to his excellence, yet . . . Friar Camillo feels artificial. As if he's hiding something."

"I hold great respect for your instincts—"

A comfort to a woman who knew what it was to have her words undervalued based on her gender.

"—and I'll suggest to my head footman that Friar Camillo be kept in sight while visiting the palace." His suggestion satisfied me and apparently him, for he moved on. "You haven't mentioned the other possibility for, at least, the attack on Nonna Ursula. My bodyguards."

From previous conversations and a knowledge of the Acquasasso rebellion, I know the history of his men. "Holofernes is your longtime friend and suffered with you in the dungeon."

"That's true." Slowly he returned to my bedside and seated himself, drank the whole goblet of wine, filled it again, and held it out for me to take.

I reached for it and realized my fingers trembled from the impact of his voice, his presence, his seduction. I didn't attempt to drink, but held the goblet close to my chest. "As with you, the Acquasasso tortured Holofernes, and you said when your father released you, you were fourteen and still overcome by pain and darkness. I assume Holofernes was the same age and had like issues, therefore would be unlikely to be able to act as your father's assassin."

"The Acquasasso demanded a ransom from Holofernes's family. They had little to give, and other sons to take his place, so he had been treated with more cruelty than me."

"He has a handsome and joyous spirit."

"I still sometimes see the dark of the dungeon. He sees only the light that came after, and is joyful."

I had suspected that truth about Cal; that he felt comfortable enough to share that glimpse of himself caused my trembling to ease, and I felt as if I could once again breathe easily.

Cal continued, "No, it's not possible for Holofernes to have killed my father. The following year, Dion came to me from my wife's family, a cousin to her, and a young but skilled warrior. He was in the nature of a gift and not in place for the assassination. Which leaves us Marcellus."

I sipped the wine and handed it back to him, and ate some of the bread crust with cheese—I wasn't going anywhere near sexual apples or sticky, sweet honey—and when it was clear that Cal waited for my words, I said, "Some months ago, you told me that the very day Elder released you from the dungeon, Marcellus appeared in Verona with the sworn intent of serving the house of Leonardi. Your father recognized his fighting skills, and the need to have protection for you, who was not yet recovered, and hired him."

"Now Marcellus commands my guard and the respect of all."

"So you have said. Yet he was in place. He could have murdered your father, and now attacked Nonna Ursula."

In an unspoken admission that yes, Marcellus was in place for Elder's assassination, Cal said, "He was fighting at my side during the attack on Nonna Ursula."

"You had him within view at all times? Because he could have obtained the tools and the accomplice to tear the grate off the wall outside her room, while he, within, slinked through the corridors and battered an old woman almost to the door of heaven."

"The combat with the flagellants was all around us." A concession that Marcellus had fought apart from him.

"If I understand correctly, the battle was pointed tooth and naked claw, a mêlée of unmatched viciousness."

"You don't like Marcellus."

I tried to decide how to explain the relationship between Marcellus and me, and finally settled on the time-honored "He started it."

Cal gave his brief burst of laughter, and the unused sound of it made me want to laugh, too. But the food and wine had begun to work its magic, my gut ached and my face hurt, and I grew weary.

Cal took the trencher out of my hands and placed it on the tray. "I would trust Marcellus with my life, and more important, with my sister's life, my grandmother's life, and your life." He leaned over me as if to kiss me.

I couldn't quite decide how to handle this. Say no? Say yes? Say nothing and let him do what he would, knowing my family was nearby?

But his face passed my face, and he picked up the icy cloth and placed it on my swollen cheek. "Now I go and leave you to sleep, and when you wake, your family will be around you, sunshine will beam through the windows, and Nonna Ursula will be awake to tell us who our villain is."

"I do so pray."

He eased a pillow out from underneath my shoulders, leaned close—

I heard giggling, and the chant I'd heard so many times about my sisters as I arranged their marriages: "Cal and Rosie, sitting in a tree, *k-i-ss-i-n-g.*"

I wanted to throw something at my darling siblings.

Cal gave a dry chuckle and straightened up. "Emilia and Cesario, I leave your sister in your capable hands. *Adio,* Rosie, and let our palms do what lips do. They pray." He offered the flat of his hand to me, and I pressed my palm against his.

A nice twist on Romeo and Juliet's meeting.

Cal walked past my family and into the corridor. He met Lysander, put a hand on his shoulder, then spoke earnestly to him. He gestured up, holding an imaginary lamp. Lysander nodded to him, then to me, and they walked away together.

Oh, good. They were bonding over lamps.

I glared at the two smirking children peering in my door . . . no, the four smirking children, and Papà holding the babies, and I halfway raised up on my elbows. "When I can stand, I'm going to make you all sorry!"

With wild shrieks, the children fled down the corridor.

I laughed. *Little snots.*

Papà lingered in the doorway, a big snot holding two potential little snots. "Mamma sends her love, and wishes she could come to you, but she needs more time."

"I know, Papà. Kiss her and give her my love. I'll be better tomorrow. I'll come to her tomorrow." My smiling lips straightened and became a determined line, and I held up one finger—not *that* finger—in defiance. "Then I'll go to the palace and I will find the one who has brought this trouble on us all. I will end this terror, if it's the last thing I do."

The babies' tiny faces screwed up and they began to wail.

"Rosaline, have I not taught you better than that?" In a rare fury, Papà advanced on me.

I cringed. "Sorry, Papà!"

"Are you *trying* to turn this into a Greek tragedy?"

"No, Papà."

To dispel the evil eye, he spit lightly on my head, then for good measure on the babies' heads, and walked out muttering, "Challenge the Fates... Used to think she was the brightest of my children... No more!"

I used the blanket to wipe the spit out of my hair, and took a moment to contemplate my biggest fault: my inability to keep my mouth shut.

Some things never change.

Chapter 47

I didn't understand how I, who had gone through so much less than childbirth, could stand before my mamma as she cradled her two new sons and still feel a nagging ache in my gut and a consciousness about my very black, black eye.

"Unless the fever takes her, a woman recovers from childbirth," she assured me. "To have my oldest daughter deliver these two wonderful boys, it's an omen from God that they are blessed, and you are blessed, and our family, so happy within the realm of glorious Verona, shall be blessed forever and ever. Amen."

"Amen." I kissed her and the babes, and held them tight. I felt her hand caress my braid, and keep my head against her chest as if I were once more her infant.

"You will be careful." It was a command, not a request.

"Mamma, I'm always careful."

"You're always impetuous, Rosaline. You fling yourself at life, imagining you are right and end battered and bruised." She caressed my still-swollen cheek and lifted my face to look into her eyes. "You may be always right, but let you not be dead right. You must always be smart, too. Be strong. Think ahead. Marry, have children, live as the heart of your family, and always, always come back home to us."

"I will, Mamma," I vowed. "I go now to the palace and I'll dig my way through the trash and the lies to the truth."

"Be wise. Your new brothers need you. We all need you." She touched my sleeve. "In your manner and your dress, you are a princess."

"Thank you." With Katherina's help, I had dressed carefully today. I wanted to reveal no more weakness than my bruised face. I wanted to be the brave, strong princess-to-be.

Well, no. That wasn't what I wanted. I wanted to be with Lysander, my One True Love, but I well knew how to face a future not of my choosing. That was now my life.

I kissed them all, first Mamma, then Adino, then Efron. Turning from the huddle on the bed, I kissed Papà, then each of my siblings, told them I loved them (knowing how uncertain life can be, speaking aloud of love had become a tradition in our household). I hugged Nurse and in a whisper commanded she care for Mamma and send for the midwife and me in case of fever or any abnormality.

I stepped out the door; the warm autumn day smelled fresh with a breeze that carried away the stench of violence. I boarded the waiting sedan chair for the palace and, with Tommaso running beside, I was carried through Verona's shouting, odiferous, homey streets to the palace. Knowing Nonna Ursula showed signs of life gave me reason to endure the jostling.

At my approach, the great palace doors opened, Tommaso helped me out, and I entered to . . . no fanfare. Not that I expected ecstatic greeting, but the palace atmosphere—gloomy, tense, and foreboding—contrasted with the vivid, recovering life in Verona.

A footman joined me and murmured, "Early this morning, Prince Escalus went out to walk Verona's streets. We await his return."

I thanked him and turned toward Nonna Ursula's suite, Tommaso on my heels.

Along the great walk, a line of soldiers waited to go into the room Friar Laurence had set up as an examination chamber. I glanced inside; Friar Camillo handed a bag of herbs to Biasio, while Friar Laurence counseled him on how to use them. As far as I could see, tired, grim-faced guards stood about or leaned against walls, suspiciously silent.

Too tired to speak? Or had Nonna Ursula taken a turn for the worse? My sudden suspicion sent me hurrying toward her rooms. Her dark, empty sitting room was stifling and without air, and my heart beat in protest at my blossoming fear. In the bedchamber, the window was closed, the drapes drawn, the fire lit—and a man's tall, bulky shadow loomed over her bed, his hands reaching for her reclining, immobile figure.

I didn't hesitate. I bolted across the room and tackled him.

With a cry of pain, he fell to the floor.

I followed him down.

From all around, a tumult of voices and cries broke out.

A woman's voice screeched, "That girl is mad!"

Princess Isabella gasped, "Rosie! What are you doing?"

The man convulsed beneath me, gasping and holding his gut, and by the sickening sweet smell, I knew at once who it was. I had landed on Duke Yago's well-clothed and exceptionally padded frame, and at that moment, I knew this whiny man was not faking an illness.

Old Maria threw back the drapes. Light flooded the room.

From the bed, Nonna Ursula cackled.

The noise froze all sound, all motion.

Nonna Ursula leaned on her elbow, thin and drawn, but alert, watching me and Yago. "Well done, Rosie. He leaned close to speak, and his breath is putrid."

I leaped to my feet, relieved she was well; but knowing I had blundered, so rather than rushing to her side, I offered my hand to Duke Yago. "My apologies, Your Grace, I saw only a man's form lurking over Nonna Ursula, and after the attack, I feared the worst. Let me help you rise."

I thought for a moment he was going to slap me. Someone

grabbed the back of my skirts and pulled me away from him, and as I stumbled backward, Lugrezia dropped to her knees beside her husband and hissed at him. "Stop making a display. Get up, get up, I tell you!" Grabbing his arm, she forcibly pulled him to his feet.

I wanted to stop her; I had recognized by his spasms of pain and his trembling gasps that I had hurt him. Something was truly wrong with this man.

But he regained his footing and his dignity, dusted at his clothing as if I'd merely insulted him, and in a voice a little higher than I remembered, he sniped, "You are a romp of a girl who doesn't deserve the honors my nephew has bestowed on you! You . . . you . . . virago!"

I placed my hand on my heart and curtsied. "My apologies, once again, Your Grace."

"He's fine," Nonna Ursula scoffed. "A little slip of a girl like you could hardly harm a duke of Verona. Isn't that right, Yago?"

He glared at her, but said, "Aye, Mamma. Now I should go and leave you to those whose breath is fresh and young. Come, Lugrezia."

They swept from the room in a rush of rich clothes, injured dignity, and that lingering stench.

I followed them, summoned Friar Laurence as I walked past his examination chamber, and not far away in the great walk, we found Duke Yago collapsed against the wall, holding his gut and moaning.

A humble monk he might be, but Friar Laurence could exert a powerful presence and he did so now. Taking Yago's arm, he walked with him to the next room and shut the door in my face.

I turned to Lugrezia. "What's wrong with Duke Yago?"

"He told everyone what happened, but he complains so much, no one listens." Her face twisted in scorn. "After the

Acquasasso defeat, he was celebrating and villains set upon him. He fought them off, but one stabbed him in the belly."

I pressed a hand to my own aching gut.

"—a minor wound, only. Long, but not deep—enough to draw blood. Not even he thought it serious, for he pranced about so satisfied with his own manly performance with a sword. He lamented the safety of the streets, but turmoil still ruled. Then Escalus was assassinated. Yago had to decide whether to seize the reins . . . and he did not."

"Out of loyalty to Prince Escalus the younger," I suggested.

She turned on me in an outraged rustle of skirts. "Out of cowardice! He wanted the riches, the power, but with Verona still the prey of scavengers, thieves, and mercenaries, and Escalus murdered, he was afraid. I told him I would be there to watch his back, and no one would touch Duke Yago of the house of Leonardi, but he wouldn't hear of it. I had power within my grasp"—she squeezed her fingers into a fist—"and it slipped away, and all that's filled the years since has been fine clothing and excellent food and bad sex with a man who complains that having an erection hurts to the tip of his manhood."

TMI! TMI!

"So he's not in much pain." She tittered.

I wanted to bolt back into Nonna Ursula's suite, but thankfully, the door opened and a grave-faced Friar Laurence assisted Duke Yago out of the room.

"Take him home," Friar Laurence told Lugrezia. "Make him comfortable for the time he has left."

She stood stock-still. "I don't understand."

Impatiently Duke Yago said, "I'm dying, Lugrezia. Friar Laurence gives me until the new moon, perhaps less, and you'll be rid of your disappointing husband."

"But I'll be a widow! In mourning! That will not do!"

Friar Laurence, God bless him, looked shocked to his sandaled toes, and taking her by the arm, he marched her toward the entrance, counseling her in his most priestly voice.

"I beg you, Your Grace, forgive me for that wicked assault." I was wretched with guilt.

"I'm already far gone. You hardly made matters worse." Duke Yago smiled wanly. "I wish you luck in your forthcoming marriage. Not that you'll need it. You'll make Cal a good wife and be an excellent princess. May God bless you with long life and many children . . . and now I go to take my farewell of my mother."

"Will you tell her it's the final farewell?"

"She pretends to be psychic, you know. She isn't, but she's a sharp old lady. I suspect she'll know." Yago leaned a hand against the wall and walked sideways like a crab back to Nonna's suite.

With one of those disconcerting pops, Elder appeared at my elbow. "Poor sap! Lugrezia commands him his whole life and now he dies a miserable death. At least he goes on without her."

"I can smell it on him. He's infected all the way to the bone."

We stood together, staring after Yago.

Friar Laurence returned from his consultation with Duchess Lugrezia, shaking his head sadly. He lifted my face to examine it. "Is it painful?"

Aware of the prince's men who had suffered so many worse wounds, I made light of my discomfort. "I come from my mother's childbed. This pain fades by significance."

"Good answer," I heard a soldier say somewhere behind me.

"Are you hurt elsewhere?" Friar Laurence asked quietly.

"A kick." I gestured to my gut. "It aches."

He stroked his chin. "That is more concerning. Let me know, Rosie, if you need a potion."

"I will." I was still spotting, but less and less all the time.

"Now I must go, or Friar Camillo will take my place as the palace apothecary." He chuckled.

"Does he wish for the post?" A question of more than usual interest to me.

Friar Laurence shook his head. "He hasn't the knowledge yet. Like you, he's an apprentice. But he's a good man, brave and upright, and he's learning quickly." He blessed me, then returned to the examination room, having answered again my questions about Friar Camillo.

Marcellus, Holofernes, and Barnadine walked past us. Marcellus and Barnadine scowled. Holofernes called out, "Nice shiner, Montague!"

I waved and said to Elder, "I've never had a black eye. Is commenting on it a ritual?"

"An acknowledgment of your newfound status," Elder confirmed. He examined my face. "You took a solid hit."

"I did." I shuddered. I expected a lecture about going out, because men seemed to receive the same dialogue over and over, no matter which character they played.

Instead Elder said, "I've made a grisly discovery." He sounded almost conversational, as if he feared I'd dissolve into a wet, weeping blob of female sorrow. "Pasqueta's in the herb garden, half-buried under the rosemary hedge, with Yorick's skull atop the mound. Whoever did it was in a rage." Unnecessarily, he added, "She's dead."

Chapter 48

Cal walked into the palace with Dion in time to see me cover my face with my crooked arm and do as Elder feared—I wept. Poor Pasqueta! Wrong place, wrong time. Seen too much and now she paid with the price of bloody death.

Cal hurried to me, enfolded me, lifted my face, and scrutinized me. "You were hurt. You should have stayed in bed."

"It's not that. I'm better. Truly."

"What evil tidings break your womanly heart? Tell me, Rosie."

New tears welling up, I said, "Pasqueta's under the rosemary hedge. Dead."

Shocked, Cal asked, "How did you find her?"

"Your father did." Cal froze, and I saw the remnants of disbelief in his face. "Cal, I haven't been out there, but I don't doubt your father."

Cal nodded stiffly, glanced around as if seeking a glimpse of the ghost who haunted me. "Go to Nonna Ursula. I'll find you there." Turning, he walked toward the herb garden, Dion on his heels.

"At least *you* believe in me." Elder sounded more worried than irritated. "I wish I could talk to him before . . ."

"Before what?"

"There's not much time. Unless something happens, I'll be nothing but a wisp of a frustrated spirit slipping through the palace corridors, unseen and forgotten."

He alarmed me with his prediction. "You said you didn't know what the rules were. You said there was no 'Welcome to the Afterlife Seminar.'"

"I don't *know* anything. I simply feel less"—he waved a hand—"here."

I stepped back and looked at him. I had thought yesterday that he looked more transparent around the edges. "Is there a deadline?" Caught by my own phrasing, I chuckled. "Deadline. An unfortunate choice of words." Yet I couldn't stop laughing, for the recent traumatic events had brought both tears and laughter.

With an indignant huff, Elder popped off.

I started for Nonna Ursula's suite and behind me heard one of the guards say to Tommaso, "I'd heard your mistress was crazy, poor thing. Too bad she's to be our new princess!"

Elder had truly complicated my life.

"Shut your maw," Tommaso said. He followed me into Nonna Ursula's rooms and took up guard position inside the bedroom.

Nonna was sleeping.

Old Maria scowled as I opened the window to let in the air. But she could hardly claim danger, for the outside iron bars had been repaired.

I knelt beside the bed and looked into Nonna's face. Her skull was bandaged, her eyes sunken, bruising crossed her forehead. Even so, what a difference food and wine had made, for her cheeks had blushed faintly with healthy color, and I thanked God for her recovery.

Knowing Pasqueta's fate would hurt her most dreadfully,

and while I had no doubt that Elder spoke true, I resolved to keep it from her as long as possible.

I knelt beside Nonna Ursula and took her hand, and she woke and smiled so sweetly at me. "Rosie, my darling girl." She ran her hand over my head and her smile widened. "Nice eye! Were you running without your bodice?"

I laughed in surprise. All the male comments didn't come close to her humorous suggestion. But then I suppose they didn't dare. "No, Nonna. My bubbies are so firm they don't jiggle."

She laughed in return. "What does the other guy look like?"

I slipped out of banter mode. "He's dead."

She patted my head as if I had been a well-trained dog. "That comforts me to know my future granddaughter can handle herself in a fight."

"I needed help," I confessed.

"Help comes when you're a woman people love."

A good thought, comforting when so much death pressed close to my body and my heart.

Old Maria bustled over, helped Nonna sit up on the pillows, and gave her a steaming cup of something, which made her grimace. "Rosie, I understand you handled the kitchen."

"I did."

"At least the gruel doesn't taste like something died in the cup." She toasted me. "Sadly, it's still gruel." She sighed. "Yago is dying. Did you know?"

"I'm sorry. I shouldn't have tackled him."

Nonna Ursula chuckled. "He and I laughed about it a bit. If he'd married a woman like you . . . but Lugrezia caught him in her claws and he never had a chance. Poor man. Poor weak man." She mourned him already.

I sat back on my heels. "Your countenance is also more colorful than when I first met you."

Leaning forward, she had a glint in her eye. "I've been waiting for you. I wanted to tell you what happened."

"Tell me who hit you?" I was all eagerness.

She frowned. "No. I don't remember anything about *that*."

"But . . . but that's what we need to know." If she could only recall who had entered her chamber and struck her down, all this mystery would be solved, the constant guards canceled, and fear could be vanquished. "While you were sleeping, did you see Elder?"

"Escalus? My son? Was he here?"

"He was, and furious about the attack on you."

As if saying his name was an invitation, Elder popped in. He placed himself close to her head, leaned close, and said, "That night she was attacked, she remembers being awake, and angry."

As before, Nonna Ursula seemed to almost hear him. "I remember being awake. So much had happened: the séance, the knowledge that my son spoke to you, that he sought his unknown killer even from beyond the grave. I sent Pasqueta off to make me a posset."

I checked that off in my mind. Pasqueta had told the truth. She'd left on Nonna's orders.

Nonna continued, "I remember being angry that I didn't yet know the answer I sought. After so many years, I should have discerned the villain who had killed my son."

"Nonna, you age, but the weight of your duties grows greater. You helped raise Princess Isabella, comforted Cal in his grief on the deaths of his father, wife, and child, counseled him in his reign."

"And all that time, the poison viper waited to strike us all down." She lowered her voice. "I saw him, savage and cruel, come into my room with iron tools, a man who spent time on the streets."

"Was it the same man who killed me?" Elder asked.

"I don't know if it's the same man who killed my son Escalus, but the villain walks a path of vengeance and destruction. Most of all, he seeks to save himself. He believed that in my séance, I'd discovered his name and he didn't hesitate to strike me down. I did know his face. I did!" She leaned back, straining to view what was in her mind's eye. "If only I could recall that moment of recognition. But those vengeful, angry eyes . . . that's all I can see. That's all."

Chapter 49

Cal walked in, his mouth no more than a thin, flat, grim line. He nodded at me, an acknowledgment that he'd found what I suspected; then he leaned close to Nonna Ursula and kissed her cheeks. "How's my beautiful grandmother?"

"I'm better," she proclaimed, then leaned back from him and searched his face with her gaze. "You seem distracted."

He put his hands on my shoulders. "I must take Rosie from you. We have much to discuss."

Nonna Ursula smirked. "Among the disorder of recent days, you two lovers must grab every opportunity for . . . conversation."

I tried to smile, to act as if romance rather than tragedy directed our actions.

Nonna continued, "Frst, I wanted to tell you what happened while I was unconscious."

Cal and I both ceased our departure and listened intently.

"What I remember is, I was very close to death. So close, I could smell the flowers my husband used to bring me. I heard his voice. As he had done so many times before, he vowed love for me. I opened my eyes. It was night, and dark in the room, and I saw him, alive and smiling, a glowing form. He told me . . . I couldn't come yet. I have more to do." She subsided with a sentimental smile. "I could have given up mint and the rosemary, and if I never smelled lavender again"—she gestured as if pushing it away—"I would be perfectly happy. When you're my age, even sneezing hurts. But you need me, Rosie, to advise you in your role as princess."

"I do, Nonna." I meant it. The simple betrothal had stirred ancient grudges, and already violent death followed.

Cal kissed her cheek. "Relax now, Nonna. Gather your strength. You're safe and well protected."

With that, Nonna fell asleep as suddenly as a babe. Old Maria rushed to cover her with a blanket—honestly, the autumn day was warm, but one could never convince the old woman her mistress needed fresh air, not stifling heat.

Old Maria followed Cal and me, trailed by Tommaso, from the bedchamber and onto the great walk. She darted in front of Cal and stopped him with a curtsy. "My prince, Pasqueta hasn't returned to her duties. I beg you, tell me where she is and what she's done." She sounded scornful and accusatory, but I thought her eyes shifted as if she feared . . . something.

"Look not for her return this day, nor any day ever again. Pasqueta has seen her last sunrise."

Old Maria straightened and stared at Cal, her dark eyes narrowing. "That man! She said she saw the ghost, and she shivered, but I knew better. Stupid girl! He got her, didn't he?"

I glanced at Cal. His gaze had fixed on Old Maria in penetrating interest. I asked, "When did Pasqueta tell *you* about this man?"

"She talked to you first, my future princess. I had to coax her to tell me what she'd told you. I told her no ghost could do to Princess Ursula what he had done, that it was a real man, a man who breathed and lurked in the palace and plotted to kill us all!" Old Maria was so pleased to be proved right.

"Did you mention her fear to anyone?" Cal asked.

"Of course not!" Old Maria's voice grew ever louder, an elderly woman making her point. "When she whimpered, I dragged her out of Princess Ursula's bedchamber and scolded her for her craven fear, while Princess Ursula was locked in battle with death's cold hands. She fled, weeping, and I never saw her again." She saw Tommaso had kept his duty to me and waited, arms crossed, eyes scanning the area for ghosts or men or any danger, and said, "Well! I'd better return and protect Princess Ursula from more mysterious men in cloaks." She swept away, oblivious to the upset she left behind.

"The villain who attacked Nonna Ursula overheard Old Maria talking too loudly to Pasqueta. That's why he knew she'd seen him." I lifted my hands in helpless despair. "You found Pasqueta? Under the rosemary hedge?"

He gave two abrupt nods.

"Elder said the killer had been in a rage."

"Rage or brutality, it's hard to tell the difference. We've sent for a layer out of the dead. She comes anon and will put Pasqueta to rest."

"Was Yorick's skull intact?"

"The skull . . . had been battered by whatever tool struck Pasqueta down, by whatever tool struck Nonna Ursula down. Bloody marks streaked and marred the bone, but the bone didn't break. Yorick triumphed."

I laughed in a like triumph, then noted Cal's grim countenance and sobered. "You believe the man who killed Pasqueta has failed twice now, in his quest to kill Nonna Ursula and to batter Yorick's skull to symbolic crumbs of humanity. You fear that he'll rampage further in frustration and fury."

"In these assaults, I perceive a frenzy of guilt and desperation yielding to nothing but the finality of death. He's loose in the palace, Rosaline, and I fear for us all."

Yes, Cal was right and my laughter had been foolish in the extreme. "Where's the skull?"

"Holofernes took it and is cleaning the dirt and blood from

its bony countenance before bringing it back to Nonna. She doesn't need to know the adventures Yorick has pursued since she used him in her séance." To Tommaso, he said, "Stay with the dowager princess. Lady Rosaline will be safe with me."

Tommaso looked to me; he hadn't yet recovered from my recent encounter with Baal.

Cal got the message. "If that's acceptable to Lady Rosaline?"

"Tommaso, if you would stay with Princess Ursula, it would relieve my mind. As you've probably overheard"—how could he not?—"we fear the man who attacked her came from within the palace, and you, who were not at the palace that night, have become our trusted mainstay. With her return to consciousness, we must be doubly vigilant, and I do vow to you, I'll be careful and wise."

"As my lady commands." Tommaso bowed, took up guard at the doorway of Nonna Ursula's suite, and inspected the passing servants until they were shied away.

Cal offered his arm, and when I placed my fingertips on it, he led me toward a wide-entranced chamber with tall double doors. "He's not happy with his new charge," he said.

"He was sent to guard me," I reminded him.

"Perhaps he fears that in the right circumstances, you're neither careful nor wise."

He ruffled my feathers. "Are you referring to my trip from the palace to Casa Montague?"

"Those were the right circumstances," he agreed.

Point made, and gracefully too. It would behoove me to remember his talents as a diplomat.

He gestured me ahead of him into a lofty room. A desk dominated the space. Doors stood open to Cal's beloved garden, and ever vigilant of my reputation (or at least when it suited him), Cal did not shut the doors into the corridor. Shelves housed scrolls and leather books, paintings of exotic flowers and statues that had been uncovered from Verona's ancient ruins; here was the heart of Cal's palace domain where he performed the podestà's work.

I grieved for Pasqueta and feared what a fetid, writhing worm stew we would find when we uncovered the culprit, yet curiosity drew me to examine the contents of the books and the art Cal chose to enjoy while he worked.

While I wandered, he took the seat behind his desk. "Old Maria made our mission easy. All we have to do is find the man in the cape."

The marble bust of a Roman general, crowned with a laurel leaf wreath, drew me, and I touched the jutting nose, marveling at the cool, smooth stone and the faint traces of paint around the eyes. "Every man wears a cape, as does every woman."

Cal looked at me. Just looked at me.

"Oh. You were being ironic." Being born into the loud, brash, romance-driven family did occasionally obscure the subtleties. "Nonna told Elder and me that although she can't quite remember her attacker, she called him a man of the street."

"'A man of the street'? Who in the palace is a man of the street?"

"Men who fight in the streets and don't die in the mud are men of the streets. Your guards are now men of the streets." I smoothed my hands over the gloriously decorated leather and wood binding on his newest book acquisition. "The man was bent on silencing her and that he didn't bother to conceal his face is telling. It wasn't an attack; it was a murder attempt."

Cal weighed my words and gave them respect. "You're right. I don't like to think of that . . . but yes. Her ruse of a séance succeeded too well and she almost died from it, and may yet if I don't discover who attacked Nonna and killed my father, and if they're the same person."

I wasn't startled to hear Elder say in my ear, "We are back where we started."

Such a discouraging thought! "The answer is there, tantalizing us, waiting for us to see what's right before our noses."

Cal folded his hands on his desk and observed me with a cool gaze. "Are you talking to me or my father?"

I half smiled at him. "Yes."

From the door, one of the footmen cleared his throat. "Prince Escalus, Lady Pulissena of the house of Acquasasso has arrived and requires attendance."

Chapter 50

As if my head was mounted on a spring, it snapped toward Cal. "Lady Pulissena? The unofficial leader of the Acquasasso revolt?"

"Here? Now? How?" Elder sounded equally gobsmacked.

Cal looked first guilty, then exasperated. "Her timing stinks like the canals of Venice at low tide. At the beginning of summer, she scripted a letter of a pleading nature, begging she be allowed to return to Verona to live out her days in the city she loves. I investigated her circumstances. She lives with her husband's niece and is barely tolerated. Of course, she was ever a sharp-tongued woman, and among the gossips, it was believed that her husband obeyed as she directed the insurrection." He waggled his head indicating he didn't quite believe that. "A female as military strategist? It seems doubtful."

"From the stories my parents tell about her, if she had been in charge, the Acquasassos would now rule Verona."

"Formidable woman," Elder agreed, "but hampered by her husband and stepson."

Cal inclined his head. "That also I remember. In my youth, whenever we met, Lady Pulissena frightened me into princely behavior. And we met often, for at one time, she and Nonna Ursula were close, good friends."

"Ah. That explains Nonna Ursula's particular bitterness toward her." I studied him; he looked almost sheepish. "You granted her petition to return."

"I did. Her petition for her and a few members of her household. The other Acquasassos can remain in the fetid air of the swamp and there rot."

That answered my question; I had wondered if Cal failed to remember the miseries of the last revolt. "It seems unlikely insurrection could be roused by the presence of one old woman."

"More than that, I've long wanted to speak to Lady Pulissena about my father's assassination. Who among them gave the directive?"

"That's my boy!" Elder said with satisfaction.

Ah. It wasn't merely kindness that moved Cal to compassion. "What if it was her?"

"Let me first make the inquiry." He came around the desk and offered his hand. "Come with me to greet Lady Pulissena."

"Let me greet her and bring her to you," I urged him. "I give her honor, and by requiring her to join you, give you consequence."

He thought, and nodded. "Be vigilant."

"As you direct, my prince." I was tired of being vigilant everywhere I went, but when the other choice was death, I could be reasonable.

Elder drifted along as I walked briskly to the outer doors of the palace and onto the great steps.

Skinny, bent, and warped in every joint, Lady Pulissena required two men in Acquasasso livery and a wooden step to get her out of the sedan chair, and more than once, she staggered and grunted in pain. She'd once been a woman of average height, but everything had shrunk from her stooped shoulders to her tiny feet.

"The years have not been kind to her." Elder sounded shocked as her two men had to almost carry her up the steps to me.

I offered my hand—she barely came to my shoulder. "Lady Pulissena, I'm Lady Rosaline Montague. The podestà sent me to greet you."

She peered up at me, black eyes wide and lashless; then in a voice like crushed gravel, she said, "You're the girl my nieces are laughing about."

She was too old and tiny to push down the stairs, so I said, "Yes, Lady Pulissena."

"I told them you caught yourself a prince. That shut them up." Pleased with herself, she smacked her wrinkled lips.

Now I was glad I hadn't pushed her down the steps. Discipline had its own reward, I reminded myself.

"I suppose he's enamored of you, too," she said.

"In his way." I said frankly, "He says I have nice *tette*."

"That'll do for a start. He was a good boy. Respectful of me even when he sent my whole family into exile. You'll have a decent-enough marriage."

"Yes, Lady Pulissena."

"I suppose that's not enough for you, though, daughter of Romeo and Juliet. You want love and passion and all that romantic nonsense."

"My parents are very happy."

"Still?" She managed to sound scandalized. "*Merda*, how long has it been?"

"Almost twenty-one years."

"That's hardly fair that one couple should have so much pleasure in each other, when most women have to settle for a stupid old man with ambitions above his station and a worthless stepson from his first marriage who dragged me down and left me alone in exile."

"Well. That was plain enough," Elder observed. "Never a

blissful union, but much disintegrated by Bastiano's rebellion, I suspected."

I offered her my arm. "Your men can wait out here." Because I wasn't inviting unvetted strangers into the palace. "I'll escort you to Prince Escalus, podestà of Verona."

"I know what his title is." She was testy, but she took my arm and we slowly, very slowly, made our way into the palazzo. As we walked, she asked, "Are the rumors true? That Ursula is dead?"

"She was attacked, but not killed." That was something else about which Cal could inquire.

"Stop!" she commanded. We did, and Lady Pulissena put her hand over her heart as her chest hurt.

Callously Elder said, "Don't let her die. Not yet! She's got information we need."

"Cal!" I shouted down the corridor. "We need you!"

"No!" Lady Pulissena snapped. "No, I'm fine. I simply thought . . ."

Cal appeared in the great walk and hurried toward us.

She watched him approach. "That's Callie? Prince Escalus? He comes when you call. You've trained him well."

I could snap as well as she could. "I haven't trained him at all."

"Yet he comes." Her gaze slid between him and me. "All the gossip is true. You didn't want this match. You want the rich boy from Venice."

"The handsome, intelligent man from Venice." I may not have been as soft-spoken as I should have been, for I took it ill she thought me so avaricious.

Cal seemed not to notice, but Elder did. "Defensive, are we?"

"Lady Pulissena, welcome home." Cal gave her his arm. "Come, we'll find you a seat."

"I want to see Ursula."

Cal cast me a surprised glance.

I shook my head, denying knowledge of this.

"I heard she was dead." As if to loosen it, Lady Pulissena tugged at the velvet over her chest. "I thought I'd missed my chance to . . . pass some time with her."

"Each hour finds her much convalesced," I assured her. "You can wait until you've had a chance to recover from your journey."

"Whoever struck her in the first place might strike again." Lady Pulissena's querulous voice grew sharp with fear.

Cal was patient. "Nonna Ursula is guarded every moment."

"She's old. She could die. I'm old. I could die. We've got no time left." She was crumpling, yet on a mission. "Take me to her."

"She always did know what she wanted," Elder told me.

Lady Pulissena had Cal's arm, and I gave her mine, and slowly we walked with her toward Nonna Ursula's room. I looked over her bent gray head at Cal, and we exchanged dubious glances, both halfway sure we were about to witness an old-lady brawl—and it wasn't going to be pretty.

Chapter 51

Lady Pulissena sized up Nonna Ursula with a single glance. She took in the cloudy eyes, the hearing horn, the heavy cane leaning against the table by the bed. She also noted the bump on her forehead and the black-and-purple bruising that extended down the side of her face into her nose, and the way she rested against the pillows, pain puckering the skin of her forehead. In aching pity, Lady Pulissena said, "Ursula..."

Nonna Ursula stared, looking through the shadows in her room toward Lady Pulissena. She must have recognized the voice, and disdained the pity, for she pointed her shaking finger; and without hesitation, she charged into the fray. "Pulissena! You ordered the murder of my son!"

"Way to tell her, Mamma!" Elder enthused, and settled down to enjoy the show.

Immediately Lady Pulissena fired back a bolt. "He killed my husband and I was left a widow in exile. Your son deserved to die!"

"Your husband tried to seize power from the house of Leonardi. *He* deserved to die."

Old Maria sat beside the fire, staring at Lady Pulissena as if she couldn't believe her eyes.

"I told the old goat he couldn't win against Prince Escalus, but he insisted we do it for his son. *His son.*" Lady Pulissena breathed hard and painfully.

Cal helped her toward a comfortable, pillowed chair by the window, but Lady Pulissena pointed toward Old Maria's wooden chair beside the bed. "There," she said. "There. If we're going to fight, I want the old grimalkin to hear me."

"You're loud enough Mephistopheles himself can hear you in hell." Nonna Ursula scowled. "Sit down if you're going to!"

"I'm getting there as fast as I can," Lady Pulissena snapped.

That was the first notice Nonna Ursula had about her one-time friend's worn and crippled joints. She watched as Cal helped Lady Pulissena hobble over, and as he and I lowered her into the seat. "You're a shipwreck!" Nonna Ursula exclaimed.

When Lady Pulissena caught her breath, she agreed. "Battered on the rockbound coast of age."

Nonna Ursula handed me one of the blankets from her bed to wrap around Lady Pulissena's knees. "There's a lot of that going around."

While the two women contemplated each other, I summoned Old Maria and commanded she send to the kitchen for warm spiced wine, bread, fruit, and cheese.

"So . . . about Bastiano's son," Nonna Ursula suggested.

"As soon as Bastiano married me, I saw the boy for what he was. A sneaking little weakling waiting for his father to die, stealing what he couldn't have for free, a jack-a-dandy, no ambition—"

"Iseppo was the greatest swordsman to run away from every fight," Nonna Ursula said.

Lady Pulissena's laugh sounded like a creaky door. "You ever had a way with words, Ursula. Iseppo died fleeing the first battle. One of Escalus's guards had to chase him down to kill him. Bastiano was shocked by the boy's cowardice, if you can believe that." She'd slipped from a confrontational mode to a conversational tone.

Nonna Ursula picked up the pace. "If it was all for his son, why did you take the reins when Bastiano began to slip? I know it was you, Pulissena. You used your knowledge gleaned from our friendship to sabotage Escalus. If it hadn't been for Barnadine's fierce defense, he would never have fought his way free. Then in the end . . . you resorted to drugs and assassins."

"I didn't!"

"Didn't use our friendship? Do you expect me to believe that?"

"No, I did that," Lady Pulissena admitted frankly. "Bastiano, who had begun the fight with all fire, in the death of his son, withered and wept, a pitiful shell of a man. He'd led us to destruction, then faded before the final battle. Yet we were condemned by his actions, and I . . . did envy you your position as mother to the podestà. I did what was needed to win. But—she held up one finger in front of Nonna Ursula's face—"once all the battles were done, and the house of Acquasasso was vanquished, I did not order the assassination of your son. I did not."

Nonna Ursula shoved that finger aside. "Who did?"

Lady Pulissena grinned, her wrinkled lips stretched tight over her teeth. "Your séance didn't uncover the butcher?" Apparently, this woman had experienced at least one of Nonna Ursula's séances.

"You know better," Nonna Ursula said without heat.

Lady Pulissena sat back. "In all the long years since, I've never heard the slightest whisper of the villain's name."

With those white, clouded eyes, Nonna Ursula stared at Lady Pulissena, forcing her to say it all.

"I came here to tell you that. I want to come home. I want to spend my last days in Verona. I want to be with my friends . . . who are left. By my sum and substance, by the divine breath of sweet Jesus, I swear I did not, in any way, wish or work for the death of your son."

I looked at Cal. I believed her. Did he?

He nodded. That answered his question without him ever having to ask.

Nonna Ursula nodded, too. "Even in loss, it seemed unlikely to be you."

"Especially in loss. Let me be practical. If Escalus had lived, I would have humbly pleaded with him to allow me to remain in Verona, and he would have cursed more blasphemously, then deemed me toothless and granted my wish."

"Now you actually are toothless," Nonna Ursula snapped.

"I still have sharp claws," Lady Pulissena snapped back.

A moment of perilous silence.

The two old ladies fell into cackles, and animosity slid away like snow in a spring rain. As they ate and drank, conversation opened, and soon became reminiscence. When they laughed about Nonna Ursula stripping off her clothes, wrapping herself in a sumptuous robe, and flashing her husband as he spoke to the cardinal, Cal loudly announced he was meeting with his men and hurriedly left, hands over his ears.

I stayed and listened, wildly amused at the two wicked women who conclusively proved the elders of Verona were not always as decorous as they proclaimed. When they both suddenly wavered, exhausted and yet unwilling to part, I arranged for a bed for Lady Pulissena in Nonna Ursula's bedchamber and made it understood to Old Maria she should care for them both.

When I left the old ladies, they were both reclining, but still talking. I knew they would soon be asleep.

Tommaso waited at the door, and tried to follow me. "You must remain on guard," I told him.

"I don't like this, my lady. I'm here for you."

"I'm young and strong, and I do swear I'll remain alert."

"You'll go at once to find the prince?"

"I'll seek him," I promised. And I did, but Cal wasn't in his office, and when I inquired of the footman, he escorted me to the large room where the guards lodged. Everyone was there: Marcellus, Holofernes, Dion, Barnadine, Biasio, others whose names I had not yet learned. Cal sat with them and led them in a discussion about the battles with the flagellants, asked for suggestions to improve on their tactics, praised his guards for their bravery, and thanked them for their dedication to Verona. The men spoke with him frankly, yet respectfully, and as I watched, I learned a few things about building brotherhood and seemingly effortless leadership.

Marcellus caught my eye and frowned—with some justification. Clearly, I was intruding on their warrior time, and before Cal could catch a glimpse of me, I backed out of sight.

I glanced into the large interior atrium. The afternoon sun and the lemon trees created dappled shadows on the pavers and tables, and pink petals of a climbing rose fluttered into the fountain and drifted along the surface of the water. For all the exotics Cal so treasured, the center of his house felt like home. For me, it would be a refuge when I needed a break from the duties of wife, princess, and mother to Cal's longed-for hordes of children. I wanted to wander there now, but who knew what killer—man or plant—lurked in the shrubbery?

Then I saw him. Friar Camillo walking slowly along a path, hands clasped and head bent. He was unaware of me, and I'd encountered him without harm before. Friar Laurence trusted him. His presence could act as my guard. No one would batter me to death in the presence of a monk, especially not a strong young monk.

I did venture to the nearest bench and seated myself close enough to Cal's guardroom to let out a full-lunged shriek if threatened. I needed quiet, the scents of good rich earth and growing things. In other words, I needed to think.

These crimes—against Elder, Nonna Ursula, me—had their roots in the past. I had assumed, as did most people, that the Acquasassos, after fomenting revolt and losing, had taken their revenge with Elder's murder before fleeing to Venice. But meeting Lady Pulissena had changed my belief. The years of exile in that damp climate had washed the canker away from the crumpled old woman, and all she had left was an iron spine, a trembling appreciation for Verona . . . and a sense of kinship for Nonna Ursula. After a few moments of testy interchange, the atmosphere between them had changed from ancient enemies to longstanding friends. Lady Pulissena viewed Nonna Ursula's sight and hearing loss with surprise and pity. Nonna Ursula had gripped Lady Pulissena's warped hand a little too hard and elicited a yelp of pain. Then they both knew what had gone before wouldn't matter when the earth soon enclosed them.

No one remembers what I remember . . . except you, Nonna Ursula had said to Lady Pulissena.

The ties of past experiences formed a unique bond, for their losses were no longer perceived in status, power, and fashion, but in lives taken by the passage of time.

As I contemplated the past, so tangled for those ladies, and the future, so unlike anything I'd imagined for myself, I reminded myself that unless I indeed discovered Elder's assassin, I might not have a future, nor Cal, nor our yet-unconceived children.

I heard a step on the gravel and turned in swift alarm, pulling the dagger from my sleeve with a thin hiss.

Friar Camillo backed up and held his hands wide in a compassionate, unthreatening gesture. "No need for that. I swear on the sweet Virgin, I'll not hurt you, valiant lady."

Reluctantly I slid the knife back. "My apologies, brother. It's a fraught time for us all."

"Would you walk?" He gestured along the path.

I truly did need to puzzle this out before someone else was hurt. On the other hand, I couldn't be rude to this pleasant young man. "That would be a pleasure."

As I joined him, he clasped his hands behind his back and strolled. "You're recovered from your attack by the flagellants?"

"I am quite well, thank you."

"I hear your family is to be congratulated on the blessed arrival of two living sons."

"My parents rejoice in their health." I glanced toward Friar Camillo. He wished to walk with me to exchange pleasantries?

He seemed to be paying me only desultory heed. His attention seemed fixed on the room where Cal spoke to the men, and I wondered why. Even with Friar Laurence's assurances, it was obvious Friar Camillo lingered where he wasn't needed and took interest in doings that were none of his business. If I was right and he wished to secure a place for himself in the palace, should he not bend himself to please me, the future princess?

He noted my study and turned to me. The sun fell full on his young face. Idly I thought how unfairly God distributed his gifts. This youth, destined and dedicated to the Church, had strong bones, good teeth, bright skin and eyes. He was in every way handsome and noble, surely the son of some great lord. When he spoke, his voice was educated, full, and rich. "With the recent events, I'm glad to see you so wary and ready with your blade. Does the prince suspect who attacked Princess Ursula?"

"He suspects everyone." Right now, so did I. Cal said he trusted my instincts; right now, they clanged like a bell, and I lagged behind Friar Camillo. The monk inquired of matters that shouldn't concern him.

"Does he consult with you?" Friar Camillo asked. "For I hear he values his future bride for her intelligence, as well as her valor."

I don't discuss the prince, my marital future, or my attributes with an intrusive monk. Which I didn't say, because although Cal and his men remained within reach of my shouts, Friar Camillo was, as I'd observed, young, strong, and no doubt swift. If death was his intention, he could kill me in an instant.

Friar Camillo continued to speak. "Your fame of last spring in defeating an evil foe in defense of your family and yourself has caused much discussion in Verona and beyond."

I backed up, never taking my gaze from him. "I should go back to Princess Ursula. She frets when I'm gone too long, and, of course, I must encourage our men to remain on the ready until her attacker is caught."

He faced me, feet planted, and his wide, pious eyes had changed, had become narrow and shrewd. "You remain much on your guard. I do encourage you in that attitude. Life is brief and precious. Treasure it while it's yours. Now I go to pray." He bowed, turned, and strode toward the shrine to the Virgin Mary.

I recognized a warning and a dismissal, and I fled like a threatened rabbit into the palace.

Chapter 52

In my panic, I entered the wrong open door and found myself at the far end of the great walk. Which didn't matter, I assured myself. Sun shone into the rooms; footmen paced and maids cleaned; Cal had the guard with him; Friar Camillo remained in the garden . . .

I caught my breath.

I needed to get back to the safety of Nonna Ursula's room.

There I'd add Friar Camillo's odd behavior into the jumble of facts in my brain and make some kind of sense of this.

I set out briskly, and as I walked past the door that led to the tower where first I encountered Elder, I heard my name wafting down from the tower. "Lady Rosaline . . ."

"I'm thinking," I snapped.

He called again, more urgently. "Lady Rosaline . . ."

"Give me a moment. I need to concentrate. There's *something* I'm missing."

"Lady Rosaline . . ."

Elder could hear me, I knew he could, but he ever acted the autocrat. No, he couldn't force me to go up to the tower, his ghostly powers didn't extend that far, but he'd proved he could annoy me enough to give me the appearance of madness. I couldn't find his killer if I was confined to a nunnery, and, let's face it, if I was confined, I was a target waiting to be pierced by treachery's swift arrow. Plus, the good sisters would be at risk, and I didn't want that stain on my soul.

Also, perhaps . . . perhaps Elder held within him a knowledge to illume this mystery. I suspected he did, although he didn't know it. I simply had to ask the right questions.

I started the climb up the everlasting stairs. It was warm in here. My sleep every night had been disturbed by horrific dreams of knives, ghosts, devil's masks, and broken bodies. I was disgruntled at being so summarily summoned. Consequently, as I climbed, I panted, and as I climbed higher, I panted harder.

I know what you're thinking. I'm a woman of twenty years in the prime of health. I should be able to climb four flights of stairs without puffing.

Please, gentle reader, let me describe my clothing on this particular day. My fashionable wide skirts were created by petticoats, petticoats, petticoats, and a heavy drape of velvet that draped from beneath my nice *tette* all the way to the floor. Under my heavy velvet bodice, I wore several layers of linen, and the bodice itself was shaped by inserting whalebone into the garment. My silk sleeves, laced on at the shoulder with sturdy gold thread, were covered in pearls and a more delicate gold thread. My headdress, a cap and *trinzale,* the net I wore over my long, thick braid, was knit and braided with beads.

Men thought of women as being dainty and fragile; I'd like to see one of them carry a weight like this up and down and around.

Consequently, by the time I got to the top of the tower, I was angry and aggravated, and I popped through the door and shouted, "Elder! What do you want that can't wait for me to *think*?"

Elder wasn't there.

Then, with that disconcerting little pop, he was. "What are you yelling about?"

"You called me."

"I did not."

My mind untangled that sticky web at exactly the same moment a living man stepped around the corner and said, "Lady Rosaline, you really are quite insane, aren't you?"

Chapter 53

Barnadine. It was a relaxed and smiling Barnadine who stood there—tall, scrawny, and with a gaze so cold and stagnant, I knew it promised death.

"Sadly, no. I'm perfectly aware what's happening here." I didn't like it, but I was aware. "You made yourself sound much like Elder, and you lured me up here to kill me."

"No, he wouldn't do that." Confidently Elder gestured to Barnadine. "He's my bodyguard. He's sworn to protect me and my family. More than once, he's saved my life as I saved his!"

If I hadn't been concentrating on putting the pieces of this tragedy together, when the call wafted down the stairs, I would perhaps have realized the voice was not quite Elder's voice. Rather than obey the call, I would have fled to Cal with my suspicions.

"He saved your life, only to take it," I told Elder in pity, for he so wholeheartedly believed in Barnadine's loyalty that I knew his no-longer-beating heart would break at this betrayal.

"Perhaps it would be better to allow little Callie to wed you and breed half-mad children. That would knock the family out of power nicely." Barnadine's once-fine clothing was still worn and stained with wine, his brown hair still thinning, but his eyes no longer shifted from side to side, nor were they bloodshot with excessive drink, and his jaw might be unshaven, but not even the concrete Roman aqueducts were so unyielding.

Somehow I wasn't surprised that Barnadine was the assassin, for what had niggled at me was a resemblance... but I was unprepared, carrying only the blade Cal had given me, and that at my ankle. "Yes, Cal and I are catapulting toward our wedding, and if you judge me mad, that surely would be a greater..."

Still smiling, Barnadine shook his head.

"Why are you doing this?" I suppose I knew, but I had to ask.

Barnadine lost the smile. "Because you might be slipping down the slope into a frenzy of hell, but as you drop, you're getting too close to the truth of the matter."

"That you killed Prince Escalus the elder? You were the assassin who plunged the knife into his heart?"

Elder leaped to Barnadine's defense once more. "That's impossible! He fought beside me in the rebellion. He rushed ahead of me, ever protecting me from the mightiest thrusts, the most fanatical attacks. Without Barnadine, the Acquasassos would now rule Verona!"

I nodded to show I'd heard, spoke to Barnadine, and gave it my own twist. "You fought beside Prince Escalus, taking him into the heart of every battle, hoping you would lead him to death. To stay true to your vow, you schemed to get Elder killed."

Elder insisted, "No, woman, listen. He—"

Barnadine interrupted the ghost he couldn't hear. "I dashed into the deepest, most dangerous part of every combat, knowing he'd consider that a challenge, and we fought back-to-back, like brothers, defending each other against any foe. Even if I died myself, I'd sworn his blood would stain the earth. But against all odds, we won. We always prevailed. We gained a fearsome reputation, enough that as long as Prince Escalus the elder was alive, no one would ever again challenge the house of Leonardi." His breath now sounded like a death rattle. "I stood alone on the battlefield of victorious honor, knowing I'd succeeded in one vow and failed in the other."

"Why?" Elder was clearly distraught and bewildered.

I had merely suspected the truth. Now I knew, and I paid attention to both men as I said, "Because Friar Camillo is more than a holy brother sponsored by your family. He's your nephew . . . and the son of Prince Escalus the elder."

"That's not true!" Elder said.

He looked so upset, so completely stunned, I addressed him gently. "Elder, Friar Camillo doesn't resemble your firstborn son, Escalus, but he does resemble *you*."

Elder reached up as if to touch his own incorporeal face. "Impossible."

"All Verona knows you don't like Callie. He trapped you." Barnadine eased one step toward me. "You don't want Callie."

I don't want to die, either. I eased one step back. "It took me time and space to see the resemblance. Elder, did you dishonor Barnadine's sister?"

"Never." Elder was insulted and emphatic. "I would never have disgraced Barnadine or his family."

Barnadine eased forward again. "You already suffer melancholy and madness. Why not make this easy for me and fling yourself off the tower?"

Elder watched his former bodyguard, dazed, disheartened, disbelieving. "Dishonoring Barnadine's sister would have been an abuse of princely power, and for such action, I stood to lose all. For to so shame the man who guarded my back would be foolish."

Elder's reasoning was so eminently logical, he gave me pause. I faced Barnadine head-on. "Elder says he didn't do it. Who's your sister?"

Barnadine stopped, and his features twisted in anguish. "She's dead to the world."

"Who *was* your sister?" One must be patient with men's need to never speak of painful events. One must be ready to draw out the story in excruciatingly slow increments.

"The fair Helena, the youngest flower of our family, born almost as an afterthought to my parents' love. She was a blessing, so pretty, so modest, so happy, the maiden who lifted our hearts. I was the oldest, one of two sons, one who would fight as my father had for the house of Leonardi. From Helena's earliest days, I listened and approved as my parents spoke of her destiny. Her purity shone from her like a golden light, and she would take her vows as a bride of Christ." Barnadine's voice grew hoarse with emotion. "Always we knew that. Always."

"Ringing any bells?" I asked Elder.

"No Helenas I recall. No golden light of purity on any—" He stopped speaking so suddenly, I knew he'd remembered . . . something.

Barnadine continued his recollections. "Before Helena entered the convent, she begged for one taste of life."

I watched Elder's revealing expression. "Life?"

"Nothing dishonorable!" Barnadine put his hand over his heart as if to contain its ache. "A party, a whirl of gaiety among the ladies and gentlemen of Verona."

We were getting close to the crux of the matter. "Where did you take her?"

"That day, we celebrated the festival of St. Peter of Verona. In the morning, the people prayed. I prayed. Helena prayed. My family prayed. In the night, revelry filled the streets. All of Verona donned masks to laugh, drink . . . fornicate."

Elder stumbled backward as if to collapse against the wall. Instead he vanished into it, which would have been funny except . . . this was in no way amusing. This was a living tragedy of brother and sister, husband and wife, illicit love, death and murder, past and present, over and over.

Now Elder knew the truth. Now, when it was too late.

Chapter 54

I watched for Elder's return and in the meantime spoke to Barnadine. "A masquerade seems a poor choice. People cover their faces to hide their deeds."

"I know that." Savagely Barnadine turned on me. "Do you think I didn't know that then?"

I could well follow the younger Barnadine's rationale. "But how else could you hide her pure countenance from the prying eyes?"

"You comprehend."

"I do. The podestà roamed the streets that night?"

"Of course. The prince of Verona, Escalus the elder—only he was not old."

"He was in the prime of life—and because of you, he'll never grow old."

"I did what I had to do." His gaze and voice were steady. "As I'll so continue."

Direct his attention back to the story, Rosie. Don't remind him he lured you up here to your death. "Did fair Helena know who he was?" I asked.

"Of course. He was the podestà. I had failed to realize that as he walked the streets of Verona, speaking to the people, she'd watched him from afar. She listened as I spoke of him. I was proud to be his bodyguard, I praised him in glowing terms: his honor, his prowess with a blade, his sadness that his wife couldn't bear another child." Barnadine spoke with contempt. But contempt for whom? Elder or himself?

"You admired him, so she admired him."

"I painted him in all the glowing colors of integrity and valor."

This was tragedy, indeed. For Helena. For Elder. Most of all for Barnadine, who had given in to his sister's pleading and would forever face the truth—his indulgence had created heartbreak for his sister, his family, and even for the vulnerable and unknowing Elder.

"That night, Helena escaped your care?" I was guessing now, backed by the knowledge of what had surely happened.

"In the wildness of music and dancing, she slipped away. I sought her in the crowds, but so many masks! Demons and devils in red and black. Courtesans and ladies in feathers and fake jewels. She didn't want me to find her, but—"

"She found the prince, for she was in love." I glanced toward the wall where Elder had disappeared. Where was he? Why hadn't he returned? Not that he could help me in physical manner, but perhaps he could guide my conversation, help me escape this loathsome trap.

"He destroyed her virtue, ruined her life, shattered my parents' hearts—"

"I know that's all true, but while Elder should never have broken his holy wedding vows, it's a rare man who resists his urges, even when his wife is available for his pleasure, which Eleanor was sadly not."

"I don't give a damn about Prince Escalus and his forced celibacy."

"While I know you hold in contempt any challenge to your plan for vengeance, you said it yourself—by your sister's very presence at a masquerade peopled with demons and courtesans, she misinformed Elder as to her status as a woman." I wished I could reach for my stiletto, but I deemed it more important to keep eye contact, for the manner in which Barnadine observed me told me I faced a warrior, cold with intent, and a wolfman who slavered with the desire to maim and destroy. "He believed her unchaste. If she also sought him out and indicated to him she was willing—"

"Shut. Up. Shut up. Shut up shut up shut up!" Barnadine squeezed his eyes closed, clapped his hands over his ears, bent as if he'd eaten stinking fish left too long in the sun.

Why should I feel sorry for him? He'd lured me up here to kill me.

Yet I did feel compassion for him and for Lady Helena. For a woman in our society, virtue meant respect. Nothing else mattered, as I myself had had amply experienced. For innocent Lady Helena to have actively reached out to a man, a man she knew to be married, and tempted him—that was walking into hellfire. Her fate had been sealed at that moment. Not even Elder had known of the existence of his son, for when Barnadine told of the time and the place, Elder's devastation was clear to see.

The man responsible for Helena's downfall stood before me. I spoke loudly and slowly. "Why are you here now?"

"As bodyguard, I'd given my solemn vow to protect my lord, the podestà of Verona, against all harm. Then he despoiled my sister, and she was with child. A babe born to that innocent maiden fathered by the very man I served. She bore a son in secret and in shame. Somehow I had to balance the scales, and at the same time pay the debt to my family, to my sister—the maiden who shone like the solace of compassion and holiness in our family." Barnadine shook like a man in the throes of a seizure of the heart.

"Elder trusted you completely. Yet you murdered the man who'd fathered Helena's child, the man you'd sworn to protect." Barnadine stepped toward me and I continued, hastily spewing the words at him. "Elder told me someone came into his room. He told me he woke, knew he was drugged, while someone with a mask of red and black crept into his room. An assassin, he said."

"Yes. Yes!" Barnadine pretended to admire me. "How well you surmise what happened."

"I do not surmise. Elder told me. He said he was drugged, couldn't grasp his sword, that it dropped from his fingers."

Barnadine appeared discomfited. "No one knows that. How do you know?"

I wasn't going to explain about Elder again. I intended to pound Barnadine's doubts down to rubble with an assault of facts. "When the assassin climbed onto the bed, Elder pulled a knife from under his pillow, and he swears he bloodied it with a thrust."

Barnadine inhaled, a big gasp of air. "That's true. He did."

"Not you."

"No." He pushed wisps of hair off his sweaty forehead. "No, I gave the task to my brother. Jamy was a gifted warrior, albeit young and unblooded. He begged to do his part to recapture our family's honor, and I thought—"

"After you had drugged Elder, you expected your inexperienced brother to triumph, thus relieving you of the stain of a vow spoken in service. But Elder rallied and—"

Barnadine took up the tale. "And Jamy hesitated. It's one thing to learn the skills of a sword and knife. It's another to thrust a blade into someone's heart and see life fade, never to return."

I nodded. I knew that from my own grim experience, and from Biasio's traumatized reaction.

"Prince Escalus was a good podestà, beloved in Verona." Barnadine wiped his nose on his sleeve. "Jamy knew him, liked him."

"Which made Jamy's duty doubly onerous." Great. I felt

sorry for the young, ill-prepared assassin. "Elder said after he stabbed, he pushed the man off the bed."

Madre de Dios, why had Elder not returned? Not that he could help me, but to leave me alone, facing the man who had murdered him, who'd attacked Nonna Ursula, who killed Pasqueta, who sought to kill me . . . I could have used his support, and I didn't understand his retreat.

"Jamy fell to the floor. I caught him. I saw blood on his ribs. Very little. I didn't realize that his tight doublet compressed the flood." Barnadine picked at his collar and stared as if seeing the scene again. "He pulled a scarf and pushed it to his gut. He gave me the mask and waved me away, up on the bed to finish the revenge that he could not."

"Still, you had to kill the lord you'd sworn to protect. Still, you had to break your vow and condemn yourself to hell." My voice rose with every word. "It wasn't victory and peace wrung from your courage and action that drove you to action. Nor was it the birth of your sister's son, a child never to be acknowledged, to be raised in secret."

Barnadine grunted as if each word was a punch to the gut.

"What drove you to take action at last was the news that while your bastard nephew was being raised in a Franciscan monastery, fated to become a penitent monk, Princess Eleanor would soon bear a babe to be exalted as royal, raised in all pomp, privilege, and honor, a child of the savior of Verona. It was the prospect of Elder's rising happiness, contrasted against your sister's fall from grace, that set the torch of vengeance to your cruel bonfire." By Barnadine's reaction, I realized my speculation was correct, for he no longer wavered between brokenhearted brother and snarling wolf.

He had become the wolf, crazed, enraged, a cold and lethal predator.

And my fatal flaw—my tendency to speak my strong, logical, unwomanly thoughts—would again cost me dearly.

Barnadine pointed a shaking finger at me. "You scurvy pox on the face of woman. An intelligent female is an abomination to God."

"Our most holy Lord God made me as I am." I spoke in a soothing tone, trying to coax the wolfman.

"Our most holy Lord God sent me on a mission to wipe you off the face of the earth. Or rather"—Barnadine glanced over the rail—"to send you down to be one with the earth."

He knew what he intended, what he'd always intended, and I knew I could never survive the fall to the ground. Nor could I successfully fight Barnadine; for all that his scrawny frame lacked muscle and his trembling hands bore testament to his longtime overindulgence in wine, he was a strong man, skilled in hand-to-hand combat.

This soldier had changed the course of history in Verona. His actions had forced Cal to assume power too soon, turned him from an obnoxious, impetuous boy into a man burdened with duty; and now here Barnadine stood, ready to once more alter Cal's destiny by murdering me.

I was doomed—unless I could confront him with his most recent crime and perhaps remind him, not of his rage but of his duty. "With Elder's murder, you avenged your sister's fall from virtue. With Princess Eleanor's death from widowed sorrow, you destroyed the happiness of his family. Why now take up the cause? Because Princess Ursula claimed to have contacted the spirits in her séance? What is your new goal? To save your own puny neck? Is that why you tried to batter that aged and gracious lady to death?"

"I didn't want to hurt Princess Ursula. She was good to me." He straightened his shoulders and proclaimed, "When she threatened to discover me, reveal me, she *forced* me to attack her."

Of course! It wasn't his fault he had violently tried to bring about Nonna Ursula's death. She'd brought it on herself. Crown him the Weasel King of Irresponsibility!

"And Pasqueta?" I asked.

With a wave of the hand, he dismissed her cruel death. "A female and a servant. Of no consequence."

"Then why did you beat her to death?"

"The stupid she-thing fought me."

I swallowed. *I* was a she-thing, and I fought him with words and, when it would be necessary, with fists and teeth and the blade of my stiletto. To be battered to death was fearsome torment, worthy of Dante's seventh circle of hell. I turned away from the knowledge and armed myself with my findings. "Unknowing of Helena's family, Elder took what was offered. When he discovered her untouched state, was he without remorse?"

"Guilt, remorse. What did that matter? He tried to find her afterward. He asked me for help. Me!" Barnadine laughed with a note of hysteria and spoke as if Elder stood before him. *"Too late to change the results, Escalus!"*

"He's not here." Oops. Barnadine didn't need to know that.

"Really?" Barnadine crooned. "Where did he go, this imaginary elder of yours?"

"You were speaking to him. Don't you know?" *Nice feign, Rosie. But too late.*

"Where's my fornicating prince now?" Barnadine glanced around, pretending to look for him. "Where's your friend and mentor when you need him?"

I tried to turn the conversation back to Barnadine and his guilt. "What does it matter whether he's here or not? You murdered him as you tried to murder Nonna Ursula. Prince Escalus the elder is of the spirit world and he has no affect upon the living."

"He's abandoned you, hasn't he? He doesn't want to stand by helplessly while I murder you." Barnadine sniggered. "But I never before thought him a coward so, admit it, he doesn't exist."

He did exist, and I needed him nagging, shouting, telling me how to handle this crazed soldier. "You seek to destroy me. Why? What's your agenda?"

"I pursue the extinction of the House of Leonardi."

I hadn't wanted to ask this question, hadn't want to point out the massive blemish in Barnadine's vendetta, hadn't wanted to point Barnadine in this direction—but time fled in the onslaught of this scourge, and if he had his way, I'd soon join Elder in his haunting of the palace.

"Why? Why me?" I said. "If you wish to extinguish the house of Leonardi, why don't you murder my betrothed? Princess Isabella is merely a woman. She'll marry and take her husband's name. It's Prince Escalus the younger who's the source of all future Leonardi generations. Why not kill *him*?"

Barnadine hesitated a heartbeat too long.

"That's it!" I waggled my finger at him. "That's it! You pigeon-livered coward, you've confirmed my suspicions! You can't beat Cal."

"I can! I helped train that featherless fledgling." Barnadine paced toward me. "I know tricks he can't even imagine!"

"Cal doesn't wallow in the pigsty of shame. He hasn't swum through purple oceans of wine. He's young, healthy, virile." I flung my hand out toward the stairway.

Barnadine glanced as if afraid I'd produced my betrothed into this field of battle.

No such luck.

He announced, "I'm not afraid of meeting him in combat. I stood at his back during the recent troubles and kept him from harm."

"Why?" My mind leaped to the only conclusion. "Because Cal's bodyguards would have eviscerated *you*."

Sulkily Barnadine said, "Marcellus suspects everyone."

"Especially a man who fights with a hand so numb it should scarcely hold a sword?"

Barnadine flexed his fingers. "I'm perhaps not so unable as I portrayed."

"A coward, a liar, and the villain who attacked an elderly woman in her bed. In pursuit of your own safety, you trod through rot and refuse, and carry with you the stench of betrayal."

"My family name requires—"

"You already killed one good man for the stain he brought on your family, breaking your vow to defend your prince. Cal is another good man, who allows you honor despite your failure to Elder." I lowered my voice to a menacing growl. "Tell me, Barnadine, how long have you watched Cal, hoping for an evil trait, a foolish failing, any excuse to do away with him? Yet he's the podestà who's brought honor and stability to your beloved Verona."

"*You* are his foolish failing. *You* distract him from his business. His sharp gaze no longer examines every aspect of his people, his city. He focuses on *you* and *your* charms."

I snapped, "According to Cal, I have only two charms and they both hold up my bodice!"

"What?" Barnadine looked merely confused.

I hastened to go back on the offensive. "It's not the house of Leonardi that's ultimately responsible for Lady Helena's fall from grace. You know who is, do you not . . . Barnadine?" I advanced on him; a foolish move, perhaps, but I intended to take him by surprise with my aggression, and, indeed, he took a step backward. "The man responsible is the man who took her to the masquerade. Instead of being the brother who would resist her pleas and keep her safe within the family compound, you escorted your beautiful, innocent sister into a wild bacchanal. She had always sensed life beyond her walls, and rather than be what you and your family intended, she seized her moment and tasted freedom."

As I spoke, a tide of red rose to stain his neck, his cheeks, his forehead. "You bitch!"

He's lying to himself. Tell him the truth, but tell it more gently. "I'm sorry Helena is dead to the world, Barnadine, but your murderous intentions can't bring her back."

My gamble could produce two results: Barnadine could realize he couldn't kill me, an innocent woman, and retreat again; or he could realize I was simply one more murder that paved his road to hell.

He chose hell.

Chapter 55

Barnadine moved with the skill and speed of an experienced fighter, and the seething ferocity of a madman. He seized my throat and squeezed.

I tried to kick, strike out, but he was a beast with long arms. His lips pulled back from his black teeth. I couldn't touch him. I couldn't breathe. My knees buckled. Red stars exploded in front of my eyes. I heard screams, but it wasn't me. I couldn't scream.

Did the sounds come from the stairwell?

Before I could grasp hope, Barnadine's grip loosened and I flew like a ragdoll.

I fell to the ground, panting, sucking in one breath, two breaths. But air was a luxury I couldn't afford. My still-clouded vision saw two men wrestling above me, feet stumbling on the floor. I scooted back, and back, until I was huddled against the rail. I pulled the stiletto from my ankle sheath and gripped it in my trembling hand.

Friar Camillo had seized Barnadine and pulled him off me, but the untrained monk was no match for the seasoned warrior. He was losing, yet Barnadine didn't grip him around the throat or pull a knife to end his life. In an awful tone, he whispered, "What are you doing here?" and grappled with the youth as if . . . as if he couldn't bear to hurt him.

Absolute and final confirmation that I was right; Friar Camillo was Elder's son with fair Helena—and Barnadine's nephew.

"Stop, in the name of our Lord and Savior, Jesus Christ, I command you!" Friar Camillo shouted.

Barnadine still wrestled with the monk, his eyes narrowing, and I could see the intent in his gaze. He might not intend to kill a monk, but he could knock him out of the fight.

Friar Camillo could also see his determination, and as Barnadine pulled back his fist, Friar Camillo said, "Stop, Uncle!"

Barnadine froze. He stared. Every line of his body bespoke horror and rejection. "What did you call me?"

"Uncle." Friar Camillo put his hands on Barnadine's shoulders and leaned close to his face. "Although Sister Agnese will soon go to glory, my mother is *not* yet dead. You know that, and you know that you're my uncle."

I dragged myself along the rail, wanting to flee, unable to stand, body bruised, fingers aching from clutching the stiletto, eyes fixed on the scene before me.

"I do." Barnadine took a quivering breath. "How do you know these things?"

"Did you think our paths would never cross?" Friar Camillo asked.

"I visit Helena. I visit her as often as I can, taking food and blankets. She never told me that the two of you have found each other," Barnadine said.

"We decided silence was for the best."

"She tells me *everything*." Barnadine managed to sound as if she'd betrayed him by keeping secret what he so badly wanted to be secret.

"She fears her sin has caused you to break your vow to protect Prince Escalus the elder. She fears you killed her lover." In a deep, sorrowful, sad voice, Friar Camillo said, "Uncle, she fears for your eternal soul."

"She can't know what I did!"

"She *fears* it," the young monk repeated. "We decided I

would watch you to make sure you brought no further harm to anyone, and when I realized what you intended for Lady Rosaline, I haunted her footsteps."

Which explained *a lot* about the sightings and warnings of Friar Camillo.

Barnadine put his hand to his eyes, then gazed at his palm as if surprised by the tears therein. "Helena *is* dying."

"Aye, so she is, and all her prayers are for you, her beloved brother. She would not have her transgression stain your soul."

"No!" Barnadine howled like a dog in pain. He struck out with his fist, knocking Friar Camillo off his feet.

The monk's neck snapped. He flew backward. His skull hit the railing with a hollow sound, and he slumped down, unmoving and unconscious.

I crawled toward the still, prone figure, whispering, "Friar Camillo, no, please. Friar Camillo!" Of course, I feared for myself, but I feared for him, too, for the brave youth who had watched over me, who had sought to save me by fighting his own warrior-uncle.

Before I reached him, Barnadine snatched me by the skirt and yanked.

I skidded backward, lost my grip on my knife, reached for it, clumsily caught the hilt.

Barnadine grabbed my sleeves, and amid the rip of thread and lacing and the clatter of glass beads, he roughly stood me on my feet and spoke into my ear. "Never mind the old prince. This is your fault. *Your* fault that Camillo knows the truth of his birth."

"Let me see if he's alive," I begged.

"Your fault I killed my own nephew!"

"Let me check him and see if I can revive—"

"You're going to pay." Ruddy-cheeked and witless, Barnadine shoved me toward the railing.

I dug in my heels. I tried to turn. I wanted to make him see what he had done, and that with the right help, it could be undone. "No. Don't. We don't know if Friar Camillo is dead. I might be able to help him."

"You're the demon behind the demon mask." The rabid wolf had been released.

I flipped my knife and blindly slashed at him. I struck flesh, I know, but Barnadine flicked the stiletto away like a buzzing mosquito and lifted me off my feet. "You must die. You must die!"

As the world twirled, turned upside down, as my hip thumped the rail hard enough to bruise, as I knew that didn't matter for death awaited me over the edge—I emitted a full-bodied scream.

Elder materialized out of thin air, shouted, "Judas!" and leaped at Barnadine.

Barnadine gave his own full-bodied scream.

Chapter 56

Barnadine heard Elder! He saw Elder!

In his terror, he released me.

I tumbled over the edge. I grabbed the wide top rail. There, weighted down by skirts, petticoats, brocade, embroidery, and beads, I dangled four stories above the ground, struggling to lift myself up and away from this plunge to my death.

As I groped to pull myself back onto the balcony, the two men were . . . well, they weren't exactly fighting. Barnadine, eyes so wide with terror that white showed all the way around the pupil, lunged at Elder, trying to grasp him, to bring him down.

Each time he did, he fell through the ghost.

Each time, lightning crackled and Barnadine shrieked in pain and horror.

With every screech, Elder taunted him. "Traitor! Murderer! Breaker of vows!" He moved like a swordsman, dancing away from Barnadine, luring him away from me and my desperate exertions, then plunging forward to meet Barnadine and envelop him for one crackling moment.

I would have enjoyed the purple-skinned panic that crept up Barnadine's neck, chin, cheeks, forehead—if I hadn't been dangling, weighed down by my clothing. The rich beading on my sleeves and bodice slipped on the stone rail. Cold sweat dripped into my eyes and my damp palms scraped along the rough stone top rail. My feet scrabbled to find a toehold. To no avail. With leisurely inevitability, I inched toward a plummet into the arms of death.

All Barnadine's attention focused on Elder. "You're dead. You're dead!" he said over and over. "You're dead!"

Way to state the obvious, Barnadine.

I wedged one leather-soled slipper between two of the upright rails and, for the first time, experienced a spurt of triumph.

Fury contorted Elder's features, ferocity marked his every move. He couldn't directly strike at Barnadine, but somehow he channeled his implacable ire into the increasingly strong lightning strikes. "*You* killed me! *You!* My friend, my bodyguard. *You* drugged me. *You* stabbed me through the heart. The man who watched my back stole life and breath and future. *Judas!*"

I turned my foot, leaned on it, used the strength of my trembling leg to lift myself the length of my smallest finger. Even that gave ease to my straining arms and shoulders. As I inched myself upward, grasped the wide rail more and more, moved my elbow to rest on the stone, I breathed more easily. I could do this!

I paused to give my shaking arms a rest, and the scene before me had changed.

No longer did Barnadine have to stumble through Elder's essence to fry in Elder's anger. Now whenever he came close, he sizzled. Faint dark smoke began to rise from his hair and his hands. His skin singed, gained the appearance of a seashell, tough and mottled with brown and specks of green and alabaster.

I could smell flesh burning. Elder was doing this. *Somehow* he was doing this.

"Stop it!" Barnadine shouted. "Stop it now. *You're dead!*"

"Righteous wrath burns the bloodstains on your hands."

"Righteous? You're a fornicator!"

"You—you kept my son from me!" Elder gestured to Friar Camillo's still figure. "Now he's dead. Murdered by his own uncle!"

Barnadine froze and stared. Stared at blood that trickled from the wound that broke through the skin on Friar Camillo's tonsured scalp. At last, it seemed Barnadine had been yanked from his crooked footpath to face the consequences of his actions.

Elder moved to stand at Barnadine's shoulder. He spoke quietly, reasonably in his ear. "You murdered me. You tried to kill my mother, the dowager princess, who welcomed you to her table, who considered you her ally. Now you've killed my son. Your nephew! You've broken every vow, every binding that ties you to family, to mine and yours. You'll face the fires of hell for your wicked deeds."

Barnadine faced him, tears in his eyes.

Hey, Elder, you could at least have mentioned me.

Then Elder made his first tactical error, and I realized why he'd been silent about my likely fate.

He hadn't forgotten that I hung four stories up . . . but Barnadine had, and when Elder glanced toward me, Barnadine smiled and nodded in a horrible parody of geniality. "If I'm doomed to burn, let me burn for all the reasons."

I saw death in the wolf's cold, dark eyes, and fueled by fear gave myself a mighty heave. I got my chest onto the rail and scrambled to get a leg over. My skirts hindered me, the weight of my clothing slowed my attempts.

Worse, nothing Elder could do—the lunging, the lightning, the insults—slowed Barnadine's approach. Barnadine grabbed my shoulders, held me in place, and grinned at Elder. "Will you try to fry me now? When I hold your beloved Lady Rosaline in my hands, and life and death are mine to dispense?"

Elder shook his head and gazed at me, sprawled partly on, and mostly off, the rail. His lips moved. *I'm sorry.*

"Touch me and your powers that weaken me will weaken her, and she—" Barnadine leaned over and looked all the way down to the ground. "The people of the palace see what's occurring. Hear them scream. Hear them cry. Yet they can't save her." He gazed into my pleading face. "You're not even insane. He really is here." Amazement and regret tinged his voice.

I clung to the rail, straining to hang on. "If you push me, Elder will put you in such pain as you have never known."

"You speak truth, so let us go down together, and you'll be my companion for the trip to hell!" Still clutching my shoulder in one hand, Barnadine slammed his other fist down on my arm.

My grip loosened. I screamed.

Elder roared and rose off the floor in fury.

From the ground below me, I heard shouts and cries, but all I could see was Barnadine's brutal face, his lips peeled back from his horrible teeth.

He grabbed for my clutching fingers—

In a rush of silent savagery, Cal tackled him from the side.

I was saved!

Chapter 57

Except that Barnadine staggered sideways and slammed me on the head with his elbow. The impact twisted me sideways. My foot slipped, my hands lost their grip, and I fell.

As the uprights flew by, I grabbed them, shoved my elbows between them.

A hand seized the back of my bodice.

I jerked to a halt; my ribs slammed against the bottom edge of the balcony. My shoulders felt as if they'd been wrenched out of their sockets. One slipper fell from my foot.

I couldn't breathe. I couldn't *breathe*.

Then I could. I sucked in one huge breath of air after another.

Above me, a man's voice shouted . . . something.

Elder? He'd done great things to Barnadine, but could he have grabbed me and helped halt my descent?

I worked my hands in and around to hook my elbows around the stone posts. The apparently corporeal hand still gripped me, and I dangled there, gasping in pain and fear, heart thumping.

I'd spent my whole life making fun of the maidens in plays who when in peril screamed and kicked. A new enlightenment took me; forthwith I understood screaming and kicking was a totally reasonable response to dangling in midair, weighed down, muscles clenched, joints straining, fighting for breath, knowing at any minute I could fall and thus end my sinful, joyous, conflict-ridden life.

I pressed my face between the uprights, closed my eyes, heard the thumps and the yells as Cal fought Barnadine.

Cal was fighting Barnadine.

I opened my eyes again.

The two men danced back and forth, each with a dagger in one hand and a stiletto in the other, so close to each other the blades flashed sunlight across their faces.

Above, the man shouted again, and this time I understood him. "I'm holding you, Lady Rosaline. I shall not fail you!"

Friar Camillo! Somehow Friar Camillo had recovered consciousness, staggered to his feet, and caught me in time.

Elder shouted, "Good man, my son!" He flung himself—his essence?—onto the floor and put his face close to mine. "Friar Camillo grasps you in one fist and has his arm braced around the rail. He can't lift you alone, and I'm afraid to help."

I shook my head vigorously. Blessed Mother Mary, no, I didn't want Elder sparking Friar Camillo. Or me. "Does he see you?" I whispered. "Does he hear you?"

"No. No."

In a louder voice, I said, "I do see you . . . and you're blocking my view!"

Elder huffed and vanished.

Cal and Barnadine fought.

I didn't want to watch, but I couldn't look away.

Cal was younger, faster on his feet, but had been lamed in the dungeon all those years ago, and as the battle continued, that slight limp grew more exaggerated. Yet his features betrayed no concern, only an expectant concentration and almost smiling calm.

Barnadine drew on a deep reservoir of experience . . . and

desperation. He'd discarded the noble mask he'd worn for so long, of grieving bodyguard and loyal citizen. His lips curled back from his stained teeth, his hands held his blades almost lightly, his deadly gaze scrutinized Cal for weakness. He fought for his sister, his nephew, his family honor. He fought to win, for he had nothing to lose. He had killed Elder, the podestà of Verona, and deserved death for such a betrayal to his lord. Cal fought to avenge his father, and that meant death for Barnadine. If Barnadine killed the current podestà of Verona, never mind hell—he would die a horrible death at the hands of Cal's soldiers.

Elder danced back and forth, watching the fight with the same intensity that enticed me to forget the horror of dangling far above the ground. I couldn't, but it was now frankly second in my mind.

"Help him!" I commanded Elder.

"I can't help him!"

I thought he meant—he was a ghost and so incapable of influencing the events. So I reminded him, "Yes, you can. You did it before. Zap Barnadine!"

He didn't turn his head to speak to me; he kept his attention on the battle. "Cal wouldn't thank me for assisting. This battle he must win himself."

"What matters is that he eliminate Barnadine!"

"Cal is a warrior. He doesn't need or want his papà's help. Have faith, child. I see what you don't."

"What?"

"Strategy."

What I saw was a man more and more in pain, leaning to one side, off balance and—

Swift as a striking snake, Barnadine's stiletto stabbed Cal in the chest.

I flinched. Cal. Sweet Mary, Mother of God. *Cal!*

Along the sides of my bodice, threads popped.

Friar Camillo's grip slipped. He shouted, "Lady Rosaline, don't move!"

Quickly, even before tears could fill my eyes, Cal dropped his dagger, grabbed Barnadine's free wrist, and twisted so hard that the bones broke with audible cracks.

Barnadine screamed.

Cal placed the point of his stiletto between Barnadine's ribs.

Barnadine lurched sideways, and in an act of defiance in the face of unbearable pain, he fell forward, using his body weight to shove his blade farther into Cal's chest—but somehow it didn't budge. Instead Barnadine impaled himself on the glittering steel all the way to the hilt. Blood gushed. He hung for a moment, staring into Cal's eyes with what looked like approval. "I taught you that trick," he breathed.

"You did. And you failed because I'm wearing the leather shirt your father made for mine. That's justice."

"Yes . . . he's here, your father. He's glad."

Cal gave a harder heave on his stiletto and hurled Barnadine back. Barnadine stumbled, fell to his knees, crumpled onto his back . . . and died.

Elder stared soberly down at his disloyal bodyguard, his hated friend, his beloved enemy. "I am glad."

I wanted to clap. I wanted Cal to yank Barnadine's stiletto out of his own chest and be well. Most of all . . . I wanted someone to pull me to safety.

It's true. As soon as the final battle was over, all my selfish concern was for *me*.

And for Friar Camillo, who now began to make groaning sounds and adjust his grip on my bodice as if his strength would fail even now. I knew how Friar Camillo must feel, holding on for dear life against the irresistible force that dragged me down to the earth where inevitably I must find my final rest. But not when life tasted so sweet. Not yet! Not now!

Cal paid no attention to Barnadine's sprawled corpse. He

turned toward me, his concentration focused on my face as I plastered it between the upright stones like a child confined to a playroom. He tossed the stiletto out of his chest, as if flicking a mosquito out of his way, and as he rushed to the rail, he wiped his hand, red with Barnadine's blood, on his doublet. Over my head, I heard his voice as he spoke to Friar Camillo, encouraging him, praising Friar Camillo's generosity and courage, promising him nursing and care for his wounds,

Cal spoke to me, not encouraging at all, but brusque and demanding, telling me my strength *would* endure, that I *had* to hang on for the brief time until he hoisted himself in place. Then he said, loudly and clearly, "Rosie, I'm directly above you. Do you see me?"

I barely shook my head. I was afraid to move, to loosen a single muscle, to change my position in any way.

"Rosie, look up!" He used the voice of a commander.

Like an obedient soldier, I looked up.

His shoulders and head hung over the broad edge of the rail. His arm stretched toward me, his palm and fingers large, reaching, open. "Friar Camillo will continue to hold you. I'm here to grasp you. All you have to do is loosen one elbow, so do that now."

Slowly I started to straighten my right arm. My weight shifted; I gasped and kinked it once again.

"Friar Camillo needs relief. Let go with one arm and grab my hand."

I stared at Cal, my betrothed . . . the lunatic.

"Rosie, there's no other way," he said. "Friar Camillo's strength is failing."

"Trust the boy!" Elder urged. "He's right. It's the only way."

Cal spoke over the top of him. "Rosie, you have to let go and reach for me."

In some part of my mind, I understood the words. I even believed him. But what he suggested was impossible. I'd scoffed at the fear of heights. Now no other thought occupied my mind except terror. Over and over, my brain gibbered the instruction: *Hold on.*

"Reach for me." Cal's hand strained closer.

I looked down and back across the safe, and now inaccessible, stretch of floor that separated the rail from the wall. Cal's feet were nowhere in sight, which meant he'd wrapped his body around the stone as support, and the largest part of his bulk hung over the railing, and—

"Reach for me," Cal said.

We could both fall!

"Rosaline Hortensa Magdelina Eleanor!" Cal commanded. "Give me your hand!"

I released a defiant bellow, abandoned safety, and *reached.*

Chapter 58

Cal grasped my wrist.

I grasped his.

Friar Camillo pulled.

Cal pulled.

"Good lads!" Elder almost danced with the need to act. He dared not act, I knew, so he served as the unseen and unheard coach.

I freed my other arm.

As all my weight transferred to the men, they grunted with the strain.

Yet I rose. Gradually I rose.

My bodice rose with me, but a little ahead, so I knew my *camicia* showed in the gap between my skirt and bodice. The pressure against my belly informed me all too clearly I still suffered from Baal's kick, and the pressure and pain made it difficult for me to catch my breath. Threads strained and popped, adding an urgency to the maneuver.

"Steady, lads." Elder kept his voice strong and encouraging. "Steady. She's almost there."

I strained up, up to the top rail, touched it with my fingertips.

"You've almost got it!" Elder told me.

I inched my hand across the stone.

Friar Camillo shouted, "The seams are going!"

"Grip her under that arm." Cal sounded as strong and encouraging as his father.

"No, wait!" I could almost reach the rail's far edge.

But I was too late.

The bodice ripped.

My gaze met Cal's.

For the merest moment, he alone held me.

My shoulder joint wrenched and popped.

His too—for a spasm of pain crossed his face.

Friar Camillo released the material and grabbed my armpit.

I was supported.

All of us shook hard under the strain.

"*Cazzo!*" Elder shouted. "They did it!"

Premature celebration did not please me, but I couldn't waste my breath with reproaches. Instead I grasped the top rail's far edge.

For the first time since my daring grasp of Cal's hand, I was able to relieve the men of some weight.

For the first time, I thought I might survive.

The line of my eyes cleared the rail. I got my elbow up.

The men put their feet on the ground. Our weight no longer teetered over the rail.

Below I heard shouts of "Huzzah! Huzzah!"

I hoped they weren't cheering the view up my gown.

Cal wrapped his fingers around my skirt's belt and steadied me.

Friar Camillo used both his hands to support me now.

The men, gasping with the effort, pulled me over the rail.

I flopped like a dead fish on the floor.

Elder shouted, "Rosie! Too much ankle. Too much! Fix your skirt!"

I glared at him. "Focus!"

"Nice ankles, good calves, and a pleasant glimpse of thigh," he advised.

Fine. Even under duress, I had to behave the part of a *lady*. Staggering to my feet, I shook out my skirts.

Barnadine's corpse rested on the floor, stained with seeping red and dried black blood. As with Baal, this *thing* was no longer a carrier of a soul, but a side of meat, carrion for flies and hell's demons who would feed on his spirit.

I was glad. I'd spent too much time fighting with words and deeds this being who broke his vows and embraced treachery most vile and heartless. Yet I knew his villainy was not without reason, and I sorrowed for Barnadine, who had failed to protect his sister; for Elder, who'd been seduced by the unexpected appearance of a pretty face; and for Friar Camillo, the innocent who knelt beside his uncle, closed his eyes, prayed for his soul, and cried sad tears.

I must have looked wobbly, for Cal leaped to support me. "I'm okay," I whispered. "How did you know to come?"

I thought he'd say he heard the shouts from below.

But instead: "I heard a summons," Cal said.

And from Elder: "I shouted loudly enough that at last he heard me."

I glanced between them to see if Cal heard his father now.

Yet Cal was blank and Elder patently disappointed.

As soon as Cal took his hands away, I collapsed, my knees so weak with residual terror the iron within had rusted to weak reddish powder. He picked me up, carried me to the wall, and propped me up. "Are you injured? Can you stand?"

I leaned against the wall, let the rough cut of the stone hold me. "I'm not injured. Not badly." Amazing how the thought of crashing onto a tile roof four stories below gave perspective to a sore gut, a wrenched shoulder, and a myriad of bruises. "Are *you* injured? Your shoulder? When I fell and you caught me, I saw—"

He put his hand over my mouth and looked at me, his brown eyes wide with some strong emotion. Relief? Exhaustion? The realization I was more trouble than I was worth? I couldn't read him.

He shook his head, paced away. Walked back, cupped my face, looked into my eyes. Shook his head. Paced away. Walked back, and when I tried to speak, he kissed me. He put his mouth on mine and kissed me until the sour stench of fear was vanquished in the rich scent of promised pleasure, until residual terror had been replaced with passion's sweet flavor, until pain had been absorbed by the clamor of my body and the knowledge of death had been exchanged for exhilaration rushing through my veins. Never mind that joints ached and bruises bloomed across my skin; I lifted my arms and slid them around Cal's shoulders and clung, for he was my guardian angel and my wildly raging tempest.

When he lifted his head, he held me as if he would absorb me into his being. Body pressed to body, all the length of us, until it seemed clothing had vanished, and muscles, bones, minds combined. Never had I experienced a more all-consuming joining . . . and need.

"Rosie," he murmured. "Lady Rosaline."

My eyes fluttered open.

"I fought to save you."

"You *did* save me."

"That is my only comfort, for my mind knows all too well I'm the reason you were in danger. If not for the betrothal I forced upon you, you wouldn't have suffered this ordeal, and stared Death in its cold eyes."

"That's true, but—"

Before I could point out I'd stared Death in its cold eyes in the spring, and Cal had had nothing to do with that, he interrupted. "I want you. You know that. But I can never again risk your life to have you. I release you from this marriage, which you would endure so reluctantly."

I shook my head. After those sublime moments—the kiss,

the fusion of our bodies—his words scrambled in my head. What did he *mean*?

"I go at once to tell your family and all Verona that I relinquish you . . . for your own safety . . . and with much sorrow on my part. I'll let it be known to all that I give my blessing to your future betrothal to . . . a worthy gentleman." Cal leaned his forehead against mine. His breath caressed my cheeks as he chuckled. "I can't say the name. Not now. Not after this . . . closeness with you. But I do gladly release you, and someday, perhaps on my deathbed, I'll not regret the loss of you, dear Rosaline, dear shining spirit whom I adore."

I stared at him, dumbfounded. "Cal . . ."

"I know. I have to let go." His arms tightened. "Give me one more minute. Just one more minute."

I breathed him in. My heart beat with his. Let me go? How was that possible? "Cal, you don't mean—"

As if my halting speech acted as the trigger he needed, he released me, tearing our flesh apart and leaving nothing behind but cold and pain and loneliness.

Chapter 59

Elder's dry, curious voice echoed in my head. "I cannot wait to see what you do now."

"What else should I do but avail myself of Prince Escalus's blessing on my union with Lysander?" A knee-jerk reaction, a reply to his taunt.

"You, madam, are as close to a princess as any woman not yet crowned with the sacred circlet must be. How do you respond to a man who saves you from certain death, who clearly loves you, yet who declares he'll forgo all his rights and his desires and yield you to an inferior man—"

Fiercely I turned on Elder. "Lysander is not inferior. He's a younger son of unusual creativity, much respected for his inventions, handsome and true."

"As you say, madam. I know not the youth who's the object of your idolatry. I only know my son declares he'll do all for your happiness, although that will mean none for himself, and indeed, all Verona will laugh at him, and even when he finds a bride, she'll be political and appropriate, none of his taste and all of his propriety."

I confess, I didn't like the idea of Younger taking a diplomatic bride. "Cal's a good man, if ruthless in his pursuits of—"

"You? How unusual is that, do you think, that Prince Escalus should abandon his thoughtful caution to gain you, your mind and your body, for his own? Are you not flattered?"

I suppose, looking at it that way, it could be construed as flattering. Irritating, high-handed, but flattering.

Elder continued. "Moreover, when the moment came when he must save you from certain death, he never doubted the scene before his eyes and killed the villain with a clever stratagem and a sharp point. He placed his weapon at your feet and declared all he wants is your happiness and you must gain your One True Love, no matter the loss to himself. So, madam, what will you do? Will you allow this noble prince to sacrifice himself to mockery and scorn so you may have your One True Love?"

"My family's history guides me to my One True Love."

"You, Rosaline, are not your family. Have your affections altered? What does your duty demand?"

Merda! Who knew Elder could ask the tough questions?

I rubbed the sides of my forehead with my fingers. "Let me think."

"Think quickly, for Cal will swiftly carry out his intention."

I closed my eyes and raised in my mind a portrait of Lysander, lovingly painted in my most precious colors, golden and smiling, handsome and droll and loving. My mind clung to him, praised him, saw only him . . . but an awareness grew of a man who stood in shadow, clad in dark clothes, unsmiling, through no fault of his own bound tight by the cords of duty. While appearing to have every privilege, he cared for none of them, but he did care for me. Unbidden, my mind produced a parade of images: Prince Escalus's fondness for his sister, his appearance on the Montague moonlit terrace to present to me his dagger, his seduction in the dark garden. Only then, I began to think of him, not as a stallion to be led to a mare of my choosing, but as a man who directed his own destiny—and interfered with mine without care to my desires.

Yet when in the Montague garden, he pressed that kiss to my palm, folded my fingers over it, and told me to keep it close to my heart. That moment made me look at him, not as the cold and distant prince, but as a man who, for reasons I knew not, maneuvered me into a most acrimonious betrothal.

Acrimonious on my part, anyway.

What had he just said before he released me and gave me his blessing?

Someday, perhaps on my deathbed, I'll not regret the loss of you, dear Rosaline, dear shining spirit whom I adore.

Now I opened my eyes and realized I once again held my closed fist against my chest, as if that garden promise kiss had branded me in ways I never knew.

I looked at Elder.

He watched me gravely, with sorrow heavy and evident. "Love is not common. Love is not to be lightly tossed aside. Yet love is not all. Minds and hearts that look through the same eyes at life and see a similar vision. A hand to help you up when you fall. Devotion Cal gives you. Passion he feels for you. What I would give to have what you so readily intend to abandon! I did that. Now, when I can do nothing, when I can no longer bring justice to an event, a life of my own making—now I know. I have a second son." He indicated Friar Camillo.

Friar Camillo, who was done with the holy rites and now grieving over his most murderous uncle, heard not a word of his father's ghostly monologue.

Elder said, "I can never know him. I can never know Princess Isabella. I can never reunite with my beloved Eleanor. I can't look for them in heaven or hell. For my sins, I'm bound to this palace."

"Wait!" In the gravity of this moment, I was glad to change the focus from my burdensome decision to Elder and (hopefully) his going. "You're here because you needed to know your killer. You do now. You can go."

"You're right. I can. I should be able to. Watch this!" He frowned intently.

Nothing happened.

"You look constipated," I observed.

"I'm not!" he snapped.

"Of course not," I snapped back. "Stop concentrating so hard! Relax and"—I wiggled my fingers—"float away."

He reacted with irritation. "Like you would know. You're alive."

"It looks as if I know as well as you!"

He narrowed his eyes at me, took a breath, and loosened his neck, shoulders, hands. His ghostly form remained as solid as ever. Which wasn't very solid, but definitely *here* rather than *there*.

He looked astonished, a man used to accomplishing what he set out to do. "This is a pigeon egg pickle."

"Maybe you have another task to perform. What would it be?"

"I don't know. I told you—"

"I know. No 'Welcome to the Afterworld Reception.'" To my surprise, I'd grown fond of Elder. Not fond enough that I wanted him haunting my footsteps forever, but enough that I wished he could finish his earthly existence and move on to . . . whatever came after for him.

As with me, he seemed glad to abandon his issue and return to mine, proving we did have something in common: evasion. "Never mind me. It's you who must make a decision. I have eternity and I have no life to worry about. Cal won't delay in upsetting this baggage cart of a wedding." When I rubbed my forehead in distress, he added, "Of course, if you've decided to marry Lysander, you need do nothing. You can leave Cal to face the scandal alone."

Elder held a bubbling pot o' muddy guilt and scooped with a big ol' ladle.

My usual clear thinking had abandoned me. Papà and Mamma were right; love opened a new world for me. Joy, yes. Passion, yes. Glory, yes. But also madness and confusion, choices made in haste that guaranteed the dawn of regrets on my horizon—

A thunder of footsteps sounded on the stairs.

Elder looked in that direction and muttered, *"Che schifo."*

Of course, Elder was disgusted, for Lysander, my One True Love, appeared in the doorway.

Chapter 60

"Lysander!" I rushed into his embrace. "Oh, Lysander!"

His dear arms enclosed me. He kissed the top of my head, pressed his cheek to his kiss, gasped and trembled. "People were looking up at the tower. I looked up, too. I saw you dangling, struggling to get your arms over the railing. I couldn't believe . . . but my heart assured me there could be no mistake. It was you. We could see a man staggering about, trying to push you, but it looked as if . . ."

"As if what?" I choked out the question.

"As if he was being hit by lightning!"

"Is that what it looked like?" Elder asked.

Lysander bent his head close to my ear and spoke softly. "I doubted you before, but now I must ask—was that Prince Escalus the elder to your rescue?"

"The boy's not an idiot," Elder said in approval. "He'd be a worthy . . . No, wait. I don't mean that."

If I wasn't already so wretchedly confused, I would have grinned at his clumsy about-turn.

"At the point at which you were about to lift yourself to safety, we shouted 'huzzah' for you." Lysander's voice sounded as if he was trying to cheer me. "On the street, over and over, 'Huzzah! Huzzah!' For you, my darling. Did you hear us?"

I shook my head. I'd known of the shouts below, but it had been the twin roars of fear and hope I'd truly heard.

"The man—it was Barnadine, was it not?"

"Good guess, since his corpse is there." Elder could apparently only be pleasant for a few continuous moments.

"Barnadine leaned over you—I thought he would hurl you and himself down, but then like a whirlwind, Prince Escalus leaped, knocked him down, and you fell . . ."

"We know what happened," Elder told him. "We saw it from up here."

Yes, and the recitation reminded and chilled me.

"I thought—" Lysander tightened his grip, and in a broken voice, he murmured, "My love, my love."

Emotion overwhelmed me. Tears started, and I sobbed aloud.

"Pull yourself together, woman!" Elder sounded disgusted.

Lysander loosened his grip. "I shouldn't hug you. I saw how hard you hit. You're injured."

I choked back sobs. "I'm fine." I wasn't, but crying made all the bruises feel worse. "What . . . Why . . . How did you get here?"

"From below, we could see two men fighting, the friar holding you, you holding on."

I moaned, "Sweet Mary, the view up my dress!"

"Woman, that's not important. What's important is—what are you going to do? Anyway, I told you, you have nice ankles." Elder seemed to think he had comforted me.

Lysander spoke over the top of him. "Comfort yourself. The tower is offset from the street. We could see nothing but your ankles and, when the shoe fell, your foot."

"My attractive ankles." In misplaced humor, I murmured, "At least it wasn't my nice *tette*."

Lysander leaned closer. *"What?"*

"Nothing. How did you find me?" I asked again.

"I watched those men lift you, saw how valiantly you struggled to pull yourself back onto the balcony, and when I knew you would survive your ordeal, I ran to the palace doors and demanded entrance. The guards would have none of it, and others from the street followed me, wanting a front-row seat to the finale of the drama they had witnessed. I had no chance. No chance to reach you, and I frantically called your name. Suddenly Prince Escalus stood there. He beckoned me, the guards allowed me in, and he told me to go to you, with his blessing."

"Oh." Inadequate. "He . . . did that."

"I ran for the stairway, up to this place where I knew you were and . . . Rosie, you're injured!"

"Yes." I pressed the side of my belly.

"*Mi amore,* you're bleeding!"

"No. What? Where?" I looked at my hands, scraped by the stone on the railing, my arms. I touched my face.

With a discreet gesture, Lysander indicated my bosom.

I looked down at myself, and he was right. Blood smeared my bodice and my *camicia,* and when I touched it, my fingers came away damp. A quick check proved it wasn't my blood, and when I realized what must have happened, I turned on Elder. "I thought Cal was wearing your protective leather shirt!"

"He was. He is! Woman, what do you think? It's not chain mail. It's light, thin, supple leather. It has stopped many a blade, but a good thrust always gets through."

"Through? Barnadine's stiletto s-s-stabbed Cal?" I could barely stammer.

"Not fatally!" Elder stopped and reflected. "Probably not fatally, although Barnadine knew how to find the heart every time."

With that, I made my decision, and turned back to Lysander.

Lysander, who watched me in confusion and concern. "You're talking to Prince Escalus the elder?"

"Yes!"

"About Prince Escalus, his son?"

"Yes!"

"Prince Escalus, his son, was stabbed protecting you?"

"Yes! He . . . he . . ." I touched the blood on my chest, then gestured toward the stairs. "I have to—"

"No!" Lysander put his hand over my mouth. "Don't say it. We can't have come this close to a lifetime of passion, love, and friendship, only to have you turn aside now!"

Gently I pushed his hand away. "Lysander, everything about you is beautiful. Your face and figure attracted me first, but the violence of my first love might have failed if not for your humor, your intelligence, your modesty, and your affections for all that I hold dear." Tears gathered in my eyes. Heartache choked my voice. Pain broke me.

"You're not improving matters," Elder warned.

"Prince Escalus encouraged me in my suit!" Lysander's voice rose.

"You would fit into my family so perfectly." My words were the lament of a loving heart.

He ran his hands through his beautiful hair, paced away, then walked back.

It occurred to me how similar in track this conversation was to my earlier discussion with Cal.

Lysander's determined chin warned me of a different tack. "I can support you in elegance, in luxury. I can invent the world anew for you, and for that, I will be paid admirably."

"My friend, my love, do you believe that I make my decision by weighing how much each of you can give me in material goods?" In a deliberately sisterly gesture, I put my arm around his shoulders. "Do you really think that of me?"

"No." He sounded wearily disgusted—I hoped with himself.

"Cal much envies you your talent and inventiveness."

"Puhlease. He's the prince of Verona!"

"As he pointed out, one of many princes past and future. You're unique and hold the prospect of everlasting fame. Cal's right; I've never met a man like you, and may never again, and my heart breaks knowing that I hurt you. Yet Prince Escalus would have me be happy."

Lysander turned and wrapped his arms around my waist. "I can make you happy!"

When I disentangled myself, he didn't try to hold me. "I have to make myself happy, and to do that, I make the honorable choice." Taking his hands in mine, I put them palm to palm, as if in prayer, and, bowing down, kissed them and wept hot farewell tears.

As I ran toward the stairway, Lysander groaned in pain, yet I resolved I would never indulge in regrets.

For once, Elder intelligently said not a word.

Chapter 61

Down the stairs I went, too fast for my still-wobbly knees, but always with a desperate urgency. Would I be too late to stop Cal from making his announcement? Halfway down the great walk, I saw Princess Isabella, skirts in hand, running toward me. "Rosie! Rosie! You've got to stop him!"

"Where is he?"

"On the balcony!"

The balcony where the podestà traditionally made his pronouncements, the balcony that was inset into the palace walls and provided protection for the prince from weather and attack.

"Come with me!" She ran through some door and up another flight of stairs, one I had never climbed—broad, shiny with wood, and on the landing a collection of noble marble busts of great antiquity.

Fittingly, I was on my way to the family's private chambers. At the top, I had to stop a moment, to gasp and hold my ribs, but Princess Isabella would have none of that. She grabbed my arm and dragged me. "Hurry! He's already speaking!" She stopped in front of a set of bronze doors of glorious workings, where Dion stood guard. "Open for us!"

I'd never heard her use such an imperious voice.

He blinked as if a kitten had slapped him with its claws, and obeyed.

I paused in my rush. "A sedan chair must at once go for Friar Laurence. Go you with it, and bid him bring herbs, potions, and tools for a bleeding wound. Hurry. Your master has need."

"Come on!" Princess Isabella grabbed my hand and tugged me through the large, luxurious, *gloomy* room, with its massive fireplace, massive bed, and massive wooden table scattered with maps, rolled parchments, and scribbled papers. From the open door at the far corner of the room, I could hear Cal speaking.

Were we too late?

In a low, rushed voice, Princess Isabella said, "Holofernes guards the door to the balcony. Marcellus guards my brother. I'll create a diversion and you make Cal see sense!" Without pause, she ran around the corner and shrieked, "Holofernes, I declare my love for you now and in front of the world!"

Well, I hadn't expected that! As I ran past the wide-eyed, white-faced Holofernes, I knew he hadn't, either.

Still in the shadow of the room, I paused. Marcellus, indeed, stood at Cal's shoulder in the middle of the balcony, where he could survey the citizenry for any threat, but now the threat came from within. He looked toward the door with a face like thunder personified.

Cal continued speaking, as if nothing untoward had occurred, and his intent expression made me think he hadn't heard or didn't care. He would finish his pronouncement regardless of the clamor behind.

Marcellus stalked toward me and, in a menacing tone, said, "You cannot stop him."

I viewed him coolly, calmly, and for the first time cleanly asserted my authority over this man loyal to Cal. "I go to converse with my prince. Now get out of my way."

Marcellus lifted his chest, straightened his spine, broadened his shoulders, showed all the signs of forming a barrier between Cal and me.

His opinion of me was of a light-minded woman, manipulative and unsuited to the high office to which Cal was raising me, and if he was being generous, a competent cook. He couldn't comprehend the force majeure it took for me to run the Montague household from a young age, nor did he understand that I easily supervised my young, strong-minded siblings. So when I used the decisive whiplash of my next words—"Marcellus, move out of my way *now*"—Cal's bodyguard fell back under the power of my personality.

I didn't rush. Not now. The unimportant obstacles had been overcome, and there remained only Cal, clad in shadow, baptized in blood, alone as no man had ever yet been before on this earth. In that deep, warm, masterful voice, he spoke, commanding the fascinated attention of the crowd gathered on the street. His thrilling description of Barnadine's assassination of Elder, his ongoing treachery in the years since, and his attempt on dear Nonna Ursula's life brought a cacophony of booing and hissing. When Cal described Barnadine's act of luring Verona's most loved Lady Rosaline Montague to the tower with evil intentions, the battle she fought courageously, and the horror of her near plunge to the ground, his words grew in volume and speed, and every man and woman gasped and moaned, feeling the terror he described.

He mesmerized, an improv actor who knew how to project an emotion: humor, revulsion, outrage. And then he began again. "When Lady Rosaline stood once more at my side, brave, strong, and true, I realized—"

It was time for my first step onstage as Prince Escalus's wife. I took a fortifying breath and charged out the door.

Startled, Cal turned at the sound of my footsteps on the balcony and looked even more startled when I projected my voice toward him—and the crowd gathered below.

"Beloved betrothed, I thank you for your constant kind assurance to my soul's well-being and your heated defense of my vulnerable woman's body, taking such a wound to your chest deep enough to kill a lesser man!" I faced the crowd and touched my chest. "After your battle with the hated villain Barnadine"—the people booed at Barnadine's name, which heartened me—"you embraced me in triumph and thanksgiving, and this bloody mark you left as a brand of your courage."

Men and women gasped as I turned from side to side to show them the smeared stain on my skin; and when I pressed my palm to the growing spot of blood on Cal's chest, I showed them that, too.

Cal flinched and, in a low voice, said, "Rosaline, don't."

I paid him no heed. "With your brave action, witnessed by so many of our citizenry, you have avenged your father's restless ghost. Even now, you bleed as you take the time to assure your people of my safety as your future wife, the assurance of your dynasty, and their own safety. Your nobility is Verona's essence, and thus I must beg our people, our citizens, to allow me to take you from them so that I may bind your wound and you will live another day, to the gratitude of your people and the delight of your multitude of friends."

Cal's citizens shouted instructions to him, to go and be well; and to me, giving advice on how to salve and bandage him, and exhorting me to be a healer and wife.

I waved acknowledgment, took Cal firmly by the arm; and when he didn't move, I shoved him toward the door.

It was going to get ugly if he refused to move.

To my surprise, Marcellus joined me, took Cal's other arm, and Cal, recognizing defeat, walked with us into his bedroom.

Cheers and shouted blessings followed us inside.

Princess Isabella unwound her arms from the red-faced Holofernes's neck, and he shut the door behind us.

Cal looked between his sister and his bodyguard. "What are you . . . ?"

Princess Isabella grinned at him. "All's well. Rosie stopped you!"

I spared a moment for Holofernes's embarrassment, but she'd reminded Cal of his main concern.

Cal gestured indignantly toward the balcony. "Rosie. What the hell was that?"

Chapter 62

"I gave you up, and now you're back?" Cal no longer used his projecting actor's voice, but his normal I'm-an-irritated-male voice.

With Marcellus's help, I steered him toward the tall bed. "The true lesson of Romeo and Juliet in the tomb is that it's not that easy to get rid of a Montague *or* a Capulet, and I'm both." I gestured to Holofernes and Marcellus, who turned down the dark brocade bedcover, and Dion brought the steps that Cal must climb to reach the mattress.

"Is *that* the true lesson of Romeo and Juliet?" At my urging, Cal climbed the steps. "If I'd known all I had to do is relinquish my claim on you, I'd have . . . Wait. No." He faced me. "My reasons for allowing you to live outside of the censorious and sometimes perilous public eye still stand. Even before our marriage, my enemies are your enemies."

"I know. Where's the justice in that?" I followed him up the steps, put my hands on his shoulders, and physically urged him to lie down on the mattress. "I can make enough enemies on my own."

Marcellus snorted.

Everybody looked at him.

He kept a straight face.

Elder chuckled. "He knows you, that boy."

Ah. Elder had come along to see the entertainment and make sure his son survived my tender care. I should have known he wouldn't whisk away on a cool, heavenly breeze. Or a hot, hellish wind, either.

"Marcellus, I need whatever bandages and medicines you keep here," I told him, "and when Dion returns with Friar Laurence, bring them at once to this room."

Marcellus bowed and departed.

Cal seated himself, then eased himself backward onto the pillows.

I observed the care with which he moved and diagnosed pain and blood loss as the reasons he hadn't remained on his feet to argue with me. "Holofernes, if you would meticulously remove the clothing from the prince's upper body, I'll endeavor to preserve his life for another day."

Cal gripped my wrist and gazed at me, his lids partially lowered over his dark eyes. "It's not my first visit to the altar of losing to win. Barnadine and I knew each other too well. For me to defeat him, I had to suffer the molestation of my flesh on his knife. It is as naught when compared to the serving of justice for my noble father."

"I wouldn't call a stab wound to the chest *naught*!" Elder said. "Listen, boy, I do appreciate your seizing the moment to avenge me, but let us not sacrifice your life, too!"

"My prince, in your youthful years spent in the dungeon, you suffered an exaggerated experience in grave wounds, which leaves you unfit for medical judgment." I watched as Cal's bodyguard unlaced his doublet and shirt and Cal eased his arms free, revealing the close-fitting leather vest. A blot of blood marked the place where Barnadine had stabbed him, and as Holofernes unlaced it, he revealed the crimson stain that spread like a malicious miasma across the white linen of his undershirt.

Elder swore.

Holofernes echoed Elder and, pulling his knife, slashed the material, revealing Cal's bronze skin, with its dark, curled hair, already scarred from the torture of his youth, and the sullenly oozing wound on his chest.

Princess Isabella gasped and turned white. "Sit down and put your head between your legs," I told her. She was twelve, and all girls of that age found the sight of blood fearsome, and knowing how the womanly years would unfold, for good reason.

Yet upon hearing Cal's casual assurances, I'd hoped for better. "Light!" I demanded, and climbed on my knees on the bed to better examine his wound.

The always hovering servants appeared, opening curtains and windows and lighting candles, which they held close.

"Bandages!" I held out my hand. Someone thrust a wad of soft cloth in it and I blotted the wound and examined it closely.

The cut was small and deadly aimed, placed exactly at the center of the chest over the heart. Indeed, the only thing that saved my prince's life was the leather vest and Barnadine's precision, for he had stabbed exactly at the thickest part of the breastbone. When Cal's blade found its final resting place in Barnadine's body, he'd been unable to complete his last act of brutal treachery against the Leonardi family.

Cal read my face and offered the obvious. "He failed."

"Barely!" Irritated, I stuffed pillows under his head and shoulder to raise them and slow the bleeding.

He continued, "However, I suspect the slender tip of the stiletto broke off and remains lodged in the bone."

"Yes." I could see its silver glint. "That's actually fortunate, for the metal blocks the heaviest blood flow. Yet . . . intense pain, I think?"

I watched Cal struggle with the need to proclaim it only a

scratch, but under my steady gaze, he admitted, "Every time I breathe, it's as if the piercing occurs once more."

I turned to the servants. "The medicine chest and more light."

Marcellus came forward, placed the chest on the bedside table, and opened it; then stepped aside for more candles to be brought close.

"Is all in order?" I asked him. "Labeled?"

Princess Isabella appeared at the bedside, still pale but steady. "It is, for after I met you, I took over its tending. What do you need?"

I lightly touched her cheek. "Thank you, dear sister. You're brave and thoughtful."

Cal did the same with a kind touch and a brotherly smile. "I feel stronger knowing my sister is nearby."

"I'm so glad to have the chance to see them together." Elder gazed at his children fondly. "They are very caring."

Princess Isabella used her royal voice to me. "What are you waiting for, Rosie? Fix him now!"

Elder chuckled. "Although she takes after *you*."

I smiled. "I hope so," I told him. After a quick calculation about the time of Friar Laurence's arrival, give or take, I said, "Cal, if you wish, I can remove the sliver and poultice and bandage this wound. It'll be a miserable few minutes, but I know not whether Friar Laurence is in his shop or out answering a call for mercy, and with so much of the citizenry surrounding the palace, I fear traffic clogs the streets and his arrival could be delayed."

"Do it," Cal said.

"No!" Holofernes exclaimed.

Cal and I looked at him.

"She's a woman! A mere apprentice!" Holofernes was ruddy with dismay. "You're the prince! Wait for Friar Laurence, I beg!"

"Holofernes," Cal said, "I'll pledge my life to Lady Rosaline very soon and put myself into her keeping."

My heart lightened to hear him uphold me.

Unfortunately, he added, "Besides, as my wife, she could end my life with a well-placed cup of poison. If she's going to kill me, might as well get it over with now."

Elder cackled.

Princess Isabella exclaimed, "Cal!"

I sighed. "You really are your father's son."

Cal didn't smile. Of course not. But he did that one-sided lip twitch and closed his eyes halfway.

And in full view of Marcellus, Holofernes, Princess Isabella, and every single servant who could crowd into the room, I went to work on him.

By the time Friar Laurence arrived, the blade point had been extracted, the wound bathed and poulticed, a temporary bandage had been put in place, and Cal, who had stoically borne the extraction process, took my hand, kissed it, and thanked me in a voice that projected to the far reaches of the corridor.

The man knew his audience.

Friar Laurence heartily approved my handiwork. I shot Holofernes the side-eye as Friar Lawrence gave Cal a lecture on what he could and could not do for the next fortnight or until given permission. Approved activities included walking, reading, talking, drinking moderate amounts of wine to build up his blood, eating the higher foods, like birds and eggs and fruit, rising late, sleeping during the afternoon, going to bed early, and devout prayer. Unapproved activities included dancing, fighting with fists or swords, practicing fighting with fists or swords, excessive wine consumption, and nocturnal activities of any nature. When he saw Cal's bodyguards smirking, he enjoined them to follow their master's lead to encourage him in his recovery.

I carefully did not smirk.

He then announced that since I'd assured Verona's populace of my firm intention to wed Prince Escalus the younger—apparently, there'd been some worried discussion among the citizens of my irked and formidable resistance—he would now bless our betrothal in front of this assemblage. He had me kneel on the bed beside Cal, had us join our hands, and went into a loud, long-winded prayer of thanks to the Virgin Mary and all the angels that I'd at last perceived my feminine duty to my prince and Verona. Then more thanks that I was a woman of chastity, who would come untouched to the marriage bed, and yet more thanks that Prince Escalus was a lord of patience, who would gently guide me into my proper role as a submissive wife.

By the time Friar Laurence said, "Amen," Cal gripped both my hands so hard I couldn't wrestle them away to take a swing at the beloved monk or the attendants, who chuckled and nudged each other.

Cal thanked Friar Laurence and asked for a moment alone with me.

I don't know what Friar Laurence saw in Cal's stone countenance, but he said, "No."

"Do not worry, Father, we're never really alone." I glared at Elder's grinning ghost hovering near Friar Laurence's left shoulder.

He glanced, saw nothing, said, "Nor will you be," and seated himself solidly in the chair close to the door.

"I'm glad this whole marriage kerfuffle is settled." Elder sounded positively smug. "Luckily for you, Rosie, I'll be here to offer sage advice for the rest of your days."

Cal turned his head as if he'd heard a voice.

"That's not necessary," I assured Elder. "I'm sure it's time for you to go on—"

"Yet it appears I cannot." Elder cut me off. "So I'll help you through the difficult early days of your marriage. I'll take command, make sure you behave with the pomp and dignity of a proper princess, realize how privileged you are to be the bride of—"

"Papà, she is not privileged. I am." Cal had interrupted his father's full-blown discourse.

Chapter 63

Hearing Cal address his father, stare at the place where the ghost hovered—that was eerie and unexpected and . . . validation.

Cal didn't wait for his father to recover his ability to speak. "Lady Rosaline will lead all Verona, show what a princess must be, for she'll set her own stamp on the task."

I wanted to lift my arms, dance the *moresca,* ring the bells. Instead I smiled demurely, folded my hands, enjoyed the thoroughly spooked expressions on every attendant's face, and waited on this outcome.

Cal continued, "I love you, Papà, and to have discovered your assassin and dispatched him lays rest to the gnawing guilt within my soul. This I could not have done without *mi cara,* Rosaline, my singed-winged messenger of compassion. We'll wed and, as all couples must, find our way into the future together. While you . . . must go on."

I couldn't remain demure a moment longer. "I told you so," I said to Elder.

For the first time, Elder seemed at a loss. "I don't know the way."

"Escalus, I've been waiting to show you." Eleanor's soft voice brought my head around, and Cal's head around.

Elder put his hand to his chest as though he had a heart to beat.

She was there/not there, a form of silver light, a warmth and a beauty so rich, I had to squint to see her.

She offered her hand.

Elder took it. "Eleanor." Emotion choked his voice: love, guilt, joy, thankfulness.

He was profoundly affected, yet she sounded practical and natural. "Escalus, before we go, do you want to offer your son any patriarchal advice?"

"Of course." Elder cleared his throat importantly. "Son, never pass up a chance to pee. Never waste an erection. Never trust a fart."

In identical gestures of horror, Eleanor and I put our hands over our eyes.

"My thanks, Papà," Cal said. "I will remember."

As Elder and Eleanor moved off, she winked at me.

Cal sank down in his chair and, clearly shaken, stared at the place where they'd been. Turning his head, he viewed me with a grave reservation. "Should we marry—"

"When we marry," I corrected him.

"Will your ghost sightings be seasonal or constant?"

"Depends on whether you have more relatives who rest uneasily in their graves." What I meant was—*Blessed Mother Mary, forbid.* I never wanted to view and hear another specter as long as I lived. "Whenever I hear a soft, clear voice, I'll think of Princess Eleanor."

"I know what you mean. Whenever I fart, I'll think of Dad."

I fell into a fit of giggles. Sometimes, despite the evidence, it seemed that Cal would fit into my family very well.

When I calmed, we stared at one another, weighing each other's thoughts, expressions, trying to see a way forward.

"Our wedding will be an event of great circumstance and importance." He spoke as if him saying it would make it so.

How lovely it would be to make a pronouncement and know it would be done! "I promise I'll do all in my considerable organizational power to create a pompous, peaceful occasion that will honor our two houses."

"Peaceful? Of course. It's a wedding, not a war."

"No . . . I suppose not."

"What's wrong?"

I hated to burst his bubble, but—"Whenever the Montagues and the Capulets get together, there's always a great sharpening of knives. Let us not forget other Veronese families have their rivalries, the men pee on the bushes—"

Cal chuckled indulgently.

"Those would be your treasured exotic bushes getting drenched with pee."

Those lazy eyes widened in fury. "I'll run them through!"

"Adulterers collide in the corridors, someone always steals the silver—"

"On the occasion of my first marriage, the great golden Leonardi lion vanished."

"See? It's not a memorable celebration unless there's a disaster or two." I beamed at him.

"You seem to take great delight in pointing out the possible catastrophes. Are you sure of your decision?"

"What decision?"

Cal looked at me.

"Oh! You mean . . . I've made up my mind to marry you for many good and logical reasons. I see no reason to change it."

Chapter 64

" 'Good . . . and logical . . . reasons.' "

Cal pronounced each word with such deliberation I suspected his displeasure, although I didn't know why.

He gestured at the watching army of servants, bodyguards, and Friar Laurence, waving them away.

They retreated to the fringes of the vast room, but not a soul left and no one took their gazes off us.

Cal patted the bed beside him. "Here. I wish to speak to you without everyone hearing."

I climbed up on the mattress and sat beside his prone form, my erect spine against the headboard and my legs stretched out straight beneath my skirts. For me to sit on a bed with him, a man of Verona, even though he was my future husband, was in every manner improper, but since I'd already been on the bed with him in front of a multitude of witnesses, and clearly had no intention of deflowering him, that seemed to have cleared the way.

In a low, stern voice, he asked, "Did Lysander not come to you carrying my blessing?"

"He did. We embraced, but in the end, my pragmatic nature won out. That night when you'd seduced me in my family's garden, and forced the issue of our betrothal, you enumerated all the sensible reasons I would be a good wife for you, and I reacted as the daughter of Romeo and Juliet must, in chagrin that you were able to make such a cold-blooded list of my attributes." I inhaled briefly, then settled myself solidly in my good sense. "But I am myself, and not my parents, and as you noted, I'm logical and practical, too. You have many worthy attributes also."

"Indeed? Besides being the prince of Verona, and my wife will live in a palace?"

In irritation, I raised my voice. "Why do men think that's all I care about?"

I viewed our avid audience, straining to hear a single word.

He shushed me. "Because for a woman, security is a sensible goal. I don't deny that, nor do I disdain that." Cal brooded over his assumption; then in exasperation, he said, "Lysander believed that, too?"

"You two have much in common." I lowered my voice, but kept the exasperation. "To me, living in a palace is not an advantage. I have no desire to manage a large household as I currently do. I'm perfectly capable—of course, you're right about that—but a lesser responsibility would be a pleasure. No, I was talking about you in yourself. Your character, which is honorable. I believe you'll afford me the honors due your wife and hostess, and the mother of your children. I don't think you'll beat me."

"Tempting!"

He had beads of sweat on his forehead. Perhaps when we were done, I'd recommend a dose of poppy juice to ease his pain. "And earlier when you held me and kissed me, you emphasized once again, as you did before, that our physical relationship will be mutually enjoyable."

"Is *that* what I emphasized?"

"Forsooth, so you did! And provided ample evidence." I

smiled at the memory. "My real concern is, at some time in the future, you'll meet your One True Love, a lady who is out of reach because you're married to me. I dread the idea of being an obstacle in such a circumstance, and I hope you'll be discreet in your devotion to her."

At this point, he . . . Frankly, I don't know what happened. I thought he appreciated my sensibilities. Why not? They were both pragmatic and sensible.

Instead he grabbed my wrist in an unbreakable hold, looked at our audience, and said—no, commanded—"Get out!"

The servants fled. His men rose in unison and as a unit filed out. Only Friar Laurence remained, and he flatly said, "I will not." Which told me he knew something about Cal's mood I hadn't yet comprehended.

A glance at Cal's face enlightened me.

His usual smooth, calm expression had dissolved into a contortion of . . . frustration? Rage? Although I didn't know why. "What did I say?" I asked.

Moving swiftly as a big cat on the hunt, Cal sat up, grasped my ankle—the man clearly had an elevated sense of freedom concerning my limbs—and pulled me down the bed. Retaining my wrist, releasing my ankle, he used his hand on my shoulder to push me flat on my back.

I, of course, was not silent during this maneuver. I said things like, "What? You . . . This isn't . . . Cal, you can't . . ."

Obviously, he could.

Friar Laurence said again, "I am not leaving these two worldly sinners!" But he wasn't speaking toward the bed anymore, and he seemed muffled and flustered.

I lifted my head and saw Marcellus, Dion, and Holofernes hustling him out. With a solid thunk, the door shut behind them, leaving Cal and me alone.

Really alone. As alone as we'd been in the Montague garden when he'd maneuvered his way beneath my skirts and into becoming my betrothed. Now I had an inkling what he intended... although I still couldn't comprehend what I'd done to provoke him.

"Cal, this is not a good idea."

"Shhh." His voice, so quiet, so soothing, was at odds with the fanatic gleam in his eyes. He did that looming trick of his, his shoulders blocking the light, his face so close to mine I could feel his breath.

I pushed on his chest with my free hand.

You'll be surprised to know that didn't work, but it did remind me that:

1. He'd been injured and he had a big bandage wrapped around the wound.
2. Other than the bandaging, his chest was bare.

I said, "You've been hurt, bleeding. You shouldn't be doing this."

"I know." His voice still held that soothing quality that I found slightly spooky, and his eyes gleamed as though possessed of a dark angel. "Yet somehow coming so close to death, I need to remind myself why Rosaline of the house of Montague continues to elude my capture."

"I haven't eluded your capture. You captured me much against my will, and we were betrothed. Since that evening, we have had adventures of many kinds, so rare for a prince who represents Verona in all its guises and a lady of... how shall I say this? Impeccable virtue." I expressed myself adroitly, I thought. "Today, after you released me, I *chose* you as my betrothed." I thought it was a neat argument, one likely to defuse his odd mood and return him to sanity.

Not so much.

He still held my wrist, but his grip had eased and he stroked his thumb over my pulse point.

I said, "We've both sagaciously agreed to this marriage." A sane argument, right?

He seemed oblivious to my sanity.

"You like my family, the possibility of my prodigious productivity, my house managing abilities, my *tette*—" I floundered on the knowledge that I should not have mentioned body parts.

"Tell me what you like about me." His voice, low and deep, whispered across my skin.

I prickled with awareness, and floundered again, trying to think what I liked about him. "You're dutiful. You . . . have a nice garden. I like your grandmother and your sister."

"You don't like to touch me. Are you repulsed by me?"

"No!"

"I'm scarred." Taking my free hand, he used my fingertips to trace the ripples caused by the burns inflicted in the dungeon. "I limp."

"I don't even think of that." True, I no longer noticed his scars. I studied him now, his mouth, his nose, his forehead. I skipped his eyes because of the way his lids drooped over his shadowed eyes as if to hide an inner hellfire of passion. I did know about that. I did believe it existed. Too much proof had been offered me. "The scars don't matter; God did not bless you with a handsome countenance, anyway."

He gave a crack of laughter.

"If you don't want to know, you shouldn't ask me." I tried to shake off his grip and roll away.

He leaned closer, using his weight to restrain me, and placed my hand on his shoulder. "You've seen my body now. The marks of the whip on my back and the brand on my chest. What of that? Will intimacy with a man whose body bears the evidence of torment and defeat repulse you?"

"I'm not so shallow." A strong, snappish reply, but I suppose he thought I was shallow, for Lysander was as glorious as the dawn. Didn't Cal realize the sunshine of my love for Lysander wouldn't have lasted if Lysander had been stupid, humorless, a brute?

"Rosaline..." Cal's voice beckoned my attention back to him. "Look and tell me what you think."

Under my palm, his shoulder flexed. I felt the ripple of muscle as he raised himself slightly, and my gaze dropped to view the brown skin, the short black hairs interrupted by the pale bandage, the taut belly.

I lifted my gaze back to his face. Safer, I thought.

I thought wrong. For now, he was watching me, the fire no longer hidden. With a single finger, he traced the line of my jaw, the roundness of my cheek.

I moaned under my breath.

He heard, for he paused. "You also have bruises and marks from your ordeal. You were handled roughly, first in the riots, then dragged you off the brink and back to life. Are you afraid of me?"

I shook my head.

"Am I hurting you?"

I shook my head.

"Good." With a touch so light it seduced my nerves, he slid his knuckles against my neck, across my chest, hovered over my fully clad and heaving breasts...

I didn't object. I could barely breathe. The man was sucking all the air from the room.

Slowly, so slowly, his face came closer, his mouth angled toward mine. He'd kissed me before—and I had liked it. Afterward, when I discovered Cal had been my seducer, I'd been enraged, but I couldn't deny I liked it. Now, in the shadowy, silent, Cal-filled moment, my lips parted. I waited...

He released me and flopped back on his pillows. "Thank you, Rosie, you've answered my questions."

I still vibrated from his touch, heard the echoes of his seductive words, knew the chill of losing that weight and warmth against mine.

Without turning my head, I looked at him out of the corners of my eyes.

He stared at the ceiling, and he was smiling, a smug, pleased, self-confident, honest-to-God smile, corners of the lips up and everything.

That insolent cur, that whoreson, that unbuttered piece of dry toast!

I took a strong, deep breath and, in one movement fueled by rage, I came up off the mattress and over the top of him. I pinned him to the mattress, my knees on either side of his hips, and yes, my skirts were between us, but if we were enacting the legend of the princess and the pea, I was the princess and that was no tiny pea beneath my *fica*.

Which gave me some satisfaction, but not enough to quench my fury. I put my hands on Cal's bare shoulders, leaned close to his face—somewhat like he'd done with me, but with different intentions—and I said, "In our marriage bed, do you think you're going to have it all your own way? Because, *my prince*"—I managed to load a fair amount of sarcasm in those two words—"I may be a virgin, as is known and celebrated by every single nosy creature in Verona, but I am also the daughter of Romeo and Juliet, and your slow, thin, bloodless seduction won't work with me. Sometimes, my friend, we'll do it my way." I bounced on him. Three times and energetically.

He groaned in pain and grabbed for me.

I slipped from his hands, leaped off the bed, and stalked toward the door. As I touched the handle, he spoke in princely command. "Rosaline."

I halted. "What?" *Hostile tone.*

He sat up on one elbow, his mouth twisted with pain, possessiveness, and humor. "I am not a virgin, I do have some experience, and I know my slow, thin, bloodless seduction was working quite well . . . on you."

I exhaled, straightened my skirts, opened the door—and faced a phalanx of men's faces, expectant, curious, worried (Friar Laurence), and hopeful. Driven by rage, I stepped out of the prince's bedchamber, dusted my fingers, and smiled the smile of a victor.

Friar Laurence asked, "Child, are you—"

Marcellus took it on himself to answer. "Nothing happened. The prince likes to take his time." He studied me critically. "And she is unruffled."

I lifted my arm like a statue of Aphrodite accepting victory in the wars of love.

Through the open door, Cal's loud, helpless laughter sounded like the pealing of a new-forged bell.

While the men stared, first at me, then in amazement into the bedchamber, I stalked down the long flight of stairs to the main floor, turned the corner, and—thank Blessed Mary, I was finally offstage and without an audience. I stepped into an empty room, shut the door behind me, and the discipline that had held me upright failed me.

Because Cal was right. That seduction had worked marvelously well.

One knee collapsed. I staggered sideways into the wall.

I rolled to place my spine against its support and slithered down to rest on the floor.

"I am the daughter of Romeo and Juliet," I whispered. "Hear me roar."

Faint and far away, from a kingdom I could not yet visit, I heard Elder chuckling . . .

Acknowledgments

First and foremost, thank you everyone at Kensington:
John Scognamiglio for his vision and daring.
Lynn Cully (Vice President of Business Relations).
Jackie Dinas (Publisher and Director of Sub-rights).
Vida Engstrand (Director of Communications) and Jane Nutter (Publicist), who brilliantly created a publicity campaign to present A DAUGHTER OF FAIR VERONA to all the readers of humor, Shakespeare, mystery, and history.

Kris Noble, who designed this bright and evocative cover that inspired the DaughterofMontague.com website and brought so many readers' eyes to the story.

Thank you to:

The librarians, high school English teachers, and booksellers who so enthusiastically embraced this reimagining of a story so famous all one has to do is say, "The balcony scene," and the world responds, "Romeo and Juliet."

Authors and reviewers Megan Chance, Kristin Hannah, Jayne Ann Krentz, Susan Mallery, Susan Elizabeth Phillips, and John Charles.

Author Connie Brockway and Shakespearean scholar Mary Bly, aka author Eloisa James, for lending her gravitas to the project.

Agent Annelise Robey for her unending enthusiasm, faith, and perseverance.

All the online reviewers who took the time to film videos, write up your opinion, and spread the word about the daughter of Romeo and Juliet.

Thank you to Lisa Laskey who steered me toward Hamlet.

Last but not least, thank you to William Shakespeare for creating plays of young love, vengeful ghosts, fateful tragedy, and family strife that has reverberated through the ages and been recreated so brilliantly in so many settings by so many actors. Language sang in your soul. Thank you, sir.